"The jewel rested there," Mistress Priscian said, and this time Liam did raise his lantern, moving along the side of the coffin to get a better look. Shallow grooves an inch wide had been cut in the effigy's shoulders and across its chest; where they met was a slightly deeper depression almost three inches wide. He suppressed a whistle of astonishment.

If that's where the Jewel lay, he thought, *it must be huge.*

He raised his lantern higher and peered at the face of the effigy. If it bore any resemblance to the real Eircnaeus, he had been a cruel-looking man. His lips were thin, compressed in a stern frown, his nose small but obviously broken once. The stone eyes were open, but they did not look unfocused, the way those of most statues did—they seemed to Liam to be attempting to bore holes through the roof of the crypt, and he did not look at them for long.

BEGGAR'S BANQUET

CONTINUING THE THRILLING ADVENTURES
BEGUN BY AUTHOR DANIEL HOOD IN
FANUILH AND *WIZARD'S HEIR*

Ace Books by Daniel Hood

FANUILH
WIZARD'S HEIR
BEGGAR'S BANQUET

BEGGAR'S BANQUET

Daniel Hood

ACE BOOKS, NEW YORK

If you purchased this book without a cover, you should be aware that this book is stolen property. It was reported as "unsold and destroyed" to the publisher, and neither the author nor the publisher has received any payment for this "stripped book."

This book is an Ace original edition,
and has never been previously published.

BEGGAR'S BANQUET

An Ace Book / published by arrangement with
the author

PRINTING HISTORY
Ace edition / April 1997

All rights reserved.
Copyright © 1997 by Daniel Hood.
Cover art by Bob Eggleton.
This book may not be reproduced in whole or in part,
by mimeograph or any other means, without permission.
For information address: The Berkley Publishing Group,
200 Madison Avenue, New York, New York 10016.

The Putnam Berkley World Wide Web site address is
http://www.berkley.com/berkley

Make sure to check out *PB Plug*,
the science fiction/fantasy newsletter, at
http://www.pbplug.com

ISBN: 0-441-00434-2

ACE®
Ace Books are published by The Berkley Publishing Group,
200 Madison Avenue, New York, New York 10016.
ACE and the "A" design are trademarks
belonging to Charter Communications, Inc.

PRINTED IN THE UNITED STATES OF AMERICA

10 9 8 7 6 5 4 3 2 1

BEGGAR'S BANQUET

CHAPTER 1

ON THE FIRST day of the holiday week called Beggar's Banquet, Liam Rhenford woke to an illusory contentment which was quickly dispelled.

The room in which he slept was a library, and the only windows were in the cupola directly above the divan on which he lay; when he first opened his eyes he saw by the diffused quality of the light in the room that there must be a layer of snow on the glass. In the Midlands, where he had grown up, Beggar's Banquet was called the Feast of Fools, and snow on the first day of the holiday was considered a good sign.

Smiling sleepily to himself, he rolled over onto his back, stretching a little beneath his blanket, and peered up at the cupola. A light dusting of snow, new since he had gone to bed, concealed the sky but allowed light to filter through, and his smile widened in the pale glow.

Good morning, master. Mage Grantaire is already awake.

The firm thought intruded on his own muddled ones, like a brick dropped through a cloud of feathers, and he started, hauling himself up on his elbows and staring down at his familiar. The dragon standing in the doorway of the library was the size of a small dog, but the intelligent gleam in its slit-pupilled eyes—and the thought it had just sent into his head—reminded him that it was considerably more than just a pet. And the name the creature mentioned quickly overrode his childish contentment at seeing snow on the first day of Beggar's Banquet: he had an uninvited guest to attend to.

"Good morning, Fanuilh," he said; then, before it

1

could object to his speaking aloud, he closed his eyes
and projected his own thought.

What is she doing?

She is walking on the beach.

Is she far away?

She is some ways down the beach, Fanuilh answered,
settling down onto its haunches and flaring its leathery
wings before folding them neatly across its back.

Can she hear us?

We are not speaking.

You know what I mean, Liam thought, trying to load
the thought with his irritation at the dragon's obtuseness.

I have told you, Master, Fanuilh replied impassively.
*No one but us can understand our projections. A wizard
such as Mage Grantaire may be aware that we are com-
municating, but she would not know what we thought.*
The dragon had told him that several times, both before
and after Grantaire had arrived, but the fear of being
"overheard" nagged at him.

With a sigh and a small groan, he lay back down on
the divan, drew the blanket over his head and thought
about his guest.

Grantaire was a wizard, apparently an old friend of
the wizard in whose house Liam now lived. She had
arrived at his door only the night before as he was getting ready for bed; his first impression of her, seen
through the glass panes of his front door, was that she
was some helpless, well-to-do lady caught out late on
the coast road to the nearby city of Southwark, and that
the lights of his house on the beach had led her to hope
for a safe place to spend the night. He had also thought
that, with her cheeks stung to redness by the cold and
her hair mussed by the wind, she was very pretty.

His first impression of helplessness was quickly dispelled: she pushed brusquely past him into the entrance
hall and shuddered once, dropping a heavy traveling
bundle to the floor.

"Gods, it's cold," she said, then unlaced her fur-
trimmed cloak and let it drop to the floor, revealing a

fairly short, plain shift that revealed a disturbing length of leg between the hem and the top of her boots. "But of course you can count on Tanaquil's house to be too warm," she went on, rubbing her neck with both hands and sniffing judiciously, as if the warmth of the house had a smell. Then she had turned to him, frank appraisal in her glance. "Or should I say, your house? You are Liam Rhenford?"

"Yes," he confessed, at a complete loss for words in the face of the woman's self-confident entrance. Tarquin Tanaquil was the wizard from whom he had inherited the house, and its warmth—along with a number of other things—was an example of the magic with which the wizard had filled it.

"My name is Grantaire. I was a friend of Tanaquil. He told me I could expect to find you here."

"You saw him?" Liam did not know why he had been surprised: he knew that Tarquin had for a brief time returned from the grave. He had seen the wizard himself, and talked with him—but he had not known that Tarquin had talked to anyone else during his return.

A sudden movement of the cloak at their feet made him jump, and then a cat poked its rumpled gray head out and directed a reproachful glare at Grantaire.

"I'm sorry," she told the cat, "but if you insist on being carried, you must sometimes be dropped." As if seeing the cat made her remember, she turned to Liam: "Where is Fanuilh?"

Things had moved very quickly from there, allowing no time for Liam to formulate the proper suspicion, let alone give voice to it. Fanuilh had entered the room and, displaying a complete lack of surprise, had ambled over to Grantaire and allowed her to scratch under its chin.

You know her? Liam had asked, barely maintaining the presence of mind to project the thought instead of speaking. *She is who she says she is?*

Of course, the dragon replied, turning its head a little to redirect her scratching.

Reassured, Liam had prepared Tarquin's old bedroom for her—he would not sleep there, because it was where he had found the wizard's body, but she had no objections.

"I am tired from traveling" was all she had said before closing the bedroom door. "We shall speak in the morning." It had sounded almost like an order.

Now the morning was upon him, and he knew nothing more about her; Fanuilh had only been able to tell him that she really was an old friend of Tarquin, and that she could not understand the thoughts they sent back and forth.

With another groan, Liam sat up, put his feet on the floor and scrubbed briefly at his eyes.

Will you have coffee, master?

"Yes," he grumbled and, forcing himself to his feet, shuffled into the kitchen. He concentrated briefly in the direction of the large oven, closing his eyes; then he opened the oven's metal door and pulled out a bowl and a mug, both steaming. The mug he sipped from himself; the bowl he placed on the other side of the kitchen table.

Fanuilh leapt lightly onto the tabletop and crouched over the bowl, inhaling deeply. It had only drunk coffee once, and hated it, but it enjoyed the smell immensely.

"So," Liam said after a few cautious sips, the coffee warming his stomach and driving the sleep from his head, "you really know nothing more about her?"

She is a great wizard, the dragon answered, without raising its snout from the coffee. *Not as great as Master Tanaquil, but great enough.*

"Yes, but where is she from? Where does she live? Why is she here?"

I imagine she is here to take some of Master Tanaquil's things. The ones you cannot use.

"Because I am not a wizard?"

Yes.

Though he had a familiar, Liam was by no means a wizard. That he was bound to Fanuilh was an accident— one he had at first thought extremely unlucky, but which he had grudgingly come to accept had its benefits.

Tarquin Tanaquil had been murdered, and on the night

of his death Liam had happened to come by the house. He had found Fanuilh dying, the part of Tarquin's soul that kept it alive rapidly departing; it bit him, taking part of his soul to keep itself alive, and incidentally binding them as master and familiar.

Strange, he thought to himself, careful not to project, *that I don't notice that part of my soul is missing.* It was not technically missing, he knew, merely residing in Fanuilh, but he found the idea difficult to grasp. *Shouldn't I notice that half of my soul is halfway across the room?*

Another sip of coffee and the sound of footsteps distracted him from this train of thought, and he looked up as Grantaire entered the room.

Her hair was just as disordered as it had been the night before, her cheeks as flushed, and her shift as short; he blushed heavily when he realized he was wearing nothing but a pair of breeches.

"The house is warm, isn't it?" she said without a trace of embarrassment, as if going half-naked in front of a strange woman was merely practical. "But I think you should put on some clothes—there's something on the beach you should see."

"What?" he said, crossing his arms, sticking his hands in his armpits and feeling foolish.

She frowned. "I think you should see it. Get a cloak." She turned and left the kitchen.

"What is it?" he asked Fanuilh, but the dragon only shook its head, then leapt off the table and padded out of the kitchen after the wizard.

Liam followed, stopping only to jump into a pair of boots and throw on a tunic. He did not imagine it could be anything important, or that it would take very long.

Tarquin Tanaquil's villa was long and low in the southern style, with white plaster walls and a red tile roof; it sat on a beach in a sheltered cove, protected by a short breakwater that touched the patio in front and still allowed the cold waves to strike the sand to the west of the house.

They gathered at the edge of the beach, clustered around the dead man, Liam and Fanuilh standing to one side, Grantaire to the other, the gray cat in her arms. Liam shuffled his boots in the sand, beating his arms and blowing on his hands, already wishing he had brought a cloak. It was winter, and the early morning air was cold.

The sea must have been colder. The body sprawled in the sand was white and bloated, the skin heavily pruned. There was seaweed laced in the fingers.

"Well," Liam said at last, "some ship is short a sailor. He must have gone overboard." He was aware of a strange intimacy between them, a set of tacit expectations arising from the dead man at their feet. He doubted she understood it, but he had seen it more than once in his life—a sort of embarrassment around the dead that drew strangers together through the knowledge that something must be done.

Grantaire pushed a wayward strand of red hair out of her eyes and gave him a somewhat contemptuous glance. "Thrown overboard is more likely, don't you think? Look at his neck."

He would rather have looked at her at that moment, not because she was pretty, but because the glance she directed his way intrigued him; it seemed to him that she had weighed him, and found him wanting, simply because he had not examined the corpse's neck. Still, he squatted in the sand by the dead man and reached out to brush away some sodden hair.

"Don't touch him," Grantaire commanded.

He frowned and looked up, suddenly feeling more sure of himself with her than he had since she had arrived. "Why? He's beyond hurt, don't you think?"

She was not listening to him, however; her eyes were closed, and she suddenly opened her arms, the cat dropping with a startled squawk. Her lips moved soundlessly for a moment, her fingers twining in strange patterns— small hands with large knuckles, he saw, the skin much creased—and then she opened her eyes again and pressed her lips tight.

"Too long in the water," she muttered. "Very well—you can move him."

"Thank you," Liam said with a slight sarcastic nod. He reached out again, this time taking the man's shoulder and pushing up, trying to roll him over. Touching the corpse did not bother him, though the skin was cold, but his eyes widened and he gave a low whistle when he saw the thin purple line stretching across the man's throat. Time in the sea had puckered and thinned the wound, but it was clear that the cut had been deep and wide.

A sharp breeze off the sea swept over them, snapping Grantaire's cloak around her heels. Liam gently let the man return to his former position, then stood up and dusted his hands on his breeches.

"Well," he said lamely, "I suppose I will have to take him into town."

"Now?" Grantaire asked, as if it were an inconvenience to her. "I need to speak a bit with you—there are things I must do here."

Liam was silent for a long moment, considering her face, which was set in a businesslike expression. There was something hard about her that set him wondering; though he had touched it without reluctance, the corpse washed out of the sea made him sad and uneasy—but she seemed oblivious to it.

How old is she? he wondered, thinking that she could not be much older than thirty, his own age. *Perhaps less.*

"We can't just leave him here," he said, gesturing at the body. "It wouldn't be right."

"Then drag him up the beach," she suggested. "As you said, he's beyond hurt—and I am pressed for time. Take him into the city later."

Master, Fanuilh thought, *you are forgetting your appointment.*

"What appointment?" he said out loud, and then, remembering: "Mistress Priscian!"

At noon, the dragon prompted.

"What is it?" Grantaire demanded.

"I have to go into Southwark anyway—I have some business."

With the slight arching of an eyebrow, she indicated what she thought of his business. "Can't it wait?"

He found himself compelled to make excuses. "Unfortunately not. It has been set for a long time, and it is fairly important." *To me,* he added silently. Gesturing to the corpse, he went on: "Besides, with him . . . I really should take him into Southwark. I have a friend in the Guard who will know what to do."

Grantaire's lips thinned, and she crossed her arms. "Very well. When will you return?"

"I'm not sure," he confessed. "I'm supposed to meet Mistress Priscian at noon, and it may take about an hour or so."

"Mistress Priscian," she repeated, and the skepticism in her tone annoyed him.

"A merchant—an elderly merchant," he said, irritation slipping into his tone. "I should be back by midafternoon, if that will suit you."

The sarcasm was lost on her, but at least her eyebrows relaxed. "It will have to do," she said, and then spun on her heel and walked off towards the house. Her cat sprang after her.

For a long moment Liam stood in the cold, angry at her and at his own lapse in manners. Despite her rudeness, she was his guest. *Uninvited guest,* he told himself, *but still . . .*

Was she always this . . . certain of herself? he asked Fanuilh, once she had entered the house.

She cannot hear our thoughts, the dragon pointed out again, and then sent another thought quickly. *And yes, Master Tanaquil often spoke of her as very self-confident.*

Liam remembered that Tarquin himself had never been much given to politeness or social niceties, but from him it had seemed an old man's eccentricity. In Grantaire, it seemed like rudeness.

Shaking his head, he set himself to moving the corpse further up the beach, away from the grasping fingers of the sea. A wave soaked his boots in the process, but they were solidly made; he cursed and jumped away from the cold water more from reflex than from a fear of wet feet. When the wave retreated, he grabbed the corpse under the arms and dragged it back from the water's edge, the dead man's feet leaving two parallel swathes in the damp sand. Fanuilh watched the whole process impassively.

Liam was sweating by the time he reached the patio, and he was happy to lay the corpse on the stone there and go back into the house. His hands were cold and clammy, covered with salt and sand that had stuck to the dead man's tattered clothing, and he held them out in front of him, eager to wash. He stopped in the entrance hall.

I will have to pick him up again, he thought with a grimace, *to get him on the horse.*

Turning on his heel, he went back out, the sweat cooling in the chill morning air and making him shiver a little bit. There was a shed on the far side of the house where he stabled his horse, and he opened the door.

"Easy, Diamond," he said, though the horse was perfectly calm, brushing a warm greeting past his ear with its lips.

Fanuilh appeared at the door of the shed as he saddled the horse. *You will take the man to Aedile Coeccias?*

"Yes," Liam said, concentrating on cinching the saddle tight with his fingertips, trying not to get too much sand on the leather. Coeccias was the friend he had mentioned to Grantaire; Aedile was his title, and he was actually in charge of Southwark's Guard, the city's chief constable and representative of the Duke of the Southern Tier. "What else?"

His throat has been cut. He has been murdered. You know what the Aedile will say.

Liam paused, Diamond's bridle hanging in his hands. "I hadn't thought of that," he said after a moment. "But that's ridiculous. He washed up on my beach, that's all. Besides, I have too much to do right now."

Nonetheless, he made no move to bridle his roan.

Since coming to Southwark half a year before, he had
helped the Aedile solve two crimes, and though he
thought their success had been mostly dumb luck, Coeccias had developed an exaggerated idea of Liam's skills
as an investigator.

In fact, the Aedile thought so much of Liam's skills
that he had offered him a special position with the
Guard. Liam had accepted, but only on the condition that
it be completely unofficial: he could choose which
crimes he would investigate. Thus far it had amounted
to little more than occasionally discussing crimes with
the Aedile, offering his opinions. Liam had enjoyed it
as a sort of academic exercise—an ongoing conversation
whose subject was always crime.

This, though, would be different. *He will ask me to
figure this out.* Liam could easily imagine Coeccias
shrugging his heavy shoulders, scratching his beard and
saying, "Truth, Rhenford, why else would the man wash
himself up on your beach, if not in the faith that you'd
con out his murderer?"

Liam's experiences had taught him to be cautious.
There were crimes he could profitably look into, and
ones he could not—a distinction it had taken him some
time to impress upon Coeccias. His arrangement of unofficial consultation had only been in place for a month,
and he guessed that his friend would try to turn the dead
man's appearance on his beach into a reason for making
the position more official.

" 'Truth, Rhenford,' " Liam muttered to himself.
"He's probably a pirate, and his ship a dozen leagues
off by now. I couldn't catch them even if I wanted to.
And that," he said, leveling a finger at Fanuilh, "is exactly what I will tell Coeccias if he gets any ideas about
my looking into this."

The dragon merely blinked at him, and after a determined pause, Liam finished preparing the roan and led
it out onto the patio. It was surprisingly calm about the
corpse, allowing Liam to hoist the dead man across its
rump and lash him in place with only a whicker and a
nervous sidestep or two. When it was done, he set

Fanuilh to watching Diamond and went back inside to wash up.

Grantaire was sitting in the kitchen, her hands folded neatly on the tabletop, which was bare except for the cold coffee. Liam felt a quick pang of guilt at his poor hospitality.

"I'm sorry—would you like some breakfast? I forgot the oven only works for me."

"Some bread," she said, but she clearly had other things on her mind. "I do need to talk to you today."

"So you said." He went to the oven and imagined fresh bread baking; in a moment the smell filled the kitchen. She had said she needed to talk to him, but he could not imagine what about, and he did not want to miss his meeting with the merchant. "I will be back later in the afternoon, but I have to be in the city soon, and with our visitor, a quick trip now makes all the more sense."

He opened the oven and pulled out two fresh loaves, juggling them for a moment, then put one in front of her. She snorted.

"I tell you, he will keep."

"Yes," he agreed, determined not to let his manners lapse again. "Yes, he will—but unfortunately, Mistress Priscian will not."

"Priscian," the wizard repeated, her eyes narrowing and her face growing thoughtful. "I've heard that name before."

"I mentioned it earlier," Liam said, taking a bite of the hot bread to mask his growing sense that Grantaire was both far more eccentric and far less sociable than Tarquin had ever been.

She waved his comment away, carefully breaking her loaf in two and nibbling a corner of one piece. "No, before you said it. I heard the name before you said it."

"In that case, you've probably heard of their jewel— the Priscian Jewel. It's a little famous, though I have to admit that I never heard of it before coming here."

"A jewel?" Grantaire said doubtfully.

"Yes. It is something of a legend in Southwark. There

are all sorts of stories about its provenance, but apparently no one has seen it for hundreds and hundreds of years until it was rediscovered a week or so ago. A niece of the Mistress Priscian I know has been making quite a stir by wearing it around town.''

"I don't recall any jewel," Grantaire said. "It was something else. The name is definitely familiar. Perhaps I'll look it up in Tanaquil's library while you're busy in town." She gave a sarcastic twist to the word "busy" which he chose to ignore. "Is that what your business with her is about? Are you trying to buy this jewel?"

"No," Liam laughed. "It's supposed to be beyond price. And if a thing is beyond price, it's also below price, useless in a way."

She frowned, digesting this and picking at her bread. "How long will you be?"

"I don't know," he said honestly. "If I leave now, I should be able to be back before sunset. But I have to clean up first," he said, pointing at a big copper basin just behind her.

Grantaire considered the basin, and for a minute he was afraid she would suggest they talk while he washed, but then she gave a resigned sigh and stood up.

"I will leave you to it," she said, as if it were a serious inconvenience. "I would appreciate it if you would come back as soon as you can."

"But of course," he responded, sketching her a quick bow and restraining an inhospitable urge to tell her not to wait up. When she was gone, he frowned down at the loaf in his hand for a full minute, wondering at her rudeness and at the strange impulse he had to be agreeable.

Why do I feel bad that I cannot stay here all day to talk to a woman who can't take the time to be pleasant? he asked himself. *She's not even that pretty.*

Liam was still trying to answer that question when he left the house half an hour later, having hastily scrubbed himself with hot water and put on his best clothes—a matching dark green tunic and breeches with white piping. Grantaire had been true to her word, and when he went to the door of the library to say goodbye, she hardly looked up from the book she was reading.

Grabbing his cloak and settling it around his shoulders, he left the house.

Fanuilh was perched on Diamond's neck, apparently oblivious to the cold; the roan waited patiently under its double burden of corpse and familiar, only snorting a little at the cold wind off the sea.

You should put something over the body, the dragon told him. *It will look strange if you carry a body into the city.*

Liam nodded and quickly gathered a tarp from the shed, which he tucked around his second uninvited visitor.

At least this one I can get rid of, he thought, then climbed into Diamond's saddle with a little grin. Fanuilh rose off the horse's neck and flew on ahead as Liam slapped the reins.

There was a cliff behind the house, and Liam rode up the narrow path that led to its top with his head sunk down in thought, his long chin resting almost on his chest. At the top of the cliff the wind was stronger, and he pulled his cloak close and kicked Diamond into a trot, still thinking, ignoring the beauty of the fresh mantle of snow that covered the bare fields. The roan located the road that led to the city on its own, and Liam let it have its head.

The red-haired wizard filled his thoughts. *What could she want from me? I'm not a wizard. And why am I worried that my meeting with Mistress Priscian will take too long? Why am I trying to accommodate her? She is pretty, but not that pretty, and I hope I am not fool enough to have my head turned that easily.*

Diamond trotted along smartly, happy to be out of its cramped shed and enjoying the brisk wind; they were halfway to Southwark before Liam came up with an answer: he felt guilty about living in Tarquin's house. From what Fanuilh had told him, Grantaire had known the old wizard for a very long time, and would have made a far more appropriate heir than Liam. And even

if she did not care about the wizard's bequest, he could
not help but feel it would make him uncomfortable to
find a stranger living in the house of a friend who had
recently died.

Tarquin died three months ago, which isn't that re-
cent, he told himself, *and she certainly isn't making*
much of her mourning. And anyway, he came back from
the Gray Lands less than a month ago and told her to
expect me, so she couldn't have been that surprised—or
hurt.

It was not a long ride to Southwark, but he arrived
quicker than he had expected, the few spires of Temple
Street and the merchants' mansions high on the Point
coming into view just as he decided to stop thinking
about the wizard and concentrate on his own affairs.

Since I came here, he noted, *I have done exactly noth-*
ing, except for helping to find Tarquin's murderer, and
getting involved in that mess in Temple Street.

Those had been short incidents, each lasting hardly
more than a week, and lately he had begun to feel more
and more that he was idling away his time. The days
had weighed heavily on him, and the short hours of daylight had come to seem far too long and empty. His
unofficial position with the Guard made him little more
than the Aedile's sounding board, listening to evidence
and offering suggestions, and he had been careful not to
let it get beyond that. There was no point in taking on
an investigation just because Coeccias thought he was
some kind of human bloodhound. The dead man behind
him was a perfect example of the sort of thing he did
not want to look into: the Aedile was far better suited
to investigating that than he was. *And that is what I will*
tell him, Liam decided.

The few things Southwark offered that he felt truly
qualified for—posts on a sailing ship, as captain, navi-
gator or even surgeon—required introductions and con-
nections which, until recently, he had not had. Until the
Aedile, realizing that Liam was unlikely to take a full-
time position with the Guard, grudgingly introduced him
to Mistress Priscian.

She was an elderly merchant, with a fleet of seven ships that were rumored to be in poor shape; rumor, in the form of Coeccias, said that was the result of bad management on the part of the captains and factors she hired. Liam had experience as both captain and factor, and what was more, he had a collection of valuable maps that could turn even seven shoddy ships into a treasure fleet. Gathered in the course of long voyages in distant lands, they were the key to rich cities of which Southwark had never heard. He even had proof: he had sold a few of the maps to two different local merchants, and both had visibly prospered in just the few months since. The Aedile arranged an introduction, portraying Mistress Priscian to Liam as a poor old woman sadly in need of guidance.

Liam had liked Mistress Priscian from the start. Within minutes of ushering him into her home on the Point, she explained that she was not a poor old woman sadly in need of guidance, "as the good Coeccias has no doubt told you. And I doubt y' are a poor scholar, sadly in need of a position. So, how shall we treat?"

They had come to a very simple agreement in only two meetings: with his maps and his practical experience as his investment, they would become partners. He would see to the equipping and manning of the ships, as well as the choosing of routes, and she would handle the accounts and provide the money and the ships.

This third meeting was to be the last of their negotiations; a week before, Liam had given her a proposal for the upcoming trading season, and they were to come to a final agreement on it and their partnership.

And even if she does not like the specifics of the plan, I'm sure we will still have a deal, he told himself, smiling slightly at the idea. At last he would have something to do.

Distant bells began to toll ten as he left the fields, and Diamond's hooves clattered as they passed from the frozen ruts of the coast road to the cobbles of Southwark proper. As always when he entered the city, his familiar left him, rising high into the sky. Liam had made it plain that he did not want its company in Southwark; people had too many reasons to think him a wizard as it was.

Fanuilh! Beaming to himself, he formed the thought into a block and projected it at the diminishing dragon, a small form high in the sky overhead. *We are going to be rich and prosperous merchants!*

Yes, master, came his familiar's reply, *as soon as you give the Aedile the corpse.*

"Spoiler," Liam muttered, but the dragon's laconic thought only made him reduce his smile to a grin. "Corpse or no corpse," he went on under his breath, "I'm going to have something to do at last."

CHAPTER 2

WINTER REIGNED IN Southwark, and the bustling crowds of summer were gone, but there were still people in the street, bundled up and moving briskly, intent on the holiday. As usual, occasional passersby displayed an awareness of his presence that made him uncomfortable. He had hoped that it would fade, that the Southwarkers would find something else of more interest at which to stare. They had a weeklong holiday to distract them, but some still eyed him furtively: Liam Rhenford, resident wizard. He pretended not to notice, trying to resign himself to it.

Even a goddess walking their streets only distracted them for a week or so, he reminded himself. There had been a goddess in Southwark recently, a new addition to the pantheon named Bellona. Liam preferred not to think about the event, except for the blessed week after her apparition, when everyone had been too busy discussing her to notice him. Now, though, things were back to normal: the odd whisper, the quickly grabbed arm of a companion, the discreet pointing. Not everyone did it, of course—just enough to make him grit his teeth and breathe a sigh of frustration.

Of course, carrying a corpse along with you won't make them think you any more normal, he thought, self-consciously tucking the tarp a little tighter around the stiffening body.

The thin layer of snow on the city square had been scuffed and kicked and ground into black slush around the edges of the cobbles, and though Liam missed the birdsellers and toy vendors that frequented the place in

17

good weather, the stands selling mulled wine and hot food were surrounded with customers; lending an air of festivity to the place. He threaded Diamond through the crowd, drawing the attention to which he had become accustomed and trying to ignore it.

In honor of Beggar's Banquet, long bundles of boughs had been strung across the imposing front of the Duke's Courts, vivid splashes of green against the stone edifice, wound artfully in and among the rows of windows. Someone, perhaps with a sense of humor, had nailed a few thin branches to the front of the building next door to the courts, a squat, ugly barracks that housed both the Guard and the city's jail.

Liam dismounted by the steps that led up to the jail and addressed the guard who stood at the top, munching on a handful of roasted chestnuts.

"Good morning. Is Aedile Coeccias here?"

"Aye, Quaestor Rhenford," the guard replied, choking down a mouthful and descending the steps. Coeccias had given him that title on the two occasions when they had worked together, and though Liam thought it was supposed to be temporary, it had caught on among the Guard, and they would not let it go. "If you'll in, I'll watch your horse."

Liam handed over the reins with a slight smile. "Watch the package there as well, if you would," he said, gesturing at the corpse. "It's for the Aedile." Then he went up the steps.

Most of the building was a single long room, with roaring hearths at either end and a scattering of benches, cots, kegs of liquor and stacks of weapons. A few Guards lingered near the fireplace farthest from the door, and Coeccias was seated at a cheap table by the other, firelight flickering over his broad back and bent head. A piece of paper lay in front of him, and the Aedile was glaring at it suspiciously, a quill protruding from the depths of his beard.

"Good morning," Liam said, pulling off his riding gloves and dropping them on the table. "And a Happy Banquet."

" 'Merry Banquet,' Rhenford," the Aedile said with
a scowl, spitting out the quill. "We say 'Merry Banquet,' not 'Happy Banquet.' "

"And a Merry Banquet to you," Liam replied, taking
his friend's bad mood in stride. Coeccias's skin was an
unhealthy white against his black beard, and the blurred
red of his eyes indicated a hangover. "You have been
celebrating it already, I can see."

"There's naught to celebrate, neither for me nor
you," the Aedile snapped, then took a deep breath and
pushed away from the table. "Truth, Rhenford, some
mornings it doesn't pay to rise in this city."

Liam guessed that there was something more to his
friend's foul mood than just a hangover. He wanted to
mention the corpse, but he hesitated, not wanting to add
to the other man's burdens and curious about his inclu-
sion in the list of those with nothing to celebrate.

"What's wrong?"

The Aedile sighed and rubbed gingerly at his temples,
his eyes closed. "Y' have an appointment with Mistress
Priscian this morning, have you not?"

"Yes," Liam said slowly. "What of it?"

"If I were you," Coeccias said, opening his eyes and
fixing Liam with a meaningful glance, "I'd postpone it.
There's trouble in the Point, and I won't make you guess
whose house it has visited."

"What sort of trouble?" Liam asked, suddenly anxious. "Has she died?" Though she was old, Mistress
Priscian had seemed remarkably healthy to him.

Coeccias waved the idea away impatiently. "No, no,
none of that. The trouble is this—you know the Priscian
Jewel?" Liam nodded impatiently. "It's been stolen."

For a long moment both men were silent; while Coeccias nursed his aching head, Liam digested the new idea.
He did not see why it should matter to him—as he had
told Grantaire, the Jewel was of almost no value, because no one had enough money to buy it. Its theft
should not affect the deal he had worked out with Mistress Priscian.

He was about to say this when he realized how selfish

it was, and he reconsidered the Aedile's news. If the Jewel had even a tenth of the value and history that rumor accredited it, its loss would certainly be a major blow to Mistress Priscian, and he could hardly expect her to put her mind to lesser things at a time like this.

"I suppose I had better not go there," he said at last, glad he had not spoken right away. He liked the widow, and the more he thought about it, the worse he felt for her. Another idea occurred to him, however, one tied to his earlier thoughts about the Jewel. "But who would steal it? I mean, why?"

"Why?" the Aedile groaned, raising his head from his hands and staring at Liam from bleary eyes. "Why not? Have you seen it?"

"No."

"I saw it just this week, Rhenford," Coeccias said, a note of awe creeping into his tired voice, "at a feast held up on Goddard's Walk. Mistress Priscian's young niece wore it, and it's as beautiful as a star. No, more beautiful than a star. It's as beautiful as a . . ." For a few long seconds the Aedile groped for a better word, and then gave up. "Anyone would want it. And I have to con out that anyone."

Entirely forgetting about the corpse on his horse, Liam planted himself in front of the table, eager to make Coeccias see his point. "Yes, anyone might want it, but who would steal it? No one could wear it, at least not in Southwark, not when everyone would know whose it really was. And no thief would steal it—who would buy it? There isn't enough money in the whole city to pay for it; you said so yourself."

Frowning, Coeccias stared up at him. "Y'have a point . . . but then, wanting to have is not necessarily wanting to show, if you take my meaning. A miser does not build a golden house, eh?"

"No, but it still makes no sense," Liam said, intrigued by the problem. "A thief who wanted it for show would be unable to show it, and a thief who wanted it for money wouldn't be able to sell it. It makes no sense."

Coeccias interrupted him, clasping his hands over his ears. "Truth, Rhenford, you make my head ache even more. It does not matter if it makes no sense—it happened. The Jewel is gone, the old woman unhappy, and I'm left to delicately foot my way through a houseful of guests with titles and privileges."

"Sorry," Liam said, a little embarrassed. He had grown used to discussing problems like this with Coeccias, and realized he had been too eager in speculating about what was merely an intellectual problem for him. For his friend, it was important business. The Aedile warily removed his hands from his ears, and Liam said lamely, "But you see what I mean."

"Aye, aye," Coeccias conceded, glumly looking at the paper in front of him. "As could anyone, which makes this even harder." He flicked a fingernail at the offending paper, sending it fluttering to the ground.

Liam bent down, retrieved the paper, and put it back on the table without reading it. "What is it?"

"A letter to one of Mistress Priscian's houseguests— or rather, one of her niece's houseguests. You know the niece?"

Liam shook his head.

"There is some small loss in that, for she's a pretty one—but the point is this: she had a houseful of guests last night, any one of whom could have made off with the Jewel. And the house was locked tight, so it had to be one of them."

The Aedile's glum expression told him that the obvious answer to that—search them all—would not do. He waited for his friend to explain why.

"The niece is a lady, married to the present Lord Oakham, which makes her Lady Oakham, and she keeps high company." Coeccias ticked the names off on his fingers: "Earl Uldericus and his wife, the Countess Perenelle, the young Baron Quetivel, Master Cimber Furseus and his sister, and Master Rafe Cawood. Do you see now my problem?"

"A little, yes." Liam knew that the Aedile had to be careful in dealing with the Southern Tier's nobility, and with the higher-placed merchants, but had never known specifically why.

"And yet it is clearly one of them—Lady Oakham swears the house was shut tighter than a strongbox, and Lord Oakham warrants it, and the servants as well. Which leaves me to send letters, cringing, fawning, sickly things," Coeccias said, his voice wavering between anger and self-mockery. " 'If it please you, milord, may I beg a moment of your time? This most regrettable crime has obliged me . . . ' And on and on. It fair makes me sick, Rhenford."

"That does seem hard," Liam said sympathetically, walking to the hearth behind the Aedile's table and warming his hands. Another idea had struck him, but he wanted a moment or two to think it through. "What will you do if they won't talk?"

"What can I do?" the Aedile said to Liam's back. "I can't compel them, and I can't clap them in on suspicion—it'd be worth my post to offend a peer or a man with the Rights of the Town."

"What are those?" He was not really interested, but he had not pursued his thought to its end, and wanted more time.

With another sigh, the Aedile explained. The Rights of the Town were a provision in Southwark's charter, granted by the Dukes of the Southern Tier when the city was founded almost five hundred years before. The merchants who negotiated the charter agreed to pay a slightly higher tax on certain goods; in return the Duke at that time had agreed that any merchants who met a certain property qualification would not be subject to criminal law, unless a vote of similar property holders agreed to it.

"Which means," Coeccias summed up, "that I cannot clap in Master Rafe Cawood—for he meets and exceeds the qualification at least twice over—until the Council of Rights sits and rules on it. And their interests are not always as close to the Duke's as one might want." He gave the last sentence a sarcastic twist, to indicate that the rich men's interests and the Duke's were most often widely separated.

Liam only half heard the explanation; he was reaching a conclusion to the strange thought that had occurred to him. Earlier in the day he had balked at Fanuilh's suggestion that the Aedile might ask him to look into the death of the man on the beach, but now he was considering offering his help in a different crime.

There were many reasons not to get involved: with Grantaire at his house and his deal in the offing with Mistress Priscian, he had more than enough to keep him busy. Besides, the woman might not like the idea of his interfering, might not like him to mix their partnership with this crime. And finally, there was his own reluctance to get involved in an investigation for which he was not sure he was qualified, something he had tried to make clear to Coeccias many times.

But then, he doesn't call me Milord May-Do-Aught for nothing, Liam thought, remembering the nickname the Aedile had once fixed on him. *Let him think me changeable.*

For there were reasons for him to get involved, despite his normal inclination. Mistress Priscian was as good as his partner, pending a final agreement, and he liked her personally; if there was any good he could do that would help her, it might also cement their business relationship, and he had come to realize that that was important to him. And the nature of the theft—all the suspects being more or less above the law as represented by Coeccias—might make his participation valuable. He had no official standing, and thus could look into things on his own, and no nobleman or rich merchant could cry up the Rights of the Town in the face of a private investigation.

They might send a bodyguard or two after you, he reminded himself ruefully; while searching out Tarquin's murderer, he had run afoul of a merchant who had done just that. He winced a little by the fire, recalling the beating the bodyguards had inflicted on him. *Still. . . . still, it would be interesting,* he admitted to himself, and he also guessed that he might be better than the bluff Aedile at wriggling around the delicate sensibilities of landed gentry and pretentious merchants.

"I wonder," he mused aloud, almost a full minute after Coeccias had finished his explanation of the Rights of the Town, "whether I might not go see Mistress Priscian after all."

He was not prepared for his friend's reaction: the Aedile threw back his chair and turned quickly, hands spread in a nervous gesture. "It would not do, Rhenford, it would not do," he said hastily. "It would not pay to go there just now."

"Why not?"

The Aedile blushed and stammered. "Look you, the widow has strange ideas, and she's like to act on them without consideration."

"What do you mean?" Liam asked, though he had an inkling, and hid a grin behind his hand.

"I may have ... planted an idea in her," Coeccias said, "when I was crying you up to her as a partner. I may have said too often what a help you had been to me, and what a one you were for solving riddles and searching out misdeeds. For that she has had problems with her factors, and been cheated, and I thought it a recommendation, see you?"

Liam was silent, rubbing his chin to pull down his growing smile, and finally Coeccias said, "And so if you go to see her today, she'll ask you to con out the Jewel, Rhenford. She as much as said so, when I saw her this morning. She said, 'I wonder what young Rhenford would make of this.' "

With a certain perverse pleasure, Liam let his smile show. "I don't know what I will make of it, but it would be interesting to see, don't you think?"

Coeccias's blush faded, and he stopped wringing his hands; a faintly suspicious look crept across his face. "Do you mean you'll take it on?"

"I was thinking about it, yes." Liam's smile grew a little troubled at the expressions warring on his friend's face—confusion mostly, with a touch of exasperation and a small amount of hope. "I don't know what I could do,'' he added quickly. "I'm not the human bloodhound you always make me out to be, but I think I might give it a try, if you don't mind.'' The hope bothered him the most; the last thing he wanted was for Coeccias to think the theft solved simply because he had said he would look into it.

"Mind? Truth, Rhenford, it would ease a great load from my mind, to have it solved so neatly.''

Liam winced, his smile completely gone. "It's not solved, Coeccias, just because I say I will look into it.''

The other man waved the objection away, rising from the table. "As near as makes no difference, once you set yourself to it.'' He rubbed his hands together briskly, a broad smile now shining through his ill-kempt beard. "Come now—we'll to Mistress Priscian's, and she'll tell you all you need to know.''

He strode purposefully past Liam, snatching a jacket from a peg and throwing open the door. "You there,'' he called to the guard at the door, "watch Quaestor Rhenford's horse! We're off to the Point!''

Liam shook his head at the fire, thinking that he had just made a great mistake. There was no way to dampen the Aedile's enthusiasm, no way to keep him from raising expectations of success in whatever investigation Liam made—particularly Mistress Priscian's expectations.

And what if I fail? he wondered, turning resignedly from the fire and following his friend. *She has agreed to this partnership mostly because of Coeccias's glowing recommendation of me—and if I fail in this, the thing he thinks me best at, what then?*

"Gods!''

The Aedile's shout interrupted his self-doubt and, suddenly remembering the thing that had brought him to the jail in the first place, he ran to the door.

Coeccias was holding the dead man's head by the hair, raising it to inspect the cut throat. The guard stood nearby, gazing with morbid fascination as the wound gaped open; a crowd, drawn by the Aedile's shout, had begun to gather.

"Do you fish now with men as bait, Rhenford?" Coeccias drew a piece of seaweed from the corpse's hair, dropped it with a little grimace of disgust and wiped his hand on his jacket. "Where is this from?"

"I found him on my beach this morning," Liam explained, jumping down the steps and gesturing for the Aedile to keep his voice down. "Washed up. You see his throat?"

"Aye," Coeccias said, stepping back and considering the body. He sucked contemplatively at his teeth for a moment, then dismissed the whole thing with another wave of his hand. "Thrown from a ship, no doubt. Another one for the morgue." He turned to the guard and snapped a series of decisive orders. "See the corpse to Mother Japh's morgue, and have her get the description out. Send a man down to the waterfront—have Balstain go, he'll ask the right questions—see if a ship's missing a man, or if any know this one. And see that the Quaestor's horse is stabled. I'll be back in an hour; mind it's all done by then!"

The Guard saluted loosely and led Diamond away toward the Duke's Courts; the crowd that had gathered parted for him with a whisper of disappointment. They had clearly been expecting something more exciting, and Liam was annoyed, if not surprised, to notice that a few of them aimed their disappointed looks at him, as if he were supposed to provide something more exciting than a man thrown from a ship.

Having disposed of the body, Coeccias took Liam by the arm and steered him across the square, in the direction of the Point. Liam let himself be drawn along, frowning crossly. The Aedile began to describe what Mistress Priscian had told him about the theft, but Liam was not paying attention. He was thinking of the other man's first question, and wondering how many people on the square had heard it.

It sometimes seemed as if everyone he knew and everything he did, no matter how innocent, were conspiring to create an aura of mystery around him, to provide fodder for the city's ridiculous idea that he was a wizard. Riding into town with a corpse behind him was bad enough; then Coeccias had to compound the problem by shouting out nonsense.

I can hear it now, Liam thought. *'You know that wizard on the beach? He fishes for sharks, with live men as bait!' In every tavern and wineshop from here to Auric's Park, they will be telling that one for days. Soon enough children will be crossing their fingers at me, and trying to avoid my shadow.*

"Why did you say that, about fishing with men as bait?" he burst out as they left the square and turned onto one of the roads leading up to the Point, interrupting the Aedile in mid-sentence.

"Eh?"

The evident confusion on his friend's face mollified him a little. "Never mind," he said. "What were you saying?"

The two men were an odd pair as they walked through the streets towards the Point: Liam tall and thin, his blond hair cut short, leather boots gleaming beneath the hem of his expensive cloak, and the Aedile short and massive, his unruly hair and beard making him look like a bear dressed up in a plain quilted jacket.

Southwark went no higher than the Point, in money or elevation, but the rich who made their homes there had built themselves into a corner. The area was small, hemmed in on the north and west by less wealthy neighborhoods and to the south and east by sheer cliffs that descended to the cold winter sea. Unable to expand, they had gone up, assembling narrow-fronted stone and brick homes of five and six stories along streets whose width and straightness made a great contrast to the twisted arteries further down the hill. Liam and Coeccias turned finally onto the last of these broad, rich streets—the highest in the city and named, appropriately enough, End Street—and headed to one of the last houses in the row.

Unpretentious for the Point, Mistress Priscian's house would still have been out of place anywhere else: it had five tall-windowed stories and an elegantly tapered roof; the bricks were respectably aged and trimmed with beige stone; and the stairs that led up to the front door were of the same stone, as were the broad banisters that flanked them.

"Truth," the Aedile said, pausing at the bottom of the steps and pitching his voice close to a whisper, "you can see that it's trickish: none in the house but close friends rich and titled, stout locks without, and the Jewel gone."

"Trickish," Liam agreed impatiently. Throughout their walk, and Coeccias's retelling of Mistress Priscian's story, he had been assailed by doubts. It was not too late to back out, certainly—he had said nothing to Mistress Priscian, and Coeccias was too good-natured to think the worst of him—but he could not. He saw himself as committed, however impulsively, to at least try, and knew that the doubts were natural, second thoughts a habit with which he should long since have learned to deal.

Let's get this begun, he told himself, and went up the steps, the Aedile behind him.

He had hardly knocked before a servant answered the door; the man nodded somberly at both men and ushered them in. "My lady is in the solarium just now, sirs, with her niece. If you will wait . . ." He did not offer them an option, turning on his heel and disappearing into the depths of the house.

Liam wondered once again at the average southerner's looseness with titles; Mistress Priscian was not noble, and in the Midlands where he had grown up, calling someone a lady who was not would have been considered something of a serious offense. *But then,* he reasoned, *we had no rich merchants, only noblemen and knights and peasants. And no one would call a peasant 'lady.'*

The house was a little gloomy, the walls and floors and furniture of heavy, unreflective wood, with thick hangings in dark colors; Liam and Coeccias waited in an uncomfortable silence for the servant to return, which he did quickly, somewhat flushed. "My lady bids you come in."

"Right in," corrected a voice from further down the dark hallway. "I bid them to come right in, and not be kept standing about the door."

Liam smiled a little and went forward towards the owner of the voice, stepping into the solarium at the far end of the hall. It was a large room at the corner of the house, with tall windows looking out onto a small garden and, beyond, to a breathtaking view of the sea. White-painted walls gathered the meager sunlight, an almost blinding contrast to the dark hall. There were two women; Liam offered bows to both.

Thrasa Priscian was in almost all ways unremarkable—neither tall nor short, with a plain face just beginning to show the wrinkles of age, gray hair pulled back in a loose but tidy bun, a plain smoke-gray dress—yet it was to her, Liam noticed, and not to her considerably younger and far prettier niece, that one's attention was drawn. He thought briefly that it was her eyes, which were sharp and intelligent, or perhaps simply her immobility: in all the solarium, she alone was still. The sea beyond the windows glinted and shifted, the naked limbs of the trees in the garden swayed silently, sunlight rippled along the walls, and her niece twisted and turned in her chair, scarcely acknowledging the two men—but the old woman simply sat on a low divan, more like stone in her dress than smoke, and commanded attention.

"Y' are somewhat early," she observed to Liam, a slight nod and a grim smile adding weight to her comment. "I imagine y' have heard something of our trouble?"

"Yes," he said. "Coeccias told me."

"I see. Duessa, would you leave us for a moment?"

As she obeyed her aunt's politely phrased command, Liam noted that the niece's eyes were red-rimmed and puffy, and her face was extremely pale; she seemed to be taking the theft much harder than her aunt, who calmly motioned the men to the two delicate cane chairs opposite her as soon as her niece had stumbled out, a handkerchief pressed to her mouth.

"I imagine also that Coeccias has told you that I'm interested in what you might have to say about it," Mistress Priscian began as soon as they were seated. "He has made much of you as a solver of mysteries, you know."

Liam smiled and at the same time made a deprecatory gesture with his hands. He liked Mistress Priscian's straightforward manner, and also recognized that she was giving him a chance to set his own terms: he could simply give his opinion, go over the things he had said to Coeccias back at the jail, or he could offer to probe more deeply into the theft.

"First, let me say that Coeccias's idea of my talents is vastly exaggerated." The Aedile snorted loudly, but Mistress Priscian merely gave a noncommittal nod, accepting the statement but reserving judgement. "And I'm not sure that any thoughts I might have to offer— or any help I might give—would be of any use."

"Ha!" Coeccias said.

"Hush!" Mistress Priscian ordered, her attention still on Liam. He found himself sitting on the edge of his seat, with his hands clasped between his knees and his back held uncomfortably straight; it was a position he always adopted around the old woman. He always felt around her as if he were presenting himself to one of his masters at the university in Torquay—a well-liked master, but a master nonetheless.

"That said," he went on, "I must confess that I am interested, and would very much like to help in any way I can."

Coeccias was fairly writhing in his seat, gripping the arms of the chair and shaking his head.

"My only real reservation," Liam continued, searching for the right words to express a delicate idea, "is that I am afraid that my looking into this might damage our business relationship. As far as I can see, anything of this kind requires asking a number of questions, and peering into corners that people might wish . . . unpeered into. Do you see?" He blushed a little at the awkward sentence, but it was the best he could do to explain, without using an example he did not want to bring up. While searching for Tarquin's murderer, he had struck up a friendship with a Southwark merchant and his wife, but the investigation had revealed a number of things about their marriage that made it impossible for the friendship to continue—and he did not want a similar thing to happen to his partnership with Mistress Priscian.

She nodded once, to show she understood. "Ah, Master Rhenford, I would that there were things in my life that would not stand the light of day, but there are not. As for my niece and her household," she went on, her face growing hard, "I have no fear of aught you may discover there, and would be sure not to hold you to blame for any of their dark corners."

It was not quite the answer he had expected, and for a moment he floundered, his hands tapping on his knees and his glance going to Coeccias, who shrugged. Then, with brisk, precise movements, Mistress Priscian stood and walked to a small desk; retrieving a large sheet of heavy paper, she handed it to Liam.

"This, I think, should allay your fears, Master Rhenford. It is our contract, and as you can see, I have put my seal to it."

Pleasantly surprised, Liam glanced over the sheet; beneath the neat, compressed handwriting of a clerk, he found Mistress Priscian's seal, a neat red oval, the edges of the wax evenly trimmed. The space for his own signature, for he had no seal, was empty.

Grinning despite himself, he looked up from the contract, and Mistress Priscian nodded decisively.

"There," she said, "y' have it. When you sign it, we are partners. Now, may we see what can be done about my family's Jewel?"

"Aye," Coeccias burst out, "may we get on with it, Rhenford?"

Liam looked once more at the contract, running his thumb along the crisp edge of the paper, and then folded it carefully and tucked it into his tunic.

"Yes," he said. "Let us see what can be done."

CHAPTER 3

"I ASSUME AEDILE Coeccias has told you what he learned this morning?" Mistress Priscian asked.

"Which was precious little," the Aedile pointed out.

"No," the woman agreed, frowning. "I am afraid Duessa was not much help. She was quite . . . excited. She has calmed down a great deal since then."

Liam did not doubt that Mistress Priscian had been the calming agent, and that she might not have been very gentle about it; the way she said "excited" made him think she would not have much patience for hysterics.

"He told me something, but I think it would be better to hear it again."

Mistress Priscian nodded, and quickly outlined the same story Coeccias had told him earlier: the Oakhams had given a party, the guests had stayed the night, and in the morning the Jewel was gone. She named the same guests Coeccias had mentioned—Baron Quetivel, the Furseuses, brother and sister, Earl Uldericus and his wife, the merchant Cawood—but where Coeccias had spoken of them with frustration, because he could not approach them, there was a coldness in the widow's tone as she listed them.

"The thief, of course, is one of those," she said finally. "There are no servants in the house at night, and there are good locks all about."

"And no sign of a break-in," Coeccias supplied sadly, as if he had hoped there would be. "We conned the house entire, and all was tight as a drum."

"I should hope not," Mistress Priscian told him, and

then turned to Liam. "I bought the locks, and made sure they were strong. So the Jewel was taken by someone in the house, which means one of my niece's guests. The question then is, which one? And, as Aedile Coeccias has explained to me, how to prove it?"

Liam was silent for a moment, a little lost in admiration for the old woman. She did not act as if she had lost a priceless treasure; she might have been discussing a minor domestic annoyance, a broken dish or a burnt meal. She steepled her hands in her lap and settled a patient look upon him, clearly waiting for him to begin solving the problem.

"Well," he said, clearing his throat, "it is tricky. Since Coeccias cannot question the guests in any official capacity, we thought I might try to talk to them unofficially, as a private person, if you see what I mean."

The old woman nodded approvingly.

"And to do that, I will need to know a great deal more about, well, about everything—the Jewel, each guest, exactly what happened last night, who slept where and that sort of thing. Little details are important, and, as I said, I may ask questions that are not easily answered."

She accepted the warning with another slight frown, and then, straightening in her chair, began to talk.

"The Jewel first, I suppose. It has been in my family for as long as it has been a family. . . ."

The Priscians were old in Southwark, one of the first families to settle there when the city was established. The first Priscian of note had sailed to Alyecir as a soldier of Auric the Great in the Ghost War, and had somehow come out of that conflict with merchant contacts in Alyecir and the Freeports. With those and some luck, he had established a small trading fleet and acquired land on the Point, where he built the house in which they sat. He had two sons, one of whom was unremarkable except in that he continued in his father's footsteps, maintaining the small family fortune and having sons of his own.

The other son, however, was different.

"His name was Eirenaeus," the widow said, "and

there are a number of family legends attached to him, most of which I think are ridiculous.''

He was supposed to have been, alternately, a goblin cradle-switched with the first Priscian's son, or a normal man who practiced black magic and trafficked with demons. Whichever the case, at some point in his life he acquired the Jewel, and bound it up with the family name in such a way that the two were, in Southwark legend, inseparable.

"You are not from Southwark, Master Rhenford, or you would probably have heard the stories. I flatter myself that they are rather widespread. Currently, the Jewel is considered no more than a priceless stone, but in earlier days, it was believed to be far more than that. My father told me that his father told him it was the crystallized heart of a demon that Eirenaeus had enslaved, though he did not himself believe it.'' She left unclear which man had not believed it, and her normally composed face grew pensive. "It is not, of course—but it is quite remarkable. I would that I could show you it. I made a grave mistake in bringing it out.''

She lapsed into a brooding silence, leaving Liam to snap her out of it with an uncomfortable cough. The rumors about the Jewel were mildly interesting, but irrelevant.

"Perhaps you could explain that—bringing it out, I mean.''

The old woman came back to herself with a self-assurance Liam could only envy, and addressed his question directly. "It is the symbol of the house, you know—much like the Goddards' bauble, or Marcius's rising sun. But we Priscians have never been much on show, unlike those two, and so for as long as I can remember it has been locked away in the family crypt. Certainly I can never remember my father taking it out— though of course we could see it, on remembrance days, or when making special prayers to the family fathers. It simply sat in the crypt, on Eirenaeus's tomb. As a child I was very impressed by it, though I never wanted to touch it.''

"But you did?"

Mistress Priscian gave a small, bitter sigh. "Yes. There are no men in my family anymore, Master Rhenford, and so, as head of the household, I must perform many of the observances usually reserved for the eldest male." The Aedile nodded sagely, and Liam followed suit, though he was not overly familiar with the southern forms of ancestor worship. He had on occasion made small offerings for his father, but more to ease his conscience than out of any real conviction. The woman directed her comments now to Coeccias. "You will know, Master Aedile, that many families offer thanks to their fathers in the weeks before the Banquet."

"Illustrious ones, certainly," Coeccias agreed, tugging at his beard. "It is common enough," he added, for Liam's benefit.

"In any case," Mistress Priscian went on, completely ignoring the Aedile's compliment, "the time came for the usual offering, but I was slightly indisposed—nothing important, a mere fever—but I was somewhat unsteady on my feet, and so I asked my niece to assist me.

"Duessa is my brother's only child," she said, pursing her mouth a little, "and has suffered all the ill effects one might expect from being raised by an indulgent and weak-willed man. What one might excuse in an older brother, one finds somewhat trying in a child. Oh, she joined me readily enough—I do not fault her there—but it was her first sight of the Jewel, and I had not counted upon her reaction. I had never wanted to touch it, so why should she?"

With a start, Liam remembered that he was not simply listening to an interesting story, though he found it intriguing enough; he was supposed to be gathering information. "How had she never seen it before? You had seen it when you were a child—why hadn't she?"

Mistress Priscian gave another sigh. "My brother would not allow it, would not allow her into the crypt. He thought the sight of so many dead would not be good for her. My brother was a peculiar man, Master Rhenford, and not a very good parent. He considered the girl too high-strung to visit the crypt. And I must confess that I never argued the point with him. Indeed, I would not have asked her there if I had not been sick.''

"But if she never saw the crypt," Coeccias said, "how could she carry on with the services?''

Liam shot his friend a discouraging glance—the future of the Priscian family's religious observances was of no interest to them.

"I hope," the woman explained readily, "that my niece will have a child—a boy, preferably—before I am unable to perform the rites. And if not, then there are other possible arrangements. A sum left to the temple of Laomedon will assure remembrance.''

"Ah, in course," the Aedile said, as though it should have been obvious. Despite the pointlessness of the question, it brought a strange thought to Liam: that he had learned more about Mistress Priscian and her family in the past half hour than he had in two weeks.

"In any case," he said, returning the discussion to the matter at hand, "she saw the Jewel then?''

"Yes, and was quite taken with it. My brother—a weak-willed man, I have said—never refused her a thing, and I have yet to break her of the habit. And so, once the rites were over and before I could say a word, she took it off Eirenaeus's breast—'' She paused at the look of horror that crossed Liam's face, and then shook her head and explained none too patiently: "Not his actual breast, Master Rhenford; it was on his effigy, on the cover of his sarcophagus.'' She clucked a little at his relieved look. "His effigy, in course. As I have said, Duessa has never been refused a thing, and I was not well. And so I allowed her to convince me that she should wear it. In public! I do not pretend that it was the proper thing—we are not a family given to show, as I have said. But there it is: I allowed her.''

"It was a success, I understand.''

"Success!'' The Aedile rolled his eyes. "It was bruited all over Southwark! Truth, you could hardly pass a man in the street without a word on the rediscovery of the Priscian Jewel!''

Mistress Priscian sniffed delicately, as if she did not wish to be reminded of the widespread discussion of the Jewel. " 'Rediscovery'! It was never lost! But it should have remained where it was, that is undeniable. We Priscians have no desire to be the talk of the town, I can assure you. Though I must confess that I did not at the time think it necessarily a bad thing." She focused on Liam for a moment. "Given our arrangements, I did think that some word might be spread of the family, to prepare the way for the announcement of our activities. I trust you have no objection?"

"Not at all," he hastened to assure her. A public display of wealth like the Jewel would have made credit easier to obtain—and they would need credit for the voyages he proposed. Again, though, they were straying from the real question, and he attempted to redirect them. "So she wore the Jewel in public?"

"Yes," she replied, with a prim moue of distaste. "It was long ago set in a necklace of gold, so that it might be worn. And wear it she did—to as many balls and feasts and dances as she could."

"So a great many people would have had a chance to see it?"

"All of Southwark," Coeccias threw in, to Mistress Priscian's discomfort, though she did not deny it.

"Yes, all of Southwark, as the Aedile says. Though I do not see that it matters—I have said that the doors and windows were locked. It must have been one of my niece's guests."

Liam held up a hand for patience. "I know, but it is best to be certain that everyone knew of it."

"Oh, they did, Rhenford, they did," Coeccias assured him, drawing another pained look from Mistress Priscian.

"Then we can assume that everyone who was staying here last night was aware that the Jewel was here? Did she wear it last night?"

"I do not think she stopped wearing it," Mistress Priscian said drily. "If I did not know better, I would say she slept with it, though she did not. I insisted that she return it to the crypt each night. I saw to it myself. And I must also say the guests did not stay here. They stayed next door, in my niece's home.''

Liam shifted in his chair, leaning forward. ''Your niece does not live here?''

''No, she lives next door, as I just said. The original Priscian father built only this house at first, and then added the second for his second son. The two are both mine, since my brother's death. I allow Duessa and her husband to live in the other.''

''And where is the crypt?''

Mistress Priscian nodded, as if she had been expecting the question. ''It runs underneath the two houses—there are entrances in both cellars. They are always locked, and were still this morning, when Duessa came over to retrieve the Jewel for whatever pointless frolic she had planned for today.''

With a look at Coeccias to see if his request was acceptable, Liam asked if they might see the crypt. Before the Aedile could respond, Mistress Priscian did, rising quickly.

''In course, in course. It is as good place to start as any. And after that?''

Liam froze in the middle of rising himself. ''After that? I suppose we should talk to your niece, if we may.''

The answer seemed to satisfy her: she nodded, and led the way back to the hallway. Taking up a shielded candle, she turned into another hall that went to a large, very neat kitchen. The servant who had let them in stopped his work at the iron stove and faced his mistress with an expectant air.

''I need your keys, Haellus.''

Haellus unhooked a large ring from his belt and brought it jingling to Mistress Priscian's waiting hand.

''We will be in the crypt for some time, I expect. I am not in to any callers.''

The servant nodded and returned to his work, stoking the stove with coal. There was a door next to the coal bin; Mistress Priscian unlocked it with one of the keys from the ring, paused to light her candle and then descended the steps beyond.

Liam went down after her, trailing one hand along the cold brick of the steep, narrow staircase, ducking his head to avoid the low ceiling. The candle showed a typical storeroom, crates and barrels and bins on all sides. Mistress Priscian went straight to a far corner of the room, where three shallow steps descended to an ancient wooden door with a rounded top. She selected the proper key from the ring and inserted it in the large lock; it turned without a noise.

The hinges of the door creaked only a little when she opened it, revealing a small antechamber with an iron grill at the far end that gave onto a dimly lit space. There were shelves cut into the stone walls on either side of the antechamber, and two primed lanterns waiting on the right shelf. Mistress Priscian lit them both, handing them to the two men and keeping the candle for herself.

A gust of cold wind suddenly blew through the iron grill, setting Liam shivering. Mistress Priscian did not seem to notice it. She unlocked the grill but held it with one hand, turning to the two men.

"I need hardly remind you that this is my family's crypt."

"In course," the Aedile said, bowing his head for a moment, and Liam nodded gravely.

Satisfied with their attitudes, she pushed open the grill and motioned them to follow her in.

The crypt was all stone, a long room with a number of bays opening off either side. Five large sarcophagi lay spaced along the middle of the floor, but what interested Liam most was the spill of light that entered from the left side of the room. His hands clasped respectfully behind his back, he walked past the silent stone coffins and the yawning bays until he reached the center of the room, and looked out on the sea.

There were five bays on the right side of the room, all lined with what looked like tiers of sailor's bunks carved from stone—each bunk containing the shrouded remains of some Priscian—but on the left there were

only four; where the middle bay should have been was
a short passageway that led to a simple balcony. Another
cold, salt-laden breeze met him as he stepped out onto
the balcony, resting his hands on the waist-high balus-
trade. Above him, an overhang of rock formed a pitted
roof, and below there was only a long drop into the sea.
He could see water boiling at the base of the Point. *No
way in here,* he decided.

"A whim of the first Priscian," the woman said from
behind him. "He wished always to be able to see the
ocean. My father often used to come here to watch for
ships, though of course few enough come from the
east."

Liam nodded, and allowed her to lead him back into
the main part of the crypt. She rested her hand for a
moment on the middle sarcophagus, the one that faced
the open balcony.

"The first Priscian," she whispered. Her hand laid on
the stone fingers of her ancestor's effigy, clasped over
the stone chest. The broken haft of a mace protruded
above and below the fingers; a foot or so of the handle
and the wickedly spiked head lay next to the stone body.
"The weapon he carried when he fought for Auric the
Great," Mistress Priscian explained. "It's been like that
for as long as I can remember." The statue was worn
and pitted from centuries of exposure, and Liam resisted
the urge to raise his lantern and examine the face; he
did not think she would appreciate his purely aesthetic
interest in her ancestor's features.

After an appropriate pause, she said, "And this is Eirenaeus," gesturing with her candle at the bay immediately behind the sarcophagus of the first Priscian.
There were no bunks in this middle bay, just a single
sarcophagus. The effigy on the lid was much larger than
that of the first Priscian; close to eight feet long, with
massive stone hands almost double the size of Liam's
and a broad chest.

"The Jewel rested there," Mistress Priscian said, and
this time Liam did raise his lantern, moving along the
side of the coffin to get a better look. Shallow grooves

an inch wide had been cut in the effigy's shoulders and
across its chest; where they met was a slightly deeper
depression almost three inches wide. He suppressed a
whistle of astonishment.

If that's where the Jewel lay, he thought, *it must be
huge.*

He raised his lantern higher and peered at the face of
the effigy. If it bore any resemblance to the real Eirenaeus, he had been a cruel-looking man. His lips were
thin, compressed in a stern frown, his nose small but
obviously broken once. The stone eyes were open, but
they did not look unfocused, the way those of most statues did—they seemed to Liam to be attempting to bore
holes through the roof of the crypt, and he did not look
at them for long.

"I placed it here myself last night," Mistress Priscian
said. "My niece being quite . . . carried away by her festivities."

Liam touched the depression where the Jewel had
lain; it was cold and slightly damp. He took his finger
away quickly and wiped it on his breeches. The wetness
did not surprise him; he was only surprised that the rest
of the room was not equally damp. He had expected
decay and the stench of rottenness, or at the very least
mold—but apart from a slight mustiness, and the sea
salt, there were no smells.

"And then you locked the crypt?"

"Yes." Her tone left no question about it.

"And gave the keys to Haellus?"

"No," she said, equally firmly. "Haellus left the
house yesternight after serving dinner, to celebrate the
Banquet with his brother's family. I used my own keys;
they were in my bedchamber all night—they are there
still."

"And the door into your niece's house?" Coeccias
asked, pointing to the far end of the room, where an iron
grate stood, a twin of the one through which they had
entered.

"It was locked as well. Haellus and I have the only

keys to the crypt." She held up the ring to make her point.

Liam threw Coeccias a questioning glance; the Aedile responded with a shrug, and the two men walked to the far grate. It swung inward at Liam's tug.

Mistress Priscian's eyes bulged, but her lips pressed against each other in a way that reminded Liam of the effigy of Eirenaeus.

"I have not unlocked that door in years!" she said. "I am quite sure of it!"

Liam looked again at Coeccias, who shrugged again. "We didn't con this one—with all the outer windows and doors tight, who'd have thought of it?"

Mistress Priscian protested: "But no one ever enters through here!"

Liam frowned. "Mistress Priscian, if it was one of your niece's guests, they had to have entered this way—unless the houses are connected above?"

For the first time, he saw her at a loss—and he did not like it. It did not seem fair, somehow, that simply because she had had the misfortune to be robbed, he should be able to observe her at such moments. *Let alone tour her family crypt,* he added to himself. *How long would we have been partners before I saw this place?*

Moreover, he did not like pointing out her false assumption: that because *she* always entered the crypt through her own basement, the thief would have, too. What bothered him even more was that Coeccias seemed to have accepted the assumption as well; he knew his friend was smarter than that. *Probably the hangover,* Liam thought.

She stammered for a moment, then nodded somewhat distractedly. "No, they are not. In course. Yes, they must have come through here. But it was locked!"

Liam knelt down next to the grate. "Hold your lantern there," he told the Aedile, and examined the lock carefully. There were small scratches on the blacked plate, and scorings around the keyhole itself. "May I see the key?" Mistress Priscian reluctantly handed it to him, the rest of the ring dangling heavily from it. There were a number of intricate teeth. He stood, handing back the ring.

"It looks like it has been picked," he said to Coeccias, and then stepped into the antechamber and pushed at the wooden door there. It opened, revealing a set of steps and a cellar much like Mistress Priscian's. The second lock revealed some of the same signs. "This one as well."

The Aedile blew out an angry breath. "What does that tell us, Rhenford? Only what we already knew—that it was someone in the house. It likes me not—"

"And to think she invited them in!" Mistress Priscian said at the same time.

Liam interrupted them both: "More than that. Think of the people who were staying there. Some noblemen, their wives, a rich merchant? Do you really think they could have picked a lock? Can you pick a lock?"

"In course not!"

"No," the Aedile said, a bit more slowly. "Y' are thinking of something, Rhenford. Unless I miss my guess, y' are thinking of someone else."

"Why not?" It certainly made sense to him, at least: he did not doubt that both entries into the crypt had been locked, and he was equally sure that none of Mistress Priscian's niece's guests could have picked both locks. One might have been luck, but two was out of the question. "We can certainly assume that one of the guests is responsible—but why shouldn't they have outside help? And it gives us another interesting area to explore."

"Aye," Coeccias agreed, catching Liam's reference. "That it does."

Mistress Priscian looked at both of them skeptically. "Say you that someone allowed a common thief into my niece's house? How can you possibly know that?"

The Aedile took the question with a small bow. "We cannot know it, madam, but it seems most likely. I'd not list lockpicking among the guests' many parts, given their eminent station."

" 'Eminent station,' " the woman snorted. "Common thieves!"

"Speaking of which," Liam said, "perhaps we had best see your niece. And her husband, as well."

For a moment, she gave him a strange look, as if he had suggested something scandalous, and then her face cleared. "In course, in course. We may as well go up through the cellar, since it is so *conveniently* open."

The Oakhams' house was built as a mirror of Mistress Priscian's: they emerged from the cellar into a kitchen, but Liam was immediately struck by the differences. Where Haellus had been performing his work in an orderly way, here there was only a mess: dirty dishes piled high, scraps of food on the floor, crates filled with empty wine bottles, and a pair of fat hunting dogs snoring contentedly around the remains of a roast.

Mistress Priscian sniffed with distaste and quickly led the way out.

The hallways were plastered white, and were much brighter than those in the other house. Liam noted that the mess from the kitchen seemed to trail out into the other rooms; there were splashes of wine on one wall, and a plate had been shattered at the entrance to the room where they found Lady Oakham.

It was the equivalent of Mistress Priscian's solarium, except that it looked out on a small terrace instead of a garden, and there were eight divans arranged in a circle, instead of the older woman's simple chairs. Lady Oakham lay on one of the divans, moaning and sobbing quietly, with one arm thrown over her puffy face. A woman knelt at her side, trying to dab at her temples with a wet cloth.

"Becula!" Mistress Priscian commanded, her hands clenched into fists. "That kitchen is filthy. This house is filthy." She took an angry step forward, crunching broken shards of plate underfoot.

The kneeling woman turned sharply, a sneer on her face. "My lady is ill, madam!" As if to confirm this,

Lady Oakham groaned and rolled over, trying to hide her face in the cushions of the divan.

"Nonsense. She drank too much, and now she is having hysterics. Go and clean the kitchen."

"My lady is ill," the servant repeated, and resolutely turned her back on Mistress Priscian. Liam and Coeccias shared an uncomfortable glance.

The old woman drew herself up. "Becula!" she barked.

Lady Oakham groaned again. "Oh, do as she says, Becca, please. I can't bear it!"

Becula rose stiffly, tossing the wet cloth down on the divan. "Yes, my lady." She strode grandly out of the room, brushing insolently past Mistress Priscian; Liam and Coeccias hurriedly parted to make room for her.

"Now, Duessa," the old woman said, advancing on the divan, "I have brought the Aedile and Master Rhenford, and you must speak with them."

"Oh, Aunt Thrasa, can't they come back later?" the girl begged, her face still hidden in the cushions. "I can't possibly see them now!"

In turning over, Lady Oakham's sky-blue robe had ridden up, and Liam found he could see all the way up to the backs of her knees. The robe hugged the rest of her body tightly. He flushed and turned to Coeccias, taking the Aedile's arm and angling him away from the divan.

"Perhaps we should come back later," he whispered.

"Aye," the other man agreed nervously. "She was not so distraught earlier."

"Come, Duessa, you are acting like a child," Mistress Priscian chided the girl. "If they cannot talk to you, they cannot find the Jewel!"

"Hang the Jewel," Lady Oakham cried. "I'm going to be sick!"

"Gentlemen," Mistress Priscian began, horror in her voice—but Liam and Coeccias were already heading down the hall.

"Mayhap we can trouble Lord Oakham," Coeccias whispered to Liam.

"We will return at another time," he called over his shoulder.

They hurried out of the house by the front door, followed by the unmistakable sound of Lady Oakham being sick.

CHAPTER 4

"OVERMUCH CELEBRATING," THE Aedile said with a wink, once they were safely on the stoop.

"I should think so," Liam said, his grin a little weaker than his friend's. He was thinking more of Mistress Priscian's discomfort than her niece's; it still did not seem fair to him that he should be granted this glimpse into her personal affairs.

It was warm on the stoop, the sun shining brightly high in the sky. The snow from the street and the walks had been swept neatly into banks all along the street, and the two men allowed themselves a few moments to admire the wealthy neighborhood, the large, well-maintained houses. A black carriage with golden scrollwork on the door panels and a team of matching black horses waited outside the house next door.

"The Goddards live there," Coeccias said, pointing out the largest house, a mansion on the northwest corner of End Street. Two well-dressed men were passing by it. "Know you they've their own theater? A true theater, albeit small, in their very house! I ask you, now, what would you do with your own theater?

"Th' Antheurises'," he continued, picking out the larger houses from north to south as he went, "the Cassillevanuses', old Rotcharius's—that's his carriage." He turned and pointed to the first house south of the Oakham's. "That's Clunbrassil's, and on the corner's Apeldoorn, a Freeporter, though no slouch as to spending."

"Freihett Necquer's," Liam said, indicating the second house around the corner on Duke Street, a place he had visited often while looking for Tarquin's murderer.

"Aye, Necquer's. He has not been seen much of late." Coeccias cleared his throat. "Two houses beyond his is Rafe Cawood's. It can't be seen from here," he added, when Liam craned his neck, trying to catch a glimpse. His friend pointed back up towards the Goddards'. "Earl Uldericus's is up there, around the corner and a short way down, just near Herione's." Herione's was a brothel the Aedile had taken him to once, in search of information.

"Huh," Liam grunted. "So close."

"Close indeed, though nothing like the Warren, for all that."

"And the Furseuses?"

Coeccias thought for a moment. "Closer to the square, I think. In the neighborhood of the White Grape. The Furseii are not as great a family as they once thought they were."

"What about the other guest? Quetivel?"

"A rural lord, of some account further north. He stays with the Oakhams, I think."

"Well, that at least makes sense."

Coeccias gave him a strange glance. "What does that mean?"

Liam gestured at the neighborhood. "Doesn't it strike you as odd that all those guests, most of whom live nearby, should have stayed the night?"

Rubbing his beard, the Aedile gave it a moment's thought, and then admitted: "Now that you say it, it does seem odd. But then, there's nothing so strange about it, really. It snowed last night, and I cannot imagine any of Lady Oakham's guests trudging home in it. Particularly not if they'd, ah, indulged as much as she seems to have." He pressed a finger over his lips and blew out his cheeks, then laughed.

Liam grabbed his arm. "Watch it."

"What—" the Aedile began, then saw that the two well-dressed men had reached the stoop and were coming up.

"Master Aedile," said the taller of the two men, smiling in welcome. "Have you caught our thief yet?"

"No, Lord Oakham," Coeccias said, bowing. "Though we hope to, we hope to."

Oakham was a handsome man in his late thirties, tall and thin, with glossy black hair trimmed neatly at his shoulders and a slightly curled mustache. He wore well-worn but elegant riding clothes, held a pair of leather gauntlets in one hand, and his eyes danced with good humor as he acknowledged the Aedile's bow with a gracious nod.

"My lord," Coeccias said, indicating Liam, "this is Quaestor Rhenford, who will be looking into the robbery."

Liam bowed, and Lord Oakham gave him a friendly smile, coming up the stairs to stand between them. "Well and well, is this the same Master Rhenford of whom my wife's aunt speaks so highly?"

"The same, my lord," Liam said, bowing again.

Oakham slapped him on the arm. He turned to the man behind him, a youth of no more than twenty, with blond hair so long it was braided. He was wiry and thin, wearing far richer clothes with none of Oakham's easy grace. "Quetivel, this is the man my aunt is doing business with. I hope her faith is well placed," he added, turning back to Liam. He spoke good-naturedly, and smiled all the while, but Liam sensed that he was being weighed in the handsome lord's eyes.

"It obviously was not earlier," interjected Quetivel, shooting a contemptuous glance at Coeccias. "Where I come from, we'd have hung the thief already. How is it that you have not caught the man already, Aedile?"

"Come, Quetivel," Oakham said. "It is not so easy as all that."

"Nonsense! Surely, Aedile, you must know the thieves in your city!"

Liam tensed, noting the anger building up in his friend's shoulders and fists.

"If I knew them, my lord," the Aedile grated through clenched teeth, "I would have clapped them in last night, before the robbery. I'd not have waited til after."

"Sheer incompetence!" the young man proclaimed. "And insolence, too, Aetius! I wouldn't stand for it—this idea that it might be one of your guests!"

"To be fair, Quetivel," Oakham said, "that was my aunt's idea."

"But he subscribes to it!" Quetivel protested, thrusting a finger at Coeccias.

"I am sure no one holds to that idea anymore, Baron Quetivel," Liam interposed quickly, to forestall an angry response from his friend. "We have good reason to believe that someone from outside the house was involved, someone with experience as a thief."

"Eh?" Quetivel said, rounding on Liam.

"I wonder, your grace," Liam went on, addressing himself to Oakham, "if I might have a moment of your time. There are a number of questions I would like to ask you about the robbery."

"Certainly," the tall man said, his lips curling with stifled amusement. "Quetivel, I'm afraid I'll have to ask you t' entertain yourself for a while. Would half an hour do, Master Rhenford?"

Liam bowed graciously. "More than enough, my lord."

"Good, then. Shall we inside?" He turned to the house.

Given the obvious antagonism between Quetivel and Coeccias, Liam paused. "If I might join you in a moment, my lord, I'd like a word with the Aedile."

"In course. Come along, Quetivel." With a nod at Coeccias, Oakham opened the door and went in, followed by the sulking youth.

"See you?" spluttered the Aedile, when Liam had led him down the steps by the elbow. "What an ass! See you why I'm no good at this? Oakham's all well and good—but that Quetivel! And the rest are as noxious as he, if not more! Ah, Rhenford, it likes me to have you on this."

"My pleasure," Liam said sarcastically. *If they are all like Quetivel, this will be harder than I thought.* "Look, can you send some of your men around to the

pawnshops? Or better yet, do it yourself. See if anyone
has been making any overtures about selling the Jewel.
And check jewelers as well. Our thief might have tried
to scout out a fence before he did his work.''

Coeccias shook his head. ''No reason in it, Rhenford—you said it yourself. There's none in Southwark
who could afford it, jeweler or broker. Any man who
even suggested it would be sent off with a flea in his
ear.''

''Exactly—and that's why I think we should check.
If there were any chance of a fence or a jeweler buying
it, there would be no point, because they certainly
wouldn't tell you. But since they were all bound to refuse . . .''

A smile grew behind the Aedile's beard. ''Truth, it
sings! Since they would refuse, they'd have no reason
not to tell me, and we might con out our thief not by
where he fenced the Jewel, but by where he didn't!''

Liam held up a cautioning hand. ''Don't get too excited, now. I still don't think anyone would steal it just
to sell it. It is just a possibility.''

''Aye, aye,'' the Aedile agreed, still smiling, ''but it's
just the thing for me. For I tell you fair, Rhenford, I'm
leaving this''—he pointed at the house—''and all
this''—he swept his arm around, including the whole of
the Point—''to you. Fine lords and ladies like me not,
and don't like me either, if you see. I give you free rein.
Go to, go to!''

''Thanks,'' Liam said, and this time his sarcasm was
not lost on the Aedile, who gave a loud laugh.

''Y' asked for it, Rhenford, you did. Enjoy!''

Frowning ruefully, Liam spread his hands in surrender. *I suppose I did,* he thought.

They agreed to meet later in the afternoon, and then
the Aedile departed, strolling briskly away as if he had
not a care in the world.

Liam lingered at the bottom of the stoop, collecting
his thoughts. He would have to be more honest with
Lord Oakham, and try to convince the man to help him
find a way to interview the guests in a way that would

not arouse their suspicions. For a brief moment he
thought back to how the day started, with a dead man
outside his front door and a strange wizard in his bedroom. And now, of his own accord, he had taken upon
himself the task of searching out a thief from among a
group of people who were practically above the law.

An old proverb from the Midlands sprang to his mind:
Never a lone wolf, but a pack.

"A very rich pack," he said to himself as he started
back up the steps. "But a pack nonetheless."

The maidservant Becula answered his knock with
barely suppressed impatience, soapy water dripping
from the sleeves of her plain frock.

"What would you?" she demanded. "Were you not
just here?"

A little taken aback, Liam said: "I was, and now I
am here again. Lord Oakham is waiting for me."

"Huh," she said, as if she did not think it likely, and
then turned and walked away, leaving the door open,
shouting as she went, "Tasso! Someone for the master!"

Another servant appeared on the stairway that ran off
the main hall before Becula had reached the kitchen, a
sour-faced man with a pursed mouth and thinning black
hair plastered to his skull.

"Master Rhenford," he said, beckoning, "this way,
please." Without waiting for a reply, he turned on his
heel and went back up the stairs.

Liam stopped for a moment, noting the thick wooden
bar leaning in a corner just inside the entrance; at night
it would have hung in brackets across the door. Then he
went up the stairs, musing a little about the quality of
the Oakhams' servants. They had certainly not been chosen for their winning way with visitors. *Though I imagine that Quetivel gets a warm welcome,* he reflected
without bitterness. He had known servants with affec-
tations before, and he guessed that a title would have
gotten him a far more gracious greeting.

He paused at the landing, having lost sight of the manservant. The second-floor hallway was dark.

I wonder what they would think if they knew that I was once a lord's son, with a chance at inheriting a domain a quarter of the size of the whole Southern Tier?

The "once" being the important part, he reminded himself. *'Once,' and a long time ago.* There was no point in laying claim to a title that had long since been taken from him—and so he only smiled a little when the manservant hissed at him from a dark end of the long landing.

"Hsst! Master Rhenford! Over here!"

Then the man opened the door at which he had been standing, letting light into the hallway. He announced Liam in a solemn manner, and held the door for him.

Casting his eyes down to hide his smile from the suddenly proper servant, Liam strolled past him and into Oakham's study.

Animal skin rugs, worn from long use, covered the floor, racks of antlers adorned the walls, and there were a few simple chairs grouped near the fireplace. Tall, narrow windows offered a view of the houses across the street. Oakham stood by the hearth, warming his hands at the fire and staring up at a tapestry hung over the mantle. It was a hunting scene, and it took Liam only a moment to recognize that the central figure, busily engaged in spearing a stag from horseback, was the lord himself.

Oakham turned, caught Liam's glance, and gestured at the tapestry. "Handsome, eh? A wedding gift from my aunt."

"It is very well done, my lord," Liam said truthfully.

The other man chuckled. "She thinks me vain, is my guess. In any case, we are not here to discuss my aunt's opinion of me, nor her taste in gifts. Tell me—have you really any hope of conning out the thief?"

Whatever the quality of the servants, Liam found himself responding to their master. The lord seemed friendly enough, and there was an earnestness to his question that gave Liam the idea he might have found an ally.

"That depends, my lord."

"On what?" He gestured to a seat. "Sit, please, and

tell me. I am anxious to have this solved."

"It depends a great deal on you, my lord," Liam said, acting on his rather sudden liking for the man. Oakham froze in the act of putting his hand on the mantle and stared hard at Liam, who went on quickly: "I was not entirely honest outside, when I said that no one thought the thief might be one of your guests. The simple fact is that someone inside the house was almost of necessity involved."

"How so?" Oakham finished putting his hand on the mantle and leaned there, frowning heavily.

"The locks on the doors of the crypt were picked, your grace, a simple enough piece of work for a trained thief—"

"Well, then . . ." Oakham interrupted, gesturing with his free hand, as if to say: There you have it.

"—simple enough, of course. But the outer door is barred at night, is it not?"

The man at the mantle closed his eyes for a moment, then nodded, grimacing a little. "So y' are saying someone from within the house must have opened the outer door for this trained thief?" He began pacing up and down in front of the fireplace, his hands behind his back.

"Yes, my lord. I understand that this is unpleasant— they are your friends, after all—"

"Give no thought to that," Oakham interrupted. "They are more my wife's friends than mine, and while I like them well enough, I harbor no illusions. A titled man can be as bad as a beggar. Though mind you," he said, pausing in his pacing and leveling a finger at Liam, "I exclude Quetivel. He is my cousin, and a personal friend, and I would trust him with my life and my honor."

"Of course, my lord," Liam said, making a mental note to put Quetivel at the top of his list of suspects. "I will exclude anyone from suspicion that you vouch for."

"I'll warrant Quetivel's innocence only," Oakham said, resuming his walk back and forth. "Now tell me, how does this depend on me?"

"The simple fact is, my lord, that the rest of your

guests are either titled or possess the Rights of the Town.''

Oakham gestured impatiently: Get to the point.

''That makes it very difficult for us to get any information from them. And information is crucial in something like this.'' Liam stroked his chin briefly, reflecting. ''I have helped the Aedile only twice, my lord, and what help I was able to give him those two times was based entirely on information. Being able to ask questions, to learn things. The more we know about the crime—what was stolen, when it was stolen, where it was stolen from—and the more we know about who might have committed it—why they might have done it, whether they had a chance to do so—the closer we will be to solving it. Does this make sense, my lord?''

Oakham had stopped pacing and was carefully following Liam's words, his eyes narrowed and speculative. After a moment, he spoke.

''I think so. What you want to do is question my guests, but because they are all highly placed, the Aedile cannot do it. I still don't see how this depends on me, however.''

Liam cleared his throat. This was the hard part, but he was encouraged by Oakham's earlier comment about his lack of illusions. ''I would like it if you could arrange an introduction for me to your guests. A letter, perhaps—asking each to help me as much as they are able, to tell me everything they can remember from last night. You could even introduce me as a friend of your aunt.''

There was a long pause, during which Oakham lightly ran the back of one finger under his mustache, smoothing it. The implications of what Liam had asked were clearly not lost on him: his eyes looked troubled, and a small frown tugged at the corners of his mouth.

''It has the complexion of a lie, Master Rhenford.''

''The complexion, perhaps, but not the essence. I am a friend of your aunt, and I do wish to help.''

''But to say that, and not say that you suspect them— that has the complexion of a lie.'' Oakham's voice dropped, as if he were thinking of something else, and his eyes were unfocused, as if he were visualizing that thing.

Liam spoke again, but he had the impression that his words went unheard. "Surely they must realize that they are suspected. Who else do they think might have done it?"

With a sudden chuckle, Oakham returned his attention to Liam. "Y' are not much of my wife's set of friends, Master Rhenford, or you would not ask that question. They would never dream that suspicion would fall on them. More, if they did dream it, then they would certainly take my sending you as an extreme insult." He stopped, staring down at the floor for a moment, and then, before Liam could respond, started again. "But come, I have another, better idea. Rather than a letter, why don't I introduce you to them in person? I can arrange things so that it appears under a different, more friendly complexion. No letters, no appeals for help. You might meet them . . . informally, as it were. What do you think?"

It seemed more like a lie to Liam than a simple letter of introduction, but he was not about to let that get in the way. Meeting them in a less than official capacity might make them more open, more prone to let their guards down. And being with Oakham might make him more acceptable; he would be a friend of a friend, instead of an agent of the Duke.

If he can justify it to himself, who am I to argue?

"It sounds like just the thing, my lord. It will certainly make my questions less confrontational, if they do not see me as some kind of inquisitor."

Oakham nodded decisively and resumed his pacing. "Good then. We'll see to this thing together, then. To start with, we can meet Uldericus tonight. Quetivel and I were to spend the evening with him; I begged off this morning, but Quetivel is still going, so it will be easy for me to rejoin the party, with you in tow. Cawood will be easy enough—we can visit him at the Staple tomorrow. I often see him there, so it will not be unusual. And if I present you as a friend of my aunt, he'll make no question about it.''

For a man who had complained about the appearance of a lie only a few minutes before, Oakham struck Liam as awfully eager to begin what would amount to a deception. But then, he told himself, the niceties of social interactions between southern nobility were beyond him. In the Midlands, the local lords rarely interacted, except on the battlefield. He had grown to the age of eighteen within a day's ride of the nearest lord, and only met him three times—once when the lord came to demand the Rhenfords' surrender, once when his army stormed Rhenford Keep, and the last time when Liam killed him.

If Oakham sees a difference between presenting me by letter and presenting me in person, I have no objections—as long as I am presented.

Still pacing, Oakham stroked his mustache furiously. "The Furseuses, now, will not be so easy. I do not have much to do with them—they are my wife's particular friends. I shall have more on it with her, later; she is indisposed just now. In the meantime, Uldericus and Cawood are a start. Is that sufficient for you?''

"More than sufficient, my lord.'' Liam rose, inclining his head out of deference. "More than I could have expected.''

"Attend a moment!'' Oakham said, whirling on Liam. "Y' are not going, are you?''

"I had thought—'' Liam began.

"But how will you proceed? What are your plans?'' He spoke heatedly, surprising Liam, and then added hastily: "I would know, so that I may be of help. This theft has upset my wife tremendously, and I would see it speedily concluded.''

"Of course, my lord,'' Liam said, blinking a little at Oakham's unexpected eagerness and sitting down again. "Well, as I said, I believe a thief must have been involved, to pick the locks. Coeccias and I will look into that, and try to find the thief.''

The tall lord took a seat next to Liam, wearing a rather

intense look of curiosity. "You can do that? Find a particular thief, I mean? How?"

"There are ways," Liam replied, and then, realizing how mysterious that sounded, added: "People who, while not thieves themselves, know of them. Pawnbrokers, certain tavernkeepers, some women—we can ask them."

"Pawnbrokers," Oakham repeated, leaning back in his chair while the curiosity faded on his face. "Some women. I see, I see. Then you will be busy, I imagine. It must be more than the work of an hour, to question all those sorts of people."

There was only one person Liam meant to speak with, and she actually was a thief, but he did not want to tell Oakham that. "Yes, my lord. But if I might ask one more thing?"

A little impatiently, Oakham said: "In course, in course."

"I wonder if you might describe your guests for me."

"I don't follow you." He straightened in his chair, a suspicious look on his face.

Liam straightened as well, holding out his hands in an innocent gesture. "Just what they look like, my lord. I know only their names—but the people I will be talking to might not know their names, only their faces."

"Ah," Oakham said, in a tone bordering on enlightenment. The suspicious look faded as quickly as his curiosity. "In course. Well, there is Uldericus. . . ."

It did not take long for Oakham to give Liam descriptions of his guests, but Liam prolonged it as much as he could, trying to read as much as possible into what the lord said. The other did not give much away, restricting himself to simple appearances—though his own feelings did show through once or twice, and Liam made careful note of them. When it finally became clear that, for the moment, there was no more information to gain in the Oakhams' house, he took his leave.

They agreed on a time to meet that evening, and then Oakham called for Tasso to show Liam out.

"Until eight, then," the handsome lord said, thought-fully tapping his lips with one long forefinger and nodding at the same time.

"Until eight," Liam responded, bowing, and then allowed Tasso to lead him down the stairs and to the front door.

Once they were out of earshot of his master, the servant made little pretense of deference, opening the front door and then shutting it as if he were shooing away an unwelcome dog.

Liam jumped down the steps and then paused on the street, taking a deep breath. He was not at all sure he was proceeding the right way—he thought, for instance, that he ought to have looked around the Oakhams' house a little more, seen the rooms where the guests stayed, tried to talk to Lady Oakham again.

But you didn't, did you? he asked himself, and realized he knew why. He had been put off by Oakham, by his nobility. *You were once nobility,* he chided himself, but it made no difference. Since the sack of his father's keep, he had been a wanderer, both within Taralon and far beyond its borders, and the company he kept had been mostly low. Soldiers and seamen, merchants, factors, spies and caravan masters, thieves and rogues of all descriptions—he was comfortable with them, knew where he stood. But he had been so long out of the company of the class to which he had once belonged that he was a little in awe of them.

And it doesn't make it any easier that Oakham is so aware of his station, he thought. *And his servants, too.* He wondered for a moment how Coeccias stood it, being treated so disrespectfully by Quetivel and even by the servants of the great houses. *It must be galling,* Liam decided, *but I guess he doesn't think about it much. Just accepts it.*

With a shrug and a promise to himself to try to follow his friend's example, he turned right, starting for Mistress Priscian's door—and stopped.

In turning, his eyes rose to the second floor of the house he had just left, and he saw Lord Oakham standing at a window, staring down at him. From his posture and the way he held aside the curtain, it seemed as if he had been watching for some time. When he saw Liam looking up, he smiled and waved once, a regal wave, almost a dismissal.

Liam bowed once again and resumed his walk to Mistress Priscian's door.

Haellus answered the door when Liam knocked, and informed him that Mistress Priscian was unavailable. "Lady Oakham has been taken ill," the servant said, inclining his head meaningfully towards the house next door. "And my mistress must attend her. Would you wait, Master Rhenford?"

"No," Liam decided, "but tell her I will call on her later in the day, if she does not mind."

The other man gave him a deferential nod, waiting until he had turned and started down the stairs to shut the door. On the street, Liam paused, rubbing his hands and thinking.

I will have to have a plan, he realized, *something more specific than just following Oakham around and hoping for a clue.* He would need more information on the guests, preferably from an impartial source, and a set of questions to ask each, as well as a suitable way to present them in a social setting. *Of course,* he joked to himself, *I could just let Oakham introduce me, and start hammering them. 'Good evening, Earl Uldericus. Did you steal the Priscian Jewel?'*

Variations on that theme kept a smile on his face as he walked away from the Priscian houses. He turned onto Duke Street, wondering about the Furseuses' re-action to a direct accusation, and then he remembered Coeccias's roll call of the Point's inhabitants. He knew Freihett Necquer's house well—the Freeporter merchant and his wife were the couple he had befriended while looking for Tarquin's murderer—and the Aedile had said that Rafe Cawood lived two doors down. Slowing his pace a little, he examined the house as he passed. Simple red brick with a narrow front and modest gables, it did not detract from the neighborhood's aura of quiet wealth, though it stood between two far larger homes. It seemed merely a pause, a comma in a long sentence of larger words, over which the eye slid without much notice.

Snapped at by a cold breeze, Liam gave a small shrug and moved on. *Does he dream of a bigger house?* he wondered. *With his own theater, maybe?* There was no way the Jewel could be sold in Southwark, or the proceeds spent there. It was simply too small a town, and a merchant's profits were common gossip, easily tallied even by strangers. So what would a thief gain?

Simple possession, perhaps. Liam had known men to become obsessed with something they did not have—a woman, a ship, a kingdom. And as Coeccias had said, a miser did not necessarily build a golden house.

The theft of the Jewel, a symbol of the Priscian family, might have been a form of revenge, or an attempt to put them at a disadvantage in trading, but that seemed highly unlikely: he could not imagine Thrasa Priscian having such enemies, and her share of Southwark's trade was very small. And in any case, symbols such as the Jewel were much less important in Southwark than in the Freeports, where they were equated with great political power as well as wealth.

The houses grew smaller, the street narrowed; Liam descended from the Point into the middle-class neighborhoods of the city, mulling over motives. Without really thinking about it, he turned off Duke Street a block before it passed the temple of the Storm King, and headed inland, towards the city square.

Cawood's modest house stayed in his mind. If the merchant had stolen the Jewel, he could not simply sell it and start spending money. He would have to make up a source for the sudden wealth, as, indeed, would any of the other guests. It might be easier for Uldericus or Quetivel, who presumably had lands somewhere else in the duchy and could claim them as sources of revenue. But then, where would they sell it?

There was not enough private money in Southwark,

of that Liam was sure. Some of the treasuries on Temple Street would have enough, of course, but no temple would deal in stolen goods. It would have to be sold in a larger city, a Freeport or Harcourt or Torquay, and that would require contacts in one of those cities. Cawood might be presumed to have those—but would any of the others? They were Southern Tier aristocracy, and from what little he had seen of that breed, he knew they were not great travelers. During his time as a student in Torquay, he had never met a single person from the Southern Tier, though the duchy was relatively close to the capital, and the scholars there drew students from all over Taralon.

So if it was stolen for money, Cawood is probably the one, Liam decided, and then shook his head. He was jumping to conclusions, and getting far ahead of himself. That sort of speculation would have to wait until he knew more about the guests; in the meantime, he would have to look in other directions.

CHAPTER 5

THE FESTIVE AIR of the square was even more pronounced when Liam entered it; the booths selling hot wine were crowded, and music drifted from the taverns and restaurants lining the eastern side. It surprised him: concentrating on the theft, he had forgotten that few other people had such unpleasant preoccupations. A day that brought most everyone else only thoughts of the week of celebration to come had brought him a corpse on his doorstep and consideration of the possible motives for theft among friends.

How does Coeccias stand it? Liam asked himself, going to the counter of a booth selling roasted chestnuts. *Always knowing the worst, and having to solve it, or clean it up.* The man behind the counter took his coin and scooped a handful of nuts into his cupped palm, with a "Merry Banquet" and an open smile. Liam nodded back and stepped away from the stall, juggling the hot chestnuts from hand to hand.

The chestnut man knew nothing about stolen jewels or sailors with their throats cut; he knew it was Beggar's Banquet, and time to sell as many chestnuts as he could. What Liam knew gave him a feeling of distance from the people around him, a sense, almost, of superiority. *They do not know what has happened,* he thought, *and I do.* He realized too that it was foolish, that what he knew did not make him superior. Even what he did about it, if anything, would not make him so. Coeccias could feel superior, because he had to deal with the city's problems all the time, day in and day out, and had somehow managed to avoid becoming jaded or bitter.

For Liam it was no more than a lark, really, a game with a potentially positive outcome, but still a game.

Except that it is not a game to Mistress Priscian, he scolded himself, *nor to that sailor.* The sailor was not his problem; the stolen Jewel, however, was, and he resumed his thinking while gingerly biting into the first of his chestnuts. It burned the roof of his mouth a little, but he swallowed it quickly and took a second one.

There was nothing he could do about the guests at the moment; that would have to wait for his introductions from Lord Oakham. The Aedile was checking into the possibility of someone having tried to fence the Jewel, or at least to seek out a fence. A remote chance at best, Liam knew, but worth looking at—he had learned more than once to leave no stone unturned. That left him with one direction to explore, one which neither Coeccias nor Oakham could help him with: the thief who had picked the crypt lock.

Which means Mopsa and the Werewolf.

In his years of travel, Liam had been many things, from clerk to sellsword, surgeon to ship's captain—and, briefly, apprentice thief. More by accident than design, he had fallen in with a legendary thief from Harcourt, who had taken him under his wing and taught him the craft. Chances to practice had never really come his way, but Liam remembered enough of the lore so that, when someone broke into his house a month or so earlier, he had been able to find the Southwark Thieves' Guild and convince them that he was a retired "chanter," as they called themselves.

The Southwark Guild was not an impressive thing, hardly more than a gang, and they had not been responsible for the break-in, but he had maintained a fair amount of contact with them. And he had also done them a service, laying to rest the soul of a thief named Duplin who had been murdered, so Liam thought they would be responsive to him. The only thief he knew well was an apprentice, a young girl named Mopsa who had been assigned to help him look for his things. All he had to do was seek her out and arrange an appointment with the Werewolf, the head of the Guild.

If you can find her, he thought. Since there was no guildhouse he could apply to, and the one hideout he knew of had been abandoned, his only option was to wander the streets and hope that he could find the girl.

Sighing resignedly, he tossed the last chestnut, now cold, into his mouth, dusted his hands, and set off for the Warren.

The Warren was not the lowest point in Southwark—the docks and the warehouse district were a little lower—but it was certainly the dirtiest and, in winter, the darkest. With the sun perpetually low on the southern horizon, even in the middle of the day the neighborhood lay in the shadow of the Teeth, the jagged fence of rock that guarded the city's harbor from the sea. Walking down Harbor Street from the city square, Liam could actually see a dark dividing line across the road, a visible border between neighborhoods, as if the people of the Warren could not afford sunlight.

Shops were open along Harbor Street, hung with ribbons and greenery and offering up holiday fare—fat plucked geese, barrels of oysters, bushels of giant lobsters—but Liam paid them no mind, pushing through the dense crowds of shoppers, his boots slipping occasionally on the slick cobbles. The shops grew fewer and farther between as he approached the zone of shadow that marked the beginning of the Warren, the buildings growing shabbier, as often as not with boarded-up doors and gaping, empty windows. Once he entered the shadow, pulling his cloak close about him against the sudden chill, even the humped piles of snow by the side of the road looked dirtier, more soot-encrusted, and the few attempts at holiday decoration seemed somehow sad to him.

He had no definite destination, just the vague idea of wandering around the Warren until he ran into Mopsa or darkness fell. His good clothes brought him a great deal of covert attention, whispers and pointing, but, sunk in his own gloomy thoughts, he paid them no mind, simply going where his feet led him.

The buildings here were mostly wooden, the rare brick or stone construction a dilapidated monument to better times, all of them rising in tottering stories high above the street. Sometimes the buildings met, overhanging floors reaching out across narrow alleys and throwing deep shadows; he hurried past these.

Once he interrupted a group of children at a game and asked them if they had ever heard of Mopsa, but they only stared at his boots and mumbled, unused to being addressed by anyone so well dressed. Liam hurried away from them as well.

After nearly an hour of pointless searching, he suddenly stopped, closed his eyes, and cursed and smiled at the same time.

Fool, he berated himself. *In a holiday week, with people out buying, why would she be in the Warren?* And a moment later, inspiration following on inspiration, he thought of Fanuilh.

I was wondering when you would call me, the dragon thought to him, as Liam looked down through its eyes at the Arcade of Scribes.

Of all the benefits conferred by their bond as master and familiar, seeing with Fanuilh's eyes was the one Liam liked the least. It often made him dizzy, and he had noticed a slight distortion in the dragon's eyesight that gave him headaches if he looked too long.

You might have suggested it before, Liam projected back grumpily. *Move a little to your left.*

His field of vision shifted—Fanuilh must have been perched on a rooftop opposite the Arcade—and he could see the professional letter-writers lined up behind the arches, some squatting by small wooden secretaries, others seated behind broad tables, and all with samples of their work pinned to boards close at hand. Some of the scribes had braziers nearby, to keep their hands and inks warm; others were bundled up, hands thrust under their armpits or deep in their pockets. There were more people than usual waiting, anxious to buy the gaily drawn Banquet messages, some done in as many as five different color inks.

He had sent Fanuilh flying over Harbor Street and the city square with no result, strolling leisurely after it, pausing when the dragon was in position. Shading his own eyes, he had shifted to the dragon's sight, but both street and square, though busy, held no sign of the young thief. A brief flight over Temple Street, where people with fat purses were going to make offerings, had proven equally fruitless. As a last chance, he had sent Fanuilh to the Arcade.

There she is.

He recognized her first by her lank, dull brown hair; she was lounging against one of the arches, looking for all the world like some innocent waiting for her parents. She still wore the clothes Liam had bought for her a month before, although the jacket was dirtier and the hem of the dress had been taken up so that it did not drag at her heels. New was the glint of steel that peeked from her clenched fist. Her gaze rested on a man on line for the nearest scribe; he was third from the front of the line, wearing an expensive red cloak that he had flipped back from his belt to expose the pouch tied there.

Liam snapped back to his own eyesight, aware of a dull ache in the back of his head, and hurried the three blocks to the Arcade. By the time he arrived, the man in the red cloak was at the front of the line, and he could see Mopsa tensing. He edged his way up next to her and, before she knew he was there, leaned back against the arch and tapped her arm.

"Avé, pickit," he whispered, and then grabbed her arm as she tried to bolt.

For a moment, seeing the fear on her face as she found herself caught, he regretted the trick, but then her look of relief made him laugh.

"You are not careful enough," he began, letting go of her arm.

"Don't do that!" she hissed. "You near frighted me to death!"

He let go of her arm. "Well, you aren't careful enough. What if I had been someone else?"

Mopsa whipped her head around, scanning the crowd, suddenly nervous. "Are there any here?"

"No," Liam assured her, "but if there had been, they might have seen your friend. I did." He tapped the hand that held her knife. "Now come on, I need to talk to you."

The girl frowned at him. "Can't. I'm working." She cast a glance over her shoulder at the man in the red cloak, who was ordering a number of Banquet greetings in various colors.

"Too late," Liam said. "He will have spent it all before you can get to him—and you couldn't cut both strings without him noticing. Come on."

"I could," she said, pouting.

He shook his head. "Come on. It's important." He gestured for her to precede him, but she hung back, suspicious.

"How important?"

"Important enough for lunch," he sighed.

Grumbling, she agreed, discreetly tucking her knife back up her sleeve. "Where will we eat?"

There was a stall selling sausages and bread nearby. "There," Liam said, pointing, and with a quick grin Mopsa darted away, shouting an order as she went. Before he could reach her, she had ordered three.

"My uncle'll pay," she was saying as he arrived, and the sausage-seller's look of skepticism faded when she saw Liam. She gave him a half-curtsy and drew three sausages from her little grill.

"And one for myself, and bread if you have any."

"Mine on bread too!" Mopsa demanded, and grabbed the first two sandwiches that the woman laid on the counter and thrust them into her jacket. The third she snatched and started gobbling.

"Hungry child," the sausage-seller noted.

"I haven't fed her for a week," Liam said, counting out his money. "It's too expensive." Dropping a few coins on the counter, he took his own sandwich, gave the woman a bright smile, and steered Mopsa away from the stand with a hand on her head.

"Over there." He nudged her toward a relatively isolated corner at the end of the Arcade. The girl went willingly, engrossed in her meal. By the time they reached the spot, she was already starting on her second sausage. Liam took a bite of his own, then grimaced: the bread was stale, and the sausage was mostly gristle and fat. Shaking his head, he handed it to Mopsa, who stowed it in her jacket without comment and without interrupting her steady eating.

Not for the first time, Liam wondered how old she was. *Twelve? Certainly not more than fourteen.* Her clothes were considerably dirtier than when he had given them to her. *But she does not look too bad, otherwise. She doesn't smell as bad, and she isn't starving.* She was skinny but not emaciated, and her face looked full enough, though there were dark circles under her eyes.

"Well," she said, finishing the second sausage and licking her fingers, "what would you?"

"I need to see the Werewolf."

"And why?" she asked, folding her arms across her chest, more a gesture of curiosity than suspicion.

"To tell him how much I love him."

She laughed and clapped her hands. "That'll set him running, sure! Honest, now—why?"

"None of your business. Just tell him that I want to see him."

"And he's to come running, like a dog to heel? I can't go to him with that!"

He had to admit that she had a point. He was not in a position to order the Werewolf to come to him—and the thief was not much given to casual meetings. "Right. Just tell him that something has gone free in the Point, and I would like to see him about it. At his convenience."

"To reslave it?"

They were slipping into thief slang, something Liam did not want to do on a public street.

"Not necessarily. Possibly, but not necessarily. I may

just want some information. In any case, I'd like to meet with him, as soon as possible. Can you tell him that?''

Mopsa gave him a little sneer. ''See you, I'm not a messenger boy.''

''No,'' he agreed, ''but you are eating my sausages. And I will make you a deal—if you promise to deliver the message and return with the answer, I will get you a Banquet gift.''

Her eyes lit up, half wary and half excited. ''What sort of gift?''

Liam gestured mysteriously, covering up the fact that he had no idea what sort of gift. ''Something grand.''

Mopsa's eyes narrowed. ''How much will you spend?''

He snorted his astonishment. ''I forgot what a little weasel you are, Mopsa. You don't ask how much someone is going to spend on a gift.''

''You do if they're only gifting you so you do them a service.''

Leaning forward, he poked her in the shoulder with one long finger. ''Listen, pickit, if you don't deliver my message, and return with the answer, not only will you not get a gift, but I can guarantee that the Werewolf will make your life very unpleasant for a very long time.''

''Go to, go to!'' She knocked away his finger and massaged her shoulder, though he knew he had not poked her hard. ''I'll tell him, I will. There's no call for rudeness. Gods.''

Satisfied, Liam nodded. ''When you have his answer, leave it at Herlekin's. You know the place?'' Herlekin's was a tavern on the city square, opposite the Guard barracks and the Duke's Courts.

''Aye, I know it,'' she said, a little sullenly. ''But it may not be today, for that the Wolf is sleeping. It may be tomorrow.''

''Tomorrow morning, then. Leave word with Herlekin.''

''When will I get my gift?''

''Gods, you are a greedy one! You'll get your gift after I have seen the Werewolf. Fair enough?''

She agreed with ill grace and, without another word, headed off to the west, down the hill and in the general direction of the Warren.

Liam remained behind a minute, shaking his head and smiling ruefully. When he could no longer see her, he turned to go himself, stopping when a particularly gaily colored Banquet greeting caught his eye. He stepped up to the board to examine it. About a foot wide and half that tall, it had a twisting border of greenery punctuated with bright red berries; the scene showed a group of impossibly fat and happy beggars in multicolored clothes singing against a background that he recognized as Temple Street.

For a moment, he was tempted—*Would she . . . ?*— and then he came to his senses. *She would hate that. Maybe a new knife?*

With a last shake of his head, he left the Arcade and headed for the city square, trying to figure out what sort of gift he would get the apprentice thief.

The noon bells had rung while Liam was looking for Mopsa, and by the time he reached the Guard barracks he realized he was hungry.

Coeccias was hunched over the same table, laboriously scratching away at a piece of paper. When he saw Liam at the door he barked a happy laugh, crumpled the paper, and tossed it over his shoulder into the fire.

"It likes me to see you, Rhenford—I was just leaving you a note."

"Have you eaten?"

"I have, for that I didn't expect you so early; I thought we'd dine, not lunch. But I can send a man for something, if y' are hungry—" The Aedile half rose, but Liam waved him back to his seat.

"No need." He brought a stool over to the table and sat facing his friend. "What was the note about?"

Coeccias sat again, leaning back and scrubbing at his cheek thoughtfully. "An interesting thing I've conned out, passing interesting. Look you, after we parted, I set straight about looking up fences, but as I happened to

go by way of the Alley of Riches—do you know it?
There are the most of our jewelers and goldsmiths and
whatnot—and I bethought me of how much the Priscian
Jewel could fetch, and how a fence might not afford it,
but a jeweler might. So I stopped in. Now there are not
so many, six or seven in all, and look you, there's a
Yezidi there, much the richest of all of them, and he told
me a man had been in asking in particular about the
Priscian Jewel!''

''Trying to sell it?'' Liam asked eagerly, unable to
believe their luck. ''What did he look like?''

Coeccias held up a hand. ''Now this is where it passes
merely interesting, Rhenford. He was not asking if he
could *sell* the Jewel—but if he could *buy* it!''

''What?''

''Here's more on it,'' the Aedile went on gravely.
''Our Yezidi friend swears up and down that his ques-
tioner was a wizard.''

''Wait a moment, wait. What do you mean, buy the
Jewel?''

''Just that! He waited on the Yezidi yesterday morning, and asked him what he knew of the Priscian Jewel.
The jeweler told him what he knew, which is what
everyone knows, and then this man asked if he thought
the Priscians would sell it!''

Liam frowned and stared at the floor. ''But that makes
no sense. . . .''

''Give me news, Rhenford; I know that. But that is
what happened, or so the Yezidi swears.''

''What did he say?''

''About whether they'd sell? He said no, that it was
the family symbol, that it was priceless and so on. And
then the man left. That's all. But a wizard, now? And
asking after the Jewel? It must connect with our theft.''

A thought struck Liam. ''Are you sure the Yezidi said
it was a man?''

''Aye. He gave his particulars—unless women wizards grow beards. Why?''

Liam gave a shrug. ''There is a wizard, a woman, at
my house now. Now that I think of it, though, she had

not heard of the Jewel until today." *Or had she?* he wondered.

Surprisingly, Coeccias winked. "At your house now, is she? Attending your return? Rhenford, your wonders never cease."

"It's nothing like that," he said, scowling a little. "She was a friend of Tarquin's, and he left her some things." The Aedile's knowing smile stayed firm, so he hurried on. "That's not important now. What did he look like, and when did the jeweler see him?"

To be honest, he was not sure what to make of Coeccias's information. It should have been a thief, someone who could pick locks, who approached the Yezidi jeweler, not a wizard—but he listened carefully to the description anyway. A man of medium height, with an odd accent and a red beard that only partially covered a purplish mark on his cheek. He had visited the jeweler the morning before the theft, which meant he had to be considered a suspect.

"With such as that," the Aedile summed up happily, "the mark and the beard, he should not be hard to con out. I'll send a man around to the better inns, and with luck we can clap him in soon."

Liam frowned, disconcerted as much by his friend's smile as by the strange appearance of the wizard. "He might not be staying at an inn. He could be staying with someone he knows. If he opened the door to the crypt, he might be staying with the person who let him into Oakham's house. He could be anywhere in the city."

Taking the hint, Coeccias dimmed his smile a bit, but did not let it go entirely. "True enough—but anywhere is also somewhere, and there is nothing for it but to look where we may. Now tell me, how was it with Lord Oakham? Did he tell you anything of note?"

"Not precisely," Liam said, and explained his appointment for later in the evening. "I think he hopes I can question his friends without looking like I'm questioning them. It's rather a fine line."

"Very fine," Coeccias agreed. "These are prickly, Rhenford, these lords and ladies. I'm not sure it's well conceived. They could easily take offense at the simplest of questions—and y' are known to be associated with me.''

''What else can we do? It seems better than just knocking on their doors. In any case, I will try it tonight with Uldericus, and if it doesn't work, we can try knocking.''

They left it at that, each mulling over his own uncomfortable thoughts. Liam was reconsidering the whole plan he had worked out with Lord Oakham; in the light Coeccias had put on it, it seemed chancy at best—but then, what choice did he have? It had to be better than simply knocking on each guest's door. In fact, he was more concerned about the addition of the unknown wizard to the situation. What would a wizard want with the Jewel? *I might ask Grantaire,* he thought, and even as he did, he remembered his promise to return in the afternoon and speak with her. He stood quickly, pulling on his cloak.

''I have to go. I have to meet someone.''

''Is it to do with the Jewel?''

''No,'' he said hastily, ''it's my guest. I promised her some time this afternoon.'' Seeing Coeccias's incipient wink, he cut it off with: ''I think she wants to hear about how Tarquin died. And come to think of it, I will ask her if she knows of any other wizards in Southwark at the moment. It might save your man a round of the inns.''

The wink did not appear, but the knowing smile refused to go away. ''In course, in course. Shall we meet tomorrow?''

They agreed on a time, early in the morning, and then Liam left, shaking his head at the way Coeccias could misconstrue the simplest situations.

Diamond was restive; Liam had to restrain the horse in the narrow streets of the city. Past the city gate he loosened the reins a little, but only enough for Diamond to reach a smart trot. A cold wind was blowing from the east, and Liam did not fancy galloping face-first into it;

besides, he wanted a little time to think before reaching the house on the beach.

What could Grantaire possibly want to talk with him about? He was no wizard; he knew little more of magic than most. What could they have to discuss?

Maybe she wants to exchange tips on how to handle unruly familiars, he thought, spotting Fanuilh in a field off to his left, waiting for him. They were a safe distance from the city, so he beckoned and projected: *And speak of the Dark. Do you want to ride?*

The dragon bounded into the air, gave a lazy flap of its wings and then two more powerful ones to counter the easterly wind. In a remarkably graceful swoop it landed on Diamond's neck, its back to Liam. The roan gave a snort.

"Nicely done," Liam commented. "Have you been practicing?"

I do not see why I cannot go into the city with you. Why must I hide?

For a moment, Liam had no answer. He had simply assumed that being seen in Southwark with his familiar would be bad, but he had never examined why he felt that way. There was no reason, really, except that he did not want to be thought a wizard.

"Did Tarquin ever take you into the city?" he asked finally.

No.

That was a relief, an easy answer. "So why should I?"

Master Tanaquil rarely left the beach, and when he did, it was for simple errands. He did not need me.

Liam laughed. "And I do?"

I found the girl.

"True," he said slowly, "but you did not have to be at my side to do that. And besides, how do you think the good people of Southwark would feel about having a dragon running rampant through the streets?"

Fanuilh's back was to him, so he could not see its face, but he imagined it might have borne a disdainful expression.

I am a very small dragon, it projected. *And I would not run rampant.*

"I'm not convinced of that," Liam said with a smile. "Who knows what trouble you might get up to? You might fall in with low companions, be led astray, visit wineshops and brothels—you could be pressed, and spend the rest of your days chained to an oar in an Alyeciran galley. I would hate to think of you as a galley slave."

When he first was bonded to Fanuilh, it had seemed to Liam that the dragon had no emotions, but he had long since learned that it had at least one, a combination of primness and old-maidish disgust. It shot that at him now, bending its long neck to peer at him over its shoulder. That drew a laugh from him, at which he could have sworn it gave a little sniff before turning its attention back to Diamond's mane.

You should project, it thought at him.

"You always say that when you don't have an answer," he chuckled, then grew a little more serious. "I will think about it. I promise nothing, but I will think about it. Now there is something more important I want to ask you about. Have you noticed any magic in Southwark recently?"

To a certain extent, Fanuilh could detect the use of magic, could sense it, like a burst of light or heat. There were limitations—it could not tell what the magic was being used for, or who was casting it—but if the unknown wizard were really a wizard, and had been active, the dragon would know.

Mage Grantaire cast a few small spells. Nothing very large. Apart from that, there has been nothing. Is there another wizard in Southwark?

Liam explained about the Yezidi jeweler and his strange visitor. "According to Coeccias, he swore up and down that the man was a wizard, though come to think of it, I didn't ask why he was so sure. After all, people think I'm a wizard. The real question is, what would a wizard want with the Jewel?"

Mage Grantaire might know.

"Huh," Liam grunted, and sank into silence, considering the suddenly large list of demands on his time. He had to try to see all of the Oakhams' guests, arrange a meeting with the Werewolf, and give Grantaire however much time she needed, to ask questions at which he could not even begin to guess. And given the contract tucked in his tunic, he really ought to begin planning the spring trading season in earnest.

You have definitely bitten off more than you can chew, he told himself, and then noticed that Diamond had stopped, waiting at the top of the cliff path. Shaking his head to clear it, he nudged the horse with his heels and started down to the beach.

CHAPTER 6

GRANTAIRE WAS WAITING at the door, arms crossed, and even though the sun was still well above the western horizon, Liam felt an unreasonable pang of guilt.

"I have many questions for you," she said as soon as he came in, but he could not tell if she was angry, impatient or merely eager to have her questions answered. She stood in his way, though, as if she meant to keep him in the doorway until they were.

A little flustered, he resorted to sarcasm, offering a deep bow. "I am at your service, my lady. I apologize profusely for the delay."

She gave him a startled, suspicious look, as if this was the last thing she had expected, and then turned and walked into the kitchen. The shift she wore was a different color from the one of the day before, but of the same cut, and as he followed her, he carefully kept his eyes on the back of her head.

"Can I get you something?" he asked, tossing his cloak on the kitchen table, but she shook her head impatiently and took a seat.

"I found out where I had heard the name Priscian before," she said briskly, while he went to the stove and imagined a large mug of coffee. "There was an Eirenaeus Priscian once, a wizard. He was mentioned in one of Tanaquil's books."

Liam had opened the oven, but he stopped his hand an inch from the steaming mug. "He was? That's strange—I saw his tomb today."

"His tomb is here?"

He pulled the mug from the oven, surprised at the eagerness of her voice. "It's in the family crypt in Southwark. The Mistress Priscian I had to meet today is a descendant of his." He sat opposite her, blowing on his coffee to cool it.

"I must see it," she said immediately. "Does she have any of his books, his papers? I must see them as well. You will arrange it?"

Liam got the impression that she was not really asking *if* he would arrange it, but *when* he would arrange it. He let that pass, however, because he was more interested in her excitement.

"I can ask Mistress Priscian, but why? He died hundreds of years ago."

"He left no records for the Guild," she said heatedly, "none of his notes or researches. If there is a chance of recovering them, I must try."

"But why?" Liam repeated, beginning to grow a little annoyed. It was as if she could not answer a straight-forward question. "Who cares about his researches?"

"He was one of the most powerful wizards of his day," she snapped. "Everyone cares about them!"

So much so that you could not remember his name earlier today, he thought, and kept the thought to himself. Instead he cleared his throat. "I see. I don't know if Mistress Priscian has any of his notes—but he did leave something else. That Jewel I mentioned to you this morning?"

"That was his?" Her eyes widened, and Liam decided that if she were not so rude, she would be very pretty. "I must see that as well! I must see that!"

"Hold on a moment," he said carefully. "Notes and books I can understand, but why the Jewel? How can that be important?"

She rolled her eyes at him and took a deep breath, as if she were dealing with a particularly idiotic child and needed all the patience she could muster. "Do you understand the difference between soul and spirit?"

"Not at all. Should I?"

"These things are elemental," she said, glaring. "Did Tanaquil teach you nothing?"

"Actually, no—"

She went on, ignoring his answer. "Soul and spirit are two major divisions within—never mind. Priscian experimented extensively with spirit, and was thought at one time to have attained the answers to certain fundamental problems. I say 'thought' because no one was ever sure. When he died, he took his work to the grave with him."

"This was all in Tarquin's book?"

Grantaire gave him another frown, and he began to feel like the idiotic child she seemed to be addressing. "He is mentioned in passing in two of them—but only mentioned. He never shared his work, and as a consequence was ... banned from the Guild." For some reason she blushed, apple-red blooms on both white cheeks.

"And the Jewel was important to his work?"

She frowned instantly, the blush fading. *The idiot child strikes again,* he thought.

"It could be important," she explained, displaying what she clearly thought was immense patience. "Some sort of physical object, something enduring like a gem or forged metal or stone, is always associated with spirit."

The mention of stone stirred a memory in the back of his head, but he put it aside for the moment, concentrating on the point he had been trying to lead up to. "So it would be of interest to any wizard? I mean, if the Jewel was associated with Priscian's work, it might be useful? Valuable?"

"Of course!"

"For research only?"

She gave him a suspicious look. "For research definitely. But also, potentially, as a source of power. It is too complicated to explain. Why do you ask?"

Why don't you finish your sentences? he wondered. *'Too complicated to explain to an idiot' is what you mean. . . .*

"It seems," he said, choosing his words with care, "that there is another wizard in Southwark at the moment, and he has been asking questions about the Jewel."

Before he had even finished his sentence, Grantaire was on her feet, looming over him.

"Who?" She was practically shouting. "Who is here?"

Liam gaped up at her, trying to master his amazement. "We don't know his name," he stammered. "He has a red beard and a mark on his face."

"Desiderius," she said, sounding relieved. Her hand strayed to her chin and stroked it in a curiously masculine gesture. "Desiderius." Her eyes unfocused, as if she were seeing the other wizard's face somewhere above Liam's head.

"You know him?" he asked. Though her initial shock had passed, he could not help but notice the way she trembled under her shift.

Stop that! he told himself.

"Yes," she answered after a pause. "I know him." With an effort, she forced her attention back to him. "Now leave me. I must think."

Liam bridled at her rude dismissal, but stood nonetheless. "There is something else you may want to know—the Jewel was stolen last night." He cringed slightly, expecting another angry outburst, but she only stroked her chin and nodded, more to herself than to him.

"Perhaps he is only here for that. Stealing, though," she muttered. "What will they not sink to?"

Liam hesitated by his chair, unwilling to bother her; she took her seat again, her hand now a fist pressed tight against her mouth, thinking furiously and completely oblivious to his presence.

I suppose my questions can wait, he thought ruefully, and backed out of the kitchen.

Fanuilh lay in the entrance hall, its head between its paws, staring at the sea through the glass panes of the front door. Beside it sat Grantaire's cat, grooming itself

with studied dips of its head, pausing between licks to
consider the view.

"Very cosy," Liam muttered, and then projected:
*Fanuilh, come here. I have some stupid questions for
you.*

The dragon lifted its head, shared a glance with the
cat, and then lazily rose to its feet and shuffled after him
into the library.

He lay at full length on the divan, staring up at the
cupola, and waited for Fanuilh to arrange itself satisfac-
torily, nose to tail, on the floor.

Comfortable? he asked.

Yes, master.

Good. He had not yet figured out how to give his
projected thoughts a sarcastic edge—was not, in fact,
sure that the dragon would even be able to interpret
that—so he put aside some of the comments that sprang
to mind. *Good. Now, in simple terms, terms even an idiot
can understand, explain the difference between soul and
spirit.*

For some reason, Liam found it easier to project with
his eyes closed; he could see the shapes of the words in
his head, and could envision pushing them away from
himself, towards his familiar. He did so now, resting one
hand on his brow while the dragon explained, interject-
ing questions from time to time.

Soul, Fanuilh began, *is the individual essence of a
person.* Spirit, on the other hand, was the life, the motive
force that allowed an individual to be an individual. No
two souls were alike, but spirit was roughly the same
for everyone. *Consider spirit as fuel, and soul as fire.
Two logs may be identical, but they never burn the same.
The fire is different.*

But no two logs are ever identical, Liam countered.
And fire is still fire.

The analogy limps, it conceded, and suggested another: *Consider spirit as food. All people eat, but none
are alike.* When Liam grunted his acceptance, it went
on: *A person may have no soul, but still have spirit.* This,
it seemed, was one of the primary purposes of famil-

iars—to separate a wizard's soul, rendering it less liable to attack. Without a soul, a person was left open to many forms of wizardry, in particular various forms of enslavement.

Simply to exist, however, required spirit; spirit animated the body and allowed the soul to inhabit it. While centuries of practice and research had allowed wizards to discover effective methods of protecting their souls, very little progress had been made in extending the length of time during which a body could sustain spirit.

Wizards can live almost double the length of time that a normal man can, it said. *Master Tanaquil was almost 120 years old.* Liam whistled, impressed, but the flow of thoughts did not stop. *Much beyond that, however, and the body simply begins to wear out. There are spells that allow a wizard to rejuvenate his body, but even so, the maximum length of time is considered somewhere between a century and a century and a half. No amount of rejuvenation will sustain a body beyond that.*

There was a way to step around that, however: stealing the bodies of other people—but that was cause for expulsion from the Guild.

"And not much appreciated by the population at large," Liam commented.

No, Fanuilh agreed, as usual missing the irony. *Wizards who take other bodies are usually hunted down and exterminated by the Guild.* Other methods of extending the lifetime of a body had been sought, but nothing reliable found. The usual method, apparently, involved constructing an object in which spirit could be stored and from which it could be drawn, without its actually entering the body. *Consider it gaining nourishment,* the dragon elaborated, *without having to consume food.*

"Aha!" Liam said, thrusting his index finger at the skylight.

A thought appeared quickly in his head: *I am aware that that analogy limps as well . . .*

"That's not what I mean," he said aloud, but the flow of thoughts did not stop.

. . . because it is not actually a question of the food

being consumed, but of the food having to pass into the
body. Consider a jug that wears out because it is con-
tinually filled . . .

"Fanuilh."

. . . *with water. Each successive filling abrades some*
of the surface of the jug . . .

"Fanuilh."

. . . *until eventually there is nothing left. If you could*
find a way to pour water without abrading the jug—

"Fanuilh!" Liam sat up and stamped one foot on the
floor. The dragon's thoughts stopped instantly. "You
may stop considering me an idiot. I think I understand.
What I want to know now is, could the Jewel be an
object like you described? An outside source of spirit?"

A long moment passed while the dragon considered
the question. *Quite possibly,* it projected at last, with a
tentative feel to the thought. *Master Tanaquil did not go*
into spirit much, but it was considered a given that the
best receptacles for spirit would be durable items—
stone, metal and, of course, gems. Diamonds were
thought best.

The mention of stone again stirred the memory that
Grantaire had dislodged, and he ordered the story in his
head before telling it.

"Some time ago," he began, when he was sure he
was remembering correctly, "about eleven or twelve
years, I was traveling north of the King's Range, and I
came by chance to the house of a wizard who was supposed to have died hundreds of years before, after turning his entire household to stone. At least, there were
statues of them all in the house—courtiers and servants
and so on, including one imposing statue that was supposed to be the wizard himself—caught in the most life-
like poses you can imagine. I had to spend the night,
alone, and I dreamed I was in another place, one that
looked just like the place where the statues were, except
that all the statues were alive. And I met the wizard, the
one who was supposed to have been dead for hundreds
of years, and all of his servants and friends were there
as well."

The dream wizard said that he removed his household to another plane of existence in order to escape the machinations of his enemies at court; the king whose court he meant had died three centuries before Liam was born. He questioned Liam closely about the new state of the kingdom, and decided that the time had come to return. "I realize that's not very clear, but does it sound like something to do with spirit?"

Again, Fanuilh's response was tentative; the thought seemed to waver in his head, as if it had come from a great distance: *That, too, is quite possible. The statues could well have been conduits for spirit from the material plane that the wizard and his household required to exist in the other plane; on the other hand, they might simply have been placeholders, a connection with the real world that the wizard required to mark the way back. I could not say for sure. What happened to them?*

Liam blew air between compressed lips, remembering the scene. "I woke up, and everything was back to normal. The house was abandoned. And then I heard a scream, so I ran to find out where it was coming from. His statue—the wizard's—was in a room where the windows were broken. The winters that far north are very harsh, and I suppose the locals had done some damage; anyway, his statue was broken as well. There was an arm missing, and the foot was broken and. . . . well, the face was . . . was rubbed away. Exposure and wind, I would guess. He cast the spell that was supposed to return them to this world and . . . I'm not sure. He died. There was a great deal of blood."

A heavy silence descended on the room, Liam brooding over his memory. He had never understood what happened. Though damaged, the wizard's statue had been standing when he first saw it; after the spell was cast, he had found it fallen over in a wide pool of blood, but still a statue, still stone. The other statues remained exactly the way they were when he first saw them; perhaps the wizard had decided to return alone.

"I heard him scream," he whispered, and then shook his head. "That's not important. I am more concerned

with the Jewel now. I suppose we can take it for granted
that a wizard would want it, assuming that a wizard
would assume that it was a relic of Eirenaeus's research
into spirit?''

The dragon bobbed its head in agreement. *If he was
researching spirit, then yes, most definitely. Though
Master Tanaquil was never much interested, many wizards find spirit an endlessly fascinating subject, despite
the immense danger associated with it.*

Liam lifted his head, drawn away from his unpleasant
memory. ''Danger?''

*If the wizard in your story was working with spirit, it
would be an excellent indication. Spirit is a fragile thing,
much more so than the soul.* Liam's soul, for instance,
could be split so that part resided in Fanuilh—but spirit
could never be so divided. Moreover, the link between
soul, body and spirit was complicated and poorly understood. *Master Tanaquil once said that more wizards
were killed attempting to protect or prolong their spirits
than from any other cause. Others go mad or . . .
change. Some think that vampires originated from experiments in spirit gone awry. You know vampires?*

''Not personally, but I am familiar with the concept.''

*There are recorded cases of wizards receiving too
much spirit. It is called blasting. They become . . . less
than human. It is hard to explain. From the moment they
are blasted, they require much more spirit than normal;
it is similar to vampirism, but they do not drink blood.
They are called liches.*

''And people wonder that I do not want to be a wizard. Why don't these people become scribes or cobblers
or blacksmiths? If you make a horseshoe and it goes
badly, you end up with a bad horseshoe. It doesn't steal
your soul and drive you mad.''

Fanuilh offered him an inquiring gaze. *Is there anything else you wish to know?*

Smiling at his own joke, Liam shook his head. ''No,
I think that will do. What time is it?''

An hour or so before sunset.

Their conversation had taken longer than he expected,

but it still left him a few hours before he had to be back in Southwark. He frowned irritably; waiting annoyed him immensely, and he was eager to get on with all the different tasks he had taken upon himself. There was so much to do, but none of it could be done right away. With an angry grunt he lay back down on the divan and began ordering his tasks in his head, as much searching for something to do immediately as actively planning.

First off there was Grantaire; he had promised her he would ask Mistress Priscian if Eirenaeus had left any papers, and whether the wizard might look at them. *Did I actually promise her?* he wondered, thinking how awkward the asking might be. The man had been dead for hundreds of years; what chance was there that anything of his would be left? Moreover, how would Mistress Priscian feel about having another person digging into her family's affairs? Bad enough to have thieves, Aediles, and amateur investigators wandering around their private matters—wizards would hardly be a positive addition.

Nonetheless, he had as good as promised, and he knew that the sooner he asked, the easier it would be for him. The longer he waited, the more it would weigh on him, and the more chances he would have to imagine the different ways she could take offense at the question.

He toyed with the idea of doing it right away, and then rejected it. For some reason he imagined Mistress Priscian as an early diner; he pictured her, in fact, as someone who did everything early. "Early awake a fortune makes," he recited, a rhyme he had heard in the Freeports and one he could easily imagine on Mistress Priscian's lips; "Early to sleep a fortune keeps." The last thing he wanted to do was interrupt her at her evening meal with an intrusive request. As if in confirmation of his decision to postpone asking, he remembered that Haellus left the house every evening; he guessed that she probably shut up the house and retired after her servant's departure.

No, he corrected himself, *she said he left to celebrate the Banquet.* But then she had said there were no servants in the house at night. She must have meant the Oakhams' house.

"Odd," he muttered, tugging at his lower lip. Duessa Oakham did not strike him as likely to give up the services of her maid at any time. It must have been just for the night, he thought, maybe in honor of Beggar's Banquet, but it still seemed strange.

Certainly worth asking about, he decided, making a vague mental note of it; one of the guests might have suggested letting the servants go for the night.

There was nothing he could do about the Jewel at the moment. The few times he had helped Coeccias investigate crimes, he had found that one of the most useful things he could do was simply think about the crime, mulling over motives and opportunities, raising hypotheses and striking them down. That, however, required knowing something about the circumstances and the people involved, and as yet he knew very little. Once he had met some of the Oakhams' guests and spoken with the Werewolf, he might be able to begin conjecturing. But until then he was useless.

The bearded wizard waited temptingly at the back of his head, but Liam dismissed him temporarily; he was there solely because he was the only suspect who had a motive Liam could believe. If the Jewel were some sort of magical relic, that would be a reason to steal it: it could not be readily sold for coin, and he had difficulty imagining the kind of envy that would prompt someone to steal something they could not display.

"A miser does not build a house of gold," he reminded himself, but still found it too strange to grasp.

His thoughts leapt fruitlessly back and forth between the few things he knew, and after several minutes he sat up on the divan, muttering: "No point to this. None at all." He stood and stretched, hearing his bones crack. A glance at the cupola told him he had killed a fair amount of time, but there was still plenty to go before his appointment. With a sigh he looked around the library, hoping for inspiration.

His eye lit on a leather writing case tucked into one

of the lower shelves, and in a single step he was on it, unclasping the lid. A neat stack of maps lay inside, his maps, the key to his partnership with Mistress Priscian. There was plenty of work there, Liam knew: he could flesh out the trading plan for the upcoming season. Courses to chart, timetables to be considered, cargo lists to draw up—there was work for weeks in cargo lists alone. What would sell in one place would rot on the docks in another, and an idea of what they would need would provide an excellent excuse for his visit to the merchant Cawood at the Staple the next day.

The paper of the maps rustled happily as he closed the lid and tucked the case under his arm. He could spread them out on the tables in Tarquin's old workroom and draw up the cargo lists until the time came to leave for his appointment with Lord Oakham. Grinning to himself, he turned to the door of the library and faltered when he saw Grantaire standing there.

They both bowed slightly; Liam almost smiled at the mirroring, and then he noticed the wizard's face. Lower lip firmly gripped by her teeth, she appeared almost hesitant, and the expression was so much the opposite of her usual one that it looked like she was in pain.

"Hello," Liam said, drawing the word out carefully, as if he were talking to a strange dog, or a potentially violent madman.

"I must apologize," she said, ignoring his wary greeting. The fingers of her right hand were wrapped around the wrist of her left arm, as if to restrain it; the words came slowly. "I have not been . . . honest with you, and I think I must be."

Liam sensed that she rarely apologized, and that it was difficult for her. "There is no need—"

"No," she interrupted firmly. "I will explain. Otherwise you will wonder."

I have enough to wonder about, he groaned inwardly; aloud, he said: "I'm thirsty, and there aren't enough chairs here. . . ." He gestured to the kitchen, and after a moment she nodded and preceded him.

The jug by the stove was beaded with condensation

even before Liam grabbed it. Grantaire took the cup he offered without really noticing it, and began talking and pacing even as he sat.

"This mage you have heard about—his name is Desiderius, and he is a representative of the Guild from Harcourt. It is possible that he has been sent to look for me. It is also possible that he is here in search of Eirenaeus Priscian's Jewel. It is equally possible that he is here on some other business entirely, but the Jewel caught his attention. All these things are possible."

She stopped speaking but continued pacing, the fingers of both hands laced tightly around the cup from which she had yet to drink. Liam did not speak; he did not think she had finished, and after a long pause she spoke again.

"I cannot, however, discount the idea that he may be looking for me. At the very least he may come here, knowing that this was Tanaquil's home, and that he and I were friends. If he does, it is crucial that he not know I am here."

If she knew that he was there, Liam could not tell it: she seemed to be speaking to herself.

"I am no longer a member of the Guild. They have labeled me Gray, as they had Tanaquil, but when he was so named it meant less. The distinction is political. It means nothing—less than nothing. At least I don't practice black magic, which is more than can be said for some of them."

Liam shivered for no perceptible reason. Again, there was the feeling that she was not aware of his presence, and that she was rehearsing some private soliloquy.

"If Desiderius finds me, he may try to bring me back. With Tanaquil's spellbooks, his library, his enchantments, I can prevent that. And if he does not try to bring me back, or kill me, he must still not be allowed to bring word back. They cannot know where I am."

Then, for the first time, she looked directly at him, registering his presence. In that look, he sensed the whole of their relationship changing. It was as if she were seeing him for the first time, and knew she needed him. *She may not be so rude from now on,* he thought with a grim, silent laugh, *but what does she need?*

She told him.

"I am sure he will come here. He may or may not ask about me, but he will come. He may demand Tanaquil's things, but you must not give them to him. When he died, Tanaquil was not a member of the Guild, and it has no claim on him. If he asks about me, you must say that you never saw me."

Easy enough, Liam thought, and realized that now he might speak. "I certainly won't give up any of Tarquin's things. And if you do not want him to know you are here, I will not tell him. But I would like to know why the Guild wants you."

He had tried to sound as indifferent as he could, but still Grantaire stiffened, clearly about to tell him that it was none of his business. She held herself in, though, and slowly nodded.

"I killed two Guild mages in Harcourt. It is complicated. They kidnapped my apprentice to draw me into the city. They let her loose in a crowd, a riot, and she was trampled. When I tried to save her, they prevented me, and she was killed. So I killed them."

"Ah," Liam said, trying to compress sympathy and comprehension into one syllable. The sympathy was genuine, but he was miles from comprehension.

"You do not understand," she said immediately, and he blushed. "They were not attacking me, and the girl was already dead. I should not have killed them. But then, I suppose, they would have turned me over to the Magister anyway, in which case I would have been killed."

To a certain extent, Liam thought he understood revenge; there had been no question of self-defense when he killed his father's murderer. "Why would you have been killed?"

Irritation flashed in her eyes but was quickly suppressed, and he knew for sure that he was in charge when she began explaining.

"At the same time I was labeled Gray, the Magister

in Harcourt declared all Grays anathema. The distinction, as I said, is political, but it has been made a Guild policy, and is being spread around the kingdom as a fact. Unless I miss my guess, various atrocities will soon be laid at the feet of prominent Grays, and the Whites of the Guild will take action.''

Each sentence left Liam even more confused. Reluctantly, with some prodding, Grantaire cleared up his questions until he thought he understood.

The Mages Guild was not decentralized, she said, like those of weavers or carters, or even thieves. When she mentioned the last, Liam squirmed a little in his seat, but she did not notice. The Guild was a united body, each city's chapter headed by a Magister who belonged to the ruling Senate. By custom, the Magister of Torquay headed the Senate, but in recent years the power of Torquay had declined, and the current Magister of Harcourt had taken advantage of that to raise himself to effective control. He had promulgated the division between White and Gray, first as an informal distinction and later as an official label.

Loosely speaking, Whites believed in a more disciplined Guild, each wizard ranked and subordinated to a strict hierarchy. They also favored direct intervention in worldly affairs, some going so far as to encourage the actual seizure of temporal power.

Liam frowned at that. ''I thought wizards were forbidden power. Isn't that in your Guild charter? They have been excluded from state affairs since the Seventeen Houses first came to Taralon.''

Grantaire glared at him, as if resenting the interruption.

''The charter is supposed to forbid it,'' she admitted grudgingly, ''but the wording is vague, and can be twisted. In any case, that is what the Whites want.''

Grays, on the other hand, favored a more relaxed Guild. They were, on the whole, far fewer in number, but vastly more powerful. ''Tanaquil was a Gray long before the name was devised. There have always been Grays, in that sense—solitary mages, who prefer their own company and their own researches. They leave the petty Guild politics to mages with less talent and more ambition. For obvious reasons, they tend to live in the countryside, or in places like Southwark, where the Guild has no chapter houses.''

For as long as history recorded, it had been like that, with some wizards keeping only the weakest ties with the Guild, and most others more or less its servants. The prohibition against political action and a general lack of interest had kept the Guild from any attempt to grow stronger. ''In Torquay then there was a real king, and the Torquay Magister was his man. But now—let us be honest, the king is king in name only. He can scarcely rule his own capital, let alone all of Taralon. As he has weakened, so has the Torquay Magister. So Harcourt has risen, and he has the power and the will to change the Guild, to make it a political power. The Grays, whether labeled or not, would not allow that for very long, however, and he knows that. So he strikes against them. To call them Blacks would be too obvious—but Gray, it implies. It hints. Who will trust a Gray mage, when they can turn to a White? And with no true king in Torquay, and most local lords weak or busy squabbling among themselves, will not people look to the strong?''

It was certainly plausible; Liam had to admit that. And he had no reason to doubt her, though he had no reason to believe her. That, however, did not matter; what mattered was what she needed from him.

''If this Desiderius comes, I won't tell him you are here, and I definitely won't give him any of Tarquin's things. But is that all you need?''

She laughed harshly. ''Not unless you can put a true king in Torquay, and root the Magister out of Harcourt.''

Despite its harshness, her answer was a relief to him. He did not need any more responsibilities. ''He may be gone by now. Desiderius, I mean. The Jewel was stolen; maybe he has gone with it.''

''Stolen by force, or stealth?''

''Stealth.''

Grantaire shook her head, sure of herself. ''Then no,

he has not left with it. If he were to steal, it would be by force. Harcourt's creatures are arrogant.'' Her mouth tensed and her eyes narrowed, as if she were remembering. ''They would buy it or rip it from the owner's neck, but they would not sneak in the night.''

Over an hour had passed. The kitchen window showed darkening shadows in the strip between the back of the house and the cliff.

''I have to go into the city tonight,'' Liam said. ''I may be back late. Tomorrow I will ask Mistress Priscian if she has any of Eirenaeus's papers. Do you need anything in the meantime?''

''No.'' She sounded exhausted. For the first time, she drank from her cup, a long gulp that made her throat and shoulders move as if she were sobbing.

CHAPTER 7

DRESSED IN THE same clothes he had worn earlier in the day, but freshly bathed and shaved, Liam rode back into Southwark. The sun had already set in the west, leaving an infinite blackness beneath the deep blue bowl of the sky. Later, when the stars were out and the moon had risen, their light would shine off the snow in the fields; for now, Liam shivered and pulled his cloak closer, turning his head rapidly from side to side, staring into the blackness and seeing nothing. Diamond, however, jogged along nonchalantly.

Fanuilh? Liam projected. He did not even want to whisper in the darkness.

Yes, master?

In the Midlands, they say that the Black Hunter rides out on nights like this, and catches unwary travelers.

Does he?

Liam rolled his eyes. *No.* He wished he could accent his thoughts to indicate exasperation.

Soon enough Southwark appeared in the distance, a cheering orange glow. Ordinarily the city was much darker at night, but he guessed that the Banquet festivities would probably keep it lit up later and later as the week went on. He spurred Diamond into a trot, and Fanuilh flew off into the darkness.

The streets by the city gate were not crowded, though Liam passed the occasional reveler. As he came closer to the city square he found more and more, so many that he had to force Diamond through thick knots of people, some going about their usual business, but most with the special shine to their faces that indicated celebrations to come.

And something to drink, he thought, as Diamond shied to one side of a congested street, avoiding a surge of boys from a wineshop, none older than sixteen and many wearing holiday masks.

There were fewer people in the city square than he had expected, though the inns and taverns that lined it, including Herlekin's, were full and noisy. He left his horse with the guard at the barracks, explaining that he would be back in a moment, and ducked across the cobbles to Herlekin's.

Heat and song blasted out of the door when he opened it, but he took a deep breath and plunged in. Each table seemed bent on outsinging all the others, and people milled in the spaces between tables, shouting encouragement or singing on their own. Many were already drunk, and Liam had to bob and weave around a steady stream of sweating serving men and women—Herlekin usually had only women serving, but he had pressed his tapsters into service for the large crowd. Liam found the fat innkeeper near the back of the common room, bowing obsequiously to a one-legged man wrapped in a tattered blanket and perched on the dais where musicians sometimes played.

"Your pleasure, master?" the innkeeper bellowed, and the beggar peered down in a good imitation of lordly snobbery. Just then a pair of men burst from the crowd, one holding a piece of some kind of cake and the other a jug. They thrust Herlekin aside and bowed unsteadily to the beggar, holding each other up and presenting their gifts. The innkeeper stepped away, smiling good-naturedly and mopping at his brow with a corner of his apron. Liam tugged at his elbow.

"Master Herlekin," he shouted, trying to make himself heard.

"Sir Liam," Herlekin shouted, bowing deeply. He spread his hands to indicate the noise and, giving an apologetic smile, led Liam through a nearby door into a dim hallway. The roaring of the holiday crowd was slightly less there, but Liam still had to raise his voice to be heard.

"Has anyone left a message for me?"

Herlekin smiled eagerly and began drywashing his hands. "Indeed, Sir Liam, a young whelp did bring you a word. She said when the bells toll nine tomorrow morning to be at the Arcade of Scribes. A most ill-mannered girl, Sir Liam."

"Yes, she is. Thank you."

A tapster came down the corridor, rolling a barrel, and Liam used the opportunity to slip back into the crowd. Coeccias had introduced him to the innkeeper with the warning that, unless stopped, he would talk forever.

Liam pressed through the crowd again, keeping a tight hold on his cloak. Near the door a woman in a low-cut gown with heavily rouged cheeks staggered into him; she whirled around to face him, a high-pitched laugh on her lips, but it died when she saw his face. She muttered something and backed away with a small curtsy. Her fingers were crossed.

Frowning, Liam left the inn. The cold air was a blessing, washing away the smell of smoke and sweat. He was sweating himself, and he walked slowly across the square, allowing the night wind to dry him.

Why did she do that? he wondered. Crossed fingers in Southwark, he knew, were the same as forked fingers in the Midlands—proof against curses or the Evil Eye. *Why would she do that?*

The answer, when he realized it, made him pause on the steps of the barracks and curse. The guard on duty flinched. "Quaestor?" he asked.

Do not trouble me, Liam thought. *I am a deadly wizard of tremendous power.*

"Never mind," he muttered, and stomped into the barracks.

Stupid, he thought, scolding himself. *Stupid, stupid.* He knew he was not a wizard, and so he often forgot that for most of Southwark that was exactly what he was, because he had been friends with a wizard and now lived in a wizard's house. And if a whore in a tavern recognized him and thought him worth crossed fingers, then any wizard from Harcourt could ask a few questions and hear the same thing.

Coeccias was not in, but Liam had not expected him to be. He could have gone to the Aedile's house—there was time, the bells in the Duke's Courts having only just tolled seven—but he chose not to. One of the off-duty guards gathered around the liquor barrel in the middle of the room found him paper, quill and ink. He hastily wrote a note, mentioning the red-haired wizard's name and asking Coeccias not to do anything regarding him until they could talk. He wrote that he would stop by sometime the next morning, and signed his name. The same guard promised to see that the Aedile received the letter, which Liam had folded but not bothered to seal.

Who would read the mail of a wizard?

Shaking his head, he left the barracks and led Diamond to a nearby ostler, who promised that his boy would be in the stables all night.

A sour mood lay heavily on him, and he could feel his shoulders sagging as he trudged away from the ostler's towards the Point. The woman's crossed fingers had annoyed him, not just because he did not want people thinking he was a wizard, but also because it had made him realize his mistake. He had practically promised Grantaire that he would have nothing to do with the other wizard, not recognizing that he would have to investigate him in connection with the Jewel. He could conceivably leave that part to Coeccias, but that would entail lengthy explanations and, he had to admit, he was not entirely sure he wanted to leave it to his friend. In many respects he admired the Aedile and thought he handled the immensely difficult job of keeping order in Southwark very well, but secretly he did not believe that the gruff man would be much of a match for a wizard. At the same time, he thought that Coeccias's estimation of his own skills was vastly overrated—and if that was a contradiction, he knew and accepted it.

So you are unsure of yourself and *obnoxiously proud,* he told himself. *So be it.* He smiled a little, an old, self-directed smile of derision with which he was well familiar. *So be it,* he thought again, and squared his sagging shoulders. There was no point in worrying about the wizard; at the moment he had to concentrate on his evening with Lord Oakham.

There was almost an hour before he was expected, so he forced himself to a slower pace, wandering leisurely on a route that would eventually bring him to the end of the Point and the Oakhams'.

Fewer revelers wandered the streets of the Point, but many of the houses were gaily decorated. Candles burned in most of the windows, and greenery festooned the gables of brick and stone, sometimes in elaborate patterns, and sometimes with colored lanterns worked in. At two he saw beggars being given food, and remembered the beggar enthroned at Herlekin's. It seemed Southwarkers took the name of their holiday seriously.

There was a group of five or six being fed outside a building he knew, the brothel owned by Coeccias's acquaintance Herione. The brothel had a long portico and enormous double doors carved with erotic bas-reliefs; in front of one door a stout woman was ladling soup from a steaming pot into bowls and handing them out.

"All well and good, mistress," one of the beggars was saying as Liam passed, "but y' have other things inside that a man needs above food."

"Go to!" the woman said, rapping the beggar's knuckles with her ladle and drawing a laugh from his companions, who were both male and female. "It's the Banquet, not the Bedding!"

Laughter trailing him, smiling himself, Liam strolled up the street, beginning to feel a little of the holiday spirit.

The brothel stood on the north side of the Point's northernmost street; only a few hundred feet further on it connected with End Street, where Mistress Priscian and the Oakhams lived. Liam had planned to wander the rich neighborhood until the time came for him to meet Lord Oakham, but now he saw a large gathering at the corner that drew his steps in that direction.

If he remembered Coeccias's list correctly, the crowd
was assembled outside the Goddards' house, a five-story
mansion easily three times the size of any other building
on the Point. The crowd waiting to go in was equally
impressive, a far cry from the ragged bunch outside Herione's; richly dressed men and heavily bejeweled
women formed a long line that spilled into the street.
Servants in what Liam assumed was Goddard livery
wandered about with trays, dispensing hot wine in silver
goblets; the guests chattered noisily amongst themselves
and awaited their chance to present their invitations to
another liveried servant standing beneath a two-story
arch. He was flanked by two halberdiers in silver-plated
armor, who stood to attention as each guest was admitted. Liam wondered whether they would use the
halberds on someone who tried to get in without an invitation.

Settling himself against the wall of a building across
the street, he crossed his arms and watched the parade
of guests with an amused smile. For a while he tried to
gauge which woman was wearing the most makeup and
which man's stock was tightest around his neck. The
odd thing was that the woman with the whitest face was
usually accompanied by the man with the reddest. He
silently awarded the prize to a purple-faced man who
was talking loudly about how few people there were
compared to previous years.

Liam found that hard to believe: he had been watching
for at least ten minutes, the guests were moving into the
courtyard at a good pace, and yet the line showed no
sign of diminishing. If anything it was increasing, as
more people in fancy attire came up the road, most walking but some riding, usually with servants in tow. When
they reached the line, they dismounted and handed the
reins over to their servants. At one point a coach rattled
up at high speed, scattering the tail end of the line and
provoking a storm of shouts from the men and squeals
from the women, until the occupant of the carriage
emerged. Apparently he was a favorite; the shouts turned
friendly and the man was quickly absorbed into the line.

So much money, Liam thought, surveying the mass of party-goers in their finery, steaming silver goblets in their hands, gold and jewels at their throats and on their fingers, furs and fine woolens and silks all around. *So many fools.* The rich in the Freeports were better, he decided, less given to show. *They have sumptuary laws to keep it that way, of course, but still . . .*

The qualifier was still lingering in his head when a polite cough interrupted him. He jumped a little, and saw Mistress Priscian beside him.

"Good evening," he said, beginning to bow. She restrained him with a gloved hand on his arm.

"Good evening to you, Master Rhenford. You are going to my niece's?" She was wearing no makeup, though the bun of hair at the back of her head was tight and neatly arranged. A stout cloak of good blue wool was pulled close around her, so he could not tell what she was wearing, but he imagined it was eminently sensible.

"Yes. Lord Oakham has arranged for me to meet some of his guests."

"I know," she said, angling her head back and frowning up at him. "He told me. A surprisingly sensible suggestion, from him. I did not think he would have the courage to stand at your side while you question his friends."

Liam coughed, unsure what Oakham had told her. "The hope, I think, is that perhaps I can disguise my questions a little."

She waved this aside. "Even so, it is more than I expected."

An uncomfortable silence ensued; Liam was thinking about Grantaire's request, a small voice at the back of his head telling him to ask right then, and a louder voice telling him to wait.

"Are you going to the Goddards'?"

She frowned down at the gilt-edged card in her hand. "Once again, yes. Every year. I suppose it is a wonderful party, if you enjoy noise and drunkards and food that is too rich to eat. I am invited every year, and I always

go, to pay my respects to Master Goddard. The Goddards also make ships, you know," she said, tapping his
arm with the card. "And he is an old friend. We may
need ships, you and I."

Liam did not think they would need more than the
small Priscian fleet; he was more concerned about
money for goods to trade, but he merely nodded.

"Not immediately," she went on, turning her gaze on
the guest line. "But someday. By that time, in course,
you will be receiving an invitation as well."

"Will I?" he laughed. "That will be nice. I like noise
and drunkards and food too rich to eat."

"Then you will be very happy," she said placidly,
still examining the line. "You will probably stay at these
far later than I do. I always leave early. Early to wake
a fortune makes—"

"—and early to sleep a fortune keeps," he finished.

She looked back at him and nodded judiciously, a
smile of approval on her lips. "Just so. When are you
expected at my niece's?"

"At eight o'clock."

"Then perhaps you will keep me company. I do not
wish to go in just yet, and in any case the line is too
long. I am not cold," she added, as if he had asked,
"though I imagine she is." With one arched eyebrow
she indicated a woman who had just emerged from a
coach wearing a bright yellow gown with short sleeves
and a very low neckline.

Liam nodded solemnly. "Very cold."

Another silence ensued, more comfortable this time.
Mistress Priscian stood upright, tapping her invitation
against the palm of her hand and studying the shifting
line of guests with a sort of regal indifference that made
Liam want to laugh. His promise to Grantaire repeated
itself in the back of his head, however, and after a few
minutes he finally brought himself to ask.

"Mistress Priscian, I wonder if I might ask a question."

She stopped tapping the invitation. "In course, Master
Rhenford."

"I have a guest, an old acquaintance of Tarquin Tanaquil—I live in his home, you know, he left it to me—
and this guest has an interest in your ancestor. Eirenaeus
Priscian, I mean. My guest is a wizard, you see—an old
acquaintance of Tarquin Tanaquil—and apparently he is
mentioned in several books as having been a wizard. My
guest was wondering if, perhaps, Eirenaeus had left any
papers, and if he had, if you might allow . . . of course,
there may be no papers, but if there were . . ." He trailed
off lamely, trying to guess from her impassive face what
her reaction was.

"Is your guest a woman, Master Rhenford?"

He blushed, and hoped that it was too dark for her to
notice. "Yes."

"And a wizard?"

"Yes, an old acquaintance of Tarquin Tanaquil."
Liam still could not guess her reaction. She reminded
him again of one of his university masters.

"I see. She would like to examine his papers. I do
not know if there are any."

"Of course," he began, but she interrupted him.

"If there are any papers, and if you will vouch for
this wizard, I see no reason that she should not see them.
Since I do not know of any, they are clearly of no use
to me. I will look tomorrow. Will that be soon enough?"

"Oh, I'm sure," he stammered. "That would be fine,
thank you."

"I promise nothing," she said, holding up a warning
finger. "And now I think I had best go." She pointed
to the line, which had shrunk perceptibly. Turning, she
paused; Liam, belatedly recognizing a cue, offered her
his arm. They crossed the street together, and exchanged
goodbyes even as Mistress Priscian had to present her
invitation to the liveried servants. Liam sketched a hasty
bow and backed away, certain that the two halberdiers
were eyeing him suspiciously. Up close they looked less
ornamental, their breastplates shining in the torchlight
but their faces decidedly menacing. Grinning sheepishly,
he walked away at a brisk pace.

• • •

It was foolish, Liam knew, but he hated being early almost as much as he hated being late, so he deliberately slowed his pace once he rounded the corner onto End Street. The windows of the Goddard mansion were unshuttered on this side, and multicolored oblongs of light lay across the cobblestones, crisscrossed by a hundred flitting shadows. Muffled music and laughter seeped out, and he crossed to the far side of the street, the better to look in.

He slowly passed the windows, each showing a different variation on the same theme of dancing, drinking people beneath enormous chandeliers, the candles of which burned blue, red and green, as well as the normal yellow.

"That had to cost something," Liam said appreciatively. "How many beggars in there, I wonder?"

There was only so long, however, that he could envy someone else's party, so he moved along, doing his best to imitate a man of leisure with no particular place to go. It was cold, though, and he wished he could walk faster, but that would have left him on the Oakhams' doorstep waiting for the bells to toll eight—which they did even as he thought of it. He hurried the rest of the way, jumping up the stoop before the bells had finished.

To his surprise, Quetivel answered the door, a cup in his hand and a snarl on his face.

"At last," he snapped, the last toll of eight still shivering in the air. "Now we can go. Oakham!" he shouted over his shoulder. "Let's to it!"

Oakham came bustling down the corridor, throwing a cloak around his shoulders.

"Good evening, Master Rhenford." He took Quetivel's cup with a wink and downed it in one gulp, then handed it back empty. "Y' are ready?" He looked Liam up and down, nodding his approval. Quetivel, meanwhile, frowned at his empty cup, then dropped it.

"Come, let's to it!" the young baron said.

Liam took a step or two down the stoop, expecting them to follow, but Oakham did not move. Eyebrows raised, he looked from the fallen cup to Quetivel and back. The baron grunted, then bent and retrieved the cup. Shaking his head so that his braids whipped around, he stalked back down the corridor.

Oakham sighed and came down the steps, putting a hand on Liam's shoulder and drawing him into the street.

"These border lords have a number of rough edges— he is still surprised that there are no rushes on the floor to soak up his messes. Now, Master Rhenford, y' are ready?"

"I think so, my lord."

"Use my name," Oakham said, smiling. "I think it will serve better." Liam nodded his assent. "Be as discreet as you may, Rhenford. Quetivel knows your purpose—I trust him implicitly—but I would that, insofar as you may, you keep it from the others."

"I will try." He could not bring himself to add the man's name, though it should not have been a problem. Many of his fellow students in Torquay had been noble, and he had been on a first-name basis with them. *You were noble too, once,* he chided himself yet again. Still, it would feel odd; it had been many years since he had had reason to think of his background, much less spend time with anyone of rank.

Quetivel emerged from the house, sulking, and as they set off down End Street, he put himself between Liam and Oakham. The young lord was far shorter than the other two men, and with his pout and long braids he seemed more like a little girl than a man out for a night of . . . *Of what?* Liam wondered. *Where are we going?* He would not ask Quetivel, though, and he did not want to talk over the shorter man's head, so he stayed silent. Oakham strode briskly, whistling a holiday song; Liam kept pace with him easily, but Quetivel had to scurry to stay abreast of them, and his scowl darkened.

Oakham stopped abruptly by the first of the Goddards' windows and peered in, brushing at his mustache. "Quite a party," he said.

"Merchants," Quetivel sniffed, and continued walking.

"Oh, I don't know," Oakham said, with a wink at Liam. "They have their points." He started walking again, though it seemed to Liam that he went more slowly, forcing Quetivel to drop back and join them.

They turned off End Street in silence, passing the Goddards' gate, where the halberdiers still stood at attention, though the liveried doorman was sipping from a chased goblet and chatting with another servant.

Oakham led them to Herione's, where the stout woman still stood by her cauldron of soup. She curtsied as they walked up the steps. "Merry Banquet, masters."

"And to you," Oakham smiled back; Liam echoed him, but Quetivel only scowled anew, tugged at the large doors, and disappeared inside. Oakham stopped Liam with a touch on the arm and chuckled. "You should look at the doors."

"They are . . . interesting, aren't they?" He was a little surprised that this was where they were to meet Uldericus, but he did not want to seem "rough at the edges," and he had, in fact, been to Herione's before. "I am always surprised that no one objects to them. Out on the street as they are," he added.

"A point," the lord said quietly, giving Liam a strange look before ushering him in.

It was mostly as he remembered—the sweeping staircase along the back wall, lined with niches containing erotic statuary, the fountain with its larger and even more explicit statue—but where before the room had been filled with bright summer flowers, now it was dressed for the Banquet, with wreaths of greenery everywhere and colored lanterns scattered about. The main difference, however, was the people. The last and only time he had visited had been during the day, and the room had been empty. Now it was almost full of young women in surprisingly modest dresses, all of the same cut, waiting on men of all ages and styles of dress. A sober-looking group of middle-aged men were talking amongst themselves in one corner, while two or three young men in half-masks whirled women around the fountain to the music provided by a trio of musicians near the stairs.

Herione was as Liam remembered, a tall, statuesque woman with an elaborately coiffed headdress of black hair. She finished cautioning one of the young men to dance a little slower and dropped a deep curtsy to the three men at the door.

"Is Uldericus here?" Quetivel demanded.

"Good evening, Baron Quetivel," she said smoothly, ignoring his rudeness. "Earl Uldericus attends you in his usual room. Good evening, Lord Oakham, Master Rhenford." She said his name without missing a beat— even as Quetivel shouldered past her—and Liam smiled and bowed in return. A good memory for names must have been a requisite, given her work, but hc was still impressed. *Particularly since you spent no money,* he thought. Even better, Oakham was directing another assessing look his way, and Liam guessed he had just gone up another notch in the man's estimation.

Which is ridiculous, he added to himself. *Because the madame of an expensive brothel knows my name. . . .*

"Alethe will show you the way, my lords." She snapped her fingers, called the girl's name. Alethe detached herself from one of the dancing boys and rushed over. "Show Lord Oakham and Master Rhenford to the Red Chamber. Merry Banquet, my lords."

Herione turned majestically away, drifting towards the group of middle-aged men. Alethe gave a deep curtsy. "If you'll attend me, my lords?" She led them past the fountain and up the marble stairs.

"Uldericus has his own room?" Liam asked.

"He gives Herione a great deal of custom," Oakham said absently. He was watching Alethe mount the steps, his eyes focused on the narrow waist of her dress and the movement of the cloth below.

"Really?"

Oakham tore his eyes away from the girl. "You would scarcely credit it, when you see his wife. She's a passing beauty. But then, I don't think he comes here to bed, if you take me."

The stairs came to a landing, off which two hallways sprinkled with doors led to left and right. Alethe led them to the right.

"Herione's girls are most talented," Oakham went on. "They sing like larks, foot it like nymphs, and keep counsel like priests. Isn't that so, Alethe?" He reached forward and goosed the girl, who whirled around, at the same time blushing furiously and managing a sweet smile.

"As my lord says," she murmured, and then indicated a nearby door. "The Red Chamber." She opened the door and ushered them in, again with a deep curtsy.

The Red Chamber lived up to its name. Walls, floor, ceiling and furniture were all done in varying shades of red, from near-orange to almost-purple. Red shades around the few candles completed the effect, which Liam found a little uncomfortable. There were too many shadows, and everything in the room seemed a little blurry, including Uldericus, who was lounging on a low couch on the far side of the room. A woman knelt next to him, draping his forehead with a wet cloth, while another sat at his feet with a closed book; both were fully dressed. Quetivel was sitting on another couch opposite the earl, looking exasperated.

"More poetry," he exclaimed, turning to Oakham for help. "He is listening to poetry again!"

"Yes," Uldericus groaned, pulling himself up to a sitting position on the couch. He kept the wet cloth on his forehead. "Poetry again. It soothes away the cares of the day, Quetivel, and the aches in my head. What's more, the girl has a lovely voice." Wearily, he dropped the cloth in his lap and clapped his hands. The two women stood, curtsied and hurried out. "Now I warrant you want a game, is that it?"

The earl was as unprepossessing a man as Liam had ever seen: thin, of medium height, with short-cut gray hair. His neck was long and his ears a little too large for his head, but otherwise his face was average-looking. He wore a simple tunic and breeches of gray, and his feet were bare.

And he likes poetry, Liam thought. *How many thieves like poetry?*

Oakham chuckled. "Some wine betimes," he said, "and some talk, and then a game. I am not as eager as Quetivel to lose. And I brought a friend—an acquaintance of my aunt's. Master Liam Rhenford."

For the first time the earl noticed him, and Liam was sure the man's eyes widened a little at his name. Liam bowed.

"My lord."

"Master Rhenford. Merry Banquet. Quetivel, there is wine in the cupboard—pour us some, if you will."

The young baron went to a red-painted cupboard and began filling cups, grumbling all the while.

"Scat yourselves, gentlemen," Uldericus said, and they occupied the couch Quetivel had just left. "An acquaintance of Mistress Priscian, eh?"

"Yes, my lord."

"Y' are in trade?"

"I dabble, my lord. It passes the time." He remembered Quetivel's sneer at merchants.

"Ah."

"Does your head still ache, Uldericus?" Oakham asked, a little smile on his lips.

"The poetry was helping," the earl said, taking up his cloth and scrubbing at his temples. "I would task you for it, and your ample supplies of bad wine, but y' have trouble enough. Has the Duke's man clapped in the knave?"

Liam's mind raced, searching for a way to exploit the turn in the conversation. Quetivel handed around the cups to the seated men, but remained standing himself.

"No," Oakham replied. "There is little enough he can do. The thief was passing clever."

"What amazes me," Liam put in, "is that the man had the nerve to enter the house with all of you in it." Both Uldericus and Quetivel turned quickly to him, and he went on smoothly: "I met Mistress Priscian this evening, and she explained it all to me. It is strange—did you hear nothing?'' He directed the last question to Oakham, who took it up smoothly.

"Not a thing. I was far into my cups," he said, and laughed ruefully.

Putting on his most innocent face, Liam turned to their host. "And you, Earl Uldericus? Not a thing?"

"I sleep very soundly," the man said, and then, inexplicably, shot a glance at Quetivel. "And so does my wife."

The baron said, "I heard nothing."

"I had the strangest dream, though," Uldericus said, as if it had just occurred to him. "I wonder if it was a sign. I dreamed I was a wolfhound rounding a henhouse, and a sly fox kept pattering on quiet feet, conning out an entrance. How does that like you?"

"Strange," murmured Oakham. Quetivel maintained a tight-lipped silence, gripping his cup tightly.

"It might be an omen," Liam admitted. "Or perhaps you heard the thief's steps, and they entered your dreams. Every time it rains, I dream that I'm at sea."

Quetivel burst out: "Nonsense! Dreams are dreams, no more."

Uldericus ignored him, staring thoughtfully at Liam. "There may be something in that, Master Rhenford. Who knows what makes our dreams? But what of it? I did not dream the knave's visage, and could not even tell the hour when I dreamed his footsteps."

"I would that you had," Oakham said, with a wry smile.

"What I most wonder, though," Liam said into the silence that followed, "is why steal the Jewel in the first place? There is not enough money in all of Southwark to pay for it—and who would buy it?"

Uldericus answered, but he was looking at Oakham. "A fool. Only a fool would buy it."

"Buy, sell, buy, sell," sneered Quetivel. "Not all things have a price, Rhenford, and the value of some is not measured in coins."

Liam smiled equably. "You are quite right, Baron Quetivel. You cannot buy happiness, for instance, or love—but a jewel? It *is* money." He had chosen his examples because they were cliches, but they seemed to strike home with Quetivel, who paled and looked down at his feet.

Now that's strange, Liam thought, and then turned back to Uldericus. Quetivel could wait; there would be plenty of chances to sound him out, but this might be his only meeting with the earl.

"I ask you, Earl Uldericus, if you were a thief, and knew you could not sell the Jewel, would you steal it?"

It was a little strong, Liam knew, too open a question, but he was worried about how much he would be able to dig, and since they were on the subject, he wanted to press ahead. The earl took his time about answering, rubbing his forehead with the cloth and looking at the rug between his feet.

"It passes my understanding, Master Rhenford," he said at last, and then looked up. "But I think we worry this subject to death. I am sure Aetius is ill with it, and it only reminds me how large a cup I crawled into yesternight." There was a bellpull by his couch; he reached out and tugged at it.

"Come, sirs, let us have a game."

CHAPTER 8

THE WOMEN WHO had been attending the earl before responded to the bellpull, and Uldericus sent them off for plain lights and a table. It must have been a frequent request, because they returned only a few moments later, followed by two manservants carrying a small table with four stools stacked on top of it. The men quickly moved the couches away and set up the table, arranging the stools; one of the women hung an ordinary lantern from a convenient hook and removed the colored shades from the candles. The room brightened considerably, and Liam began to like it more.

The other woman had brought two decks of cards and a lacquered box, in which were neatly stacked wooden counters painted in blue, red and white. As soon as the stools were in place Uldericus sat and began deftly shuffling the decks, seven times each.

"Come, sirs, come," he said. "What game shall it be?"

"Alliances," Quetivel said, taking a seat and dropping a heavy sack on the table.

"In course," Oakham said, doing the same. "For what stakes, though?"

Liam sat as well, disturbed for no reason he could name. He knew how to play Alliances, and before leaving the house on the beach he had filled his purse with a fair number of coins, just as a precaution. When Uldericus announced the stakes, he breathed a mental sigh of relief. But the unease remained.

"Whites a silver, reds five, and blues a crown. Agreed?"

The other men readily agreed, and Liam opened his own purse, reaching in for a handful of coins.

"Rhenford, I think I may have not mentioned this to you," Oakham said, concern in his voice. "I can advance you a stake—"

This drew an arched eyebrow from Uldericus and a snort from Quetivel, but Liam merely smiled and shook his head, drawing a handful of gold coins from his pouch.

"Not at all, Oakham. I am always prepared." He stacked the coins on the table in front of him, and was happy to see that Uldericus nodded approvingly.

"A happy state," the earl said. "And do you know the game?"

That, Liam realized, was why he was not entirely comfortable. "I do," he said, which was true. He knew the rules, which were fairly complicated—he knew the rules for many card games. The problem was that he was no good at them. Cards were, he had long since decided, a combination of good memory and luck. He had a good memory, but for some reason could not bring it to bear on remembering all the cards in a deck; he also had good luck, in most things, but it had never extended to games of chance. So he said: "I have played from time to time, but I must warn you that I am far from the good."

Oakham smiled good-naturedly. "No matter. Quetivel isn't either."

The young baron frowned and tossed one of his braids over his shoulder. "I will trounce you all." There was nothing friendly in the way he said it.

Uldericus took their coins, stacking them neatly in the lacquered box and replacing them with the colored chips. Then he started dealing.

Alliances—and Generals, a version for three players—was popular in the Freeports, where there were entire taverns devoted to it; Liam had learned it there, between voyages. There were two decks, the first of which was dealt out, while the second was left in the center of the table for drawing. From the thirteen cards originally dealt them, each player was supposed to field an army, laying it out face up. An army had to be led by a king or queen, called generals, and be composed of at least three cards from the same suit. At the beginning of each turn, a player drew an extra card from the second deck, and at the end threw a card to the dead pile. In between, they could attack the other players' armies. A general could lead an extra army out of the player's hand, as it could for the player attacked, while existing armies could be reinforced. The rules of engagement were fairly simple—after reinforcing, the cards in each army were counted up and the player with the most powerful army took the loser's army. Later, if the loser was forced out of play, all of the armies he had lost could be bought into the hands of the winners. More important than winning cards, Liam knew, was that each action cost money.

Keeping an army out cost a red chip each turn; drawing a card cost a white; each card brought out to reinforce an army not under attack cost a white; an army under attack could be reinforced with one card for free, but each additional card cost a red; one army with a general could be laid out each turn for free, but to lay out an additional army on the same turn cost a blue. A player could pay to draw extra cards, or to avoid discarding, or to proclaim himself neutral for a number of turns, or even to ransom armies lost in an attack—in short a player could pay, and pay, and pay, and pay.

When Liam had learned in the Freeports, the game had not seemed so expensive. *You were playing with sailors*, he told himself, *for coppers*. He could not remember ever having put more than a few silvers into the warchest over the course of an entire game.

The idea was to force other players out, by attacking them until they could no longer field armies, either because they had no generals to lead or not enough cards of the general's suit to back them up. With three players, the game continued until only one was left; with four, the last two players left usually broke the warchest into shares equaling the number of armies left in play, each taking the same number of shares as they had armies.

It was not a fast game.

In the first of the five hands they played, much to his surprise, Liam split the warchest with Uldericus, taking two shares to the earl's seven. In the second, Liam drew a poor hand and Quetivel attacked him relentlessly, weakening himself so that Oakham and Uldericus split. The third was called a truce, because Liam had no generals on the deal, and could field no armies. Quetivel, with the strongest hand, took the meager warchest, a white ante chip from each player and a red indemnity from Liam for not being able to field.

The fourth hand was longer than the first three combined. No one seemed willing to attack, building up their armies slowly and husbanding their strength. Liam had the weakest position on the field and very little in his hand to reinforce with; when the attacks finally began, they were centered on him. He was forced to buy heavily to defend himself, but eventually, after a long, drawn-out and expensive series of defenses, he was put out of the game and left with a tiny pile of chips. Uldericus declared himself neutral for three turns, paying three blues for the right, and in the flush of victory over Liam, Quetivel turned on Oakham and put him out of the game.

"Alliance?" Uldericus asked. His forces were untouched, and his smile seemed to indicate that he had a strong hand in reserve. Quetivel, though, had most of Liam's and Oakham's armies; for a heavy fee he could field them and try to take the whole warchest himself.

He hesitated, swaying in his chair a little. He had filled and emptied his cup more times than the other three men put together. Screwing up his eyes, he surveyed the table, inspecting the armies Uldericus had laid out, the discard pile and the hands Liam and Oakham had laid out after their defeats, as if he were searching for something.

"Alliance," he mumbled at last, and stumbled away to refill his cup. Liam and Oakham stood as well, stretching, while Uldericus split the warchest into shares.

"Shall we try a final hand?" the earl asked, eyes still on the pile of chips.

"Yes!" Quetivel shouted from the far side of the room. "Another!"

"I'll venture," Oakham said. "Rhenford?"

Liam shook his head and waved a hand at his tiny stake. "No. I can hardly field an army."

Oakham smiled. "Come, I'll vouch for you. You can repay me tomorrow."

Uldericus looked up, frowning. "Y' are not doing so well yourself, Aetius."

"I have enough for another hand—and I'll vouch for Rhenford. What say you?"

Oakham was looking at him, but Liam waited for Uldericus, who looked back and forth between the two standing men. The earl thought for a moment, one finger tapping his chin, and then drew the lacquered box towards him.

"Thirty?" He started counting out chips.

"Thirty to start," Oakham said with a bright smile. "And ten for me, if it please you. You and Quetivel can't have all the luck."

"I hope not," Liam said, taking his seat and accepting the new chips Uldericus sent his way. Borrowing the money did not bother him, because he knew he had more than enough at home to repay Oakham; besides, he was having fun.

Enjoy your losses all you want, he scolded himself, *but are you learning anything?*

He was learning things, in fact, but nothing that was of any use. Early on he had tried to start a conversation, but his comments had fallen flat, the other three men concentrating solely on the game at hand. He gave up trying to start them talking, and focused on their playing.

Oakham was bold but careless, laying his armies out in full strength, with very little in the way of reserves. He attacked Liam and Quetivel recklessly, laughing when he won, laughing even louder when he lost. He bought very little, however, relying mainly on the strength of the cards he was dealt and what he drew, so that even though he had lost twice, it had not hurt his pile too much.

Quetivel, on the other hand, made a great show of trying to be canny, carefully examining all the armies laid out and making an effort to remember all the cards in the discard pile and those held prisoner. He kept large reserves, paying heavily to bring them in when attacking and defending. In the first two hands he had only attacked when someone was weakened by previous attacks from other players, and then only Liam and Oakham. In the fourth, though, emboldened perhaps by the wine, he had attacked almost as often as Oakham, though still maintaining reserves. Still, he avoided fighting the earl, though he frequently shot calculating glares at the man. Even with his share of the fourth warchest, it was clear that he had lost money.

Uldericus was the only consistent winner. His pile of chips was much bigger than anyone else's, despite the fact that he almost never attacked. He had bought neutrality for himself in the fourth hand, but Liam could not see why: neither Oakham nor Quetivel had ever attacked the earl, and Liam had only done so in the first hand, when he had the strength. At first Liam had worried that the other two men might have been refraining from engaging the earl out of deference, but Uldericus had taken no offense at his attacks, so he put it down to fear of the man's pile of chips, with which he could afford to buy enormous reserves.

Quetivel came back to the table with another cup of wine and brilliant red spots on each pale cheek. "I shall trounce you all," he announced, as if he had a grudge against them, and sat. Uldericus began dealing the fifth hand.

From the moment he picked up his cards, Liam knew he was going to lose. He had only one general, a queen, and the rest mostly low cards scattered among the suits. Oakham and Uldericus arranged their cards in silence and with blank expressions; Quetivel sneered happily at his and immediately, before it was his turn, laid out an army. The earl frowned and laid out his first army, Liam and Oakham following, skipping Quetivel's turn.

The play started even slower than in the hand before. Oakham and Uldericus drew normally and laid out no more armies, Quetivel fielded a general each turn until he had four, and Liam bought extra cards, hoping for another general. He drew neither kings nor queens, but managed to get a few decent reserve cards, including one of the two dragons in the deck.

Thus it went around the table for several rounds, with Liam's pile of chips steadily dwindling as he sought vainly for generals. Both Oakham and Uldericus had laid out extra armies and then, suddenly, Oakham attacked, laying out a third army and directing it at Liam. Led by a king and with high cards to back it up, it easily beat both what Liam had showing and his reserve cards—except for the dragon.

The dragon was an expensive card to play, but he had little choice. Oakham called for his defense with a small smile. Liam payed out the equivalent of five blue chips, which left him with only ten white chips and two reds, and played the dragon.

Oakham's jaw dropped. The army he had attacked with, his strongest, went to the dead pile, as did the dragon, and Liam was allowed to counterattack. He chose the lord's weakest army, reinforcing his queen-led army with two high cards and paying the fee into the warchest.

"I have nothing," Oakham stammered, and watched Liam scoop up his weakest army.

It was Uldericus's turn. With a sour look at Oakham, he bought neutrality for two rounds. Quetivel was champing at the bit, and as soon as the earl had paid his fee, he paid the upkeep fees on the four armies he had, laid out a fifth, and attacked both Liam and Oakham.

Without reserves, Oakham handed his last army over. Liam stayed in a little longer, using his last three whites to buy in strong cards to support his queen, and the last red to field the army he had taken from Oakham. Quetivel, though, had strong reserves as well, and when he bought them in, he took both.

Liam nodded graciously, impressed by the quick move, and handed his armies over. Quetivel snapped them up.

"It seems I bought neutrality to no purpose," Uldericus said, a hint of bitterness in his voice. "Alliance?" He reached forward to split the warchest. Quetivel reached out unsteadily and stopped the earl's hand.

"No. No alliance." His voice was husky, wavering, and he cleared his throat. "No alliance. I'll trounce you all."

There was something in his tone that made Liam lean forward, a feeling that Quetivel's words had some significance he could not catch. Oakham did not seem to understand the young lord's meaning either; he watched both Quetivel and Uldericus with an expression that combined confusion and anxiety.

"Well enough," the earl said at last, pulling his hand from underneath Quetivel's. "My draw, then."

He paid his fee, drew, and paid another to avoid discarding. Quetivel paid, drew, paid to lay out another army, and discarded a low card. There was a sudden tension around the table, and Liam found he was holding his breath. He let it out slowly between his teeth; after all, he had already lost all of his money. *Oakham is out too,* he thought, *but he is as nervous as I am.* It was true: the lord's handsome face was pale, his glance flickering back and forth between the remaining players.

Quetivel glared at his opponent, his eyes narrowed to slits; his head jerked forward from time to time in rapid pecks, and he rubbed his lips together hungrily. Uldericus appeared not to notice, nonchalantly paying the proper fees to draw and lay out a strong army. Then he paid for three reserve cards, the most he could draw in a turn, and discarded one of them, a red two.

"It is not too late to call Alliance," Uldericus said, but Quetivel ignored him, drawing and starting to field all of his armies. He had five led by kings and three by queens, and even though he had fumbled a great deal with his hand to lay them out, he still had an impressive spread of reserves.

"Trounce," he said, with a mean and happy smile. He attacked with all his armies. There could only be sixteen armies in the field—eight kings and eight queens. Quetivel held eight, and one of Oakham's was in the dead pile, untouchable, which meant that Uldericus could only field seven.

With a wry smile, the earl laid out seven armies. "It would like me to play this out," he said.

"If y' enjoy a slow trouncing," Quetivel said with a flourish of his free hand. "Go to."

Uldericus placed his seven armies in order against Quetivel's eight. "Reinforce?"

Quetivel swayed forward and blinked deliberately, studying which armies had been placed against which, and then reinforced the first. Sudden beads of sweat stood out on his brow and cheeks, obstinately refusing to run. Uldericus laid out enough reserves on his first to make the two armies equal—and they went to the dead pile. The second and third armies for both men went the same way, tied and discarded, and Liam began to see the earl's strategy. He was husbanding his strength, using cards just strong enough to match and leaving his highest reserve cards in his hand.

Oakham licked his lips nervously and left the table for a cup of wine.

Three more armies went to the dead pile, and Uldericus had only one left, his strongest, matched against Quetivel's strongest. Quetivel's eighth lay unopposed, and the young baron laughed. "Trounced!"

"Would you reinforce?" Uldericus asked pleasantly.

"Why?" Quetivel demanded. "Even if you take it, it cannot be fielded until your next turn, leaving mine the only army in play. No, I'll not reinforce! Take it, if you will—the warchest is mine."

"Unless the only army left is unfielded," Uldericus said. Paying and reinforcing his seventh army, he took Quetivel's, then threw five blues into the warchest and played a dragon against the last army on the field. "And that army is now mine." With a satisfied smile he sat back.

Quetivel stood, knocking over his stool, and planted his fists heavily on the table, leaning over the wreckage of his game. "Impossible!" he shouted. "No!" He threw his head back and practically howled. "Oakham! It's impossible!"

Leveling a stern glance at the angry baron, Uldericus called out: "Aetius, I think our young friend needs some air."

"No!" Quetivel cried, and he would have lunged across the table if Oakham had not caught him by the shoulders and pulled him back. The wiry baron struggled briefly, but Oakham easily caught him around the waist and carried him out of the room. Liam would have thought it funny—Quetivel kicked and shouted like a child—if Uldericus had not been staring so thoughtfully at the departing pair. When they were gone, he stood and stretched, then went and shut the door behind them.

"Well and well," he said, rubbing his chin. "He should neither drink nor game, I think. He should learn to lose from you, Master Rhenford."

"I am very good at losing," Liam said with a wry smile. "I do it much quicker than anyone I know."

Uldericus waved the sarcasm away. "I mean the squalling. It ill becomes a man." He found a pair of boots and began pulling them on. There was a precision to his movements that interested Liam, a neatness and economy to each action that suggested they had all been planned in advance. His dealing had been the same— deliberate and careful.

"I suppose I should go," Liam said, looking about for his cloak. He had learned a little, though nowhere near as much as he would have liked.

"Nonsense," the earl said. "It likes me to leave, but only for another place. Accompany me—for that y' are a man who can lose and smile. And if y' are out of pocket," he gestured at the large pile in front of his seat, "you will be my guest." He finished pulling on his boots, blousing his long gray breeches just so, and fished a matching gray cloak out of one of the cupboards.

Liam bowed his thanks and found his own cloak lying

on one of the divans. He did not particularly wish to stay out longer—it had been a long day, and his eyes had begun to feel gritty—and he was not entirely sure he liked Uldericus, or the offhand manner with which he had assumed Liam would stay out longer simply because that was what the earl wanted. Still, he was not asleep on his feet, and he hoped that a chance might present itself to get more information about the previous night.

So they left the Red Chamber together, Uldericus pausing for a moment to study the table at which they had played, and went downstairs. The masked youths were gone, but most of the middle-aged men were still there, though now comfortably seated and very closely attended by the modestly-dressed young women. Herione stood by the fountain, her lips pressed thin, directing a servant in mopping up a puddle.

"Madame," Uldericus called, striding across the marble floor, "we have concluded. If you would see to the room, and the money there—and I'll tell you, I know it to the coin. See that it is all accounted for when next I'm here."

Herione curtsied deeply, murmuring, "In course, my lord," but Liam could see she held her head down to hide an angry blush at the insult.

"Coming, Rhenford?" The earl walked on to the doors and began rummaging through a tall basket tucked in one corner. Liam hung back, waiting for Herione to rise, offering her a bow and an apologetic smile when she did.

"Merry Banquet," he said.

She nodded, an answering smile gradually draining the anger from her face. "And to you, Master Rhenford."

No harm in being polite, he told himself, going on to the door where Uldericus waited. *Besides, she may be able to answer a few questions. . . .*

Uldericus held up a heavy walking stick as Liam approached. "See you this?" He swung it two or three times through the air, smiling at the whistling sound it made. "A life preserver. An uncommonly useful thing, with all these knaves about. Go to." He pushed the door open with the head of the life preserver and gestured for Liam to precede him.

Oakham leaned against a pillar, arms folded across his chest, watching a servant slop water over the steps. Uldericus stopped in the doorway, the stick over one shoulder, and gave a sharp sniff.

"Our young baron is much taken with the customs of the Banquet," he said to no one in particular. "He shares my wine with everyone, it seems."

The servant sloshed more water on the steps, emptying his bucket.

"I ducked him in the fountain," Oakham said, "and he seemed the better for it, and quieter, but when I got him outside—well." He nodded at the servant and the mess he was trying to wash away. "Then he ran off, to Pet Radday's, unless I miss my guess."

Liam circled around the servant, avoiding the stains. Uldericus let the door close with a snort. "Radday's, eh? Will there be baiting, then?"

The night was clear and cold, with no moon; once his eyes adjusted, Liam could see the dim outlines of the street by the stars' faint light. He had not drunk much, trying to concentrate on the game and the players, but the fresh air felt good and cleared his head a great deal.

"It's likely," Oakham said doubtfully. "But will Quetivel like company?"

Uldericus laughed and set off down the street, away from the Point. "Damn him—I want to see the baiting."

Liam and Oakham followed him in silence. It was too dark to see the lord's face, but Liam could tell that he was concerned. The situation reminded him of his university days in Torquay—the pointlessly complex play of hierarchy in friendship. *Oakham wants to play with Uldericus,* he thought, *but feels responsible for Quetivel. And Quetivel refuses to play nicely.* Drinking too much and throwing up on the steps of a brothel was not behavior calculated to endear—and the baron had come dangerously close to calling Uldericus a cheat. And there was that strange exchange about the earl's dream, how his wife slept soundly, sly foxes and guarding the hen-house. What did that mean? *I would try to keep them apart too.*

Uldericus walked briskly, completely at ease in the dark streets, tapping the life preserver on the cobbles in time to his steps. They headed north, towards Auric's Park, passing the entrance to Temple Street, still brightly lit despite the late hour. Apart from the occasional late stroller, and one or two parties of torch-bearing holiday-makers, they had the streets to themselves.

Liam wondered about Quetivel's near-accusation. Had Uldericus cheated? He had certainly done very well—Liam had lost the forty-odd crowns he had brought with him, as well as the thirty he borrowed. Oakham was down whatever he brought with him along with most of the ten he had borrowed. There was no guessing at Que-tivel's losses, but he had thrown huge sums into the last warchest. Uldericus had split three warchests and taken the last all for himself. They had used his cards, in his room, where Quetivel had apparently lost before.

Don't get carried away, Liam thought. *You played badly. You always play badly, so of course you lost.* Oakham had not played well, either—but Quetivel had. Still, there had been nothing unusual about the game, and the baron was drunk. *And a rude brat as well,* Liam added, surprised at how much he disliked the young man. *He is, though. An obnoxious little lordling. He deserved to lose.*

"Have you been baiting, Master Rhenford?" Uldericus was speaking to him. Liam begged his pardon, and the earl repeated his question.

"No, my lord."

They had been walking for almost twenty minutes, and were far into Auric's Park, approaching Northfield, where Southwark straggled loosely into the countryside. The streets were wider, the houses set farther apart, and the road they were on had turned from cobbles to dirt.

"Radday's the best—they say he sends to the Mid-lands for his animals, and he's ever open, though not always with baiting. Cockfights, ratcatching, wrestling, boxing, he always has some sport.''

Liam made a noncommittal noise; he had never been baiting because he had no interest in blood sports. Even while growing up in the Midlands, he had disliked the formalized aspect of the hunt, though at least there they ate what they killed. Staking a bear or a boar in a pit with a pack of dogs and watching them kill each other seemed vicious to him.

''And there it is,'' the earl said, pointing out a strange building standing alone in a large lot. It was long and low, a roof of wood raised up on thick posts with canvas walls. Two rows of smoking torches led to the entrance. Uldericus led them in, paying three silver pieces to the large and unfriendly men who guarded the door. Liam ducked through the flap in the canvas with the others, but almost immediately wished he had not. The space was filled to bursting with a strange mix of classes— from men as well dressed as Uldericus or Oakham, some even better, down to the most ragged beggars—all talking, shoving and jostling over the dirt floor and churning it into mud. A few more torches were fixed over the pit in the center, a good fifteen feet deep and walled with heavy logs; the air was thick with smoke and an eye-watering smell, animals and unwashed men packed too close, cheap torches and fresh blood.

Uldcricus shouldered his way right into the crowd, straight for the pit, Oakham in his wake; Liam pushed in the opposite direction, putting his back to the canvas and sliding along the wall. There would be no chance for questions here, but since he had come all this way he decided he might as well wait, and hope for an opportunity on the way out.

An animal roar rose suddenly over the noise of the men, drowning and finally silencing it; then the crowd was shouting, men calling out bets, others acknowledging them, markers passing back and forth. Hands and heads flashed around Liam; as far back into the canvas as he pressed, he was surrounded by the crazed mob of men, jostled and pushed back and forth.

"Six dogs," a man near him cried. "That one'll take down six! Who's got six?"

Another man asked, "How many's Radday loosing tonight?"

"Sport," Liam muttered angrily, and began to shove back, making a way for himself towards the back of the room, where it looked like there was more room. The roar came again—a bear, he guessed—and dogs began to bark and howl. The crowd grew frenzied.

He kept pushing, and then, suddenly, he was through, in a canvas corner of the room that was almost empty, and face to face with Quetivel.

The young baron was filthy, stains across the front of his tunic, the hem and much of the rest of his cloak clotted with mud. He leaned bonelessly against the corner post, a tall jar of wine dangling by its neck from one hand. His face was gray, studded by the same obstinate beads of sweat, but his eyes lost some of their glassiness, focusing weakly on Liam. He mumbled something.

"Baron Quetivel," Liam shouted, "are you all right?"

The barking and roaring from the pit were continuous now, punctuated by cheers and cries from the crowd. Quetivel straightened a little, gestured vaguely with the jar. "How does it like you to be cheated?"

He really is an ass, Liam thought. "You are drunk, my lord—come outside!"

Quetivel shoved aside Liam's offered hand. "Cheated," he repeated, his voice rising. "Cheated! By a man who can't keep a wife!"

Liam goggled; involuntarily he turned his head, hoping not to see—Uldericus, a grim look on his face, the life preserver on his shoulder. Oakham stood behind him, pale and fearful. Liam whirled back to the drunken baron.

"Come on!" he shouted, pulling at Quetivel's arm. The crowd was howling now; a high-pitched yelp of pain tore through the noise.

"Where's your wife?" Quetivel shouted at Uldericus. "You goddamned cheat!"

Even over the noise of the crowd Liam heard the crunch, though he had not seen the life preserver leave the earl's shoulder. Quetivel crumbled, his nose spurting blood and lying at an ugly angle to the rest of his face.

For a long moment no one moved: Uldericus held the stick just where it had hit Quetivel, Liam gaped in shock, and Oakham cursed. Then the lord took hold of Uldericus's arm and tugged him gently away; the earl let himself be led, a grim smile forming on his lips.

Liam was left to look after Quetivel, who lay moaning incoherently in the mud.

A quarter of an hour later, Liam had managed to haul the baron to his feet, stanch the flow of blood, and half carry him out of Radday's. The sounds from the pit followed him out into the night, even when the canvas flap shut—the weakening roars of the bear, the deep-chested barking of those dogs still on their feet, the high yelps of the hurt.

The cold air seemed to do Quetivel good: he stirred groggily and opened his eyes. "What—" he murmured, then groaned.

Oakham hurried to help, propping the baron up from the other side. Together they brought him out to the street. Uldericus waited there, the life preserver held across his chest, parallel to the ground. Torch-shadows flickered over his face. He was not smiling anymore.

"I'll have satisfaction," the earl said. "When he is recovered, we'll meet. Master Rhenford, you witnessed all—you'll be my second. Attend me tomorrow noon, at my home." Without another word, before Liam could respond, he turned on his heel and stalked off into the darkness.

A few seconds later, Liam cursed and stamped his foot. "Ah, gods! As if I haven't enough to do!"

Oakham spat bitterly. "Count yourself lucky. I'll end as his second." He nodded at Quetivel, who was slowly regaining control of his legs. They got the baron a few more steps before he started straining against them, groaning and muttering.

"Come," Oakham said at last. "This is foolishness. We need a horse. Yours is at a stable?"

"Yes." He mentioned the ostler's name.

"Well enough—I know the man. Fetch yours, and have them send one to me. I'll watch the boy."

Liam quickly agreed, slipping out from underneath the baron's arm. He hesitated a moment, having seen the results of blows to the head a number of times. "Keep him walking until the horse comes, and make sure he sits up. When you put him to bed, keep him sitting up. And if he vomits, do not let him go to sleep. Do you understand?"

Oakham nodded impatiently. "Go to, go to."

He hesitated again, staring the lord in the face. "I think there are some things we should talk about, Oakham." He stressed the name. "I do not think this will work the way we are going about it. You must tell me more about your guests."

"Aye, aye, I see that now," the lord said, sighing wearily. "Come tomorrow in the morning. Near ten or so. We'll to see Cawood, and we'll talk."

Liam waited a moment, trying to read Oakham's face, and then gave up. He left the two men in the torchlight and walked off into the darkened streets. After a few minutes, when the torches outside Radday's were mere pinpoints of light in the distance, he stopped and projected.

Fanuilh!

Yes, master?

Are you nearby?

I will be with you in a few minutes.

"Good," Liam said to himself. He was angry, angry at the things Oakham had obviously not told him, at Uldericus's imperious manner, at Quetivel's rash and obnoxious stupidity, but beneath the thin layer of anger was a deeper current of exhaustion. It had been a very, very long day. Tired, and distracted by his anger, he did not want to walk the streets alone. *It would be just the thing,* he thought, *after losing almost eighty crowns, be-*

ing dragged into a bear-baiting pit and a duel, to be knocked on the head by robbers.

He heard more than saw Fanuilh's descent, the flapping of its leathery wings. It was a black shape blotting out the stars in front of him, hovering with slow wingbeats.

Master.

"Ride on my shoulder," Liam said. "Keep me company."

The dragon leapt into position, landing so lightly that he barely felt its claws. It seemed to weigh nothing. He started walking again.

The stableboy brought Diamond out in record time and began saddling a second horse before Liam had even finished asking for it. Exhaustion had overwhelmed anger on the long walk. His feet, hands and nose were cold; all he could think of was his bed.

"You know Radday's?" he asked.

"The baiting pit," the boy stammered, and Liam suddenly realized that the boy was not looking at him, but at Fanuilh.

Too late to do anything about that, he thought, too tired to care much.

"Go quickly, boy." He fished the last silver piece out of his purse and tossed it. The boy instinctively caught the coin, and then juggled it as if it were hot.

Liam grinned tiredly and swung up onto Diamond's back. He guided the horse as far as the city gate and then let it find the way home.

"Well," he said, "you have made your first appearance in Southwark, and scared the wits out of a stableboy. Happy?"

He will recover.

Liam laughed, a small, happy chuckle that eventually trailed off to a sigh. They traveled the rest of the way in silence, Diamond instinctively heading for home. Huddling in his cloak to escape the cold, Liam could only think of how miserable he was, and even when the horse started picking its way carefully down the cliff path, his only thought was: *Bed.*

CHAPTER 9

THE HOUSE WAS ablaze with light, and as Liam led Diamond across the patio to the shed, he guessed that Grantaire was still awake.

He grumbled to himself, sure that there was no way he was going to get to sleep soon. Fumbling the saddle off the roan, he gave the animal a barely adequate currying and trudged back to the house through the cold, exaggerating his own weariness.

She will want to talk, he whined to himself, *and talk and talk and talk.* Once on the patio, though, he hung his head for a moment, composing what he hoped was a cheerful-but-not-interested-in-extended-conversation face—*She is my guest, after all*—and entered the house, Fanuilh at his heels.

Grantaire was in what Tarquin had called his trophy room; Liam called out, "Good evening," hung his cloak on a convenient peg and, hoping to forestall conversation as much as possible, went to stand in the doorway. He could not have gone much further, in any case.

The trophy room was dominated by a set of waist-high cabinets with glass lids, in which Tarquin had stored a collection of wands, flasks and various pieces of jewelry, all of which Fanuilh had assured Liam had magical properties. The walls were hung with enchanted items as well, including a sword and shield, what appeared to be a stringless lute, and a rug which flew.

Grantaire had taken everything out of the cases and off the walls, and arrayed it on the floor. She sat cross-legged in the midst of it all, the gray cat in her lap.

"Good evening," she said, looking up at him innocently.

Liam took the room in at a glance, leaning against the doorjamb with his arms folded across his chest. "You've been busy," he said, as nonchalantly as he could.

"I don't know how Tanaquil expected me to find anything," she said sourly. "There was no way to identify all of this." She gestured at the mess around her.

"Fanuilh knows what it all is," Liam said. "I'm sure he would be happy to explain."

"Well, neither of you was here, so I did it myself. I've figured them all out—I'll be taking most of them with me, but there are a few things I will leave for you."

Liam nodded and cleared his throat, still a little taken aback by the mess she had made. She stood then, a smooth, graceful motion, and dusted off the back of her shift.

"I wonder, would you mind making me some dinner?"

He started guiltily. *Some host,* he thought. *The oven will not work for her.* "Oh—yes, yes, I'm sorry. Come on." He led the way to the kitchen and asked her what she wanted. She had no preferences, though, and left to his own devices, he imagined a typical Southwark sea pie.

"They eat these a lot around here," he explained as he laid the dish in front of her. "It's mostly fish."

She nodded her approval and cut into the pie, nodding more at the fishy smell that spread through the room. She ate quickly, with little ceremony, but he found himself fascinated by her movements, even the way she picked out a piece of fish and fed it to the cat. He knew he was staring, but he could not help it; he was tired, and the effort of moving his eyes away seemed too much for him.

When she was finished, she pushed the half-eaten pie towards the cat and sat back, closing her eyes with a look of contentment. "That was very good," she murmured. "I haven't had fish in a long time." Her throat was firm and smooth; Liam shook his head, forced himself to move. He paced a little, and then remembered:

"I spoke to Mistress Priscian about those papers you were interested in," he said. "She said she would look and see if there were any this morning."

"Wonderful! And she said I might see them?" She sat up straight, genuinely pleased, her mouth open a little, expectantly, eyes wide and hopeful. Her lower lip was fuller than the top, and Liam thought the way her hair just brushed her shoulders, auburn against the white skin, was very pretty. He stirred himself. *What are you thinking?*

"Yes," he said, "but she was very clear that she did not expect to find anything. He lived—and died—quite some time ago."

"Life and death mean much less to mages," she pointed out, "and if there were anything . . ."

"Also," he went on, looking away from her, "she is a very proper woman. I mean, a little formal, if you know what I mean."

Annoyance briefly wrinkled Grantaire's face; then she forced it down, and plucked at the shoulder strap of her shift. "I think you mean this. I will certainly wear something more appropriate, and I shall bow and be polite. Mistress Priscian will have no cause to regret my acquaintance—if she has anything to show me."

"You understand, I hope," Liam said, feeling vaguely as if had insulted her. "She is an old woman, a little prim, I mean, but I like her, and we are partners. It's all right around here, on the beach."

"Is it, though?" Grantaire wondered, and then said lightly: "Every time you see me, Liam Rhenford, you blush. This is not what I expected from Tanaquil's diary."

Predictably and quite involuntarily, Liam blushed, then tried to move the conversation away from Grantaire's clothes. "Tarquin kept a diary? You've read it?"

"It is in the library. It is really more of a record of his experiments, but on occasion he included little personal notes. He mentioned you more than once."

"Did he?" Was that why her attitude towards him had changed? "I'd like to see that."

She shook her head. "I do not think you should. He said a number of complimentary things, but he was also a scrupulously honest man. There were one or two things that might sting."

Liam chuckled. "Those are exactly the things I want to read." Of all things, he hated this sort of teasing worst; he knew that for a long time he would wonder what Tarquin had written about him.

"In any case, I will be taking those books with me. Most of it would be of no use to you anyway."

Suddenly he realized that he was quite happy to talk to her, that he was not ready for the conversation to end. He went to the table and took a seat opposite her.

"Tell me something—why is it that you haven't asked me about Tarquin's death? I mean, you have traveled half the length of Taralon to be here, but you haven't asked about that."

"He told me about it," she said. "I told you that he appeared to me."

"Ah," Liam said lamely, "of course."

To his delight, she went on: "What I do want to know, though, is why he came back at all. He said he had business in Southwark. Do you know what it was?"

He did, but he did not want to talk—he wanted to listen to her. As quickly as he could, he outlined what had brought Tarquin back. "It was Laomedon, or his servants. They needed his help freeing one of the god's servants, a gryphon. There is a new goddess now, named Bellona; some of her worshippers had captured the gryphon and were going to sacrifice it."

"Bellona," she said. "I've heard the name. All the way south people were saying that she had appeared here." Liam confirmed that she had, and Grantaire digested this for a moment, eyebrows raised. "It is not every day that a new goddess appears, or that one walks the earth. And you were there?"

"Yes," Liam said hesitantly. "I was helping Tarquin."

She nodded, as if this was what she had expected, and then rose. "I think I'll go to bed, now. It has been a long day."

Not just for you, he thought sourly, irritated that the conversation was at an end. He rose, though, and smiled. "Yes, it has."

They started out of the kitchen, Grantaire in front, and then she stopped short and turned to him, holding out her hand so that her fingertips just touched his chest.

"Tell me—the gryphon was freed?"

"Yes." His throat was inexplicably dry.

"And who freed it, you or Tanaquil?"

For a moment, he recalled hanging from the roof of Bellona's temple, picking the lock of the gryphon's cage. "We both did."

He was terribly aware of how close they were, but he did not step back. Neither did she.

"Tanaquil told me you found the woman who killed him. Is that true?"

Liam nodded, and then stammered, "It was luck, mostly. I am very lucky."

She nodded, her eyes fixed on his. He was much taller, and she had to crane her neck to do it, but she gave no indication that it was awkward. Her eyes were green, he noticed.

Her hand just rested on his chest, but there was nothing sensual about it; she was merely holding him in place. And her face was completely blank, unreadable; her lips were parted, but her teeth met behind them. There was nothing inviting about her, but he was quite sure that he could kiss her. *I could kiss her now,* he thought, somewhat surprised. *I could.*

More important, he did not think she would object.

It was an amazing moment to him, so amazing that he thought again, *I could kiss her!* and he paused too long, trying to grasp what, to him, was the enormity of his realization. *I could kiss her.*

Liam waited too long, reveling in the idea; she dropped her hand and turned away.

"Good night, Liam," she called, turning down the corridor to her bedroom.

For a long minute he stood in the entrance hall, his eyes wide with disappointment. Then he closed them and tilted his head back, stifling a groan in the back of his throat.

Fanuilh trotted into the entrance hall from the trophy room and paused, cocking its head at Liam's strange posture.

Master? Are you all right?

He let his head drop to his chest and trudged heavily into the library.

The dragon followed, and watched as he undressed and crawled onto the divan.

Are you all right? it asked again.

Liam sat up suddenly, a disgruntled look on his face. He formed the thought and shoved it at the dragon: *Did you see that? In the entrance hall?*

Fanuilh sat back on its haunches and peered quizzically up at him.

What, master?

"Oh, never mind," Liam said, and let himself slump down on the divan. He was asleep before he knew it.

However long Liam had been asleep—he could not remember what time he had come home—it was not enough. The sockets of his eyes were filled with sand, his mouth tasted foul, and he was in no way ready for the long list of tasks that lay ahead of him. He sat on the edge of the divan, head in his hands, and groaned twice.

It is almost half past the hour, master.

Fanuilh had woken him at seven, and he had lain there since, "resting his eyes" and muzzily dreading his day.

"I'm getting up," Liam said, and dragged himself from the divan, pulling on his breeches and undershirt from the day before. He slouched out to the kitchen, Fanuilh at his heels. Grantaire sat at the kitchen table; he wished her a good morning and went to the stove. With the image of his breakfast fixed firmly in his head, he poured a handful of water from the jug and splashed it on his face, then opened the stove and pulled out a platter. He parceled out plates and cups on the table: mugs of coffee for himself and Grantaire, a bowl for Fanuilh, and a plate of hot sweet rolls. The dragon hopped up onto the table.

"Good morning," Grantaire said, an odd smile on her face. Her cat stepped from her lap onto the table and sidled over to Fanuilh's bowl. With a dainty sniff, it inspected the coffee. The dragon sat back on its haunches and looked at Liam.

Perhaps the cat would like a bowl of his own.

"Mm," Liam said, his mouth full of honeyed roll. He swallowed. "Does your cat want something? Milk? A dead mouse? A gutted sparrow?" While he did not dislike cats, he did not much appreciate their eating habits.

"Milk, I think."

Stuffing down another roll, Liam went back to the oven and imagined up a bowl of milk, which he set down before the cat. It left Fanuilh's bowl, and the dragon took over, breathing deep.

"Why is his so dark?" Grantaire pointed at the dragon's bowl.

"He likes it that way," Liam said. Coffee was not drunk in Taralon; he had encountered it in the course of his travels. "It's better with milk and sugar, but then, he does not drink his. Do you want yours plain?"

She shook her head and reached out for a roll. "No, it's good as it is. The smell is nice."

The change in their relationship that he had felt the night before was still there, an easing of tension. She also seemed to have gotten over her panic on learning about the other wizard in the city—but she gave no indication of what she thought about that moment in the entrance hall.

For a few minutes they sat and ate, Liam eating each roll whole, Grantaire tearing hers into shreds, chewing and swallowing each piece separately. When he had finished five, he leaned back, nursing his coffee in little sips. She was still wearing the same shift as she had the night before; her shoulders were pure white, and he thought they would be soft to touch. He vividly remembered the scene in the entrance hall, and he picked over it, wondering what he had missed. *Should I have kissed her?* He tried to imagine what would have happened if he had.

"Rhenford," she said suddenly, waving a hand in front of his face, "you're staring." It was not an accusation at all—she might have been pointing out that he had spilled some coffee—but he jumped guiltily.

"Excuse me," he blurted, averting his eyes and hiding his embarrassment in his mug. Searching for a way to change the conversation, he remembered suddenly that it was possible he and Coeccias might be meeting Desiderius later in the day. "I have to go into the city soon—this thing with the Jewel is going to keep me busy. But I will see Mistress Priscian this morning, and let you know if she has anything for you. There is another thing though, something I forgot yesterday."

"Yes?"

"The wizard, Desiderius—he was asking about the Jewel before it was stolen. You said that sneaking it away was not like him."

"No. He is too proud for that."

"We'll take that for granted. Now, what if someone tried to sell it to him? You see," he said, holding up a finger for her to wait while he explained, "I can't see what anyone would do with it in Southwark. Where would they sell it? Who would buy it here? There isn't enough money in the town. But a wizard might have the money—or be able to get it."

"So?" She seemed to have completely forgotten his staring, and he was not sure if he was relieved or disappointed.

"So, the thief may try to sell it to him. It's a long reach, I know—a thief who wanted money would be more likely to try to sell it elsewhere, in Torquay or Harcourt, even the Freeports. On the other hand, wizards rarely go unnoticed, particularly in a city the size of Southwark. And who knows what people might remem-

ber of the Jewel, or Eirenaeus? He has been dead for
centuries, but you know how legends like that can grow.
So the thief might approach Desiderius.''

''You are working up to something,'' she said suspiciously.

''I am,'' he admitted. ''Coeccias—the Duke's man
here, a friend of mine—already knows there is a wizard
here who was asking about the Jewel. He told me about
it. And he will naturally want to find this wizard. What
I'm wondering is if you think it will be dangerous for
me to approach Desiderius.''

She thought carefully before answering, gently biting
the tip of her thumb. ''I cannot say. I do not know why
he is here. If he is looking for you, he could easily find
you here, so there is no secret lost there.''

''I wouldn't mention you, of course.''

''No,'' she said, shaking her head absently, as if the
possibility had never occurred to her. ''He must not
know I am here. If he is looking for you, your approaching him might take him by surprise. He might not press
whatever claims he has as hard.''

''And if he is looking for you, I might be able to
throw him off the track.''

''Subtly, of course. Desiderius is very subtle. And if
he is not here on account of either of us, there can be
no harm in it. You should be careful, but no, I cannot
say that it would necessarily be dangerous. So you know
where he is?''

Color came to Liam's cheeks again, and he cursed to
himself. *When did I start blushing so much?* ''Actually,
no, but Coeccias—the Duke's man—is looking. He
should not be hard to find.''

''No. He will not be hiding.''

There was a great deal to do. Liam rose and started
gathering the dishes, putting them all on the platter and
returning them to the oven.

''I will be in the city most of the day, but if Mistress
Priscian has anything for you, I will send Fanuilh to let
you know.''

Grantaire nodded her approval, sinking into some internal reverie even as he left the kitchen to wash and dress.

Liam was on the road to Southwark less than half an hour later, huddled in his cloak and trying to plan his day. He had to be at the Arcade of Scribes at nine, and then he wanted to see Mistress Priscian and Oakham, and he needed to stop at the Guard barracks and talk to Coeccias. Uldericus had practically ordered him to come at noon, but he was not sure if he would. Dueling was high on his list of foolish things, along with bear-baiting and love poetry. It was not a moral objection, but a practical one: the idea of the field of honor was flawed. He had never known a case where the injured man won simply because his cause was just—duels always went to the better fighter. Being better with a sword was no proof of virtue.

Granted, Quetivel had thrown out some serious insults, but he had been drunk, and why Uldericus could not take satisfaction from what he had already done to the baron was beyond Liam. It made him wince just to think of the sound of the life preserver crushing Quetivel's nose.

Finally, he knew that the real reason he did not want to wait on the earl was that he objected to being ordered around. Had his father ever been as arrogant as Uldericus? Had he ever been as irresponsible as Quetivel? No. Even when there was still a Rhenford Keep for him to inherit, he did not think he had been so high-handed. And if being noble naturally led to that sort of behavior, perhaps he was lucky to no longer *be* noble.

Worry about that later, he told himself. *Concentrate.* There were too many things to do for him to race off on tangents. He needed to meet Cawood and the other two guests, the Furseuses; he had never had a chance to talk with Lady Oakham. There was the wizard, and his meeting with the Werewolf. Too much, far too much.

Most important, he still could not imagine a real reason for stealing the Jewel. There were reasons, of course—money, mere greed, or even, according to

Grantaire and Fanuilh, magic—but none of them rang true, at least so far. If Grantaire was right, magic was unlikely, since this Desiderius would not resort to theft. Neither Quetivel nor Uldericus had struck him as the covetous sort, and they both seemed well supplied with money.

"My money," Liam said ruefully, his hand straying to his purse. He had shoveled enough into it to pay his debt from the night before. There had to be a better way to interview the Oakhams' guests than losing money to them.

Cawood and the Furseuses might turn out to be desperately poor, but that still left the question of disposing of the Jewel. After visits from the Guard, no fence or jeweler in Southwark would touch it, and selling it in another city would require contacts.

His stomach grumbled. "What?" he demanded, but he knew the answer. He had eaten nothing the night before, and the rolls, though good, were small. There were places near the Arcade to get food, and he promised himself another breakfast.

Southwark was mostly asleep when he passed the city gate, an indulgence only explained by the Banquet. Quetivel was not the only one with an aching head, Liam knew, but at least the others had done it to themselves. A few people were wandering down Temple Street as he rode by, carrying offerings from temple to temple, but apart from the devout, the streets were empty and more than half of the shops were closed.

He left his horse at the stables, waking the boy from the night before. Hay in his hair and awe on his face, the boy treated Diamond with a respect bordering on fear, handling the reins gingerly and even, once, bowing to the horse.

I should bring Fanuilh with me more often, Liam thought, chuckling to himself and setting off on foot. When he reached the Arcade there were only a few scribes in place, and even they were just setting up their tables and booths. The stand where Mopsa had bought her awful sausages was, unfortunately, the only place open that sold food; he bought two in rolls and settled himself on the steps of the arcade. He shook the sausages into the gutter and contented himself with the grease-soaked bread, which was not quite as stale as the day before.

Licking his fingers and brushing crumbs from his tunic, he turned his face to the meager sun, closed his eyes, and waited.

The bells began tolling nine, and he opened his eyes, scanning the Arcade and the street. There was no sign of Mopsa. He stood, rubbing some warmth into the seat of his pants, and started walking the length of the Arcade, examining the few displays. He walked and examined for about five minutes, drawing a few curious stares from the scribes, and once or twice the beginning of a sales pitch, which he cut off politely. Then he saw the Werewolf coming down the street.

Liam had expected Mopsa to come, to lead him to someplace secret; the Werewolf had once boasted to him that he never went out in the daylight. Still, there the man was, eyes narrowed balefully, darting glances left and right as if he expected an ambush. Liam stepped into the street as the man approached.

"This'll not do," the head of the Southwark Guild growled. "We'll walk." Liam nodded agreement and the two stepped away from the Arcade, heading down the hill toward the Warren. As always when he saw the Werewolf, Liam wondered which had come first, his nickname or his appearance: a grizzled black and gray beard welled up from his chest, over his chin and cheeks, ending in sharp points beneath his eyes, which were a disturbingly bright green, and his canine teeth were pronounced. Ordinarily he made a point of showing them in a feral grin, but now his mouth was tightly closed.

"This'll not do," he repeated, keeping his voice low. The shoulders of his much-patched coat kept rising and falling, and his fists punched at the insides of his pockets. "I know what you would, Rhenford, and I cannot help you."

Liam stopped, touching the Werewolf's elbow. "What

do you mean? How do you know what I want?''

The other man scowled and walked on, forcing Liam to keep up. ''What else would it be, but this damned Jewel? I told him no commissions, but he'd not listen— and now's dead. So I cannot help you.''

''Wait, wait, wait,'' Liam said. ''It was one of yours who stole it?''

The Wolf shot him a withering glance. ''In course it was—that lock cried out for one. But I tell you now, if I'd known you would concern yourself, I'd have made good the ban. Not that I'd need to. Soon as he heard you were on it, he fair soiled himself, so sure he was you'd con him out.''

Frustrated with the man's cryptic talk, Liam demanded: ''Who? Who are you talking about?''

''Japer,'' the Werewolf said. ''Japer picked it. On commission from another.'' For a moment, Liam's heart leapt; it must have shown on his face, though, because the other man quickly said: ''But I know not who. Japer wouldn't say.''

''All right, wait a moment. Start over. Start from the beginning.'' He knew who Japer was—a sour, stupid thief who had hit Mopsa one too many times for Liam's liking—but otherwise his frustration was growing.

''No games, Rhenford,'' the Werewolf said, glaring at him. ''I've things to do, and you know enough.''

''I know nothing,'' Liam said, grabbing the man's arm and forcing him to stop. ''And I want you to tell me everything, from the beginning, now.''

The Werewolf shook off Liam's hand, but he stayed still, breathing out a long sigh. ''Well and well. In fine: Mopsa brought your word yesterday, and I was vexed, for we'd done nothing I knew of to interest you. But Japer did, and was sore frighted, and all came out. He'd taken a commission to pick that lock. I'd have taken him up for it, but he was near wooden with fear. Said a beggar had brought him the job, one we know, named Malskat. Said Malskat brought him to the house, and this man let them in, but then there was a quarrel.''

''Wait—did they get the Jewel?''

"Aye, or the man did who let them in. Japer knew him not, said he was noble. There was a quarrel, though, in that tomb, and the man killed Malskat, cut his throat and pitched him from a window to the sea."

Thus the corpse on my beach, Liam realized, but put the thought aside as near useless. "He let Japer go?"

"Aye, and when Mopsa said you were asking questions, he told all. So I sent him to the beggars, and they took him off." The Werewolf's voice was full of remorse.

"Why did you send him to the beggars?"

"For to tell them that we'd nothing to do with it," the other man said incredulously. "Why else?"

"And now he's dead?"

"Aye," the Werewolf said heavily, then snarled: "They killed him for that Malskat, and I sent him there!"

Liam shushed him, and started them walking again. "You are sure he is dead?"

"We found him in the Warren, not two hours ago, Rhenford: I'm sure he's dead."

"Are you sure the beggars killed him?" Liam asked, feeling his way cautiously. He thought it more likely that it was someone else.

"Who else, then? I sent him there, he left us to go to them, and that was the last of him. Until this morning. Where do you go with this?"

Liam shrugged. "I would think it was the man who commissioned him."

The Werewolf snorted bitterly. "I think not. If you'd seen Japer—he was as frighted of him as he was of you. Would say nothing of him, how he looked, his name, naught. In any case, it matters not. Look you, Japer is dead, and I've told all, so there is nothing in it for you to bother us."

"No," Liam said, his mind racing to conclusions. "I suppose you are right." His steps slowed as he tried to arrange what he had learned.

"I came only to tell you this, for that you did for Duplin. It was good in you."

Liam stirred himself, putting away his conjectures for a moment. With two of his thieves killed in the space of a single month, it was clearly a hard time for the Werewolf. Liam watched the other man's mouth work angrily, and his shoulders bunch, and felt a pang of sympathy. "I am sorry about Japer."

"The fool," the Werewolf grated harshly. "The fool. I told him no commissions. But we'll make it good."

Liam cocked his head at the dangerous words. "What are you going to do?"

"What think you?" As if the answer were obvious.

"You don't know the beggars killed him."

The Werewolf said nothing, staring hard into Liam's eyes.

"You don't know."

Still the other man said nothing.

"Look," Liam said desperately. "Look, just wait on it." The simple theft he had agreed to investigate was suddenly growing bloody. Two deaths had already come out of it, and Uldericus's challenge would probably lead to another. He did not want some sort of vendetta added. "I cannot believe it was the beggars. Give me a chance to find the man. That's why I asked to meet you—I want to find the man, and the Jewel. Wait until I find him."

The silence dragged on, as did the Werewolf's luminous green stare. Liam returned it as strongly as he could. At last the thief relented.

"If you find him, what then?"

"We find out if he killed Japer."

"And if he did?"

Liam shrugged uncertainly. "I don't know. Give him to the Aedile."

"No good." The Werewolf set his jaw stubbornly.

The last of Liam's patience fled. "Good enough," he said angrily, raising his voice, "and all you are going to get. If he killed Japer, the Aedile deals with him. And you avoid a feud with the beggars. If you kill one of theirs, do you think they will let it go? You cannot risk that when you cannot be sure they did it. And if you do risk it, and then find they did not kill Japer, what then? Wait, I say!''

The Werewolf flinched a little, backing up a step.

''Will you wait?'' Liam demanded.

The thief's mouth moved silently, then he brought out: ''Until tomorrow night. I'll send Mopsa to you.'' Before Liam could agree he turned, walked three steps, and then started running.

Liam raised a hand and began to call out to him, then let his hand fall to his side and muttered a mild curse. He started back up the hill, in the opposite direction from that the Werewolf had taken, heading for the city square and the Guard barracks.

Today is going to be even longer than yesterday.

Liam never felt completely comfortable in the barracks. The guards all knew him, called him Quaestor, and let him in without question whether Coeccias was there or not, but he still felt like an outsider. Though they gave him a title, he was not really one of them; they tolerated him because he was the Aedile's friend.

He warmed himself by one of the fires, waiting while Coeccias gave orders to a number of guards, two of whom had bloodstains on their hands and clothes.

''You two,'' the Aedile was saying to the bloody men, ''report to the Sergeant of the Day, then scrub up and take you home. Sergeant, split the rest, keep the half here, and send the others home, to report back this evening for night patrols. We'll go light on days for the rest of the Banquet, and I want the men walking through the night, Sergeant; pass it on, if you please. Constant patrols. And look you, tell all the men of those two children—the boy and the maid.''

The sergeant dismissed the men, and then he and the Aedile discussed the added patrols for a few minutes. Not for the first time, Liam was impressed by the range of Coeccias's responsibilities. He watched the burly man talk with the sergeant, rattling off street names and neighborhoods, hours and the number of men for each patrol. When the sergeant had repeated everything to his satisfaction, he came over to the hearth where Liam stood.

"Truth, Rhenford, I hope you've good news. Your note said you knew this wizard?"

"Just his name," Liam said, then hesitated. What he had learned from the Werewolf made the wizard a dead end, since the man who hired Japer had been inside the house. It also ruled out the two women, he realized. That made his task a little easier, but presented the problem of how to relate the information to the Aedile. He could not just say that he had met with the head of the Thieves' Guild.

"I do not think we need to concern ourselves with him," he began, feeling his way cautiously. "I heard some things this morning. There was a thief involved, a professional, and he was let in by one of the Oakhams' guests."

He stopped, waiting for the Aedile's reaction. The other man gave him a searching look from beneath lowered eyebrows, but said nothing.

Liam cleared his throat, fixed his eyes on the fire, and went on: "Someone killed the thief last night. It's complicated, though, because the person in the house met the thief through a beggar, and the beggar was murdered, too."

"Ah," Coeccias interrupted, "that I know. We found him this morning, though we did not know the why."

"What?" Liam asked sharply.

The Aedile frowned at his tone. "The beggar—we found him this morning."

"No," Liam said slowly, "I found him yesterday. The man I brought in yesterday morning. He was the beggar. His name is Malskat. Was Malskat," he corrected himself. "Who are you talking about?"

Coeccias rolled his eyes to the ceiling. "And here I'd hoped you'd solved it all. We found a beggar this morning in the street. His head was fair crushed, most vicious. For that I made the night patrols stronger. You say this isn't your beggar?"

"No," Liam said, horrified, wondering for an instant

if the Guild had already acted—and then dismissed the idea. The Werewolf had spoken only of future action. "The man I brought in yesterday was Malskat. He was killed by one of Oakham's guests and thrown out of the crypt. You remember the balcony? And that was two nights ago. The thief who picked the lock was killed last night. The person I spoke with thought it was the beggars, because of Malskat. But I think it was probably the man who killed Malskat."

"Aye, aye, I doubt the other. The beggars are not so forward. I know their chief, and for all he's a rogue, he'd see through to the right of it. So the man is a murderer twice over, eh?" He did not sound in the least bit happy about it.

"Probably. At least once. It limits where we have to look—the wizard is out, and the women, too. Which leaves just the four men, Cawood, Furseus, Quetivel and Uldericus. I'm going to meet Cawood this afternoon, and I have to arrange about Furseus. But I saw the others last night."

He narrated the events of the previous evening, including what happened at Pet Radday's and the subsequent challenge. "Uldericus was very quick with the life preserver," he finished up.

"No stranger to blood, then, eh? It hangs together—but it is not enough to clap in a pecr."

"No," Liam said. "But why would he want the Jewel? Besides, I'm not sure Quetivel would have any qualms about killing a beggar or a thief. He lost a great deal of money last night, and I gather he has done it once or twice before. Perhaps he is deep in debt, deep enough to consider desperate measures. Though where he would sell it is still beyond me."

"Truth, it is a pretty riddle. You must sound out the other two before we can go further."

"I will." He nodded absently, staring into the fire. Pine boughs had been hung on the mantle; he braced his hands on the stone and leaned forward, feeling the heat from the fire on his chest, smelling the scent of the needles. The single large log was slowly breaking apart into glowing chunks. A hazy idea came to him amid the crackling of the fire.

There was no place to sell the Jewel in Southwark, he was sure of that. Moreover, knowing that the guest who had arranged the theft had then killed two people, he could not believe that it had been done solely for possession. No one would kill to have a bauble they could never show in public, would they? He refused to believe it. So it must have been done for money, and that meant selling the Jewel in another city, which would take time and contacts. *But if they thought they could sell it in Southwark . . .*

"Have you found the wizard?" he asked.

Coeccias grunted, taken by surprise. He had been gazing into the fire too, his heavy eyebrows knit together in a furry bunch. "The wizard? Not as yet. I've a man on it, but there're a lot of inns."

"If you can spare more men, have them look." The idea Liam was toying with was still rough, but if it was even to be considered, knowing where Desiderius was would be important.

Sketching a deep bow, Coeccias said: "As you wish, Milord May-Do-Aught." He had given Liam the name while they were investigating Tarquin's murder; it meant that he would never be surprised by anything Liam did.

"And if you can, don't let him know that you are looking."

"As you wish," Coeccias repeated, bowing low again. When he rose, though, there was no humor in his face. "That still leaves me with the second beggar. Rathkael'll tax me with that." Seeing Liam's questioning look, he went on: "The chief of the beggars. He'll tax me with the beggar's death."

"I thought you said he was not 'forward'?" Sometimes the southern dialect left Liam wondering if he fully understood anyone.

"Not in that way, no. He'd not take off the thief until he was sure he had the right of it. He's patient, but a grudge-holder—more a poison than a sword, if you take me. I suppose a beggar must be. This, though, he'll tax

me with, for that the streets aren't safe. And I confess,''
the Aedile said with a sigh, "that he'll be right, in a
way. Even beggars shouldn't be taken off in the streets,
most especially during their own feast.''

Liam thought of the Werewolf, and his threat. He was
not sure whether he should tell Coeccias about it. If he
could find the Jewel by the end of the next day, he would
not need to; and from what the Aedile said of Rathkael,
the beggar chief would not make any rash moves. On
the other hand, he could not be sure that the Werewolf
could control the Guild. After all, if he had been able to
enforce the ban on commissions, the Jewel might never
have been stolen. *And if you had only met with the Werewolf last night, Japer might not be dead today.*

There were simply too many ifs. He cleared his throat
again. "If you do see this Rathkael, you might tell him
what we know about Malskat and the thief. You might
tell him to warn his people to be careful tonight.''

"Why?" Coeccias asked, genuinely puzzled.

"Well, you could tell him that you have it on good
authority that the Guild thinks the beggars are responsible for the thief's death.'' The complex constructions
were becoming awkward, but he held to them. "You
could also tell him that they have done nothing about it,
and will not, and that the second beggar is not their
work.''

Speaking slowly, fixing Liam with his stare, the Aedile said: "I could say that, but I would need good authority. Do I truly have it?''

"Yes." *I hope so.*

"Truth, Rhenford, I hope so. I do not need a war in
these streets during the Banquet, or at any other time.
Southwark is just growing normal again, after all that
with Bellona. Can you vouch for the Guild?''

"I can," Liam said, almost completely sure that he
could.

"Then I'll do my best with Rathkael. I am glad you
told me this, Rhenford. I can at least say who did not
kill his beggar, and the rest will give him something to
worry on.''

The bells in the Duke's Courts started ringing ten; Coeccias heard the sound and shook his head, while Liam stepped away from the fire, counting the hours. If he wanted to see Oakham alone, then visit Cawood with him, and go to Uldericus's by noon—he had still not decided whether he would obey the earl's command or not—he would have to move quickly.

"I should go," he said. "It's going to be a very busy day."

"It already is," Coeccias countered. "I've to con out who took off this other beggar, and gather up some lost children."

"Children?"

Coeccias made a noise of disgust in the back of his throat. "It is nothing—a boy and a maid from up the Point, out masking and caroling too late. Their parents fear they've run off together. More likely they're hiding at a friend's, bussing and spooning like innocents. It is nothing. Look you, will you dine with me?"

"Not lunch," Liam said from the door, "but perhaps dinner. Are you free?"

"Leave word here," the Aedile said, waving him off. "Go to, y' are busy. Dinner can wait. I've work of my own."

Liam left.

CHAPTER 10

LIAM WALKED QUICKLY, eating up the cobbled street with long strides. There were many things he needed to know, and Oakham was going to have to tell him most of them. The others he could find out in different ways—among other things, he thought a talk with Herione might prove worthwhile; the brothelkeeper had given him and Coeccias valuable information before. But Oakham would have to provide most of it.

And he will, too, Liam promised himself. He needed to know more about the guests, much more than he could learn in a social setting. The idea had been a bad one, and he should not have agreed to it. All it had done was cost him a pile of crowns and embroil him in a duel.

He was still undecided about whether the fact of the duel told him anything. Though it was premature, he thought Uldericus the most likely suspect, primarily because of the way he had lashed out at Quetivel. The earl did not need the money, as far as he could see, but the two murders had almost overtaken the theft in his mind. *One proven murder,* he corrected, *and one assumed.*

Quetivel, on the other hand, was certainly quarrelsome enough to have started the argument in the crypt, and arrogant enough to have thought nothing of killing a beggar and a thief; the size of his pocket was a mystery.

Still, Liam was putting his money on Uldericus.

"For now," he said firmly, "I'll wait on Cawood and Furseus." He could not allow himself to jump to conclusions; he needed information, and soon.

He deliberately avoided the most direct route to End Street because it led past Uldericus's house, choosing instead to go up Duke Street and come from the south. The maidservant he had seen attending Lady Oakham the day before was kneeling on the stoop, scrubbing the steps.

"Good morning," Liam said. "Is Lord Oakham in?"

"I wouldn't know," Becula replied in a surly tone, dipping her rag in a bucket of water, wringing it out and scrubbing at some rusty stains. "You'll have to ask inside."

"That might work better if you splashed some water from the bucket right onto the steps," Liam suggested.

The girl flipped the hair out of her eyes and stared hard at him. "It would work better if certain ones wouldn't go bleeding all over the stairs." Her look clearly challenged him to come back at that; he declined.

"And a good day to you," he murmured behind a smile, and went up the steps.

Tasso answered the door, offering him a very slight bow. "Lord Oakham is in the study; he said to bring you up."

The Oakhams have bad taste in houseguests and *servants,* Liam thought. "Lead away, then, and let the trumpets sound."

Tasso repeated his slight bow even more stiffly, and went up the stairs. At the door of Oakham's study, he called out Liam's name in the same solemn way as before and held the door open for him, the picture of the respectful and unobtrusive servant. Liam resisted the urge to kick him as he passed into the room.

Oakham was standing by the fireplace, head down beneath the tapestry of himself hunting. He chewed his underlip anxiously.

"I am glad y' are here, Rhenford," he said, signing for Tasso to shut the door.

"Oh?" Liam stayed by the door after the servant closed it. He was afraid he sounded too cold, but he wanted to make sure that Oakham understood things were going to change.

"Aye," the other man said, starting to pace, throwing a look across the room from time to time. "I wonder, how much longer do you think this will take? How long before the Jewel will be returned?"

"I do not know," Liam said, quite honestly. "I hope to finish it by tomorrow evening." Just how, he was not sure—but he wanted to keep the Werewolf in check. At the very least he needed to be able to show some real evidence of progress.

"Tomorrow? Gods!" Oakham's face was a comic mask of surprise. "So soon?"

"I hope so. Again, though, it depends on you."

"How so?" The lord sounded defensive, so Liam pressed.

"I mentioned last night that things were going to change—and they will, if I am ever to find the Jewel. I need information, and you must provide it for me. I need to ask you questions, and you must answer them, or . . ."

Oakham raised his chin, bridling. "Or what?"

"Or I will not be able to find the Jewel, and it will be lost to your family forever."

A long moment passed, Oakham glaring down his nose at Liam, Liam returning the stare impassively. Oakham gave first, turning to the mantle and crossing his arms behind his back.

"Very well," he said quietly. "What would you know?"

Liam became brisk and businesslike. "First, how long ago did you invite your guests? And did they know they would be staying the night?"

The guests had been invited a week earlier, Oakham told him, and spending the night had been understood from the first. The Jewel had made its first appearance at about the same time, but it was still plenty of time to arrange the theft, Liam knew.

"And had all the guests been in your house before at some time?"

They all had; the Furseuses visited often, Cawood and

Uldericus had come to dinner once or twice, and Quetivel had been staying at the house for almost two weeks.

"Did they all know where the Jewel was kept?"

Oakham was sure that they must have; his wife had told the story of its "discovery" in the crypt any number of times.

"Those were all simple questions," Liam said, "with no harm in them. Now, however, I am afraid I must be specific. I hope you understand—I simply cannot learn enough doing things the way we did them last night. You will have to tell me something."

Oakham stiffened, but he did not turn around. "Go to."

Liam nodded, gathering his thoughts. "Do you know if any of your guests have money problems? Debts they cannot pay?"

"Debts?" Oakham's voice came out a little strangled.

"For instance, gambling debts," Liam said quickly. "For instance, Quetivel—he lost quite a bit to Uldericus last night. Has he been gambling much since he came here? Losing a great deal?"

"It is not Quetivel!" Oakham snapped over his shoulder.

Liam waited for a moment. When he spoke at last, he made his voice as quiet and firm as he could: "I will tell you something I learned this morning, Oakham. I know for a fact that it was a man who let the thief into your house. I also know who the thief was—but Aedile Coeccias cannot arrest him, because he is dead. The man who let him into your house killed him. He has also killed another man, an accomplice. So this is no longer just about the Jewel. One of your guests killed two men, and he cannot get away with it. Do you see that?"

Oakham had spun around when Liam said that the thief was dead, his face a pale mask of shock. Now he groped his way to a chair and sank into it, one hand fluttering feebly at his forehead.

"Two men, you say? How can you know this?"

Liam waved the question away. "That is not important. I know it. What is important is that we catch the

man who did it. Your reticence is honorable, Lord Oakham, but dangerous, and undeserved by at least one of
your guests. As for the others—I promise you that nothing I learn from you will go beyond these walls. You
can trust me."

"Yes, yes," Oakham said, covering his eyes with his
hand. "Ask."

Masking a small, grim smile of triumph, Liam took a
deep breath. "Do you know for a fact that Quetivel did
not do it? I mean, can you prove it? Are you absolutely
sure?"

"He is my cousin." It sounded like a plea.

"I know that, but are you absolutely sure of him? I
have known men to betray far more than a cousin over
far less than this Jewel."

"No," Oakham whispered. "I am not sure."

"Then does he have any debts that you know of?"

The answer came slowly. "He gambles a great deal,
but I have never seen him give a marker. He loses often,
though . . . more than I think he can have."

"Always to Uldericus?"

Apparently not. Oakham had known him to drop large
sums at Pet Radday's, in tavern games, even at one or
two horse races.

"And Uldericus? I cannot imagine that he has any
problems with money."

Oakham knew of none. He also knew nothing of Cawood's finances; as far as he knew, the man was a fairly
successful merchant, with his own fleet of four ships.
"The Furseuses are not rich," he said, hastening to add:
"But they live very modestly. Their father was a knight
in the Duke's service, pensioned off with a living, something in the courts. They collect that. I have never known
them to live beyond their means, and they are my wife's
oldest friends."

So Quetivel and the Furseuses might be interested in
the Jewel for its value, Liam decided. Cawood had
money, and Uldericus had too much—*Seventy-five
crowns too much,* he thought—to need the Jewel. Greed

could not be discounted, he told himself, but he was beginning to wonder.

"This question will be more difficult," Liam said. "Did anyone ever say anything about the Jewel? Express any interest in it?" He sought for the right word: "Covet it? Did anyone covet it?"

"Everyone did," Oakham said, very quickly. "I forget—you have not seen it. It was . . . wonderful." Awe softened his voice. "Ah, Rhenford, anyone would covet it."

This was not what Liam wanted to hear. "So it would seem, Lord Oakham, but that does me no good. Did anyone covet it any more than everyone else? Cawood, for instance. A merchant. Did he ever ask how much it was worth?"

"No," Oakham said miserably. "He knows something of stones. *He* told *me* how much it was worth."

"He did?" That was interesting.

"Aye. He said it was worth nothing, or everything."

Liam smiled grimly; it was his own thought. "Anyone else?"

Oakham took a deep breath. "Poena Furseus admired it extremely, but she admires everything extremely. As I said, she and her brother live most modestly. Countess Perenelle also . . . admired it. I believe she and my wife had some words about it. The countess wished to borrow it, and Duessa quite rightly refused. They quarreled, but they had made it up by that night. It was over."

Neither woman interested Liam; it had been a man, after all, who cut Malskat's throat. But what Oakham said next caught his attention completely.

"Earl Uldericus." He paused, rubbing his hands on his knees. "Earl Uldericus asked to buy it from me."

That was something. That was something indeed. Liam tried to keep the eagerness from his voice. "And you refused?"

"In course!" Oakham exclaimed indignantly. "It was not mine to sell!"

"How did he take your refusal?"

The other man's indignation deflated. "He was most

vexed. He doubled his offer—an amazing offer, in truth—and when I refused again, stormed off. He was . . . most vexed.''

Careful, Liam warned himself, trying to control his excitement. *Be thorough.* ''When did he make the offer? Did he ever mention it again?''

''Four or perhaps five days ago. The day escapes me. And he never repeated the offer.''

''Did he say why he wanted it?''

He had not, according to Oakham, who looked as if he wished he had never brought the whole thing up. Liam felt sorry for him; the sort of delicacy and sense of honor that would make a man keep such things to himself in the face of a great loss were rare. *And it has to kill him that one of his guests does not deserve it.*

The whole thing began to point strongly in Ulderic-us's direction, though Liam had to admit that money could not be a motivation. If he had been prepared to pay for it, that meant he wanted the Jewel for itself.

''Do you have any idea why he might want it?''

''No,'' Oakham said, standing suddenly, brisk now. ''As I said, no one who saw it could help but desire it. It was magnificent, Rhenford.''

''Hm. So you said.''

Pacing again, Oakham waved his hands, trying to indicate the Jewel's attraction. ''It glows, unlike any diamond I have ever seen, and its depths . . . there are no words. Anyone would want it.''

''I have one other question, for now. It will seem foolish, but . . . well, do any of your guests have an interest in magic?''

''Magic?''

''Yes. The Jewel was Eirenaeus Priscian's, after all, and there are the legends about him—wizardry, sorcery, that sort of thing.''

Oakham laughed weakly, but with genuine humor. ''Gods, no! Whyever they may have coveted it, it was not for any magic it could do, I assure you.''

That's good news. Liam smiled. *It only leaves money and pure covetousness.* For some reason the word appealed to him, something about the sibilance. *Covetousness.* "I think that is all for now. I need to meet Master Cawood and the Furseuses. I know we were supposed to go to see Master Cawood now, but I have to see your aunt, and I would like to speak with your wife, and then I have to go somewhere at noon. Can we go to the Staple afterwards?"

"I am at your service," Oakham said, then started to say something else, but stopped himself.

"Is it inconvenient? Is he waiting?"

"No, no," the lord said hurriedly, clasping his hands firmly together. *To keep from wringing them,* Liam guessed. "We can see Cawood at any time. It is my wife. I wonder, Rhenford—"

"I promise you," Liam interrupted, with what he hoped was a suitably earnest expression, "I will be far more . . . delicate with her."

"Thank you," Oakham breathed. "We are men, in the end, and can stand things. Duessa is not, is not . . ."

"I understand. I do not have many questions for her, and you can join us, if you wish."

Oakham shook his head, insisting that that was not necessary, that he trusted Liam completely, and he only asked that Liam not mention the murders. "You will be delicate, I know. She is with her aunt now, next door."

Offering a final assurance that he would, indeed, be delicate, Liam started for the door. "I will come back some time this afternoon, around one o'clock, I hope."

Following after him, Oakham asked: "Are you attending Earl Uldericus?"

"Yes," Liam said, and both men frowned. They went down the stairs together, and Oakham opened the door for him.

"Quetivel will be abed for at least another day, I fear. His nose was, well—you saw. I pray you, see if you can't get Uldericus to drop this. There has been quite enough blood. And, Rhenford—I am sorry you have been dragged into this."

"Not to worry," Liam said, starting down the steps to the street. "I will come back around one, I hope." In fact, he was guiltily grateful for the duel: he wanted another chance to talk with the earl.

Mistress Priscian was in and expecting him, her servant told him at the door. Haellus took his cloak and said, "If you will follow me?" Without waiting he turned back into the house and walked down the main hall, the cloak folded neatly over his arm.

They went to the solarium, the servant announcing "Master Rhenford" and slipping unobtrusively away. *She should choose her niece's servants,* Liam thought, and then saw that the niece was there, as well as a man and woman he did not know.

"Master Rhenford," Mistress Priscian said, nodding graciously to him. "Y' are well come." He bowed, hearing the way she separated the words, and once again noticing that she commanded attention by stillness. Her niece fidgeted in her chair, half twisting to shoot a glance at the woman beside her, who was perching her plump body on the edge of her seat, straining towards him. The man rose fussily.

Mistress Priscian made the introductions: Lady Oakham he had met; the man was Cimber Furseus, the woman his sister Poena. Liam offered them each a bow, taking in details.

"Oh, Master Rhenford," Poena Furseus said breathily, "speak of the Dark! Lady Oakham was fresh from telling us of you, and you appear! Come, tell us, will you catch this low caitiff?" She was a pleasant-seeming woman, fat in a matronly way but with a young, eager and very plain face. In her plain linen dress and her snood, she looked more like Lady Oakham's governess than her friend, though she could not have been more than three years older.

"Do say, Master Rhenford," her brother piped in, and Liam instantly ruled him out as a suspect. He had his sister's dull brown hair, and large horselike teeth that he bared in what Liam imagined was supposed to be an encouraging smile. He was also considerably plumper than his sister, and he wheezed when he rose. Japer had been a big man, well muscled, and even the beggar Malskat would not have fallen to Cimber Furseus. "It sounds passing exciting! Lady Oakham has told us everything!"

"Yes, she has," Mistress Priscian commented drily.

"It is not really exciting at all, I am afraid," Liam said. He was not sure what Lady Oakham knew, or whom she knew it from, but he was annoyed that she had been talking. She seemed to sense it, too, or perhaps she was merely responding to her aunt's tone: she sat stiffly in her chair, straightening the pleats of her dress, her chin in the air and a little defiance in her eyes.

"Come, Master Rhenford," she said, accenting "master" in a condescending way, "surely it is. This can be no ordinary theft." Recovered from her hangover, she was pretty in a fragile, doll-like way. Blue-black ringlets framed her porcelain face.

"I am no expert on theft," Liam said, "but I think it is." For some reason he had taken an instant dislike to Lady Oakham. How could she be so stupid as to tell the Furseuses about his involvement with the theft? She did not know that it was a man who had let Japer into the house, and she did not know that that man had to have been stronger and far more agile than Cimber Furseus. Not to mention more threatening. *What is she thinking? Is she thinking?* "And I wonder if I might ask you a few questions—I think they will prove just how unexciting it is."

"In course," Lady Oakham said, as if she were granting a boon. "Would you excuse us?" She swept the others with an imperious gaze, faltering only when she reached her aunt, who gave no evidence of noticing it.

The Furseuses started bustling, but Liam held up his hands. "Actually, it would be good if you could stay. You may be able to help." Since she had chosen to tell them "everything," they might as well stay, and hear what he had to ask. A very small part of him whispered that he was forgetting his promise of delicacy to Lord Oakham, and that he was also being petty.

The siblings were more than happy to stay; Cimber settled himself back into his chair with an excited wheeze. Mistress Priscian offered Liam a chair, which he took gratefully, using the time to settle his conscience and discard all the rude questions that had sprung to his mind. *She is just a merchant's daughter who married well*, he reminded himself. *Let her have her airs.*

So he did not start by saying how glad he was that she had gotten over her indisposition of the previous day; ladies did not drink too much and throw up the next day, and if they did it was impolite to refer to it. But he wanted to.

"First," he said, "do any of you know anyone who might have expressed a special interest in the Jewel?"

Lady Oakham held her head cocked primly to one side, and spoke very patiently. "Everyone expressed an interest in it, Master Rhenford. It is a passing thing."

Liam gave a very wide smile. "So I understand, Lady Oakham. But what I meant was, did any of your friends express a special interest in *having* it. For instance, I know Earl Uldericus was quite taken with it."

One of the Furseuses snorted; Liam was not sure which one, because Lady Oakham suddenly uncocked her head and raised her voice. Little spots of red appeared as if by magic on each cheek. "I do not know what you can intend by that, Master Rhenford. If y' are implying that the earl had aught to do with this—"

"Come, Duessa," Mistress Priscian said, none too gently, "this is given. We have discussed it."

"No, Aunt Thrasa, I will not have it! Some thieving knave breaks my house and steals my Jewel, and you accuse my friends! I say I will not have it!" She stamped her foot, most of the effect lost because she was sitting. This time Liam caught the Furseuses' expression: identical wide-open mouths and eyes. Poena leaned over and touched her friend's arm.

"Duessa, is this true? Are we accused?"

"Gods," Cimber wheezed. "Gods! Me, a thief!"

Lady Oakham shot to her feet, her arms rigid at her

sides and her fists clenched. "No! No, I tell you! I will not hear it!" Then she put her fists to her ears and stormed out of the solarium, leaving a deafening silence in her wake.

Poor Oakham, Liam thought.

Mistress Priscian broke the silence at last. "I am sure you two are not accused of anything," she said to the siblings, and to Liam it sounded less like an assurance than a condemnation.

He quickly agreed: "Oh, yes. You are completely in the clear. . . ." He trailed off, unsure how to address them.

The Furseuses seemed disappointed by their innocence.

"Damn," Cimber said with a chuckle. "It rather liked me to be thought a thief. A cunning, desperate rogue." He mimed a few passes with a sword.

"To think, we ate with a very thief," Poena said, wonder in her voice. "I wonder who it was? I'll wager money it was that Quetivel."

"The servants," Cimber guessed. "That Tasso has more than a touch of the hungry dog."

"No, he was out of the house," Poena said.

Cimber conceded that this was quite true. "Still, it happens so often. You remember the silver plate Antheuris lost?"

They began to remind each other of thieving servant stories they knew, completely oblivious to Mistress Priscian and Liam, and he took the chance to ask the older woman for a moment alone.

"Certainly," she said, gathering herself up from her chair. "We'll talk in the kitchen."

Liam stood, and the Furseuses noticed. "Oh, do excuse us, Mistress Priscian; we are quite rude. We should go."

"No, please," Liam said quickly, "stay just a moment. I have a few questions."

They settled back in their chairs, puzzled but willing, and Liam went with Mistress Priscian to the kitchen. They stood by the worktable.

"I assume you meant it when you said the Furseuses were . . . 'in the clear'?" she asked. Liam nodded. "That is to the good. They are the best of Duessa's lot, and they had a good father. What do you want of them?"

"I hope they can answer some of the questions Lady Oakham would not."

"Ah. My niece is—" She paused, searching, then gave up. "As I said, she was brought up strangely. But the Furseuses should do admirably. They love talk." She rubbed her hands together then, as if ridding them of previous business. "I assume you wish to know if I have found anything for your friend."

"Yes. If you haven't, it is not important."

"I have, though I do not know if it was what she sought. There are some books with his name in them, which I presume are his work. They were deep in the attic, and in passing good condition, given their age. I do not wish them to leave the house, so she may look at them here. There is a very quiet study upstairs that she may use. The light is good. When will she call?"

"Whenever is convenient," Liam said, "and thank you very much. I believe she thinks this is important."

"I could make nothing of them. She may come this afternoon, if she wishes, and during the day for as long as she needs. You will bring her?"

"Yes," Liam said, thankful and eager. "This afternoon, I think. She was very interested in anything you might have. And thank you again."

"It is nothing," she said. "I will expect you later in the afternoon, then. You can tell me what progress has been made. I am anxious to know."

She did not seem anxious, Liam thought, but he promised to give her a full report. She started briskly out of the kitchen. "And now I think we have kept the Furseuses waiting too long."

The Furseuses were waiting in the hall, cloaked and hooded. They explained that they did not wish to impose on Mistress Priscian anymore, and should in any case be returning home; but if Master Rhenford chose to accompany them . . .

"Of course," Liam said, and before he could ask, Haellus was behind him, helping him into his cloak.

Once outside, they surrounded him, each taking an arm, complaining cheerfully about the cold.

"Have you known a winter like this?" Cimber said, though he was heavily bundled up. He panted as they walked.

"It is the very coldest," Poena threw in, from behind a long, thick scarf wrapped three times around her neck. Liam did not think it was particularly cold, but he meant to agree; the Furseuses, however, did not give him a chance. They were already discussing Mistress Priscian, leaning in front of him a little as they walked down End Street.

"Aunt Thrasa seemed most displeased with Duessa, didn't you think?"

"Passing displeased," Poena agreed, and then added for Liam's benefit: "We call her aunt, though she is not: she is an old friend of our dear father's, though somewhat fierce. Don't you find her so?"

"When we were young," Cimber said, while Liam was still trying to open his mouth, "we were sore frighted of her. And I think we still are!"

"She is most kind, though, on further acquaintance; I'm sure you'll find her so," Poena said soothingly, patting Liam's arm.

"Oh, I already do," he said quickly. "I admire her a great deal. But there are those questions. . . ."

"Quetivel," Cimber said, allowing no doubt. "Baron Quetivel is your man."

"And what of Earl Uldericus?" Poena asked. "He would want it for the same reason."

"Yes, but Quetivel is the younger man—the juices of passion flow more strongly in him!"

"Oh, juices," his sister said disparagingly. "What do you know of juices? And what do you mean by them? Baron Quetivel is shallow, unpersevering, he lacks sap. The earl hopes to revive his marriage. It is self-evident.''

They turned off End Street, heading down past the Goddard mansion and towards the center of the city.

Cimber countered, ''The baron is hot-blooded, and young. I believe the earl has quite given up. Does he not pass all his evenings there?'' He nodded at Herione's, just a few yards down.

Liam took advantage of the pause to yank gently on their arms, as if he were reining in a team of runaway horses. He was getting dizzy from trying to follow their conversation. ''Please, I am not sure I understand. Why would both Quetivel and Uldericus want the Jewel?''

The siblings shared a look of surprise, and then launched into an explanation. Countess Perenelle, apparently, was quite enamored of the Jewel. Poena described the ''quarrel'' Oakham had mentioned as more of a brawl. After that, the countess had made no secret of how much she wanted the Jewel, and how she would give anything to have it—though never in front of Lady Oakham.

Now, they explained carefully, it was common knowledge that all was not well in the earl's home; Uldericus spent most of his evenings unhappily at Herione's, and there were rumors—Cimber stressed the word ''rumors'' in such a way that Liam guessed they were more than rumors—that his wife was receiving visitors at home. Furthermore, it was plain that Quetivel wished to be one of these visitors.

''In fine,'' Poena summed up, ''whoever has the Jewel has the countess's heart.''

''And welcome to it,'' her brother added, still puffing a little, though they had stopped walking. ''For all of me, she is not worth it.''

''Not everyone thinks that,'' Poena warned. ''Many men would gladly steal more than the Jewel for but one kiss.''

They rambled on a little more, but Liam was not paying much attention. He should have thought it all through before—Quetivel's comment before the game about some things being worth more than money, Uldericus's odd dream and the way he had looked at the baron after recounting it. And, of course, the insults that lead to the duel. It should have been obvious, he thought, but refused to scold himself. He had been right, in a sense: neither Uldericus nor Quetivel wanted the Jewel for itself, or for money, or for the magic it was supposed to possess. They wanted it because it was the key to possessing the countess.

Her wanting it is ridiculous, he judged, *but* their *wanting it . . .* He would have to see her in person to decide about that.

"Is it true?" Cimber said, interrupting Liam's train of thought. Brother and sister were staring at him with expectant eyes.

"What?" He had not been listening to their chatter.

"That the earl and the baron will duel, in course!"

"Ah," Liam said. "Ah. No challenge has been given yet." He wondered how long it was before noon; Uldericus's house was nearby. It would be worthwhile to get a look at the earl's wife.

"There will be," Poena said, wagging a finger at the two men, and wearing a knowing smile that said she looked forward to the event. "Mark me, I'll warrant it."

Liam gently disengaged himself from their clutches. "You remind me of something. I have an appointment with Earl Uldericus very shortly. His house is near here, isn't it?"

"Over there." Cimber pointed it out, a narrow-fronted building three doors up from Herione's. "Is it about the duel?"

"Will you dissuade him from it?" Poena asked.

Cimber snorted and flapped a hand at his sister. "Who could dissuade him? Or Quetivel, for all that?"

"Oh I wish we could have spied his nose!"

"Oakham's Tasso said it was quite flat," Cimber giggled. They began to wonder gleefully whether Quetivel would be permanently disfigured.

Liam took a step backward, bowing. "Thank you very much for talking with me," he said. "I really must go." He took another step backward, and to his relief, they hardly noticed him, caught up in their speculations.

Turning, he trotted off to the house Cimber had pointed out.

CHAPTER 11

THOUGH THE PLACE was undistinguished on the outside, the inside of Uldericus's house laid to rest any lingering questions Liam may have had about the earl needing money. A servant let him in the front door, took his name, and disappeared up a grand staircase, leaving him alone in the entrance hall. There was money everywhere, in the intricate patterns of the rugs that muffled the servant's footsteps, the gilt-framed portraits on the walls, the gleaming brass fittings of the tiled fireplace. To his left, double doors opened on a dining room, a sideboard laden with silver plate, a long oak table flanked by matching chairs, legs and arms carved and turned elegantly, and an enormous chandelier of crystal.

As if he needed my money, Liam thought. *Probably had to hire an extra servant just to polish the plate.*

The servant returned. "Earl Uldericus is not in; he is not expected until noon. The countess will receive you in her sitting room."

Liam allowed himself a small smile as he followed the servant up the grand staircase. He had expected Uldericus to be at home, but hoped that his early arrival might gain him just a glimpse of the earl's wife, a chance to judge how much of an incentive to theft she was—and now he would get to speak with her. The question, of course, was, what would he say?

The countess's sitting room was on the second floor, the first room off the stairs; the servant announced him and then left them alone. Liam bowed, keeping his gaze on her face to avoid staring at the room's furnishings, a vague impression of crystal, gold and silk crowded around a low divan much like the one in his library. Hers, though, had gilded legs, and the upholstery was laced with gold and silver threads in an elaborate pattern of birds and flowers; beside it stood a water pipe of brass and purple glass and a delicate lacquered table with a golden plate of sweetmeats.

"Master Rhenford," she said, "do come in." She had been lying back on the divan; now she swung herself around to sit on the edge.

Liam smiled blandly, narrowing his eyes until all he could see was her face. *I would steal the Jewel for her.* Countess Perenelle was quite possibly the most beautiful woman he had ever seen. It was undeniable, though he knew that a great deal of it was artifice and attitude— the studied grace with which she swung her legs over the edge of the divan, the subtle bend at the waist that emphasized the strain on the upper part of her dress, the makeup that delicately enhanced her natural pallor and made her lips so red. Her voice was high but soft, her face composed and curious. A sweet, flowery scent radiated from her direction. Liam tried not to think about her dress. He wanted to whistle.

"Excuse me for disturbing you, my lady," he said with a bow. "I was hoping to see your husband."

Her eyes trailed languidly over him, a slow sweep from boots to head. He fought an urge to square his shoulders and throw out his chest.

"We expect him shortly. Can I offer you something while you wait?" Her knees shifted minutely.

One of those, Liam thought. He was not entirely sure what he meant by "those," but the image of a predatory cat came to mind.

"No, thank you."

"I imagine it is to do with this challenge?" Her lips curled into what might have been a smile.

"Yes," he said regretfully. "It is an unfortunate thing."

"I am not so sure." She began to busy herself with the water pipe, filling it with quick, deft gestures. "It is a little flattering. A lady's honor must be upheld.''

She smiled sweetly at him, and he decided he did not like her. *So many unpleasant people,* he thought. *And this one wants men to fight over her.*

''Certainly,'' he agreed. He was at a loss; if Uldericus or Quetivel had stolen the Jewel, would they have given it to her already? She wore no jewelry, but that meant nothing, because she could not wear it in front of strangers. And anyway, if either suitor had stolen the Jewel, they would hardly have spent the previous night gambling—the man who had it would have run right to her with it.

The countess finished priming and lighting the pipe, put the mouthpiece to her lips and puffed gently. She was looking at him.

Liam closed his eyes and thought. Might the thief have waited? What would be the point? When he opened his eyes, she was examining him again, a smile quirking her lips around the mouthpiece. She was not drawing on the pipe.

''Still,'' he said, clearing his throat, ''I hope the duel might be avoided. Baron Quetivel was drunk.''

She seemed to find this funny; she giggled, putting the mouthpiece down on the table. Smoke curled lazily around her, its odor mixing with her own sweet smell. A dreamy haze stole across her face. ''Think you he'll apologize?''

''I hope so.'' Why wait to present her the Jewel? She was beautiful, leaning back now on the divan, drawing her legs up under her. *Enough to steal for?* Liam did not like her, her casual attitude towards the duel, her obvious self-absorption. *Perhaps.*

It was complicated. To suspect Quetivel and Uldericus, he had to assume that the countess was their motive. But neither of them, as far as he could see, had claimed their prize. Did that mean they had not stolen the Jewel, or were they waiting? If they were waiting, what for?

There was still Cawood to consider; he might be the thief. Liam found himself hoping that would prove the case.

"I don't," Lady Uldericus said, putting a hand to her mouth and yawning behind it. Liam had to admit that he had never seen a yawn more perfectly executed. "It will clear the air."

"My lady?" Had she really just said that?

"My husband," she said, closing her eyes, and Liam heard footsteps on the stairs.

Uldericus entered a moment later, stopping in the doorway. His face was cold. Liam bowed.

"Master Rhenford." He paused, taking in the scene. Then he gestured to the hallway. "If you will attend me." He let Liam go before him, and shut the door firmly behind them. "We will speak in my sitting room. Y' are early."

"I was in the Point on other business, my lord, and finished early. I thought you would be at home."

"My wife does not receive visitors," Uldericus said, scowling. "You should have come at noon."

"My apologies," Liam said, though he wanted to say something else entirely. *Easy,* he counseled himself. *You do not want to be involved in a duel yourself.* Instead, he smiled innocently. "Your sitting room?"

The earl grunted and led the way a little down the hallway, to a room half the size of his wife's but just as expensively furnished. He seated himself behind a massive desk, its top a single sheet of polished wood, in the surface of which Uldericus was blurrily reflected. He did not offer Liam a seat.

"I propose that as soon as Baron Quetivel is recovered, we should meet. I will accept no apologies. He may choose the weapons. I believe that is clear enough."

"Perfectly clear," Liam said, heaving a sad sigh. "But are you sure you wish to refuse apologies? The baron was not himself; he was drunk."

"There will be no apologies."

"But he may—"

Uldericus pounded his fist once on the desktop. "Master Rhenford! Y' are not here to offer advice! He may make his apologies, but I'll not accept them! Is that clear?''

Once again, Liam put aside his instinctive response. ''Perfectly,'' he said. Then, a beat later, responding to a whim whose origin he was unsure of, he went on: ''And of course, there is this rumor about Quetivel and the Priscian Jewel. It would be good to put an end to that, I suppose.''

Uldericus's head snapped up. ''What rumor?''

''It is nothing.'' Liam waved a hand dismissively. ''I should not have brought it up—and please do not mention it to Lord Oakham. It would upset him a great deal.''

''Do they say Quetivel stole the Jewel?'' the earl demanded, his mouth set in a tight line, fists clenched on the table. Liam immediately regretted his whim. He could practically hear the other man's mind racing, reaching certain conclusions.

''It is just a rumor,'' Liam hastily put in. ''I don't believe it myself. What good would it do him?'' The instant he spoke the words he realized that they, too, were a mistake.

''No good at all,'' Uldericus said, the words hissing out between his teeth. Bright red spots appeared on his cheeks, the cords of his neck standing out like taut rigging. ''Deliver the challenge, Master Rhenford. I'll expect a response.''

He rose and stalked to the door.

''You can show yourself out.''

Liam stepped out of the room to let him pass, then went to the head of the stairs. Uldericus, trembling, took a deep breath at the door of his wife's sitting room, then shoved the door open and went inside. After a moment, Liam went down the stairs, staring at his feet and shaking his head.

Well, what did that tell you?

The answer, he thought, was absolutely nothing—but he would have to think about it.

The servant who had let him in was waiting by the front door. He bowed at Liam's approach and silently held out a folded piece of paper. Liam took it with a nod and stepped out into the street.

The note could wait. It smelled faintly of perfume, and at the moment he was more interested in organizing what he had learned—if anything—than in whatever the predatory countess might have to say. He walked slowly down the street, stopping outside Herione's.

Uldericus thought having the Jewel would do Quetivel no good, Liam reflected. The way he had said it was ambiguous, though.

The earl must have known how his wife felt about the Jewel—that she had promised "anything" for it—and thanks to Liam he now probably guessed that Quetivel knew as well. But he had said that the Jewel would be of no use to the baron, which made no sense to Liam. Did it mean that Uldericus could prevent his wife from fulfilling her promise, or that he could prevent Quetivel from using it? Liam feared he would never know which.

Of course, it did show the lengths to which the earl would go. His barely controlled rage had not been faked, and Liam guessed that he would not flinch at killing a thief and a common beggar.

It seemed unlikely, though, that Uldericus had the Jewel; if he did, why had he spent the night at Herione's? He should have been home claiming his prize. The same held true for Quetivel.

The steps of the brothel were swept clean; he gathered his cloak underneath him and sat down, closing his ears to the noise of the street and trying to concentrate.

He needed something else. The idea he had had in mind when he asked Coeccias to find Desiderius would not work. Simply put, he had hoped to let the guests know that there was a wizard in the city willing to buy the Jewel. Beyond that, the idea had been vague—putting someone in an inn, as far from the one where Desiderius was staying as possible, and luring the thief there. But since neither Uldericus nor Quetivel would have stolen the Jewel for money, it was no longer a plan worth considering.

Unless it could be applied to Cawood. *Gods, let him be in debt,* Liam prayed. The trap was the only solution he had at the moment, and he could think of no way to differentiate between Uldericus and Quetivel. If it was either of those two, he would need to come up with another plan entirely.

Further thought was pointless, he decided. He had to sound out Cawood, and talk to Oakham. *Coeccias, too.* The Aedile might well be able to shed some light on the question, or come up with another plan. For that matter, discussing it with Fanuilh could be valuable. In the three months or so that they had been linked, he had found the dragon an excellent sounding board.

Thinking of Fanuilh reminded him of Grantaire, waiting at the house on the beach. He leaned back against the stone steps and closed his eyes.

Fanuilh! he projected.

Yes, master? The response was almost instant.

Please tell Grantaire that she can come see Mistress Priscian this afternoon. She should leave soon.

Liam had already begun to form his next thought when the dragon replied: *I cannot, master.* He cleared his throat and closed his eyes even tighter.

What do you mean, you cannot?

I cannot give Mage Grantaire a message.

In his head, Liam's thought was capitalized and very large: *WHY NOT?*

I cannot speak.

"Oh," Liam said aloud, a moment later. "Right." Growling to himself, he sent a final message: *Fine, forget it. I will come out.* He opened his eyes and got to his feet, brushing behind him, where the seat of his pants was cold despite the cloak.

The piece of paper Uldericus's servant had given him was still in his hand, neatly folded and sealed with a perfect circle of purple wax. The paper crackled as he opened it.

Master Rhenford, it read. *Come to me this evening at eight bells—my husband will be away.*

It was not signed, but there was no question whom it

was from. He held the note to his nose and inhaled. No question.

What does she *want?*

He folded the paper and tucked it inside his tunic, starting to walk down out of the Point.

By the time he had reached the stables, he had decided that what Countess Perenelle wanted was beside the point. He could guess, though an inborn modesty made him laugh at the idea. "How bored can she be?" he chuckled to himself. Still, it did not matter: what mattered was what he could learn from the meeting, and cuckolding the earl was not on his list at all. Was there any information to be gotten from her? If either of her suitors had given her the Jewel, he could hardly expect her to confess, and in any case he did not think either had. Otherwise, why would she be making assignations with him?

"It may not be an assignation," he said to himself, "much as that may hurt your pride, my boy." But if not that, then what? He assumed she did not know that he was looking for the Jewel, so it was doubtful that she wanted to give him information.

Out of the Point, he passed a shop selling mirrors and glassware. He stopped and examined himself briefly in a large mirror in the shop window. Tall, close-cropped blond hair, a youthful face with a long, narrow nose. He ran a finger down the length of that nose, first trying what he thought might be a seductive expression, then grinning at his own reflection.

Liam Rhenford, lady-killer, he thought. *She must be very bored. How do I turn that boredom to good use?*

Liam was still considering the question, pulling it back and forth in his head and getting nowhere, when he arrived at the beach. He had pushed Diamond hard, and the cold wind had numbed the tip of his nose and blasted his face red. He left Diamond saddled on the sand and ran quickly to the door.

Fanuilh was waiting just inside.

Hello, master.

The cold ride and his frustration at the course of his investigation had put Liam in a bad mood. "You," he said, aiming a finger at the dragon, "you I do not want to talk to. Why didn't you tell me you could not give her a message?"

You did not ask, his familiar responded, *and I did not know you wanted me to.* It flared its wings once. Liam closed his eyes and started to count to ten. Grantaire spoke when he was at five.

"Good afternoon. Have you spoken with Mistress Priscian?"

He opened his eyes. "Yes, I have. She is expecting you this afternoon." She stood in the library door, wearing a gray, ankle-length dress with long sleeves and a high neck.

"Will this do?" She indicated the dress, tugging at the tight collar. Liam grinned at her discomfort.

"Perfectly. You will make a good impression. But can you leave now?"

"Of course. A cloak." She went into the bedroom and returned a moment later, drawing on her fur-trimmed cloak. Liam explained Mistress Priscian's conditions, to which she had no objections, and they went outside.

She followed him to Diamond, and he realized that she had no horse. *How did she get out here?*

"I suppose you will have to ride behind me," he said hesitantly, and she said, "Yes," as if it were nothing. He mounted, and she climbed up behind with ease, sitting sidesaddle and wrapping her arms around his waist.

Liam set Diamond going at an easy pace, mindful of Grantaire's position—and her hands, snug around him—though he was anxious to be back in the city. There was so much to do, so much to figure out. He wanted to sit down with Coeccias, perhaps over dinner—the Aedile thought best over meals—and go over what he had found out. Quetivel and Uldericus were his main problem. If either was the thief, he could think of no way short of searching them to find the Jewel.

Near the city gates Grantaire pulled the hood of her

cloak down so that it obscured most of her face.

"We will take the shortest route there?"

"Of course," Liam said, remembering that she would be worried about meeting Desiderius. He should have thought of that earlier. "I will introduce you to Mistress Priscian, and then there are some things I must take care of. I'll come back for you later."

They passed through Temple's Court and turned up the Point's northernmost street, riding past Herione's and the Uldericuses' to End Street. Grantaire jumped lightly off when he stopped outside Mistress Priscian's; Liam dismounted and tied Diamond's reins to the hitching ring discreetly bolted to the stoop.

"This is it," he said, and they went up the stairs together.

Haellus let them in and led them directly to the solarium. There was not much sunlight, but Mistress Priscian was standing by the windows, staring out to sea.

"Good afternoon, Master Rhenford," she said, turning from the view.

"Mistress Priscian, this is the friend I mentioned—Mage Grantaire." He was not sure if that was the proper way to introduce her, but it was what Fanuilh called her, and he figured the dragon would know. He was vaguely aware that true wizards preferred the more arcane "mage," but he had never known why. In any case, she did not object, dropping a very creditable curtsy at the older woman.

"Allow me to thank you for this opportunity, Mistress Priscian. It is a great privilege."

The older woman nodded, as if this was only proper. "There are a fair number of papers and two books to examine. I imagine it will take some time."

"I hope not to inconvenience you," Grantaire murmured.

Mistress Priscian laid a hand on her chest. "It is no inconvenience to me," she said. "But come, Master Rhenford grows restless. I am sure he must have pressing business."

Liam had not thought his restlessness was obvious,

but he nodded. "There are some things I must see to. I
will leave you to it, if I may."

"Certainly," Grantaire said.

"In course," Mistress Priscian said at the same time.

He promised to return by five, and left the two women
alone.

Tasso let him into the Oakhams' and led him to the
rear room on the first floor. It had been cleaned up since
the last time Liam saw it, some of the padded couches
removed, the remaining ones grouped by the fireplace.
Oakham was lying on one, but he sat up as soon as he
saw Liam.

"Y' are back." There was a cloak folded over the
end of his couch; he gathered it up and stood. "We'll
to the Staple, then." He spoke heavily, as if it were a
duty he would rather not fulfill, but knew he must.

"I saw Earl Uldericus a little while ago," Liam said,
unsure of the etiquette surrounding duels. "He gave me
a challenge for Baron Quetivel."

Oakham paused with his hands on his hips, grimacing.
Then he shook his head. "There is no point, just yet.
He's in no condition to receive it—can scarcely think
straight. I think it'll keep."

Liam agreed. "I suppose it will. Has he eaten?"

"He has, and's kept all down. I'll warrant his health,
if he's given a day or so." He clapped his hands together, as if bracing himself for a hard job. "Come, the
Staple."

They walked down Duke Street, Liam leading Diamond. There was a stable on the way. He was thinking
about the rest of his afternoon—after the Staple, he
wanted to sit down with Coeccias. Would it be worth
his while to stop by Herione's? She had offered him
good information before; he would ask the Aedile about
that.

He stole a glance at the lord beside him. Oakham
walked slowly, his head down, studying his feet. He was
chewing one end of his mustache, and a heavy vertical
line creased his forehead.

This is getting to him, Liam thought. *And why should it not? It was not even his, and one of his friends stole it.* Thinking of Oakham's friends reminded him of something. He drew his purse from his belt.

"I forgot, my lord." He started to count out crowns, looping Diamond's reins awkwardly around his arm. "It was thirty, wasn't it?"

"What's that?" Liam had meant to distract Oakham from his brooding, but the man was acting as if he had been offered a live snake. "That's not for me." He shook his head, rejecting the money. "That's Uldericus's. You'll pay him."

"But you vouched for me," Liam said slowly. "I thought—"

"The money is Uldericus's," Oakham repeated, sharply this time. "We'll have no more on it."

Liam slipped the money back into his purse, wondering at the other man's attitude. Duke Street bent at a right angle, and they passed the temple of the Storm King.

"Perhaps you can tell me something about Master Cawood," Liam said, determined not to be put off by Oakham's bad mood.

With an exasperated sigh, the lord told him what he already knew: that Cawood was a merchant, with several ships.

"Yes, I know that," Liam said patiently. Oakham refused to meet his eye, looking anywhere on the street but at his companion. "I was hoping you might tell me something else. For instance, how did you meet?" Cawood was the only guest who had no social rank—even the Furseuses were the children of a knight.

"At the baths," Oakham said. "He enjoys sparring, as I do."

Liam was vaguely aware that the southerners did more at their baths than just get clean. They held debates, races, contests of strength, wrestling and boxing matches—almost anything that could be done indoors.

"Sparring? With swords?"

"No," Oakham said, sighing heavily, clearly resigning himself to Liam's questions. "Boxing, you might name it, with helmets and padded gloves."

"Ah. Is he good?" He was trying to imagine boxers wearing helmets. Even with padded gloves, he would not want to smash his fist into a war helmet.

"Yes, he is very good." Oakham tugged the end of his mustache out of his mouth and smoothed it. "I see your direction, Rhenford." He sighed bitterly.

"What direction is that?" Liam asked, genuinely ignorant.

The other man finally met his eye. "You wish to know if he could have killed the thief. That I can't tell you. I only know that he's a good boxer."

I wish that had been my direction, Liam admitted to himself. However, there was no reason for Oakham to know it was not, and it allowed him to ask some other questions.

"What about Earl Uldericus? And Baron Quetivel?"

Once more fixing his eyes on the ground, Oakham spoke reluctantly, weighing each word. Uldericus was not a soldier, but was known as good with a blade. He had a private tutor, and had from time to time participated with success in practice matches at one of the more exclusive baths.

"These parts do not sum up a murderer," Oakham cautioned, and Liam agreed.

They had turned off Duke Street and reached the stables; Liam arranged for Diamond to spend the afternoon, not bothering to haggle with the ostler. He hurried back to the street. They headed for Harbor Street, Oakham resuming his talk.

Quetivel was from the northern parts of the duchy, bordering partly on the Midlands and partly on the wild mountains around Caernarvon. Noblemen there were bred to fighting, particularly on horseback. "He is partly in Southwark now to pay obeisance to that new Bellona. He's made an offering and said prayers at her fane."

Liam raised an eyebrow at this: Bellona's worship in the Southern Tier was only a month old, and though the goddess had actually appeared in the city, he did not think word would have spread so fast. More, though, he could not reconcile his image of Quetivel as a gambler and a rakehell with the idea of the baron praying and making offerings.

"I am sure he can couch a lance and draw a bow," Oakham went on. "On the marches, every man is a warrior, and from a young age. But again, that does not sum him up a murderer."

That was certainly true, Liam knew. A man could do things in the heat of battle that he would never consider in cold blood. Moreover, the sort of skills Oakham had described were meaningless—Japer and the beggar had not been run through with lances or beaten to death with padded gloves. Their throats had been slit.

"I note you do not ask after Cimber Furscus," Oakham said.

Liam shook his head. "No. I met him this afternoon, and I saw both the men who were killed. Furseus could not have done it."

"Y'are sure? Even a strong man can be taken by surprise, and it is but the work of a second to cut a throat."

One moment information had to be dragged from the man, the next he wanted to implicate another man. *Does he want to find the Jewel or not?* "No," Liam said insistently, "it was not Furseus."

They passed off Harbor Street onto straight, narrow streets running between the high walls of warehouses. Winter was slow for Southwark's merchants, and with the Banquet in progress, there were even fewer people than usual in the neighborhood. Gull screams from the nearby docks echoed off the warehouses, as did the men's footsteps.

"Rhenford, do you still think you can recover the Jewel by tomorrow?"

Liam could not read the other man's tone, but it was as if he had read his mind. He had just been thinking that he had vastly underestimated the amount of time he would need. If Countess Perenelle was really the cause of the theft, he could imagine no way to find the Jewel. *If we could just search them—all of them! The gods know there's reason enough to suspect them.*

That was out of the question, though: gossip, however close to the truth, was not cause enough for accusing noblemen of theft. Even the truth was not enough, for that matter. He would have to have proof, concrete proof. It was no wonder that Coeccias had been eager to hand the investigation over to him. Still, there was no sense burdening Oakham any more. The lord looked worn down by his cares.

"I hope so. At the very least I hope to know who did it. Proving it will be harder, but once we know who it is, we can figure out a way to prove it." *No sense raising his hopes too much. . . .*

Oakham nodded, as if this confirmed his own thinking. "If that's the case, there is something I'll tell you. I wish to leave Southwark. This affair has put a great strain on Lady Oakham—and on me, for all that. I have family in Torquay, and it would like me to pass some time there."

"I can imagine." It was hardly strange, though Liam was a little surprised that Oakham would tell him about it.

"I have booked a passage for us on a ship, the *Sourberry*. It parts Southwark in three days."

"That soon?" Liam blurted. He was by no means sure he could have the Jewel back by then.

Oakham nodded grimly. "The city oppresses me, Rhenford, but I think most of my wife. This has been passing hard on her."

"Of course" was the only thing Liam could think to say, but he felt panic rising inside him. There was no way he could have the Jewel back in three days, not at the rate he was going. He might know who had stolen it—would have to know who had stolen it, he reminded himself, to satisfy the Werewolf—but having it back was another thing entirely.

"I have not told my wife or my aunt," Oakham added, "and I would consider it a kindness if you would not mention it to them just yet. It is a delicate thing, and I wish to do it myself."

"Of course." It was still the only thing he could think to say. Three days seemed a very short time.

In a solemn silence, they walked on past the warehouses.

CHAPTER 12

THE STAPLE WAS out of place in the warehouse district, a rectangular building neatly plastered and painted a delicate blue. Large windows marched down its sides, clean white shutters framing each broad expanse of glass. A tall tower rose above the gently sloped roof of gray tile, topped by a gilded statue of a woman shading her eyes with one hand to gaze out to sea, and holding a piece of paper in the other. The building fronted on a small square, more a fortuitous gap between the surrounding warehouses than a planned space, and two shallow flights of steps met in a broad landing in front of the entrance. The whole effect was surprising, a strange apparition of grace among the squatting brick and wood shells all around it.

Liam had seen it once or twice, in rambling walks around the city, and the week before, when it had begun to seem as if his partnership with Mistress Priscian might really materialize, he asked Coeccias about it. It was little different from similar constructions in the Freeports and Harcourt, a place for merchants to meet and arrange cargos, to exchange goods they could not sell for those they could, to barter and to cheat. The name was odd, but Coeccias had explained that; the Duke held a monopoly on wool in the Southern Tier, and to ship a bale of it out of the city, the bale had to be marked with a staple, a foot-long red wicket. Originally, it had been a warehouse full of wool and red staples, from which the Duke's agents would sell the bales. The trade had long since grown too big to operate out of a single building, and when the old warehouse had burned down some fifty years ago, the merchants of Southwark had erected the present building, providing offices for the Duke's wool agents and booths and a trading floor for themselves. No goods actually moved through the Staple now, just invoices and bills of lading, but if it had not been for the deals made there, most of Southwark's ships would have sailed empty.

They went up the stairs and through the entrance, through a small vestibule and down onto the trading floor. Literally down, because the floor was sunken, three steps down to stone flags that stretched across almost the entire first story. Massive white posts rose every so often, branching out into braces and struts supporting the ceiling beams; on three sides wooden dividers reached from the outermost posts to the walls, creating stalls for individual merchants. Many were empty, at others single men sat alone, waiting for business, and at a few there were groups of men. It was only slightly warmer inside the building than out, and all of the occupied stalls had braziers. There were a few groups of men in cloaks or heavy coats scattered around the trading floor itself, though they did not seem to be working hard. A wine jug was being passed around one group, and another was laughing at some joke just told. Liam was sure he recognized one of the laughing men from Herione's. At the western end of the room, a uniformed guard sat on a broad flight of steps leading to the second floor, his pike leaning against the banister.

"I do not spy him," Oakham announced after scanning the room. "We'll visit Denby—he'll know of Cawood."

Frowning, Liam followed the other man across the trading floor. He should have guessed that Cawood might not be there—it was winter, after all, and the trading season did not begin for another few months—but he had assumed Oakham was sure of the man's whereabouts. The lord was unconcerned, however; the anxious look he had worn on the street dropped away, replaced by a light smile, as he walked towards one of the stalls manned by a lone merchant.

"Master Denby," he called, jumping up the three steps, "how are you keeping?"

Tall, thin and stooped, Denby unfolded himself from his chair and offered a bow as if he were falling over. "My Lord Oakham."

"Master Lons Denby," Oakham said, "Master Liam Rhenford. Master Rhenford is joining with my aunt in a venture."

Denby blinked mildly and offered his hopes that it would be profitable.

Liam thanked him. "With luck it will be."

"Tell us, Master Denby, have you seen Rafe Cawood? I had hoped he might show Master Rhenford the Staple."

"There is not so much to see," Denby said, blinking again and digging solemnly at his ear. "Nor would Master Cawood be the man to show it. Not this day."

"And why not?" Oakham asked with a pleasant smile.

"For that he's there," Denby said, pausing in his digging long enough to point at the stairs, "with the wool agents."

"Are they so terrible?"

Denby shrugged, blinked. "No, they're not." He blinked again. "But he's two cargos to pay for, and the ships not in."

Liam's heart leapt, but he tried to hide his eagerness. "Not in?"

"Not in," Denby agreed, nodding slowly. "And the Duke's agents can be fierce with those who can't pay."

"Surely it is a mere gap," Oakham said, practically pleading. "A temporary shortfall. When the ships are in . . ."

"The Duke is not patient," Denby responded solemnly, as if he were a judge passing sentence. "And the ships are more than a month out. The agents'll guess them lost." He said the last as if the consequences were obvious, and Liam thought they were, at least as far as he was concerned. If the agents assumed the ships were not coming back—had sunk, or been taken by pirates—

they would call in Cawood's debt for his wool. That meant he would need money, and if he needed money, he had a reason to steal the Jewel. Most important, it was a reason Liam could understand, and one he could work with.

"He may be down shortly," Denby went on, digging in his ear again. "Though he may not be in the mood to take Master Rhenford on the rounds of the Staple. Such as it is."

"Will he be long?" Liam asked. "I was hoping he could answer a few of my questions."

Denby shrugged. "Who can say? He may be coming down presently, or not for hours. But it may be that I can answer your questions."

"I don't think so, Master Denby," Oakham said. The news about Cawood had not pleased him, and once again he refused to meet Liam's eyes. "We had hoped to speak with him directly."

"We can wait a bit, Lord Oakham," Liam said, a little annoyed at the other man. "And Master Denby may be able to answer some of my less specific questions."

He was, and he and Liam spent a few minutes discussing the way the Staple functioned, as well as trade in general. Denby, it turned out, was a sort of general factor, dealing in tapestries produced by the peasants of a Midlands lord, wine from Alyecir, and ore from some small mines near Caernarvon, among other things. Liam was particularly interested in the mines—one of the ports to which he wanted to send Mistress Priscian's ships needed metals of all sorts.

Oakham fretted the whole time, folding and unfolding his arms, tugging at the ends of his mustache, but refusing to participate in the discussion.

"Perhaps we can walk around ourselves," the lord burst in at last. "We don't want to keep Master Denby from his tasks." It was a transparent lie, since no one had come anywhere near the stall since they arrived, but Denby accepted it, shrugging and blinking.

"As you will, my lord."

Liam cast a sharp glance at Oakham. "I would like

to speak with you some more," he told Denby. "Are you here often?"

In a tone that clearly wondered where else he might be, the merchant said he was there every day, and bid the two men good day as they turned away.

"I am sorry, Rhenford," Oakham said, as soon as they were out of earshot. "I cannot listen to such pratings. I've too much on my mind."

Liam waved the apology away. As much as Oakham's scruples annoyed him, as much as they made his investigation more difficult, the loss was still Oakham's, and the lord's problems were far more serious than any Liam faced. He should have remembered that. "It doesn't matter. What does matter is that we know Cawood is having money problems."

"He never told me." There was sorrow in Oakham's voice. "He has never told me much of his business, in course, but such a blow! Two ships!"

"Yes, but the Jewel would more than make up for that," Liam pointed out, wanting to make sure that Oakham understood. "It puts suspicion strongly on him."

Oakham admitted as much with a heavy sigh, then stiffened, his eyes fixed on the stairs at the far end of the trading floor. The guard was scrambling to his feet to make way for someone to descend. A man came into view a second later, dressed in a jerkin and plain hose, a short cape over his shoulders. A floppy cloth hat was balled up in his fists, and his face was red with anger.

"Cawood," Oakham whispered, pointing.

"Speak to him," Liam urged, taking the other man's elbow and propelling him gently towards the stairs. "Arrange a meeting with him later today or early tomorrow, just the two of you."

"Why?"

"Just do it, please." Liam said, pushing harder. Cawood had reached the bottom of the steps, and Oakham, with an angry glance at Liam, raised his voice and hailed his friend.

Cawood heard, and stopped, but he made no move to meet them, waiting while they hurried over.

"Cawood," Oakham said, "how are you keeping?"

"Not well," the merchant growled. He was tall and thickly muscled; his head seemed to grow from his shoulders, with no intervening neck. His lower jaw was large but rounded, and he jutted it at them now. "You'll excuse me, Aetius, but I'm not fit company."

Liam put on a suitably sorrowful face as Oakham said, "We've heard of your troubles. It's a sad pass."

"Aye." Cawood clearly did not want to talk.

"Cawood, this is Liam Rhenford, an acquaintance of my aunt."

Cawood bowed stiffly. "Master Rhenford." Liam returned the bow.

"I had hoped you might show Rhenford around the Staple, but you've got worries of your own. It can wait."

"It must, I fear." Cawood twisted his hat, eager to be gone.

"I understand," Oakham went on, "but look you, Rafe, perhaps we can meet later. At the baths—a round with the gloves might be just the remedy."

He shook his head, apparently about to refuse, then took a deep breath. "Y'are right, Aetius. A round might be the thing. Though I cannot vouch for your health if you stand against me."

Oakham laughed sympathetically. "I'll wear two helmets," he promised. "This evening?"

"Later, though," Cawood said, then added grimly, "I have business to tend to."

They agreed to meet at eight, and Oakham expressed his sympathy again. Then Cawood took his leave, his bow to Liam less stiff this time. Once he was gone, the two men started walking slowly towards the door. Oakham waited to speak until they were out on the street again. He could just see Cawood, going out of sight around a corner.

"What is this meeting for, Rhenford?" His voice was low, almost dangerous.

"You will not like it," Liam said.

"Go to, Rhenford."

Hearing the mounting anger in the other man's voice,

Liam took a deep breath. "I want you to tell him, as casually as you can, that there is a wizard in Southwark who wants to buy the Jewel. You must make it sound like gossip you have heard, and I'll give you the name of an inn where he is supposed to be staying."

"You would have me trap him!"

"Lord Oakham," Liam said, summoning his patience, "it will only be a trap if he stole the Jewel. And if he stole the Jewel, he is not your friend. If he did not do it, then it will be just a piece of harmless gossip."

"Why didn't you do it, then?" Oakham asked. "He was there—with us! You could have set your own trap!"

Liam shook his head. "No. I do not know what inn to use yet, and I could hardly ask to meet him again just to tell him that."

Sputtering, the lord grabbed his arm and stopped him. "You don't know what inn? What does it matter? Pick one!"

"I cannot. The point of the trap is that no one but a wizard would have enough money to buy the Jewel— or at least, no one would think so. The problem is that there really is a wizard in Southwark who wants to buy the Jewel."

The color drained out of Oakham's face in an alarming way. "What?" He sounded strangled.

Without mentioning Grantaire, Liam explained what he knew of Desiderius, including the wizard's visits to jewelers. "So I have to be sure what inn not to use, you see? And I do not know where he is yet—Coeccias is looking into it."

None of this reassured Oakham. He grew frantic, grabbing Liam by the shoulders. "How can you be sure he is still in Southwark?" he demanded. "He might have parted already! You must find him, find him now!"

"The Aedile is looking for him even now," Liam assured him, speaking gently. "He does not have the Jewel." A small, mean part of Liam's mind reminded him that, for all he knew, Desiderius might have the Jewel, but he could not help that. He did not promise that the wizard had not left Southwark. "We will find the inn he is staying at, and then choose another one for the trap. Now come, I must see the Aedile now."

He managed to get Oakham moving, though he was chewing the ends of his mustache furiously, roughly knuckling the middle part of it. "Gods, Rhenford," he muttered, "gods. If this wizard should buy the Jewel . . ."

Oakham was still shaken when they parted near the city square, though he had regained much of his composure. Liam felt bad leaving him, but he very much wanted to speak with Coeccias—and he was also uncomfortable with the lord. He had promised Mistress Priscian that whatever dark secrets he uncovered would go no further than his own ears, but even the simplest of facts were painful to Oakham. There was only so much of his unhappiness that Liam could take.

Small stabs of guilt needled him on the way to the square, heightened by his relief at being rid of Oakham. He had enough to worry about, he told himself, without being overly sensitive to other people's distress. It was not his fault that the Oakhams chose their guests poorly, or that they had thieves among their acquaintances.

Recognizing how unfair his thoughts were, he forced them in another, more specific direction, trying to order what he knew. There were facts and there were suspicions, guesses, hints and rumors, but it seemed to him as if there was not enough of anything on which to base any useful speculation. And he knew that was his strength, or at least the tool he had used most successfully in the past: speculation, potentially elaborate games of "What if?" and "Why?" in which the point was to try to assume a different perspective on the information he had.

The information, though, refused to cooperate, slipping around inside his head, unwilling to point out profitable avenues for his imagination. His frustration mounted as he entered the square by the barracks.

Coeccias was in, and though it was past three, too late

for lunch and too early for dinner, he leapt to his feet, grabbed a coat and suggested they go across to Herlekin's.

"Truth, Rhenford, I'm sick to death of this place. I need air, and something hot."

Liam did not argue, and they crossed to the tavern, Coeccias pausing in the middle to take three or four deep breaths, rubbing his chest with both hands and commenting on how good it felt. Even then, though, Liam noticed that the Aedile's eyes scanned the crowd, an almost automatic movement. His look of satisfaction seemed to stem as much from the quietness and placidity of the square as from the cold air in his lungs.

For a moment, Liam gained a sense of perspective: Coeccias looked after an entire city, thousands of people and all their concomitant problems, worries and troubles. What was his own search for the Jewel compared to that?

All the tables on Herlekin's ground floor were occupied, but there was none of the claustrophobic crowding Liam had met the night before, and the customers were much better behaved. Herlekin himself came forward, a clean apron spread across his wide belly, and led them to a fairly secluded table on the second floor.

"Does he never sleep?" Liam asked, when the innkeeper had bustled away to fetch a serving girl.

"Eh?"

"It seems that, no matter what time we come in, he is always here."

Coeccias smiled and leaned across the table. "I'll give you a secret, Rhenford. Did you see his apron? Clean, eh?"

"Yes."

"He's just woken. When we leave, it'll be so spattered you'll swear he's been here an age. He does it himself, in the kitchen. I have seen him take a leg off the fire and rub it on an apron as pure white as the snow, and his wife crying rivers." They laughed at the idea, and the serving girl who appeared smiled with them.

"Y' are merry, sirs; would you dine?"

Liam said he would, and ordered a sea pie and beer;
Coeccias said he had eaten already, and ordered the
same.

"Aye, it's rare that Herlekin does any work," he went
on, "but he gives the appearance of it. But y' are not
here to fathom his arts, Rhenford; you wore a world of
care on your face when you came into the barracks. This
with the Jewel is not going well?"

Liam shook his head shortly, choosing to ignore his
friend's comment on how his face looked. "No, not at
all. I have an idea or two, but . . ."

"But they don't satisfy?" Coeccias said helpfully.

"No, not at all."

The serving girl brought their drinks and, sensing the
change in the mood of the table, solemnly promised that
their pies would be ready shortly.

When she was gone, Liam glanced around the room—
half of the tables were full, but Herlekin had seated them
at a window far away from the other customers—and
then put his elbows on the table, leaned forward, and
started talking.

He laid out what he knew first: that someone inside
the house had let Japer in on the night of the theft, and
presumably Malskat as well. In any case, Japer had
picked the lock, the Jewel had been stolen, and whichever guest had let them in slit the beggar's throat.

"We know it was a man, and I think we can assume
it was a big man, both because he was able to kill Malskat and because the lockpicker was afraid of him." He
did not mention Japer by name, but Coeccias made no
comment; instead, he nodded.

"Aye, it would follow."

He described Cimber Furseus, and the Aedile agreed
that he could be safely dismissed from suspicion.

"But that still leaves three—Master Cawood, Earl Uldericus and Baron Quetivel. What know you of them?"

"That's my problem. I'm stuck between them. Neither Quetivel nor Uldericus has any money troubles that
I know of. Uldericus certainly doesn't." He briefly described Uldericus's house, and then explained the game

of Alliances. "Quetivel played with his own money the whole evening. Oakham says that he has lost a great deal since coming here, but he still seems to have coin—and I think he was more upset at losing the game than at losing the money, if you see what I mean."

"It may have been his last."

The serving girl appeared with their pies; they sat in silence while she put them on the table and waited until she was gone before talking again.

"I don't think so; and anyway, I cannot see stealing something so large because you were out of pocket. If you had large debts, perhaps."

"But not for that you lacked the ready; go to, I see where you lead. You do not think much of the earl or the baron, then." Coeccias spread his hands as if the answer were obvious. "It must be Cawood, then. I'll warrant he has debts, eh?"

"As a matter of fact, he does," Liam admitted. "Some ships of his are long overdue, and apparently the Duke's wool agents are pressing him hard. So he certainly has debts, and large enough ones that the Jewel makes sense."

The other man raised an eyebrow, though his hands were busy manipulating knife and fork. "Truth, Rhenford, there is more. You don't put much credit in Cawood, but I can't see why not."

"Oh, I put credit in him. He's as likely as the others—and that's the problem. They are all equally likely." He took a bite of his pie, and realized that he was very hungry. Around mouthfuls he outlined Countess Perenelle's reaction to the Jewel, how much she admired it, the argument she had had with Lady Oakham, and what she had said she would do for the man who brought it to her.

"Anything," he repeated, putting down his beer and emphasizing the word. "Have you met her?" Coeccias shook his head. "She is the kind of woman whose 'anything' would make many men do anything in return."

"And that puts Uldericus under a cloud again?"

"Apparently he tried to buy the Jewel from Oakham. But it also puts Quetivel under as well."

Coeccias stopped eating long enough to raise a bushy, questioning eyebrow. Liam nodded, and told about the young baron's reported obsession, the countess's rumored indiscretions, and the comments that had led to the duel.

"A duel, eh?" The news did not seem to bother him; the Duke fully approved of the field of honor, and the Aedile rarely saw reason to disagree with his master. "It's a shame, but Quetivel's words would sting. Still, that does put them both back under a cloud."

Liam sighed. "Exactly." Both the earl and the baron appeared to have a reason to steal the Jewel; however, he explained, that was not the real problem, as far as he saw it. The problem was that neither man seemed to have produced the Jewel and claimed the prize. "Both spent the night gambling with Oakham and me. If one of them had taken the Jewel, wouldn't he have gone straight to her?" He did not mention the note the servant had given him, but it more than anything else convinced him that the countess had not yet surrendered her "anything."

To his surprise, the Aedile laughed, a deep, happy bark. "Truth, y' are wooden, Rhenford! If neither has claimed the prize, then neither stole the Jewel! It is as plain as your nose!"

Listening to his friend chuckling, Liam realized that he was probably right. He had been trying to think of a reason why Uldericus or Quetivel might put off giving the countess the Jewel, never considering that the most likely reason was that neither had it. It was a simple answer, so simple he had not thought of it—and so simple he mistrusted it. *Nothing is ever simple,* he told himself.

Coeccias, though, was beaming with pleasure. "It needs must be Master Cawood, then. Look you—he has a reason, in his debts, and the same chance as the others. In fine, all that's left is proving it. With proof, we can get round the Rights of the Town, and the other merchants'll be quick to let us have him. Nothing puts a man down in their eyes like a failure in business, whether it can be helped or no. So, how do we prove it?''

Liam put aside his doubts concerning the other two suspects, and addressed himself to the question at hand. "I have an idea about how we might do that. With the wool agents pressing him, Cawood would want money quickly. No one in Southwark has enough money to buy the Jewel for anything near its real worth, correct?''

"Aye—the Goddards might, if they marshaled all their wealth, but they would not. So say no one.''

"And no one would buy it, even if they could, except Uldericus or Quetivel, but forget them for a moment. My idea is that if someone were desperate enough to steal the Jewel for money, they would want the money as soon as possible. Now, if there were someone in Southwark they thought could buy it, wouldn't they jump at the chance?''

"Y' are thinking of the wizard," Coeccias said doubtfully.

"In a sense. Not Desiderius himself, but a wizard. Someone claiming to be a wizard, and offering to buy the Jewel. If we can let Cawood know there's a wizard in the city who would buy, I think he will try to sell. All we have to do is be there.''

The beaming smile returned to Coeccias's face. "It likes me, Rhenford, it likes me. It is a sweet trap. Now I see why you wanted me to find this Desiderius—so that we can make sure our trap is nowhere near him.''

"Have you found him?''

"Not yet." He gestured negligently. "A little later this afternoon. I've a man going round the inns. If he's still here, we'll know where by dinner. My question is, how do you let Cawood know of our wizard without making him prickle? And who will our wizard be?''

Liam explained the meeting Oakham had arranged at his urging. "I hope he can drop the hint without giving it away. As for who our wizard will be, I'm not sure yet. I had thought I might do it myself, since everyone in Southwark seems to think I'm a wizard, but then people know I'm associated with you, which might scare him off. I have someone else in mind, but it may end up having to be one of your men in disguise.''

"You'll ask your guest?''

As always, the Aedile surprised him with his insight. "I would like to. She would give an air of authenticity to the whole thing.''

"Aye, that she would, but if she'll not, one of my men can. Truth, it seems finished to me!''

Liam picked uneasily at his pie. "I suppose.''

With a mouthful of pie, Coeccias still managed an incredulous laugh. "Y' have not given up on Countess Perenelle, have you?'' he accused good-naturedly.

Blushing, Liam admitted that he had not. "It just seems too simple. At first I didn't think that there could be any good reason for stealing the Jewel. But I have seen Quetivel and Uldericus do so many strange things, and I have this feeling that neither would hesitate a second over killing the lockpicker or the beggar.'' Which, he knew, was a product simply of having spent more time with them than with Cawood. For all he knew, the merchant might spend his spare time sharpening a dagger specifically meant for beggars and thieves. Still, despite his earlier inability to believe any motive, he now could not rid himself of the suspicion.

"Look you,'' Coeccias said, more serious now, "what does it matter? We try this with Master Cawood. If it works, and he's the thief, all is well. If he is not, and the Jewel is with Uldericus or Quetivel—well, at least it does not part Southwark, and we can search it out in some other way. Does that satisfy?''

"Yes, yes. I'm just worrying. It may be that I don't like putting all our eggs in one basket.''

"There is that,'' the Aedile allowed. "Then go on with the other. Seek out Countess Perenelle. Press the Furseuses for more. Go see Herione—she'll know something of Uldericus, and the others as well. She casts her net wide, and'll part with news for that y' are with me.''

Liam nodded, not mentioning that he had already

planned to. Coeccias was right: if either of the other two men had stolen the Jewel, then it was unlikely that it would leave Southwark. That was small comfort—he had promised he would know who had killed Japer by the next night—but it was still comfort. And he could do no more than the Aedile had suggested.

He took a few more bites of his pie. Coeccias had long since cleaned his own plate, and held his mug in both hands, studying Liam over the rim.

"I had the right of it about Rathkael," he said at last.

"Eh?"

"He tasked me hard—at first. Your good authority, though, stopped him fairly quick. He grew thoughtful of a sudden, and said he'd mind it." He peered nonchalantly into his mug, then asked, with apparent indifference: "That will hold, eh? Your good authority?"

"Yes." *As long as the Guild does nothing—and as long as I can find the Jewel.*

Coeccias nodded, as if this was exactly what he had expected.

Liam wanted to change the subject. "When do you think you will know about Desiderius?"

"If he's lodged in a public house, then in an hour, two at the most. I could only spare a single man, for that I've doubled the night patrols, and I had to send another man out looking for those maskers."

"Maskers?"

"The boy and the maid," Coeccias said. "Their parents taxed me almost as much as Rathkael."

"Ah," Liam said, vaguely remembering the Aedile's other problem.

They fell silent, moodily nursing their beers and their problems. The bells in the tower across the square started tolling four o'clock. Liam found himself counting each hour. As four shivered in the air, a thought formed in his head.

Master, there is magic near you.

Despite himself, he jumped, nearly knocking over his beer. He grabbed wildly at the mug, righted it. Coeccias stared at him.

"What?"

"Nothing—someone on my grave." He shook his head; the Aedile shrugged and turned to the window, looking out over the square.

Liam focused and projected. *What do you mean?*

The thought came instantly: *Someone is performing magic near you.*

Grantaire, Liam replied.

No, Fanuilh sent back. *It is not in the Point—and it is not just near you, master. It is directed* at *you.*

Liam stood hastily, pulling coins from his purse and dropping them on the table with fingers suddenly gone clumsy.

"I have to go," he said, and grabbed his cloak.

CHAPTER 13

LIAM FOUGHT AGAINST panic, thinking, even as he reached the stairs, that he was over-reacting. He felt nothing, no magic, no spell—nothing. Could that be right? Could you have magic directed at you and not feel it? And if you could not feel it, could it harm you?

Where are you? he projected, walking into the first-floor common room. His eyes tracked uneasily around the customers, though he had no idea what he was look-ing for—unless it was a red beard and purple mark.

I am on the roof of the courts, master. The magic has stopped.

Where was it? Who did it? What was it?

He was moving quickly, threading through the tables, but he brought himself up short by the door, even as he projected his last question. Once before he had gone bolting out of Herlekin's, and it had landed him in the middle of a battle between the devotees of two different war gods.

Now he stopped, one hand on the doorknob, waiting for Fanuilh's reply.

It was in the square, the dragon told him. *I would imagine it was Mage Desiderius, but I do not know what he was casting.*

His arm was shaking, and he realized the doorknob was cutting into his hand. He let go, debating whether or not he should open it. If Desiderius meant to harm him, he would be harmed already.

The door swung open; Liam jumped back, and two men he had never seen before entered, glanced warily at him and pushed right by, heading for the table from which friends called to them.

"Idiot," Liam muttered. "You look like an idiot." Sheer embarrassment made him take the few steps out the door, but he flattened himself against the outside of the inn and started scanning the crowd.

Can you see him?

No, master. I am too high up.

He was overreacting, he told himself, repeating the thought over and over again. Grantaire had said that Desiderius might seek him out, and if the wizard meant to harm him . . .

"I know, I know," he muttered through grinding teeth. He saw no red beards, but the sun was lowering on the far horizon, half its bulk hidden behind the roof of the courts. Most of the square was in shadow; he had never noticed how quickly it could become dark there.

It was cold, too, and he held his cloak bunched in one hand. Slowly, trying to keep his eyes on all parts of the square at once, he pulled it on, shrugging it onto his shoulders and tying it loosely at the neck.

Beside him, a voice spoke up: "Mage Rhenford?"

Liam's head snapped towards the voice, and he knew that his face was a mask of fright. Deliberately, he closed his eyes and gave a long sigh of relief.

"Gods, you startled me," he said, and was pleased that his voice obeyed him.

Liam stood much taller than the wizard, but he sensed no advantage from the fact. From beneath a broad triangle of a hood, Desiderius offered him a polite smile.

"My apologies," the wizard said. His beard was merely red, but the mark that covered the entire left side of his face was a vivid, unnatural purple, a fascinating color. Liam found his eyes tracing the border between the mark and normal skin. "I did not mean to startle you, Mage Rhenford, but I have been meaning to speak with you since I arrived in Southwark."

Fanuilh, Liam projected, *let me know the instant you notice magic.* He smiled back at the wizard, masking the dryness of his mouth. "Really?" He tried to feign embarrassment. "I am afraid I don't—have we met?"

The other man chuckled. "No, but I have heard of you. My name is Mage Desiderius. I come from Guild Magister Escanes." His smile was confident, as if that explained everything.

His mind racing, Liam tried to stall. "Did you say 'Mage Desiderius'? Are you a wizard?"

"A mage, much like yourself," Desiderius said, with a polite inclination of his head.

"Oh, I'm not a wizard," Liam said, and held up a hand when the other man raised his eyebrows. "I know everyone in Southwark thinks I am, but I am not, really." The white of Desiderius's left eye seemed particularly bright against the purple of his skin. The man's manner was not threatening, but Liam still felt nervous. "Did you say you were from the Guild?"

"Yes." His smile shifted slightly, a tinge of disbelief shading his confidence. "We have heard of Mage Tanaquil's death, and I was sent to look into it. You were his apprentice, no?"

Liam faked a laugh. "No, no, no. Just a friend. He left me his house, and so a great deal of foolish talk has spread around, but I am definitely not a wizard."

The disbelief grew more marked, the wizard cocking his head as if to say they both knew better. "Come now, Mage Rhenford—apprentices are supposed to be registered with the Guild, but it is no crime. Mage Tanaquil was forgetful."

What would I say to him if I had never heard of him? Liam dropped his smile and grew earnest. "Honestly, Mage Desiderius, I am not a wizard. Please take my word for it—I am not a wizard, have never been a wizard, and never will be a wizard." His nervousness grew. He did not like the way the conversation was working; he felt a little as if he were being judged, and he wanted more control. *Coeccias can help.* "But it is cold here— why don't we go inside?" He jerked a thumb towards the door of the inn. "We can have something hot to drink, and discuss this."

"Very well."

With a bright smile, Liam held the door for the wizard. "I cannot tell you how often people make this mistake, Mage Desiderius. People are forever coming to the house, begging spells and potions and so on." He walked behind, steering the other man with gentle taps on the shoulder. "We will go upstairs, if you do not mind—it's much less crowded."

Desiderius made no objection, walking ahead of him and pausing to look around the second floor room. Liam peered over his shoulder and saw Coeccias still sitting where he had left him. The table had been cleared.

"Aedile Coeccias!" he called happily. To Desiderius, he said: "A friend—I am sure he can clear all this up." He led the way to the table and introduced the two men, using their full titles. "Coeccias is the Duke's man in Southwark. Mage Desiderius is from the Guild." He gave the Aedile a broad warning smile, hoping he would play along.

"Good day to you, Mage," Coeccias said, rising from his seat. "You'll have something to drink?"

Desiderius said he would, and sat at the table, completely at ease. Coeccias found the serving girl, ordered, and returned to the table, sitting opposite Liam and the wizard.

"Mage Desiderius has been misled," Liam began. "The same old story about my being a wizard."

To his relief, Coeccias chuckled convincingly. "Truth, have you not laid that to rest? Look you," he went on, addressing Desiderius in a friendly tone, "Quaestor Rhenford is no more a wizard than I am. It amazes, how these rumors breed. My house was once a shoemaker's, but am I a shoemaker?"

The serving girl arrived and handed out goblets of mulled wine. Desiderius sipped appreciatively at his, closed his eyes for a moment with a gentle smile. When he opened them, his smile turned sad. "Ah, well—it seems we were mistaken. I hope you will accept my apologies, Quaestor Rhenford. It is important for the

Guild to keep track of those who practice magic. It is a question of proper control."

"Not at all," Liam said magnanimously. "I understand completely. I am just glad you believe me. Now, if you could just convince every heartsick girl who wants a love potion . . ."

Desiderius gave a polite laugh. "There I must leave you to your own devices, I am afraid." He grew serious then. "However, there is something else I would like to ask you about. Mage Tanaquil had a number of, shall we say, artifacts. Items of power, magical power. They would be of no interest to you, and the Guild would very much like to have them. I wonder—"

Liam had thought about this. He grimaced, as if he had bad news, and interrupted the wizard. "I am afraid I have to disappoint you, Mage Desiderius. As you say, they were of no interest to me—so I sold them."

The other man's eyes widened slightly. "Sold them?"

"I am afraid so," Liam said. "I had no idea someone would come for them."

The wizard's voice was calm, but it was clear he considered it a blunder. "Who to?"

"A merchant from Torquay," Liam lied. He paused, searching his memory for an appropriate name. "His name was Hincmar. He seemed to think he could get something for them, and I had no use for them. There were some books, as well, but I could make neither head nor tail of them. I sent them to an old tutor of mine, Master Bahorel. You may have heard of him?" Bahorel actually existed, and had been Liam's tutor; he had also been considered an expert on old books.

"The name sounds familiar, though I am not often in Torquay. You say he has Mage Tanaquil's books?" Liam nodded, trying to appear as remorseful as possible. "And this Hincmar—he was from Torquay as well?" Liam nodded again. Desiderius frowned, then forced a wry grin. "Well, I think my journey will be a little longer than I thought. Torquay is not so far off, I suppose."

For an instant—a very short instant—Liam felt sorry

for the wizard. Then he remembered what Grantaire had said about him, and the fact that he himself was lying. *What is wrong with you?*

Through the same instant, no one else spoke. Then Coeccias cleared his throat, and began hesitantly: "Mage Desiderius, I wonder if you might not help us with a matter."

What's he doing? Liam wondered, suddenly nervous.

"Concerning what?" Desiderius's face was open and affable.

"As Quaestor Rhenford said, I am the Duke's man in Southwark. As such, I needs must see to the resolution of all the varied crimes committed within the city. Quaestor Rhenford is an invaluable help in this. Of late there has been an incident that has exercised us a great deal."

It was rare for Coeccias to produce anything like a polished statement, and whenever he did Liam was always impressed. This time, though, he was more concerned about where his friend was heading.

"Go on," the wizard said, pulling closer to the table and giving Coeccias his full attention.

"One of the local merchant families has lost an invaluable treasure—a stone of passing beauty and worth. In fine, it has been stolen. It is called the Priscian Jewel." The Aedile paused, wiped some wine from his mustache, and looked up at the ceiling, as if weighing his words.

"I have heard of the Priscian Jewel," Desiderius said shortly. His face had gone blank.

Coeccias smiled. "Ah—did you perhaps visit several jewelers just a few days ago, inquiring about it?"

"And if I did?" The wizard spoke warily, looking back and forth between Liam and the Aedile.

Liam laid a soothing hand on his shoulder. "Oh, please, Mage Desiderius—you must not think the Aedile is accusing you of anything. Not at all. We know for a fact that you were not involved." He turned to Coeccias. "I was so surprised at meeting him that I didn't even think of that."

"It only just occurred to me," the Aedile said, and then addressed the wizard: "As Quaestor Rhenford says, we know you were not involved. The matter I was curious about was why you took an interest in the Jewel."

"You see," Liam put in, "we have narrowed down the number of people we suspect, but we are unsure of their motives. If you could shed any light on the matter, we would greatly appreciate it."

Though he was not sure where Coeccias was taking them, Liam preferred the way the conversation was going. He was not in control, but at least his friend was—and Desiderius looked off balance, his eyes moving back and forth. He was on his guard.

"It is of no use to anyone but a mage," he said. "It has certain . . . *properties* that would make it interesting as an object of study. But only for a mage." He stopped, letting that sink in, then asked suddenly: "Is one of the people you suspect a wizard?"

Liam shook his head sadly. "No, unfortunately not. That might make it easier."

"How?" The question was snapped out suspiciously.

"It would give our suspects different parts," Coeccias said after a beat. "As it stands, they are as alike as peas, all wanting the Jewel for money."

The answer seemed to satisfy Desiderius, but he did not let his guard down. "Is there something else I can help you with? It seems I must now arrange a journey to Torquay."

"Actually, there is," Liam said, looking a question at Coeccias. The other man shrugged. "Since all our suspects are interested in money, we believe they may try to sell the Jewel somewhere. It is priceless, though, so buyers are few and far between."

Coeccias nodded. "To put it bluntly, none in Southwark could part with enough for it. Whoever stole it would have to know that. They might, however, think that a wizard could."

The wizard's eyebrows shot up, but before he could speak, Liam did: "It is possible that the thief might approach you, and try to sell it. Southwark is a small city, and we do not get many wizards here. So word of your presence might spread.''

''And the thief may hear of you, and try to sell you the Jewel,'' Coeccias said.

''And if he does?'' It was practically a challenge.

Liam and Coeccias shared a glance. ''We would appreciate it no end if you would inform us,'' the Aedile said.

''Ah.'' Desiderius took a deep breath, let it out with a nod. ''Of course. I would be happy to.''

''It would be a very lucky thing for us,'' Liam said, sounding—even to himself—remarkably grateful.

Desiderius shrugged. ''It would be nothing. I should report it in any case.''

''That is a sentiment I would we heard more often,'' Coeccias joked. ''And tell me, Mage Desiderius, if we should have any more questions, are you lodging somewhere convenient?''

Liam wanted to applaud: the question had come out completely naturally—and the wizard answered after only a moment's consideration. He was staying at the Three Foxes. Liam did not know it, but Coeccias nodded.

''Well and good, well and good,'' the Aedile said. ''I imagine that is all. Our thanks for your aid, Mage Desiderius. I do not wish to keep you, and Quaestor Rhenford and I have pressing business to attend to.'' He stood.

That, Liam thought, *was a little much,* but the wizard took the near-dismissal in stride, staying in his seat and regarding the Aedile with cool eyes.

''I must prepare for my journey to Torquay,'' he said, ''but if I might, I would have a word with Quaestor Rhenford, in private.''

''In course,'' Coeccias said. ''I will leave you for a moment.'' He stepped away to another table out of earshot and slid heavily into a seat.

The good feeling that had kept Liam going through the conversation suddenly left him. Desiderius turned his seat so that he was facing Liam, less than a few feet away. He licked his lips once, his eyes gone cold. He spoke with odd pauses between the phrases, and with extreme clarity.

"Someone may visit you, a woman named Grantaire. She will call herself a mage, but she is not. The Guild has expelled her. She has murdered two people, and if we catch her, we will kill her."

Liam nodded, unsure what to say.

"If she comes to you, do not listen to her. Do not help her. She may want some of Mage Tanaquil's things. Tell her the same story you told me." When Liam started to protest, Desiderius cut him off fiercely: "Be still! You have Tanaquil's things. You may have killed him yourself, for all I know or care. But if we find you have helped this woman, we will come for you, Mage Rhenford. Do you understand that? The entire Guild will come down for you."

"But I am not a—" Liam began, stammering.

"Hush," Desiderius said softly, rising. "Good day to you, Mage Rhenford."

Leaving Liam speechless in his wake, the wizard walked to the stairs, giving Coeccias at his separate table a friendly wave.

Liam did not see Coeccias rejoin him; he had the heels of his palms pressed firmly to his eyes, and was groaning in the back of his throat.

"That went ill, I take it," the Aedile said.

Liam let his hands drop to the table. "Ill? I suppose being threatened by the entire Mages Guild could be called 'ill.' Yes, I think so."

Coeccias' head jerked up. "Threatened? How so?"

"They don't like my guest—the one I told you about. They parted on bad terms."

"They cannot threaten you. I'll not have it. Shall I pay a visit to the Three Foxes?"

Liam shook his head quickly. "No. Definitely not." He did not think Desiderius would do anything to Coeccias, but he did not want to stir the wizard's suspicions. With Grantaire actually in his house, he did not want to draw any more attention to himself, as much for her sake as for his own. "I don't think anything will come of it— just bluster." That was untrue; he had a feeling that he had let himself in for far more trouble than he wanted. How hard would it be for the Guild to find out that Grantaire had visited him? More importantly, would they really follow through on Desiderius's threat?

If you have to make enemies, he told himself, *why make any but the best?*

"The real question is," he went on aloud, "do we really believe that he would tell us anything?"

"Not for a moment," Coeccias said immediately. "He'd never. So we put a man on him?"

"Can you?"

He thought, counting on his fingers, then: "I think it can be done. But then, do we still go on with your trap?"

"I don't know. I'm tempted to turn Desiderius into our trap, but that would be dangerous. So, no, I don't think so. Have a man watch the Three Foxes, and keep track of him if he goes out. See if he gets any messages. I doubt he will, but just in case."

"Well and good. In the meantime, you'll continue with the trap? And you'll see Herione?"

"Yes. Probably tomorrow morning, though. There are a few other things I have to do tonight." He needed to see Oakham again, and arrange to take Grantaire back to the house, and then there was his appointment with Countess Perenelle. He wondered if he ought to go to Mistress Priscian's right away, to let Grantaire know about Desiderius—and then discarded the idea. For all he knew, the wizard might be watching him, and he did not want to lead him right to her. Instead, he formed a thought and sent it to Fanuilh.

If you notice any more magic, let me know immediately.

Yes, master.

Any magic, anywhere.

Yes, master.

"It is curious," Coeccias said, then stopped.

"What?" He thought he knew what was coming.

The Aedile toyed diffidently with his wine. "It is curious," he repeated, "how you of a sudden have to leave, but come back in a moment with the wizard himself. Happenstance, I'd wager." His expression showed that he doubted it.

He already knows about Fanuilh, Liam reflected. "No," he said, drawing out the word. "Not happenstance. He was looking for me, using magic. Fanuilh warned me."

"For all y' are not a wizard, Rhenford, y' act as one. You know that?"

"I know," Liam said miserably. "But I'm not, I swear." *Depending on your definition,* he added silently. Living in a shoemaker's house did not make Coeccias a shoemaker, but then he did not get his meals by making shoes, and his closest companion was not . . . Liam cursed the limp analogy, but knew the basic sense of it was true. He lived in a magic house, ate from a magic oven, and his closest companion was a miniature dragon that could cast spells and send its thoughts into his head. He used magic every day—and what was a wizard but someone who used magic?

Coeccias was grinning at him. "Truth, Rhenford, when I think of the charlatans and knaves who spend their breath trying to convince the world that they are wizards, and see you fighting tooth and nail to convince that y' are not, it likes me enormously."

"Laugh," Liam said, standing up with a sardonic grimace. "Laugh away. But think about this—wizards have notoriously poor senses of humor. I might just turn you into a toad." Coeccias cringed in mock fear, and Liam had to laugh himself. "Failing that, I will perform a very simple piece of magic: disappearing and leaving you to pay."

Ignoring the Aedile's protests, he strolled out.

His amusement faded shortly after he left Herlekin's, as Liam realized he did not know where to go. He wandered aimlessly through the square, at a loss. It was near

five o'clock, so Grantaire might conceivably be finished—and Mistress Priscian would probably want her
to go soon anyway. He imagined the older woman
throwing out not-so-subtle hints about the lateness of the
hour, and the younger one blithely oblivious to them,
deep into some musty paper or other. He smiled a little
at the idea.

The sun was already sunk beneath the roof of the
courts, and the winter night was coming on fast. If he
picked up Grantaire, it would mean making the trip out
to the house immediately, and he wanted to be sure that
there was nothing else he could do in the city before
dinnertime. It was a little late to visit Herione; she would
be preparing for the evening already. And though he was
plagued by a premonition that he was forgetting something important—omitting some crucial and probably
obvious step—he could think of nothing that needed doing right then.

With a frown, he started off for the stables.

"Tramp, tramp, tramp," he muttered to himself. He
seemed to spend a great deal of time walking, and wondered if anyone else in Southwark covered as much of
the city as he did. Coeccias certainly, and the Guard, but
were their walks as pointless as his seemed to be?

Stop that! he scolded. It was ridiculous to depress
himself, when everything around him conspired to do so
already. He tried instead to concentrate on the town
around him. As night fell, holiday candles were lit in
many of the windows he passed. There were wreaths of
pine boughs on many doors and colorful ribbons, mostly
red, hung from practically every other gable and win-
dowsill. In the courtyard between the stables where he
had left Diamond and the inn it belonged to, he saw a
group of servants—the women wore white aprons and
mobcaps, the men heavier aprons of brown, all cut the
same way—gathered around a small bonfire.

With tremendous enthusiasm, they sang a song he did
not know, passing a jug, oblivious to the cold. As he
watched, two or three of the women and one of the men
left the group and went into the inn; a minute later three

different women came out and demanded a chance at
the jug. They were granted their wish amid a storm of
laughter and the beginning of a new song.

Reluctantly, he called the stableboy away from the
bonfire and asked for Diamond. The boy brought it in
record time, hardly waiting for his tip before dashing
back to the fun. Liam would have liked to ask about the
songs they were singing, but he could not bring himself
to interrupt again.

Instead, he swung himself into the saddle, took a last
look at the happy group, and set Diamond to an easy
pace towards the Point. He breathed deeply of the cold
air, noting with a sudden pleasure the expressions of the
people he passed—all variations on happiness, from the
simplest contentment to the most extravagant joy. A lone
boy tramped along beside him for a few steps, shouting
one of the songs Liam had heard at the inn, and when
he turned off onto a different street, Liam was tempted
to follow him.

In the midst of his own worries, it had been easy to
forget that Southwark was celebrating—and in the midst
of the celebrating, he knew it would be easy to forget
the dark business he was investigating.

He rode up Duke Street, surrendering himself to the
beauty of the houses dressed for the holiday. The further
up the street he went, the more candles shone in windows, the more greenery and decorations festooned the
homes. A house three down from the Necquers' was
covered from cornerstone to rooftop in red ribbons that
had not been there earlier in the afternoon, when he
passed with Oakham. Even the house that Coeccias had
identified as Cawood's was brightly lit, candles in all the
windows, lanterns and wreaths around the door.

End Street was a little more subdued; though he could
still see candles in almost every window—the Goddard
mansion spilled such pools of orange light onto the street
that it looked as if it were a furnace—there were fewer
boughs and no ribbons.

Nonetheless, he was in a good mood as he looped
Diamond's reins through the hitching ring on the Oak-

hams' steps. They had candles lit like the rest of South-wark, and he went up the steps lightly. Even Tasso's sneering welcome could not shake him, and he wished the sour-faced servant a very Merry Banquet.

"And to you, I'm sure," Tasso muttered, and disappeared down the front hall. A few seconds later, Oakham came to the door.

"Good evening, Rhenford." He was not happy to see Liam. "I'm with Quetivel now. Have you learned anything?"

"Is he awake?" Liam asked. He had never delivered Uldericus's challenge, but he guessed from Oakham's wince that it was not a good time for that.

"But barely," the lord said quietly. "And in no condition for this business with the earl. It'll have to wait. Have you found the wizard?"

"Yes. He's at an inn called the Three Foxes, down the hill from the city square."

Oakham nodded. "I know it."

"What's the Three Foxes?" a peevish voice behind him said. "And what knave's at the door, Aetius?"

Quetivel loomed out of the corridor like a ghost. The top of his head was wrapped completely in linen strips, so that only his bruised and swollen eyes showed above his lips. His braids had been cut off.

"Is it that Rhenford?" He put a hand to his head, swaying a little, unsteady on his feet.

"Come, coz," Oakham said gently. "You should not be up."

"It is!" he exclaimed, jabbing a wobbly finger at Liam. "Y' have news for me," he accused.

"Now is not the time," Oakham interrupted, laying a gentle hand on the younger man's shoulder. Quetivel brushed it off weakly and lurched forward a step or two.

"I say it is, and if Uldericus's whining dog has something to say, let him speak his piece!"

Liam's good mood lay shredded at his feet, but he kept still.

"Well?" Quetivel demanded.

"Coz!"

"Coward!" the baron shouted, and then swayed on his feet and pitched forward. Oakham just barely caught him, and struggled with the dead weight for a moment before Liam stepped forward and helped. They caught him up between them and carried him back to the first floor sitting room.

"My thanks," Oakham said, when they had arranged Quetivel on one of the couches. With a groan, the wounded man stirred and flung one arm out.

"Does he know about the challenge?"

Oakham frowned. "One of the servants' needs must have told him. It likes me not—he should not think on such things now. It was a shrewd blow."

"I can see." Beneath the linen, Quetivel's nose was a misshapen lump, too far over beneath one eye. As Liam looked, the baron's eyes flickered open briefly, then shut firmly.

"The challenge will keep," Oakham said, gesturing for Liam to lower his voice. "What of this wizard in the Three Foxes?"

"Let me see." Liam was silent for a moment, pretending to collect his thoughts. He was listening to Quetivel's breathing—except the young lord was not breathing. "I met him this afternoon." Liam frowned and lowered his head, looking at the couch from out of the corner of his eye. "He was indeed interested in the Jewel, but only as an object of study."

There. Quetivel's chest rose shallowly. His eyes were half-lidded. *He's listening,* Liam thought. *Why?*

A possibility occurred to him. "He said he had come here all the way from Harcourt in the hope of buying the Jewel. He even said he could cast a spell that would create a replica, so that you could have the appearance of the Jewel while he studied it."

"So my aunt could have the appearance," Oakham corrected carefully.

Liam accepted the correction with impatience. He hoped Quetivel was hearing all this. "Yes, yes, your aunt. He seemed very disappointed that it was stolen—said his trip was wasted, no profit in it at all." He broke off, because Oakham was giving him a curious look. "Never mind—it is not important."

"Strange, though," the lord mused. "So much interest in the Jewel, just now. What did you say the man's name was?"

"Desiderius," Liam replied. He forbore mentioning that he suspected the wizard's interest in the Jewel was secondary. *He was looking for me,* Liam thought with an inward shudder, *and for Grantaire.* "It is strange, but not really relevant."

Oakham turned away, pensive. "Stay a moment. It is so strange. The Jewel is found, and presently this wizard comes to Southwark for to see it." He turned back to Liam, but his eyes were still a little dreamy. "Do you believe in Fate, Rhenford?"

"No. It is a coincidence, no more." *And not even that,* he thought. "The Jewel was not even really lost, Oakham. Mistress Priscian knew where it was all along."

"That is true," the other man admitted, and roused himself from his reverie. "And not to the point, as you say. What do I tell Cawood?"

"Tell him that there is a wizard in Southwark who has expressed interest in the Jewel. You can tell him that Aedile Coeccias told you, and that the man has a great deal of money with him. Also, that he is leaving the day after tomorrow." He added the name of the inn where he had seen the servants singing. It was on the opposite side of the city square from the Three Foxes. "Make sure he knows that the wizard is leaving the day after tomorrow," Liam said.

"What of the real wizard? Does he stay in Southwark long?"

"I am not sure," Liam said, which was the truth. He did not put much faith in Desiderius's story about going on to Torquay. For what he hoped was Quetivel's benefit, though, he mentioned it. "I gathered he might be leaving tomorrow or the day after."

Oakham nodded absently, and suddenly Quetivel groaned loudly, giving what Liam thought was a convincing portrayal of awakening from a faint. "Aetius?"

"I'll go," Liam said before Oakham could say anything. "Do your best to be convincing with Cawood."

"I'll try," the lord said, not bothering to hide his distaste at deceiving a friend. He went and knelt by his cousin's side, uttered a few soothing words, then led Liam to the front door.

"How long will you be with Cawood?" Liam asked.

Oakham shrugged. "We meet at eight—perhaps an hour or two."

"I may be back in the city at eight, for an appointment. If you don't mind, it might be good if we could talk afterwards."

The lord frowned for a moment. "I don't know. I'll be very tired." There was more, Liam could tell: the man simply did not wish to see him. "Look you, come by after your appointment. I put the candles out when I go to bed—if they're still lit, knock. Else, and I'll see you in the morning."

It sounded like the best he would get, so Liam accepted. He began to think he had pushed the lord too far.

But what else could I do? he wondered, alone on the stoop after Oakham had shut the door. *What else?*

CHAPTER 14

HAELLUS ANSWERED THE door at Mistress Priscian's, and when Liam wished him a Merry Banquet, he returned the wish happily.

"Mistress Priscian and Mage Grantaire are in the study, Master Rhenford," he added as he led Liam up the stairs. The houseplan was the same as the Oakhams'; Haellus rapped respectful knuckles on the door that corresponded to Oakham's study.

"Come," Mistress Priscian called, and the servant opened the door for him.

The room was well lit, filled with heavy, dark furniture. Mistress Priscian sat at a massive trestle table of unfinished wood, a tidy stack of paper at either hand, an open ledger before her and an inkstand just beyond that. Grantaire sat at an identical table just opposite the older woman, with a similar arrangement of papers and inkstand, though she was reading from a folio-sized leather book, not a ledger. Both looked at the door with nearly identical expressions and postures: patiently expectant, bodies forward and heads cocked to the door.

Liam almost laughed at the mirroring—they might have been mother and daughter, or some allegory of age and youth—but he did not think they would appreciate the observation. He bowed instead, and wished them a good evening.

Both women nodded their acknowledgement at the same time.

"Good evening," Mistress Priscian said. "Have you had a successful day?" She indicated a vacant chair. Liam perched on the edge of it.

"More successful in some ways than others. Mostly it has just been confusing."

She sniffed. "Lord Oakham had the foolish idea that you would have the Jewel recovered by tomorrow."

Wincing, Liam shifted uncomfortably in his chair. "I am afraid I gave him that idea. There is a chance, but I think I was overhasty."

There was a riffle of paper, and Grantaire closed her book with great care. Mistress Priscian looked in her direction, her mouth twisting between a smile and a frown.

"Mage Grantaire believes she has learned some interesting particulars about the Jewel. And about my ancestor, it seems."

The younger woman's hands were pressed flat on the cover of the book, as if there were something inside that might spring out if she let up the pressure. She was chewing her underlip, but out of thoughtfulness, not embarrassment.

"Yes, I think I have. Eirenaeus was a genius."

"And a monster," Mistress Priscian said, her tone an odd mix of hauteur and pride, as if Grantaire had suggested something improper but nonetheless impressive.

"That too." The wizard looked at Liam, tapping the book. "The things he writes here are . . . amazing."

Liam craned his neck to look at the book, but it still seemed like an ordinary folio volume, significantly aged but normal. "What is it?"

"His notebook. There is a code, but it is relatively simple. Still, the things here . . ." Words failed her, and she made an expressive gesture: the book had made a tremendous impression on her. "He has laid out everything so very simply, and solved problems with ease and a sort of style that have eluded the Guild for centuries."

"But he's a monster?"

"He was studying black magic," Mistress Priscian confided, as if she were relating the naughty antics of a favorite grandchild.

"Not exactly black magic," Grantaire corrected, and Liam was a little annoyed to notice that she did it gently, with none of the patronizing tone she had once used with him. She turned to him. "Do you remember when I said he studied spirit?"

"Yes."

"His work on spirit is all it was rumored to be, and more."

Mistress Priscian interrupted. "Tell of the Jewel."

Grantaire nodded. "The Jewel was the focus of his work—he wanted it to be a source of spirit."

"So that he could draw spirit without his body having to sustain it?"

The wizard tilted her head, regarding him with curiosity and surprise. "Yes. Exactly." She shook her head, and Liam silently promised to be nicer to Fanuilh. "He made the Jewel in such a way that it could hold and supply spirit to a body indefinitely. According to his notes, he seemed to think it would work. I have not finished the book, but from some of these other documents"—she ruffled the pile to her left—"I think he could not solve the last real problem."

"Where to get the extra spirit," Liam guessed, and was rewarded by another curious glance.

"Yes." She flipped carefully through the pile, and withdrew an ancient parchment. She held it by the edges and placed it delicately on the end of the table nearest Liam.

He stood and crossed to the table. The paper was browned and the ink had faded, but he could see that it was an official document: there were three cracked seals at the bottom and a number of signatures.

"It is his expulsion from the Guild," Grantaire explained. "In a very wordy way it says he was stealing spirit from people."

Liam had just reached that part: " ' . . . this most heinous and vampiric practice,' " he read aloud. "So he did it."

Both women nodded. "The Guild thought so," Grantaire said, and tapped the pile on her left again. "There is an order in here authorizing a reward for the death or capture of the vampire thought to be plaguing the city then. It is dated a few months after the Guild order—and the interesting thing is that he signed it. Eirenaeus, I mean, along with a group of merchants.''

Mistress Priscian shuddered. "As I said—a monster." All trace of pride was gone.

Liam thought Eirenaeus's signature on an order calling for his own death indicated a certain twisted sense of humor, but he did not think Mistress Priscian would agree. He scratched his chin, thinking of Desiderius.

"Interesting, interesting. You say you have only gone partway through his notebook?"

"You must finish," Mistress Priscian insisted immediately, her voice a little thin.

"That would be good," Grantaire said simply. "May I come tomorrow?"

"By all means. What time shall I expect you?"

Grantaire looked at Liam. "Master Rhenford?"

"I need to be in the city in the morning. Would nine o'clock be too early?"

The older woman snorted, as if nine were ridiculously late, and they agreed that Grantaire would come at eight. When they left her, Mistress Priscian was standing by Grantaire's table, chin clamped firmly in one hand, squinting balefully at Eirenaeus's book.

Once again uncomfortably aware of Grantaire's arms tight around his waist, Liam guided Diamond out of the Point at a smart trot. He had told Grantaire to pull her hood close around her face, and she had done so without objection.

The stars were out already, the cold winter night wide open around them. At any other time of the year Liam would never had made Diamond go at anything above a leisurely walk, but the candles in the windows gave him enough light to see and avoid passersby.

Fanuilh, he projected.

Yes, master?

Would a wizard know if you were watching him?

Not unless he looked, master.

Where are you?

Above you.

Liam stifled an involuntary impulse to look. *Are you cold?*

No, master.

Not at all?

No.

He told the dragon where to find the Three Foxes. *Go there, find a place to watch from. Let me know if Desiderius comes or goes.* Coeccias would certainly have put a man there—but he wanted to be sure.

Yes, master.

Wait, he thought, and brought to mind the faces of Oakham's guests. *Look at these.* Through their link, Fanuilh had access to Liam's memories—could ransack them at will, in fact, though Liam had made it clear that the dragon was not to do so unless invited. *Can you see them?*

Yes.

Good. Let me know if any of them arrive—particularly the men.

As you wish, master.

Outside the city Liam pulled Grantaire's arms even closer around him and touched Diamond lightly on the ribs; the horse broke into a swift, exhilarating gallop. He wanted to explain about Desiderius, to ask her a number of questions—but he wanted to ask in the house. In the three months that he had lived there, he had come to view the house as a sort of ultimate sanctuary, a place apart from the world. He felt more secure there than he would have in a fortress.

Grantaire waited on the patio while he put Diamond away, and they went into the kitchen together. He left his cloak in the entrance hall; she dropped hers on the kitchen table, unhooking the high collar of her dress.

"Do you want something to eat?" He had only eaten part of the pie at Herlekin's, and thought that the news about Desiderius could wait at least until they were eating.

"Something small," she said. "Mistress Priscian gave me lunch. She is not at all what I expected." She stood by the table, one arm tucked under the other, her free hand barely caressing her neck. He went to the stove and imagined a meal, aware of the appraising gaze she bent on him and wondering what it portended.

''How do you mean?''

The oven produced two bowls of soup, an oily brown stock thick with onions, and a loaf of bread. He laid the meal out on the table.

''You painted her an ogre of propriety. She was very pleasant.''

They sat at the same time.

''You wore the right dress,'' he pointed out. He broke the loaf and handed her half. ''You . . . dunk it.'' The soup was from Alyecir, and not well known in Taralon.

''And I was very proper and respectful,'' she assured him sarcastically. Looking at him over her spoon, she continued in a more neutral tone: ''She told me a number of interesting things about you.''

''Really?''

''Things the Aedile had told her. She is very impressed with you. Were you really the first to greet Bellona when she appeared?''

Liam choked on his soup. ''That was an accident,'' he said, when he had regained control of himself and wiped off his chin. ''I was in the wrong place at the wrong time.''

She made a noncommittal noise, as if she were reserving judgement. ''And have you been all the other places she says you have?''

''Yes. Most of them at least.'' He considered his travels differently from his experience with Bellona. The former had been his choice, a conscious accomplishment in which he took a little pride, if only because he knew no one as well travelled. Meeting Bellona had really been an accident, completely unintentional and not entirely pleasant. ''Where did she say I had been?''

''Everywhere.''

''Ah. Well, I haven't been everywhere. I may have been everywhere that matters, though.'' He chuckled at his own joke, but Grantaire made no response, turning her attention to her soup.

They ate in a silence only broken by the purring of her cat, who wandered in and started rubbing at their ankles. Liam dipped a piece of bread in his soup and offered it, but the cat made a disdainful face and slunk up into Grantaire's lap.

The wizard ate on, rubbing a piece of bread around the inside of her bowl and licking her fingers to get the last of the soup.

"That was very good," she said. "I like onions."

Somehow that did not surprise Liam. He gathered up the bowls and put them back in the oven, then imagined two mugs of coffee and a bowl of milk.

He set the milk on the floor, and the cat leapt from Grantaire's lap. Then he got the coffee.

"I met Desiderius today," he said, and put a mug in front of her. He was gratified to see that she did not jump, though he could see her tense, her arms grow rigid on the tabletop. She pulled the mug closer, blew on it.

"When?"

He recounted the whole story, down to the wizard's parting threat. "So I think we can safely say he is here to look for you."

She pushed her mug away and ran a hand through her hair. "Yes."

"Now I need to know some things. If he got the Jewel, would he be dangerous?"

"No more than he already is," she said bitterly. "Which to you is too dangerous. You should not have spoken with him."

Liam waved that away. "I had no choice. Would he be more dangerous to you?"

"No." Her lips were pressed together in a thin, unhappy line. "No. Now that I have Tanaquil's spells and his things, he is not really dangerous to me at all. I could face him. The Jewel does not change that. It is merely a repository of spirit, an inert thing. He might use it to live longer, that is all."

That was good to know. "I have set Fanuilh to watch

him, so we will know if he tries anything. Do you think he will?''

''Not here.'' She gestured around her, at the house. ''Tanaquil has warded this place well. It would take something very powerful to pierce his spells.'' Then her voice grew harder, and she seemed to shake off a certain apathy. ''Still, he must not be allowed to have the Jewel. If he should have it, or give it to Escanes . . .''

''Escanes? That's the Magister? What does it matter if he gets it?''

''I have not given you the correct impression of him,'' Grantaire said, fixing him with a stern glance. ''If Escanes were to get the Jewel, he would be practically immortal.''

Liam let out a little, incredulous laugh. ''But you said the Jewel wouldn't work without spirit from—'' He cut himself off, and began to realize he had made a great mistake.

''He would do it. Just imagine what that would mean—a man who would achieve immortality that way, what would he not do? And with the power of the Guild behind him? He could tear Taralon in two.''

It was, strangely, a prospect Liam could easily imagine. In his mind's eye he saw the kingdom as an Alyeciran slave galley, its progress across a stormy sea marked by the crack of whips and the screams of the rowers. But the picture palled beside his growing realization of what he had done.

The hints he had dropped in Quetivel's hearing had been meant as a test. At the time, he vaguely imagined that they might force the young baron to some sudden action, and that from the results he might learn something. Just what, he was not now sure. He had tried to slant the story so that Quetivel might imagine he could buy a replica of the Jewel; if he went to see Desiderius, that would show that he had not stolen the Jewel.

Looking back on it, however, Liam saw that he had bungled that: his words might inspire the baron to visit the wizard whether he had the Jewel or no. If he had the Jewel, Desiderius would get it; if he did not, and found that the wizard had no replicas, he would undoubtedly reveal who had given him the information. And that, Liam imagined, would draw the wizard's attention to him in a very, very unfriendly way.

Why did you do that? he demanded of himself, knowing full well that mostly he had been angry, stung by Quetivel's insults, and moved to an ill-conceived action by his own dislike.

He cursed, suddenly and with great feeling.

"Rhenford!" Grantaire exclaimed. "What is it? You look sick."

"I feel sick," he said, though he did not. There was a sort of electric tingle all over his body, but his arms and back felt strangely limp. *What have I done? What do I do?*

He groped for his mug, then checked his hand and shook himself. He would simply have to fix it—make sure that Quetivel would not go to Desiderius.

Grantaire reached across the table and slapped his hand. "What is it?" she demanded.

His mind raced. "I told Oakham about Desiderius. I was going to set a trap for someone."

Her jaw dropped. "With Desiderius? Are you mad?"

"No," he snapped. "Of course not. In a different inn, with one of Coeccias's men posing as a wizard. I had to explain about Desiderius to Oakham, so he would be careful." Now that he thought about it, there had been no real reason to tell about the wizard, but that did not matter. Grantaire's face was a mask of incredulity and confusion.

"Wait. Oakham is Mistress Priscian's nephew?"

"Yes, her niece's husband. He is helping me look for the Jewel—introducing me to the guests who might have stolen it." Her confusion was deepening, but he plowed on. "I had to explain, but Oakham is not the problem. When I told him, one of the guests was there, a baron named Quetivel. He has been . . . ill, and might have been asleep, but—"

"He might have heard." She stood suddenly, her

chair scraping back harshly. "And he might have the Jewel, and he might go to Desiderius."

"He might go even if he doesn't have the Jewel," Liam said. Much as he wanted one, he could not think of a lie to explain why Quetivel would seek out Desiderius. "I didn't think he was asleep. I let him hear, because I thought I might be able to trap him, too." As briefly as he could, wincing at her occasional exclamations of dismay and disgust, he told about the countess's promise. It was a not very coherent account, but Grantaire understood enough.

"So now he'll go—to sell the Jewel or to try to buy a replica. Gods, Rhenford, what were you thinking?"

Thankfully, she did not seem to expect an answer. Pacing the kitchen, she continued: "If he sells Desiderius the Jewel, then Escanes gets it. If he does not, then Desiderius will seek you out and demand an explanation. Mark me," she said, "he will. I know Desiderius, and he will not take this sort of thing lightly. Particularly after his threat of this afternoon."

Liam cleared his throat. Watching her grow more agitated, he had gradually calmed down. "Now wait, let's not get carried away. I will simply have to make sure Quetivel does not go to visit him."

"And how will you do that?"

He bridled at her tone, at the way she implied he could not do it. "I'll tell him the truth, or whatever convenient lie comes to hand. And if that fails, I'll knock him out and tie him to his bed. I'll think of something." What he would do, he realized suddenly, was talk to Oakham. Oakham might be able to manage it.

He stood. "I'll go now. Oakham has to go out at eight, but I might be able to catch him."

"It's not Oakham that—never mind." She picked up her cloak and started putting it on. "I'll go with you. I need to make sure of this."

Liam did not object; secretly, he was relieved not to have to go alone.

• • •

Tramp, tramp, tramp, Liam thought to himself,
though Diamond was far from tramping. Grantaire had
her face buried in the back of his cloak, and he was half-
blind with tears from the wind, his cheeks numb and his
nose aching. The bundle Grantaire had insisted on bringing—an odd assortment of things from the trophy room
and a small satchel of her own—dug into the small of
his back.

He was completely calm, almost unconcerned; they
had almost certainly overreacted. Quetivel was in no
condition to go out looking for wizards, and Liam
thought it unlikely that he would go at night. Not that
he thought they should not be rushing into Southwark:
it was he who urged Diamond faster, not Grantaire. It
was his mess, after all, his responsibility.

And even as he shook his head at his own stupidity,
he wondered if there was a way to turn the situation to
his advantage.

Fanuilh!

Yes, master?

*Has anything happened there? Messengers or anyone
we know shown up?*

*No. Mage Desiderius has been here for the past few
hours, and has not gone out. Some people have gone in,
but they have stayed.*

Good. Are you cold?

No.

Hungry?

I have eaten.

Liam almost asked what, but stopped himself, obliterating the thought in his head. He did not want to know.
Then an idea struck him. *Go to Oakham's and watch
there. You can find it?*

Yes.

*Good. Let me know if anyone leaves or enters—par-
ticularly any messengers.*

He could not imagine that Quetivel would go himself,
not if he wished to keep up the pretense of being seriously wounded. Liam considered it just that—a pretense,

probably to put off Uldericus's challenge. *And he called me a coward!*

They had reached the city gate when Fanuilh's next thought appeared in his head.

Master, Lord Oakham has come out.

Liam cursed. Oakham had gone to meet Cawood. He considered not going to the house—Fanuilh could watch, and he did not much relish the idea of having to talk to Quetivel alone—but he did not think Grantaire would accept it, so he urged Diamond on. The bells started tolling eight as they turned onto End Street.

The candles were out in Mistress Priscian's house, but next door they still blazed. When they had dismounted, Liam held the reins out to Grantaire.

"Stay here. I will go in and see to Quetivel." She started to protest, but he held up an imperious hand. "I will take care of it. If I need you, I'll come back out." He could not see her expression, but she took the reins with a jerk.

He turned with a nod and went up the steps.

Lady Oakham answered his knock, opening the door only partway. Her face turned hard when she saw who it was. *Servants gone,* Liam noted, as well as the fact that her expression robbed her of her limited beauty.

"Lord Oakham is not in," she said coldly.

"I know, Lady Oakham." She took offense at his knowledge, drawing herself up for some stinging comment; he hurried on. "Actually, I was hoping to speak with Baron Quetivel. Is he in?"

She blinked once, and then all of her features conspired to produce one of the most remarkable expressions of disgust Liam had ever seen. "In?" she shrilled. "In course he is in! He's in his couch, where he has lain this last day, his head near broken in!"

Poor, poor Oakham. "If I could, I need to speak with him," he said, as mildly as he could. "It is a matter of some importance."

She goggled at him, astounded by his effrontery. "Y' are mad!" she stammered at last.

"Has he sent any messages to anyone?" Liam asked quickly.

"No! How could he? He is sore hurt, and asleep, and I for one have had enough and too much of you!" She slammed the door in his face.

"Merry Banquet," Liam said to the brass knocker, and turned and trudged wearily back to Grantaire. Her voice was a hiss in the night.

"That was impressive."

"Baron Quetivel is asleep, and has sent no messages," he said, taking the reins. "Fanuilh will watch the house—if anyone comes or goes, we will know. We will be fine for the next hour or so, and then I can see Oakham. With him I can make sure Quetivel does nothing."

"Rhenford," she said, grabbing his arm fiercely, "I don't think you understand how important this is."

His arm twitched underneath her hand, but he stilled it, and made himself speak calmly. "I think I do. But what would you have me do—knock the woman over? Quetivel will keep for now. And if he doesn't, remember that I'm the one Desiderius will come for first. Now, there is something I need to do. Will you let go of my arm and let me do it?"

He heard her take in a hissing, angry breath, and then she let go of his arm.

"Very well. What are we doing?"

Liam swung up into the saddle and offered her his arm. "I am going to visit Countess Perenelle, to have a little talk." About what he had no idea, but he would think of that later. Probably on her doorstep, in between knocks. "I'm not sure what you are going to do—we'll have to figure that out."

"This is the countess who will do anything for the Jewel?" she asked, and it seemed to him that she pulled harder on his arm than she needed to to get herself up behind him.

"The same."

"And my presence would undoubtedly spoil the atmosphere of your little tryst."

He stiffened, then turned awkwardly. "Do you want to walk?"

"What?"

"I asked if you wanted to walk." A sudden wave of anger rushed over him, the uprush of two frustrating days. "It is a holiday here, Grantaire. The past two days have been a holiday here. Do you know how I have spent them? I have spent them in the company of people who sneer at me, running all over this damned city to prove to a decent man that one of his friends is not just a thief, but a murderer as well. I am trying to find a man who cuts throats for fun, and I am not doing very well. I am making mistakes—I am aware of that—but I will do my best to mend them. And to add to all my fun, I have had the pleasure of entertaining you, for which pleasure the Mages Guild has threatened me with death." He paused, out of breath. "So I ask you if you want to walk, because I do not particularly wish to ride with you."

"I am sorry," she whispered after a moment, and his anger deflated at once: there were tears in her voice. "Sorry to have brought this on you." She started to climb off, and he grabbed her hand brusquely.

"Don't be stupid." He kicked Diamond and the horse started walking. He regretted his outburst intensely. *How fair was that?* Having the entire Guild as an enemy was only a threat for him, but for her it was a reality. And it had been his choice to investigate the theft of the Jewel. His troubles seemed small in comparison to hers.

As they turned off End Street, she quietly asked him where they were going.

"To the Aedile's house." He did not want to leave her at an inn or a tavern, and Coeccias lived fairly close by. "He won't mind letting you stay for a little while."

She said nothing, but her hands tightened a little around his waist.

Coeccias was not at home, but his servant let them in with a broad smile.

"Quaestor Rhenford! A Merry Banquet to you!"

"And you, Burrus. Burrus, I have to attend to a little business—official business—and I wonder if Mage Grantaire might stay here for an hour or so."

Burrus swept a grand bow in Grantaire's direction. His head, entirely bald, reflected the myriad candles in the windows. "In course, in course. I'm sure Coeccias wouldn't mind. He's seeing to extra rounds just now, but he'll be back presently."

"Thank you, Burrus." Liam shook the other man's hand briefly. "I'll leave Diamond by the door, if I may, and be back in an hour."

"No hurry, Quaestor. I am just brewing something for the holiday; Mage Grantaire can help me test it, if she will."

Grantaire nodded gravely at the man's happy smile.

"An hour," Liam said, and left.

An hour would be more than enough time. Coeccias lived on the edge of the Point, where it mingled with less wealthy neighborhoods, and the earl's house was less than five minutes away.

Liam walked quickly, rubbing his arms against the cold and berating himself. *Why can't you keep your mouth shut?* What he had done with Quetivel was an enormous mistake, but it had been pure meanness to lash out at Grantaire. Her situation was bad enough—alone, in a strange city, with the Guild after her. *Why can't you think before you speak?*

Two days gone by, and what had he accomplished? Nothing. Exactly nothing. He had made Oakham lie to his friends, had become party to a duel, and had potentially made an enemy of the Guild. Noblewomen slammed doors in his face, and he was nowhere near to finding the Jewel. He stopped short of blaming himself for Japer's death, but he wondered if he could have prevented it. *If you had gone to the Werewolf earlier,* he thought.

Then he cut the thought off: that way was madness. He could only do what he could do, and the first thing

would be to pay more attention to his words, to think
before he spoke, before he acted.

Vowing to do that, he strode past Herione's, and a
voice called his name. He checked his stride, quickly
scanning the portico. There were no candles in the
brothel's windows—there were no windows—but lit
torches had been set in brackets all along the wall. He
could see the stout woman with the pot, serving out
bowls to two silent beggars; a few feet further, two men
came down the steps towards him.

"Master Rhenford," Earl Uldericus called again in a
stern voice. "Whence this headlong rush?"

Going to see your wife, Liam thought wildly, and then
he recognized the man with Uldericus.

"You're supposed to be with Oakham," he said ac-
cusingly.

"Have you seen him?" Cawood asked. "I attended
him at the bath for a while, but he never arrived."

For a long moment Liam simply stared, unable to
think. Then he managed to say: "How long did you
wait?"

"Long enough, in faith," Cawood said. "I gave him
up for lost only a few moments ago, and was on my
way to his house to rate him for his absentmindedness,
when I chanced on Earl Uldericus."

"Come inside, Master Rhenford," the earl said. "You
can tell me how the baron took my challenge, and then
we'll have a game."

Liam still could not think. Where had Oakham gone?
Had he decided not to go through with it? *What is that
idiot thinking?* He knew the two men were staring at
him, thinking him the idiot, with his jaw on the ground.

Pull yourself together, he demanded. A stray thought
came to him, and he started fumbling with his purse. "A
game—no. No, thank you. I have an appointment. But
I believe I owe you some money from yesterday evening." He started counting out coins with numb fingers.

"Come, you'll have a game with us, proper Generals,
and perhaps you can win it back."

Liam scarcely heard him. Why would Oakham miss

the appointment? He reached the right sum and handed it to Uldericus, who dropped it negligently into his own purse.

"Well," he said, "I wish all debtors paid so quickly. Oakham could learn something from you, Master Rhenford."

Oakham, yes. Oakham. Where is he? His words to Grantaire came back to him: *I am trying to find a man who cuts throats for fun.* Oakham had said something on the way to the Staple, something about it not necessarily being difficult to cut a throat—that anyone might do it. He had been trying to dissuade Liam from completely discounting Cimber Furseus as a suspect.

"Master Rhenford?" Cawood sounded cautiously concerned. "Are you ill?"

Liam mouthed the words to himself: *I never told him the beggar's throat was cut.* He gulped, trying to bring some moisture to his arid mouth.

"Does he owe you money?"

"I beg your pardon?" Uldericus sounded offended.

Damn that, Liam thought. "Money!" he snapped. "Does he owe you money?"

"I don't think—" the earl began, stiffening dangerously.

"How much?" He was shouting.

"Master Rhenford!" Cawood exclaimed, sounding shocked.

Uldericus's voice was a low growl. "I will not be spoken to in that tone."

Liam uttered a strangled curse, whirled, and started running to Coeccias's house.

CHAPTER 15

LIAM RAN, HIS cloak spread behind him like wings, wanting to stop, to pound his chest, to kick something, to beat his head against a wall. He settled for pounding his feet, slamming them down on the cobbles with unnecessary force. A mad rage had settled into his head, a whirlwind of curses and evil desires. He wanted to pound Oakham, to kick the man, to beat *his* head against a wall.

He watched me! He put himself at my side! That bastard!

Coeccias's house was just a street away, and he slowed his pace, stopped, bending over and groaning out his frustration. He could not go in just yet. He stood straight and started pacing. His run in the cold had burned his lungs ragged, but he hardly noticed. A hot flush suffused his face.

All that time he watched me, and knew where I was going. He told me not to suspect Quetivel, and knew that I would. And then he let me, oh so unwillingly. Gods!

Liam's anger did not cool, but he gained control of it. He began to think clearly.

Oakham had been brilliant. Brilliant! There was no other word for it. He had doled out damaging information about his friends, always at just the right moment, always with just the right degree of reluctance—Uldericus's attempt to buy the Jewel, his wife's promise, Quetivel's gambling losses. Cawood's debts he had not revealed, but he must have known of them, and he must have known they would be mentioned at the Staple. The loss of a fortune would not go unremarked.

Gods, Liam thought, gritting his teeth. *How he must have laughed!* A muscle jumped over his eye, and he erased the thought, refusing it consideration. However much of a fool he had been, brooding now would not help him. He concentrated on Oakham.

There had to be debts, he knew. Uldericus had not said so, but he had not said no, and to Liam that was as damning as a full list of losses. Would it be gambling? Those stories he told about Quetivel—the money lost at horse races, at Pet Radday's, in the Red Chamber at Herione's—were those really his own stories?

The Oakhams' house belonged to Mistress Priscian. She could afford to have a live-in servant, but the Oakhams could not. He had borrowed money from Uldericus when they played cards.

An electric shudder ran through Liam. "He cheated!" he said aloud. Cheated—but not for himself. He had attacked and attacked, recklessly, carelessly, squandering his own forces and weakening everyone but Uldericus. And in each hand, the earl had come in at the end and split the pot.

Liam stopped that thought, too. There was no proof of that, and it was not to the point.

The point . . . the point reached through his anger, chilling it, leaving him aghast in the dark.

Oakham had the Jewel, he wanted money, and he knew all about Desiderius.

Fanuilh! he projected desperately. *Go to the Three Foxes! Go now!*

Yes, master. The answer, as calm and precise as any of the dragon's thoughts, went a long way towards keeping Liam from panic. He stopped pacing and took three deep breaths, squaring his shoulders. He knew where Oakham was going—was sure of it. That was not the point. The point was, what would he do about it?

Burrus had put a blanket on Diamond, Liam noticed, and he stopped on the doorstep, absently stroking the horse's nose. Then he squared his shoulders again and went in without knocking.

Coeccias and Grantaire stood by the hearth, cups in their hands, talking in low voices. Both looked up when he entered.

"Rhenford, what news?" The Aedile nodded in Grantaire's direction. "Mistress Grantaire tells me something about Baron Quetivel and that wizard of this afternoon. Is it true?"

Grantaire did not notice the incorrect title. "I had to explain," she said to Liam, as if she had revealed a secret and wanted forgiveness.

"Fine," Liam said briskly. "But Quetivel is not the problem. The problem is Oakham." As coherently as he could—new thoughts kept coming to him, half-remembered shreds of Oakham's conversation and behavior—he told what he thought. Spoken aloud, it sounded unconvincing to him, a mass of speculation, open to different interpretations. Uldericus had not actually said that Oakham owed him money; the hints and rumors Oakham had supplied him might not have been meant to be misleading; even the lord's comment about cut throats was ambiguous: could Liam be sure he had not mentioned it?

Liam knew it was true, though, felt it as deeply as he did the urgent need for immediate action. It made sense, more sense than anything else, and as he watched Coeccias and Grantaire digest the news, he felt his earlier rage rising again.

The only decent one of them, he sneered at himself. *How could I have thought that? One and all, a set of . . .* There was no word strong enough, and that insufficiency brought him back to the room, to the other two.

Grantaire was pensive, clearly not prepared to judge. She looked expectantly at the Aedile, who found a chair and sat heavily, expelling a long, whistling breath. He moved his head from side to side, but he was not denying Liam's argument, just trying to express his shock.

"Aye," he said at last, "aye. It makes sense."

"I am not sure I understand," Grantaire said hesitantly. "Why would he steal the Jewel? It is his, is it not?"

"No," Liam explained patiently. "It belongs to Mistress Priscian, to the Priscian family. I suppose it would eventually come down to him, through his wife—but he must have needed the money now. He talked about going to Torquay, said that the stress had been too much for him and his wife. He probably planned to sell it there—but I think now that he means to sell it to Desiderius." An unimportant thought strayed across his mind and was gone: *How many passages did he take for Torquay?* Liam was willing to bet there was only one.

"We must stop him, then," Grantaire announced. "Desiderius cannot have that Jewel."

"No," Coeccias said, drawing the word out. "No. It would not do." He stood and looked at Liam. "What would you do?"

"That depends." He frowned, not liking his own tentative plan but unable to think of another. "I think he has gone to Desiderius now. We'll know shortly—from your man or from Fanuilh. If he has, then we can try to arrest them."

Grantaire objected. "You won't find Desiderius easy to arrest."

"I know. If we can, we want to avoid confronting him. The real question, though, is whether Oakham has taken the Jewel with him or not. I would guess not."

"Not if he has any wit at all," Coeccias said. "He knows that this wizard knows the Jewel was stolen. He'll bargain. And if he does not have it with him, our arrest is wasted."

"Exactly. So we can wait until they part. When they do, we can take Oakham. For that, we should wait until he gets home, I think."

"And do what?" Grantaire wanted to know, a little lost in the back-and-forth between Liam and the Aedile.

"Confront him," Liam said. "I'll do that." He did not know just exactly how, but neither Coeccias nor Grantaire asked him. "And that will be that."

There was an uncomfortable silence, and finally Grantaire broached the topic no one wanted to address. "And what if he has given the Jewel to Desiderius already?"

Liam glanced significantly at the bundle of things from the trophy room. "Do you still think you can face him?"

She laughed, a harsh bark with no humor in it. "I can, but I do not want to."

"With any luck it won't come to that. I will go to him and explain that we have Oakham—which we will—and that we are sure he was unaware that he was sold stolen goods. I will give him back whatever he gave Oakham. Then, if he refuses, it will be up to you. But remember, he doesn't know you are in Southwark. You will be able to surprise him."

"There is that," she allowed; then, not as if she were troubled by the idea but rather as if she were seeking permission, she asked: "But you understand that I will have to kill him?"

"You had better," Liam said.

Coeccias said nothing, his face grim.

"What do we do now?"

"Wait," Liam told them, and took the chair next to the Aedile's.

Burrus had come with cups of some hot drink and, sensing the mood of the room, quickly withdrew. Liam held his cup absently, not drinking, staring at the floor between his feet.

What if he was wrong? What if Oakham had not gone to the Three Foxes? *Then the wait is for nothing,* he told himself, but he did not think it would be. He had no doubt where the lord was. There had been more than enough time between when Fanuilh had seen him leave his house and when Liam had ordered the dragon back to the inn. Oakham was there. The question was, what was he doing, and when would he leave?

It was an effort not to pester Fanuilh with questions, but Liam restrained himself, confident that his familiar, at least, would make no mistakes.

Burrus came back with a steaming pot to refill their cups. Coeccias alone had drunk his, but he waved the

pot away. The servant was going into the kitchen when
the thought came into Liam's head.

Lord Oakham is coming out of the Three Foxes.

Liam closed his eyes and mouthed a silent prayer of
thanks.

"Oakham is leaving the Three Foxes," he told the
others. Coeccias half rose from his seat, but Liam waved
him back down. "We will wait until he gets home."

Coeccias stood anyway. "I'm thinking of putting another man on the Three Foxes, and I needs must check
in at the barracks in any case. I'll return before he gets
there."

As he left, Liam projected: *Fanuilh, follow Lord Oakham home. Let me know the moment he arrives.*

Yes, master.

He held the thought in his mind. Why could he not
be more like Fanuilh? More logical, more competent.
More humorless. Perhaps he did not want to be completely like Fanuilh.

It was strange, how at ease he was. Ordinarily he
hated waiting more than anything else. Now, though, he
felt only a calm eagerness, if such a thing could exist.
He had mastered his anger, and was enjoying it in a
strange way. With a self-conscious laziness he rose and
strolled to the fire, rubbing his hands slowly before it.

Grantaire was sitting on a low stool by the hearth. She
turned her face up to him, and he was surprised to discover that she was scrutinizing him, an abstracted, assessing expression in her eyes.

"What?" He laughed a little, but it sounded nervous,
so he stopped.

"I am wondering what you will do when you see this
Oakham."

"Spank him soundly and send him right to bed,"
Liam replied. This time when he laughed, it sounded
normal to him. Grantaire shook her head impatiently.

"No. I wonder."

He was wondering too, but about something different.
Should I bring something? No. Oakham had used a
knife; a knife was not much, after all, and he would be

on his guard. He was sure the beggar had not been—
and the Werewolf had said Japer was nearly beside himself with fear. *Besides, I might kill him.*

That surprised him, and his eyebrows drew together
as he stared into the fire. *Would I?* He dismissed the
idea immediately. Wounded pride, no doubt, and there
was nothing to be gained from that. It would be much
more satisfying to see Oakham tried—and hanged. The
prospect of Oakham at the end of a rope gave him a
certain grim pleasure, but he dismissed it, too, a little
reluctantly. There was no guarantee of it, after all: Oakham was titled, and a beggar and a thief did not count
for much against that.

At that, who knew why he had killed them? Thieves
quarreled, Liam knew, and though the quarrels rarely
escalated into violence, Japer had been a hothead. And
the beggar—who knew? Oakham had laid himself open
to all sorts of threats.

Liam shook his head. Whatever came of that, there
was still the theft itself, and at the very least the lord
would be disgraced.

In a gust of cold air, Coeccias returned; the extra man
to watch the Three Foxes had been arranged. "And the
oddest little girl was waiting on you, Rhenford. Filthy
as a frozen midden—she's outside."

It was Mopsa, about as dirty as Coeccias had said,
patting Diamond's foreleg nervously. Liam squatted
down beside her, shivering—he had left his cloak inside.

"What are you doing here?"

"The Wolf sent me," she said, "and for that I'm
ruined!"

"What are you talking about?"

"I'm ruined!" she wailed. "If the whole Guard
doesn't know me by now, they will in the morning—
and the Addle himself!"

Liam had no time for this. "What does he want?"

"To know what y' have found," she said, sulking.
"And to say we're attending your results. It's beyond
me why he couldn't just wait—or why he couldn't send
someone else. Why me? And now they all know me!"

"Mopsa," Liam interrupted, "shut up. Go to the Werewolf and tell him I know who did it, and it's not the beggars." She was still moping, so he caught her by the shoulders. "This is important! Tell him it was not the beggars, and that I will have the man shortly. Can you remember that?"

"In course I can." She wrenched free from his grip. "Small lot you care, if I'm ruined! Some chanter! I can't work crowds now, do you see?"

He did see; he understood that she thought herself compromised. "I know—but there is nothing I can do about that. And you have to tell the Wolf what I said."

"Huh."

"And tell him I will come to him when I can, to explain. Will you do that?"

Mopsa scowled, barely mollified, and finally nodded. "I'll tell him," she muttered, and then burst out: "And what of my gift?"

Liam winced; he had forgotten. "You will get it," he promised, "but you must go to the Werewolf now."

She glared suspiciously at him for a moment—he strove to look trustworthy—and then she stalked off into the night without a word.

Liam shivered once, all over, and went back inside.

"That was my good authority," he told Coeccias, knowing that he might be compromising her even more. *I will make it up to her,* he promised himself. "We will be able to wrap that up tonight, too."

Before the Aedile could do more than nod, Fanuilh's thought came: *Lord Oakham has come home.*

A cold smile lit Liam's face. "Lord Oakham has returned home, and will see us now."

They stopped at the end of Duke Street. The Oakhams' house was just visible around the corner; a single candle burned in one of the first-floor windows.

"He's expecting me," Liam told the others. "He said he would leave a candle burning if he was still awake." In fact, he was surprised to see the signal; when they had parted earlier Oakham had given Liam the impression that he would have been happy never to see him again—and given the business the lord had presumably just transacted, the signal seemed doubly unlikely. Nonetheless, there it was, winking at him, shedding a yellow glow on the sill and the mullions, the edge of the light just barely illuminating the front door.

"Well," he said, rubbing his hands together, "there's nothing for it."

"Rhenford, this is wooden," Coeccias said, waving a shuttered lantern at the house. "Why don't we both go?"

"This will be trickish," Liam said, using the Aedile's word. "Count to ten thousand, and if I'm not out by then, come after me. I want him alone for a little while." *If I'm lucky, I may get to hit him—just once.*

He threw a smile at them and started across the street, fast enough that he only heard the Aedile begin to mutter something about having to stay out in the cold.

Jumping up the steps two at a time, he put his hand to the knocker, thought better of it, and rapped gently with his knuckles.

Oakham opened the door almost at once, a lantern raised above his head. His handsome face was pale and strained; he grabbed Liam's arm and pulled him through the doorway.

"Gods, Rhenford, y' are well come. Something passing strange has happened!"

Liam allowed himself to be pulled along a few steps without resisting, completely taken aback. This was not the greeting he had expected at all. They were halfway down the corridor before he dug in his heels and forced Oakham to stop.

"Come along!"

"What is it?" Apart from the lantern, the hall was dark; their shadows stretched behind them, grotesque monsters.

"The Jewel!" Oakham whispered. "It has returned! Come along!"

The lord tugged at him again, and Liam allowed himself to be led, out of the main hallway, down the white-plastered corridor towards the kitchen.

This was not right; this was not the way it was supposed to be at all. He stopped again, forcing Oakham to face him in the doorway of the kitchen.

"Oakham, where are we going?"

"The crypt! It's there!" He hurried into the kitchen alone, disappearing through the door to the cellar.

The light from the lantern faded almost immediately, and Liam had to hurry after or be left in the dark. He followed the light down the stairs, always just at its edge, hearing Oakham urge him to hurry, not to dawdle so.

A box crept out of the shadows and caught Liam's shin a shrewd blow; he stifled a curse and went on, to the end of the cellar, the entrance to the crypt vestibule.

"It's here!" Oakham was standing at the far end of the anteroom, one hand on the iron gate, the other holding his lantern. Another lantern burned somewhere beyond him, deep in the crypt.

Liam took two steps into the anteroom, then stopped, deeply regretting the weapon he had not brought. *Wasn't I going to think before I acted?* Still, he was on his guard, and Oakham had entered the house alone.

Two steps more brought him to Oakham's shoulder, and he gestured for the lord to precede him.

"Show the way," he said. Oakham nodded eagerly and walked into the room, holding his lantern high.

"It's amazing," he said, then turned around, a puzzled look on his face. "Aren't you coming?"

"Yes," Liam said softly, wary, his uncertainty growing every minute. He took three steps into the room, looked around. The second lantern whose light he had seen was perched on the central sarcophagus. Oakham stood next to it, beckoning Liam on.

"It's here! It's where it's meant to be!" He was practically dancing with excitement, the lantern bobbing in his hand and throwing his shadow over the stone walls, the great bulks of the sarcophagi. Whistling in the narrow hallway from the balcony, a cold wind snaked into the room, coiling around Liam's ankles.

He went to Oakham, his eyes jumping around the room, his boots grating on the floor. His arms hung loose and ready at his sides, fists clenched.

"Rhenford! Come along," the other man said, exasperation drawing out his words.

Liam came, stopping at the edge of the bay that held Eirenaeus's tomb, uncomfortably aware of the shadowed recess at his back, the thick blackness that filled the other bays. Oakham stepped back, holding the lantern higher.

"Look," he commanded, nodding his head towards the bay.

For a long second Liam stared at him, trying to puzzle out this strange behavior, trying to figure out what was going on. He could not; slowly, unwillingly, he turned to look at Eirenaeus's coffin.

Movement flickered in the corner of his eye—Oakham's free hand darting to his waist—and Liam jumped back with a loud shout, a burst of fear and energy exploding through his body. For a moment, his feet tangled beneath him, he was going to fall.

He caught at the wall, righted himself, lurched forward.

Oakham had shouted as well, skipped back a step, and now he stood tall, the lantern in one hand, a thin piece of wood clenched in the other. Liam froze, staring at the piece of wood, and distinctly heard the other man take two ragged breaths.

With his eyes locked on Liam, Oakham brought his thumb against the wood and pressed, bending the sliver over, almost double, and then it snapped.

For another long second, neither man moved; then Liam started cautiously advancing, knees bent in a fighting crouch. He remembered the broken mace head from the first Priscian's effigy, and spared a glance. It was no longer there.

No matter, he thought, and his lips twisted in a small smile of anticipation. Whatever the stick had meant, it would not stop him from taking Oakham.

"Stay where you are," the lord commanded, holding out a hand, palm out. "Not one more step."

Liam let his lips part, his smile widening. He flexed his hands.

Master! Fanuilh was in his head. *There is magic down the hill.*

He froze again, cocking his head. *What—*

The thought was only partially formed when he saw the shimmer, an insubstantial gleam, like light reflecting from a spiderweb. He blinked, and Desiderius was there, standing at the far end of the first Priscian's sarcophagus. His arms were thrust out, fists clenched, his face in shadow.

"Take him!" Oakham shouted.

A trap, Liam thought, dazed, terrible realization sapping the strength from his knees. *They set a trap for me!*

"It is not so easy," Desiderius snapped, and then, almost hesitantly, he opened his fists, flicking his fingers in Liam's direction.

A visible wind sprang from his fingertips, mottled white ribbons of cloud that melded together and barreled at Liam, wrapping his legs, his waist, his shoulders. He was encased in the ribbons; they flowed ceaselessly from his toes to his shoulders. He pushed against them, but it was like being wrapped in a wet carpet. He could twist a little, and wiggle his fingers, but nothing else.

Master, there is magic with you now!

"I know," he whispered, staring fearfully at the wizard. Desiderius let his arms drop, staring back, a curious expression on his face. After a moment, a happy smile split his piebald face, a flash of white teeth in the unnatural purple.

"You really aren't a wizard! You really aren't!"

"Kill him!" Oakham shouted.

Desiderius held up a single, commanding finger. "A moment. He isn't a wizard!" He put his fists on his hips, savoring the words, an ugly pleasure sliding across his face.

Master—

FANUILH! Liam interrupted the dragon's thought,

obliterating it in his head with his own thought. *GET COECCIAS! GET COECCIAS!*

"Kill him!" Oakham repeated. "The thief said he was a wizard!"

Liam licked his lips and fixed his eyes on Desiderius. "I told you I wasn't a wizard."

"Oh yes, yes, you did," the wizard agreed with a chuckle. "Sometimes I am too clever by half."

"But the thief said—" Oakham began, and Liam cut him off with a snarl:

"Is that why you killed him?"

"He wanted to give the Jewel back!" The lord came forward till he was right next to Liam, peering intently into his face. "He said you were a wizard, that you could see men's souls."

"Which he clearly cannot," Desiderius said, enjoying himself immensely. "I would have thought Mage Tanaquil could do better."

Deliberately casual, Liam cursed him, in no uncertain terms, and then prayed: *Let them get here soon.*

"This is interesting," Desiderius said, his smile gone. "I wonder, now. I did not believe you were not a wizard, but I did believe you had not seen Grantaire. Could I have been wrong both times?" He gave a gesture, and the ribbons of cloud tightened suddenly, crushing Liam's arms to his side and grinding his knees together. "Could I?"

Liam gave a startled cry, but the pain was negligible, only a hint.

Over the wizard's shoulder, he imagined he saw a shadow in the hallway to the balcony.

He screamed then, as loud as he could, making it last as long as he could. Desiderius's face twisted in an angry grimace, and Oakham jumped forward, clamping his fingers over Liam's mouth. Liam bit down as hard as he could, catching a fold of flesh in his teeth. He spat it out and screamed again, as if he were being murdered. Oakham drew his arm back and punched him hard on the side of the head.

His head snapped to one side. Where was Fanuilh?

Squirming sparks of gold swam in his vision, and suddenly Oakham was gone from his field of vision, and he could see one of the sparks, glowing in the middle of Desiderius's chest. The wizard was staring down at the glowing mote, his cupped hands framing it. He looked up from the spark, straight at Liam.

"You—" The word was the beginning of an accusation, but he did not finish it.

Other sparks appeared, on his legs and shoulders, on his hands. He opened his mouth to speak again, and there were sparks on his tongue, sparks everywhere. He was like a congregation of fireflies, and then he was a solid mass of glowing gold, back arched in pain but silent except for a low crackling sound.

The mottled ribbons faded to nothing, and Liam stumbled, suddenly free. He spun from the molten mass that was the wizard, and saw Oakham pressed back against the far wall, eyes wide in horror.

Liam did not see the sparks brighten suddenly, and then collapse like a broken log. He did not see the cinders float to the ground and go out, leaving only a thin scattering of ash.

He only hit Oakham once—but it was enough.

CHAPTER 16

THE CRYPT FILLED up quickly: Liam's screaming woke both houses. Mistress Priscian arrived first, stern and tight-lipped, Haellus's incredulous face peeping over her shoulder. Quetivel came in a moment later from the opposite entrance, propelled from behind by Lady Oakham. Catching sight of her husband lying at Liam's feet, she shoved both Quetivel and Coeccias aside and bolted across the room, oblivious to Grantaire, who was stirring all that remained of Desiderius with the toe of her boot.

With a wild cry, Lady Oakham threw herself down beside her husband and began stroking his forehead and chafing his hands.

"They've killed you!" she wailed, over and over again, with minor variations.

Just before her spectacular entrance, Liam had made sure the man was still breathing—in reeling from Liam's punch, Oakham had managed to clip his head against the wall—and now he turned away and met Mistress Priscian's inquisitorial eye. With a nod at Lady Oakham, he moved her aunt back into the antechamber. Haellus disappeared into the cellar, and Coeccias joined them.

"This all has some meaning, I'm sure," Mistress Priscian said, her head held high. She was wearing a nightdress, and her unbound hair fell in gray strips down her back, but she still reminded Liam of his university master.

"It does," he assured her. "I wish it could have been done in a more discreet manner, but the Aedile and I have to arrest Lord Oakham for the theft of the Jewel."

248

She turned to Coeccias, seeking confirmation. He looked extraordinarily uncomfortable, but he nodded and managed to meet her eyes.

"Aye, it's true. We'll need to clap him in."

She nodded thoughtfully. "You have proof?" It was not a challenge, only a request for information. Coeccias directed the question to Liam.

"He admitted it."

"I see. It is very strange, but not altogether out of character. Very well—arrest him. I will see to my niece."

This caught both men unawares; Liam had expected some sort of protest. Evidently, Coeccias had too: "Y' are sure? I mean, you could extend him the Rights of the Town—he's a relation—"

"I will do no such thing," she interrupted sternly. "Please remove him presently." She swept past them, back into the crypt.

They drifted after her, sharing a look of surprise, and found her kneeling by her niece, holding her firmly by the shoulders.

"Come along, Duessa. The gentlemen have some business with Lord Oakham."

"Look on him," the young woman wailed. Oakham's eyes fluttered weakly, and he mumbled something.

"He will be fine," Mistress Priscian said. "Now come with me. Y' are overexcited." She rose, drawing her niece, suddenly compliant, with her, and steered the young woman towards the door.

"What will they do with him?" Duessa asked.

"Hush, child," Mistress Priscian counseled, and they were gone.

Coeccias looked embarrassed, but Liam, strangely, felt nothing but satisfaction. He knew he should feel sorry for Lady Oakham, but he simply could not bring himself to do so. He motioned to the Aedile, and between them they brought Oakham to his feet. The lord shook his head groggily, as unresisting as his wife, and they started helping him to the far end of the crypt.

Suddenly Quetivel was before them, trying to sound firm but licking his lips nervously.

"Now, what is this all about?"

His bandages were askew, showing the stubble of his shaven scalp in places, and Liam fought down an urge to laugh—not just at the ridiculous-looking baron, but at everything. The side of his head throbbed where he had been hit, and his limbs felt hollow, scoured out by fear and nervous energy, but it was done. *Done!*

"Lord Oakham is under arrest for the theft of the Priscian Jewel," he said. "And for two murders."

"As well as attempting the life of one of the Duke's officers," Coeccias added. "I think perhaps you might go with Mistress Priscian, my lord. Lady Oakham will be sorely distressed." His tone was hard, indicating that the most important thing was that Quetivel get out of their way.

Licking his lips again, Quetivel shot a glance at Oakham, lolling drunkenly between Liam and Coeccias, then hurried after the two women.

Liam and Coeccias moved Oakham along at a brisk pace, with Grantaire walking behind, Fanuilh on her shoulder and a lantern in one hand.

The dragon had alerted them, Grantaire told Liam, dropping out of the sky onto the street in front of them. When they did not take its meaning quick enough, it flew behind them and nipped the Aedile, which had induced them to enter the house.

"By then, though, my cat had told me about magic in the house," Grantaire explained, "so we were somewhat prepared."

"Somewhat," the Aedile grumbled.

You bit Coeccias? Liam projected.

He would not move. I did not draw blood.

"He is very sorry," Liam told his friend, privately amused. "He won't do it again."

Coeccias grunted sourly. "It likes me not that we did not guess their purpose. That could have been dangerous."

"Could have been?"

"Not a simple spell," Grantaire mused. "Matter transferral is never easy. He must have guessed we were watching him."

"Wait," Liam protested, remembering the way the ribbons of cloud had tightened, "*could* have been dangerous? *Could?*"

"There is still the Jewel," Grantaire reminded them, ignoring Liam. "We must find it."

"He hasn't got it with him," Liam said. He had checked Oakham's pockets along with his breathing.

"But he'll know," Coeccias said. "I doubt me he'd already given it to the wizard, but if he has, we can search the Three Foxes. Unless I miss my guess, though, it'll be somewhere in the house."

This satisfied Grantaire, and they walked down Duke Street in silence. As they went further down the hill, they began to pass people, small parties and occasional individuals, many masked, many drunk. After one particularly sodden youth tried to pet Fanuilh, Liam suggested that the dragon make itself less conspicuous—which it did by taking flight from Grantaire's shoulder in full view of a wagonload of drunken farmers.

Watching their panicked faces, he sent an inadequately ironic thought after the dragon: *You have just made this their most memorable Banquet ever.*

Fanuilh did not deign to respond.

With his familiar gone, Liam realized that they blended in quite well with the growing crowds—just another group laden with a drunk. Oakham began to come around as they entered the square, getting his feet under himself and taking a few stumbling steps.

Holidaymakers seemed to fill the square, but they were loosely packed, the cobbles covered and uncovered in swirls and eddies of laughing, singing people. They plowed easily through, a little confused by the sounds and the constant shifting movement, bumped and jostled from time to time; a drunk in jester's motley erupted into raucous greetings when he saw them, then quickly subsided when he recognized the Aedile's bearded face, and ducked into a concealing group.

They washed up on the steps of the barracks, where a frantic guard leapt down on them.

"Aedile Coeccias, there's something," he panted, "something—something!"

Coeccias rolled his eyes. "Aye, aye, Taenus, in a moment. Let us get this in."

The man balked, trying to stammer out his message, but Coeccias cut him short.

"Let us get this in," he repeated, bulling forward, dragging Oakham and Liam with him. The guard jumped out of the way. "I'll talk with the Sergeant of the Night."

The guard followed them up the steps, still stammering. "But the Sergeant's not there, Aedile Coeccias, for that he's gone to this, this thing!"

Liam pitied the poor man, trying to get his meaning across to the Aedile's unresponsive back, but Oakham had begun to stir and protest, dragging his feet a little, and he wanted the lord behind bars as soon as possible.

The barracks was almost empty, with an air of having been hastily abandoned—stools were overturned, and a poker lay half in and half out of one hearth, its tip beginning to glow. Mopsa stood at the liquor barrel in the center of the room, sniffing cautiously at the contents of a tin cup.

"Away from there!" Coeccias roared; the girl dropped the cup and skipped backward, a defiant sneer quickly replacing her look of drop-jawed surprise. "Taenus! Can't you even keep a child out of a barrel?"

"Come on," Liam said, wondering what had possessed the apprentice thief to return to the barracks. "Let's get him in a cell, and then you can find out what is going on."

He had never seen more of the barracks than the main room; a single heavy door in the rear wall led to the cells, he knew, but he had never been there. At Coeccias's command, Taenus found a ring of keys and opened the door, fretting and fumbling, and then ran ahead of them to find an empty cell.

The door opened on the middle of a long corridor, the far wall of which was lined with bays in what was, to Liam at least, an eerie echo of the Priscian crypt. The bays were barred off, and there were far more of them—eight that he could see, and a staircase at the right-hand end of the corridor might lead to more—but they were almost exactly the same size, and in the uneven glare of a pair of fitful torches, they made him shudder.

The three nearest the door were full, and their occupants erupted into drunken shouting at Taenus's entrance. In one, four masked young men began serenading the guard with a filthy version of a Banquet carol; they broke off when Grantaire entered, and one of them offered her a slurred apology and attempted a low bow, which ended with his head clanging against the bars.

Grantaire pursed her lips and suggested a cell farther away.

They eventually settled Oakham in the cell closest to the stairs, letting him slide to the ground in a graceless huddle. For a moment they all stared at him: Coeccias with a satisfied nod, Grantaire with an air of impatience, as if he were secondary to the actual recovery of the Jewel, and Liam with a faint sense of wonder. With his hands flopping ineffectually at his hair and his legs sprawled out before him, Oakham cut a pathetic figure, and Liam found it unbelievable that he could have stolen the Jewel, and then killed two men and kept up a masterful two-day charade to keep it.

And let's not forget that he tried to kill you, he reminded himself. That, too, was unbelievable. *How much did he take off the price of the Jewel to get Desiderius to do that? Or did he just throw it in for free?*

He clapped his hands, assuming an attitude of briskness to block out the thought. "We will need some water, I think."

"Aedile Coeccias," Taenus began desperately. "This thing . . ."

Coeccias turned to him wearily. "Aye, aye, I'm with

you. Rhenford, you'll do this?'' He pointed at Oakham.
''Search out the Jewel? Master Taenus'll burst if I do
not hear him out. I'll join you in a minute. Now, Master
Taenus, unburden yourself.'' He started out of the cell.

The guard's voice was quickly lost in a renewed burst
of song from the young men's cell, and Liam offered
Grantaire a shrug.

''I imagine they must be busy all throughout the Banquet.''

She nodded at Oakham. ''I think you hit him too
hard.'' The lord was rocking his head back and forth
now, cradling it in his hands.

''Not hard enough,'' Liam corrected her. ''A little water will bring him around.'' His conscience stirred a little, though: it had been an unfair punch. ''I'll get some.''
He left the cell and went back down the corridor, ignoring the rowdy men in the middle cells.

Mopsa was back at the liquor barrel, sipping from the
cup. Liam hurried over and took the cup away. ''What
are you doing? And what are you doing here?''

''What's it to you?'' she sneered. ''If I'm ruined,
and'll never chant again . . .''

''Well, why did you come? They would never have
thought twice about you!''

''I didn't mean to come,'' she whined, ''not the first
time. I was just attending you, out of the way, quiet, and
that damned guard caught my eye and demanded my
business! Well, I had to tell him, didn't I? And when
they heard it was you I was laying for, it was 'Quaestor
Rhenford this' and 'Quaestor Rhenford that,' and nothing would do but that I wait inside by the fire, and the
Addle—the Addle himself!—pats me on the head!'' Her
shoulders slumped, and she looked truly miserable.
''And for that I'm ruined!''

Liam raised his hands, helpless. ''Mopsa, I am sorry.
The Werewolf should never have sent you—''

''Too right,'' she muttered.

''—but why did you come back?''

She spat on the floor. ''The Wolf made me. For that
he says he must see you, tonight.''

Liam shook his head. "I cannot. Tell him I will come when I can—sometime tomorrow. Meet me at the Arcade tomorrow, at noon. I will bring you your gift." When this did not cheer her up, he started ushering her to the door. "Now go—and keep a low profile for a while. The guards will forget you soon enough." He believed it, almost, and she let him steer her out the door.

Taenus was standing on the steps, a halberd in his hand, watching the milling crowds in the square. He gave Mopsa only the briefest of glances.

"Where's the Aedile?" Liam asked, as much to find out as to distract the other man from Mopsa's forlorn departure.

"Gone to see," the guard said. "It's a murther!" The southern slur irritated Liam.

"A mur-der, eh?" He deliberately split the word, emphasizing the "d." "Will he be back soon?"

Taenus shook his head emphatically. He was young, hardly more than sixteen. "I doubt it, Quaestor. The Sergeant said it was most frightful."

Liam grunted sourly and went back inside. It was not his business, though it would not surprise him if Coeccias tried to make it that. *I'm finished,* he told himself. It had been a long two days.

There was no water to be found in the main room, and he guessed it was probably kept in the cellar. He was still holding the cup of liquor Mopsa had been drinking. With a shrug, he went back to the cells.

A very long two days, he thought. He was tired, but the tension he had felt earlier was gone. Walking down the cell corridor with the cup in his hand, he felt quiet, walled off from the shouts and songs, quite alone. There were only a few things left to do.

Grantaire was standing over Oakham, arms folded, listening. The lord, his eyes clear and his head bent back to look up at her, was saying something about his study. Liam paused at the entrance.

". . . a tapestry. It's behind that."

The wizard nodded curtly.

"There was no water," Liam said, as if he had just returned. "But it looks as if he doesn't need it."

"I woke him," she said with a shrug. "He says the Jewel is in his study, behind a tapestry. Do you know where that is?"

Liam glanced back and forth between the two. Oakham was staring fixedly at the wizard, his mouth working soundlessly. "What did you do to him?"

She looked annoyed. "Nothing—I just woke him up, and cleared his head for him."

"Hm." He squatted by the lord's side and held out the cup.

"Perhaps he is remembering Desiderius," Grantaire suggested.

Oakham's hands trembled around the cup, but he managed to raise it to his lips without spilling any. He sipped cautiously, his eyes now roving between Grantaire and Liam.

"Can we get the Jewel now?"

"In a moment, in a moment. I want to ask him some things." He ignored Grantaire's exasperated sigh and focused on Oakham. "If Desiderius hadn't been here, what were you going to do with it?"

A spasm of anger flashed across the lord's face. He looked up at Liam and cursed him in a low whisper, then glanced fearfully at Grantaire as if awaiting her reaction.

Liam sucked on his teeth for a moment. "All right. It will all come out in the end."

"Can we go now?"

"Yes." He stood. "Good night, Lord Oakham." Oakham did not respond, only let his head sink down onto his chest. Liam motioned for Grantaire to precede him out.

The key was still in the lock, and as he closed and locked the cell, Liam realized that he had no idea what came next. Returning the Jewel, obviously, but what about Oakham? Would there be a trial? Would he have to confess, or would Liam's word be enough? The Jewel itself would be damning evidence, but then there were the murders, for which he had no physical proof.

He walked slowly down the cell corridor, oblivious to the racket and Grantaire's impatient stare. There were judges in Southwark—he had heard Coeccias name one or two of them—but he did not know how they worked. The Duke's Courts were next door, but he had never seen a trial there; he had only visited the first floor and the basement, which were taken up with administrative offices and a place called the morgue, where unclaimed bodies were stored, under the supervision of a witch named Mother Japh.

Justice in the Midlands was a rough sort of thing; his father had held "court" whenever and wherever necessary—in Rhenford Keep, in a barn, in a field. Issues were brought before him, and he simply decided. That could not be the case in Southwark, Liam knew. The Duke was too far away, and the duchy was too large. Hence the judges Coeccias had mentioned—but he still had no idea how the process worked.

Grantaire made another impatient noise, waiting for him at the door to the main room. "Come along, Rhenford! I won't rest easy until that thing is safely locked away!"

Her anxiety puzzled him, but he quickened his step anyway, pulling the door closed behind him and locking it hastily. "Who do you think is going to take it?" He nodded at the locked door. "Oakham is back there, and Desiderius is dead, and we are the only people who know where it's hidden."

She scowled, but did not answer.

"Exactly," Liam said, as if her silence were an admission. "No one. But we will go anyway—because we should restore it to Mistress Priscian. All right?"

"Whyever, Rhenford, as long as we see it safely locked away." She went to the door and out.

Liam rolled his eyes, wondering at her insistence. *Why is she so nervous about this?* And then he thought about Desiderius's end—had she winced when he mentioned that the wizard was dead? That could well be it: he had known only a few people who could kill and think nothing of it. *And I didn't like any of them.*

So it was a way of coping, he decided, like a soldier he had known once who, after every encounter, spent hours cleaning himself, his weapons, his armor—all of his equipment, even things he had not taken into battle. It had been a harmless mania. *We'll lock the Jewel in the crypt, and then get some sleep, and she will feel fine in the morning.*

And all he would have to do was buy Mopsa a gift and talk to the Werewolf. Both ideas bothered him; he knew he should have arranged to see the thief that night, but he was just too tired, too fed up with all the things he had to do. *My word ought to be good enough,* he thought. *He doesn't need to see me in person.*

As for Mopsa, it would have to be a large gift. It was not exactly his fault that she had been seen by the guards—the Werewolf should never have sent her to the barracks—and he really did not think it would make much of a difference, as long as she was careful. But she was taking it very hard, and he felt bad for her.

"A very large gift," he said, shook his head, and went outside.

The crowd in the square was thinning; it was growing late, and the revelers had begun to break up.

Liam took a deep breath, enjoying it, reveling in the knowledge that he was done. *Tomorrow night I'll be out there,* he promised himself, eyeing a group of young women, half-masked, kicking their legs high in a ragged dance just in front of Herlekin's. A cheering, clapping crowd had gathered around them. *Right in front.*

Then Grantaire called his name from the bottom of the steps.

"Coming, coming," he said, and joined her.

"Rhenford, can't I make you see that this is important?"

"No," he said, grinning. He took her arm and started across the square. She started to pull away, then stopped and let her arm hang limply in his, muttering something he did not catch.

They had only gone a few steps before the crowd parted and a furious Coeccias appeared before them, flanked by two guards.

"Rhenford!" he barked. "We've a problem."

"What?" Liam snapped back, letting go of Grantaire's arm. The Aedile's tone annoyed him.

"Come with me," was all Coeccias would say, grabbing him by the shoulder.

Liam went, dragging his feet a little. *Haven't I done enough?* he grumbled to himself. Aloud, he said: "What is it?"

Coeccias pulled him close and hissed in his ear. "Three beggars, Rhenford, dead. Where's your good authority now?"

He jerked away in surprise. "Where?"

Grantaire thrust herself forward. "What is it?" she demanded.

"In the Point," Coeccias said, ignoring her. "Will you see?"

"Is it—was it thieves? Do you know?"

"Who else?" Coeccias growled, pushing Liam along by the shoulder.

Two more guards with lanterns marked the entrance to the alley, a narrow lane between the high, blank walls of two modest houses in the middle of the Point. They had walked in silence, the Aedile's grim and angry, Liam's fearful.

"In there," Coeccias said. "Take a lantern." Liam could see a spill of light farther down the alley, but he did as his friend said, taking the lantern the guard held out to him. Then he closed his eyes briefly, shook his head, and started in.

Behind him, he heard Coeccias begin to speak, and Grantaire cut him off.

"I should think not," she said, and a moment later she was behind Liam, almost on his heels, one hand tentatively holding his elbow for guidance.

A wind Liam had not really noticed cut off as they moved down the alley, the walls rising around them, enclosing them; it felt almost perceptibly warmer, though he could still see his breath. They came to a bend, a jog where the first alley twisted and expanded to meet another alley coming from the far street, where the light was.

It was a ghoulish scene: an old woman shrouded in black, a lantern held high above her head, bending to examine the shattered corpses, three of them, sprawled around the little space like discarded dolls in a toybox. The blood that splashed the walls glistened black in the lantern light, and Liam stopped, hoping he had not walked too far. The men had not been dead long; the blood had not even begun to freeze.

The old woman looked up at their approach.

"Good evening, Liam Rhenford," she said, and he recognized her.

"And to you, Mother Japh," he answered. They both let their eyes drift to the wreckage around them, mutually acknowledging the horror of the scene.

"See you," Coeccias said from just behind him, and Liam could hear the frustration in his voice, a thin layer just underneath the anger. "Three of them."

"I see," Liam said, meaning to say more but unable to think. He knew what the Aedile was thinking, and was thinking it himself: that the Werewolf had done this, despite his promise. From their clothes, the men were clearly beggars, and what had drawn them to the little alley—the way it cut off the wind, the two entrances— had made it an easy place for an ambush.

So, Liam thought, squatting carefully, bunching his cloak up to keep it off the ground, *this is my fault. Japer was not, but this . . .*

He heard Grantaire ask, "You know who did this?" and Coeccias replied, a terrible accusation: "Rhenford does."

He could tell it had been brutal, the way the blood had splashed, the terrible wounds. The man nearest him was lying propped against the wall, as if he had been thrown there, and most of his jaw was missing. The second's arm hung at his side, bone showing at shoulder and elbow; he lay face down, a deep indentation at the back of his head mostly covered by matted hair. Mother Japh was between him and the third man, but an odd thought had occurred to Liam.

"Did anyone see it? Or hear anything?" He rose, stepping over the first two men and joining Mother Japh by the third. She was shaking her head, clucking sadly.

"No," Coeccias answered shortly; Liam heard the unspoken addition, that it did not matter, since they both knew who had done it. Then the Aedile did add something: "They used clubs."

Liam shook his head, wondering about his odd thought. "I don't think so." He closed his eyes, trying to remember, picturing the blood-soaked aftermath of a battle, and a surgeon taking him through the tent where the wounded groaned and screamed, or sometimes lay silent. The surgeon pointing out wounds, telling what had made each and how he would treat it.

The third man's face had been battered unrecognizable.

"It looks like maces, or ball-and-chains. Morning stars. Why would they use those?" He had addressed the question to himself; Coeccias grunted, but Mother Japh touched Liam lightly on the arm. They had met a few times; he liked her, and believed she liked him. *Of course, she doesn't know this is my fault.*

She frowned quizzically up at him. "How can you know that?"

"The wounds, the . . . holes. They are too precise, too small. The spikes have cut through the skin, as well. Clubs don't mangle like that." He pointed at the third man, the missing face.

"Maces, morning stars or three-masted caravels," Coeccias said with disgust, "the how does not merit attention. It is the who—and where to find them."

Liam ignored the Aedile for the moment, frowning down at the third man without really seeing him. He had thought about a mace earlier, had wanted one. "Pris-

cian's,'' he muttered, and remembered the broken piece
of statuary. *So?* he asked himself; he could think of no
reason why it would be important. *Unless Mistress Priscian is using it to massacre beggars.* The sarcasm tasted
sour; there was nothing funny in the alley.

"These are just like the other," Mother Japh said to
Coeccias, and Liam turned fast enough to see the Aedile
nod.

"Aye—vicious."

"What other?" Liam asked, and then answered his
own question: "The beggar from the other night." A
dim spark of hope flashed in a corner of his mind. "It
was the same as this?"

"The wounds, aye," said Mother Japh, clucking
again. "Terrible things. And you know who did this?"

"No," Liam said, straightening up and facing the Aedile. "No, I do not. Not if it is the same as that other
one." The Werewolf said he had taken no action after
the beggar was killed, and Liam believed him. *And he
still hasn't done anything.*

Coeccias exploded. "That's ridiculous!" he shouted.
"You know whose work this is—and y' are going to
find them, and bring them to me!"

"Coeccias, listen: I don't think it's them. They promised—and they know we have caught the man. I sent
them a message hours ago." Which was not quite true,
but close enough.

The Aedile glared, restraining himself, his whole body
quivering, and then he turned on his heel and stomped
away down the alley through which they had entered.
Grantaire stepped forward to Liam.

"You do not know who did this?"

"No," he said, confident now. Little things occurred
to him: the thieves would only have killed one man, and
Mopsa's words about how they were "attending his results." *And they would never use maces—how would
you hide a mace? Or climb across rooftops with it in
the dark?*

So . . . who did this? He looked around the little space,
at the slaughter. It was like a frozen abattoir.

Grantaire took a deep breath with a hitch in the middle of it. "You said something earlier, about maces. Something I did not catch. What was it?"

He looked blankly at her, shaking his head.

"It sounded like 'Priscian,' " she said.

"Oh, that." He waved it away. "I was thinking of maces. There was one in the Priscian crypt."

"I didn't see it," she said anxiously. "Where was it?"

"It's gone. Mistress Priscian pointed it out to us when she first showed us the crypt. It was part of one of the sarcophagi, but it was broken. She must have taken it." He realized that she was not merely curious, that she was hugging herself; he poked her shoulder. "You are thinking of something. What is it?" How many times had Coeccias asked him that?

She spoke too quickly, avoiding his eyes. "Nothing, nothing. Listen, Rhenford—you stay here. I'm going to get the Jewel and return it." Before he could say anything she was running down the alley. He stumbled after.

"Wait!" He slipped, horribly aware of what he had slipped on, almost fell, and recovered by windmilling his arms wildly. The lantern swung in wide arcs, pieces of slaughter swinging in and out of the light.

CHAPTER 17

WHEN LIAM WAS steady, he decided it was too late to go after Grantaire—and he did not think Coeccias would let him go anyway. He heard the Aedile coming down the alley.

"Truth," the big man said, "what brought her to such a hurry?"

"I don't know," Liam replied, puzzled by her sudden departure. It was not the mania he had imagined in the barracks; her questions had not been prompted by some desire to avoid thinking of what she had done to Desiderius. She was worried about something, and remembering himself what she had done to the wizard, he could not imagine anything that would worry her.

It had to do with the Jewel, and the news of the missing piece of statuary had set her off. If Desiderius had not been able to match her, what was she afraid of? He was the only wizard in the city, and he was dead. *And if she's going to be afraid of dead wizards, why not add Tarquin and Eirenaeus. . . .*

The name hung in his mind, taking on substance and weight like one of Fanuilh's thoughts.

"Ridiculous," he said aloud, but the name would not dissipate in his head, his other thoughts trying to roll around it.

Tarquin came back from the dead, but he was brought back, brought back by the gods. It's ridiculous. How could he come back? And why now?

The Jewel had been moved, the Jewel that sealed his tomb, but Liam refused to accept that. It was gone for a week; why would he have come out tonight? The name disappeared as he built this strange train of thought, piecing it together as he went. *He didn't come out tonight, he came out two nights ago, and killed the beggar. He would need spirit after those centuries in the dark; so he killed the beggar. And the two children, the maskers that had disappeared, what about them?*

Liam frowned, shaking his head. Just because Grantaire took it seriously was no reason for him to; she was jittery because she had killed a man, and he could think it through clearly.

She was a wizard, though, and she had read Eirenaeus's book; she knew what he might be capable of.

He was tired suddenly, bone tired, exhausted, and thinking was too difficult for him. He turned to Mother Japh. She called herself a ghost witch; he knew there was a vast difference between wizardry and witchcraft, but he did not think that would change what had to be basic things.

"Do you know the difference between spirit and soul?"

She cocked her head at him, as if she had not heard him right and said, tentatively, "Yes. . . ."

There was a trick she had done once for him, proving to him that a body in her morgue belonged to a ghost then haunting Southwark. He reminded her of it. "You said the soul was gone, that it always was when there was a ghost." She nodded. "If the spirit had been taken, would the result be the same? I mean, if you did the same thing with these"—he swept his arm out, indicating the dead men around them—"would you be able to tell if they had any spirit?"

Her lips twitched while she considered the question. "It is possible," she said at last. "What you saw was the soul guttering; it has the form of a flame as a symbol, if you see. It is the soul breaking the last of its ties to the body, expending the last of the spirit. A ghost is a soul and spirit without the flesh; a ghost has no flame, for that the spirit and the soul have been bundled, tied together for some reason outside the flesh. So—aye, aye, no flame, no spirit, though it is the soul that interests us most.''

"Can you do it here? For them?''

"Rhenford,'' the Aedile said, "what are you thinking?''

Liam noticed that the anger had faded from his friend's voice, replaced by his usual wary curiosity, but he ignored it. He was trying to make himself think, to concentrate on the problem at hand—*The new problem,* he thought with weary disgust—and he knew that if he thought at all of Coeccias, it would be with anger of his own.

He repeated his question to Mother Japh, and the old woman shrugged.

"If you wish,'' she said, as if it did not matter to her in the least.

She held out her right hand and slowly opened the fingers wide; a small ball of pure blue flame rested on her palm, floating an inch above the skin. As she drew her slightly cupped fingers down, the circle expanded, stretching out to become a plane.

Liam had seen this before, in the morgue beneath the Duke's Courts, but he still held in his stomach and his breath when the shimmering blue broke around his waist, circling him and spreading beyond to Coeccias. He heard the Aedile gasp, and then the plane filled the little space, and it was like they were deep in a glowing blue well. He even noticed that there was a meniscus along the walls, where the blue light curled up slightly against the stone.

"This is not so easy,'' Mother Japh said, her lips twitching again, and then she brought her hand out from underneath the field of blue, turning it palm down and pressing, fingers still cupped.

In the morgue, the bodies were laid on stone slabs, all at the same height, and the shimmering plane had remained flat; it billowed now, as she pressed, like a sheet thrown out over a bed, drifting towards the ground. Soundlessly it settled, touching the ground at Liam's feet, shrouding the head of the first man, propped against the wall, folding and dipping to touch the mouths of the two others, face down and face up. It was like a landscape of blue, hillocks and valleys, and coming through it were the faces of the dead.

Nothing stirred; there should have been flames burning over the mouths of the dead men. There were none.

Mother Japh closed her hand, tucking her fingers into her palm, and the blue landscape shredded like mist. They were left blinking, the two lanterns suddenly insufficient. The ghost witch cleared her throat, looking expectantly at Liam.

"One, even two lacking might be, but all three—it's unnatural."

Liam nodded absently, his eyes fixed on the face of the first man, where the flame had failed to appear. *So it might be.* He played with that thought, repeating it in his head three times over. After the third time, he turned his head slowly from the corpse, blew out a long breath, and rubbed at his face.

"All right," he said to Coeccias. "I have to go to Oakham's. You should go back to the square, and try to find that girl—the one who brought me the message." He would find Grantaire and see if he had guessed correctly about what was worrying her, but he could not ignore the fact that he might be wrong, that the Werewolf and his men might be responsible. And if he was wrong, he would prefer to find out about it alone. "Find her if you can, and tell her I need to see her friend. Mother Japh, there should be two other beggars in the morgue—please check them as well."

"Think you I'll find the same?"

"Probably." He turned back to Coeccias. "I will come to the barracks as soon as possible. Find the girl if you can." Then he turned and started past Mother Japh, down the opposite alley, the one by which they had not entered.

"Rhenford—"

Liam called back, "I won't be long," and forced himself to a trot, the lantern tossing back and forth.

Better to be wrong alone, he thought.

• • •

Once out of the far alley, Liam slowed to a walk, feeling fatigue in every limb. He was complaining, too, silently, scowling wearily as he walked. Coeccias was not being fair, not fair at all. He could hardly be held responsible for the Werewolf's broken promise—if, indeed, he had broken his promise—but Coeccias had acted as if Liam had killed the beggars himself.

If he gets blamed for something, it's 'Oh, they tax me with everything,' and 'What am I supposed to do?' but when something might possibly be my fault, he jumps on it with both feet. And it's not even my responsibility! It's his city, not mine!

The alley gave out on a cross street just a short distance from Duke Street. Liam turned that way, heading up the Point, indulging his sense that he had been wronged, wallowing in self-justification. Tired as he was, long as his day had been, it felt good to tell himself that he did not have to do this. That he could have stayed home, that he could even go home, right now, but he would not, he would see it through.

He had almost reached End Street before doubts began to creep in—beginning with his usual reflection that Coeccias had so much to worry about, such a heavy load of responsibility—and by the time he stood before the Oakhams' house, he was shaking his head at his own complaints.

You would have been angry too, he told himself, and further knew that, as much as he wanted to, he could not go home just then. He had taken the responsibility on himself, however unwittingly, and knew that he would not be able to live with himself if he did not see it through.

No lights shone at the Oakhams', the windows black and lifeless. There was nothing frightening about it, just a house shut up for the night, but there was something that held him, staring at it. The cold pried at his cloak but he did not mind it, trying to figure out what it was that kept him there, looking at the blank facade.

And then he knew: it was the very normality of the house, the quiet respectability that fit in so nicely with the rest of the street. *Who would know?* he thought. *Who would walk by and say, 'Bad things have happened here'?* Liam had known places that you could not see without sensing the evil that had gone on within—black castles, ruins, temples devoted to hideous rites—and he had known places that gave that impression but belied it inside. Like the temple of Laomedon, an evil-looking building a few streets away in Temple's Court, behind whose high, foreboding walls the priests smiled cheerily and tended beautiful gardens.

The Oakhams' house, though, showed nothing; to Liam it was a smiling mask facing the street, with a bloody knife behind its back—and a mace, he imagined now, striped with gore.

He shook himself and trotted over to Mistress Priscian's, where a light was showing.

Haellus answered his knock, much disheveled and hardly his usual polite self.

"Master Rhenford," he said, as if he had been expecting Liam, "come—they're in the study." The servant practically ran up the stairs, Liam in tow, and began announcing Liam's arrival even before they reached the study.

Grantaire was sitting where she had earlier, the enormous folio open to her left and another, smaller book before her. Her finger traced her reading, darting up and down the pages; she read with impossible speed and complete concentration—she did not even look up when Liam came in. Mistress Priscian, though, standing by the door, turned anxiously to him.

"Oh, Master Rhenford, it likes me to see you here!"

"I'm sorry to disturb you so late," he began, but she went on, taking his arm and propelling him to Grantaire's side.

"It matters not. If what she says is true . . ." The voice of the older woman trailed off; she was unable to imagine the consequences.

"Well?" Liam asked the wizard. "Is it?"

She did not answer, holding up a hand for silence, her finger moving faster down the pages of the small book. It was a diary, Liam saw from over her shoulder, neatly written in fading ink. The pages crackled as she turned them; the binding was coming apart, and many of the pages were entirely loose. Grantaire handled them carefully, turning them over as if they were still attached.

The sound of her breathing reached Liam's ear; it came out between her working lips, matching the cadence of her finger as she read to herself. He tried to follow along, but she was hunched over the book and he could only catch glimpses of the page. He saw the name "Eirenaeus," and gave up; he had guessed correctly.

Right, he thought, taking a step back. She was worried about Eirenaeus, but was she right to be? And if she were right, what would that mean? He thought of asking Fanuilh, but he did not think the dragon would know; besides, Grantaire was stirring, closing the diary on her finger and reaching over to turn to the last pages of the large folio, then reopening the diary, as if checking the two against each other.

Whatever she had checked apparently was enough for her; she closed the diary with a snap and pushed it decisively away from her.

"Well?" Liam said anxiously. "Is it Eirenaeus?"

"It could be," she said, not at all surprised at his question. "I would have thought of it earlier if I had read all of his book." She tapped the folio, her lips twisting ruefully. "It is clear that the Jewel did not really work as he wanted it to. It allowed him to store his spirit, but it had to be 'primed'—his word—supplied with spirit from some other source, and even then he could only use a fraction of what went into it."

Liam was aware of Mistress Priscian standing at his elbow, listening to the wizard's explanation; he wondered briefly if she should hear it, but Grantaire continued without a pause, stroking the folio absently with her fingertips. It struck him that her recital was as much for herself as for him and Mistress Priscian, as if she was working it out aloud.

"He writes that the Jewel took spirit from him, draining him, and that the more he was exposed to it, the more it took. By the end, he had to feed the Jewel two or even three lives a week to get enough spirit just to live. The Jewel was a sort of parasite, taking all the spirit he stole and only returning a small amount of it; but because he had made it, and tuned it to himself, he could not destroy it without doing himself tremendous damage.'' She spoke with a calmness that was strange to Liam, as if she were describing nothing more serious than a recipe gone wrong.

"Grantaire," Liam interrupted, "I don't mean to be rude—but what does all this mean? Are you assuming that Eirenaeus is back from the dead, that he killed those beggars?"

She stood, shaking her head impatiently. "He is not back from the dead, Rhenford," she said, as if that should have been obvious. "He never died. Now come, let's deal with this."

Grantaire brought the diary with her, and a small sack that had apparently lain in her lap while she read. Mistress Priscian followed her without question, falling in behind her before Liam could begin to ask the many questions that sprang to mind. Foremost among them was just what the wizard thought she was going to do. He grabbed his lantern, still lit, and hurried after them.

She marched straight downstairs and into the kitchen, as if it were her own home. Mistress Priscian hurried to open the cellar door, producing a ring from a pocket of her dress and searching for the proper key. Liam took advantage of the pause to ask his question.

"Why, seal him up again," Grantaire said, irritatingly sure of herself. She held up the diary. "It is all here. His brother kept this. Eirenaeus feared the Jewel as much as he needed it—he kept it at a distance, in one of the family warehouses. The brother—''

''Dorstenius,'' Mistress Priscian supplied in a troubled whisper, gesturing to the open door. Grantaire took Liam's lantern and started down the steps, speaking over her shoulder to him.

''—The brother discovered that Eirenaeus was behind the murders, and used the Jewel to stop him. The closer the Jewel was, the weaker Eirenaeus grew, so the brother forced him into the sarcophagus and sealed it with the Jewel. Without a source of spirit, he was helpless, drained completely by the Jewel.''

They passed through the cellar, Liam feeling as he were being pulled along, barely keeping up, and quite sure that whatever Grantaire was doing was not safe.

''The Jewel is proof against him,'' she was saying, waiting by the door to the crypt while Mistress Priscian unlocked it. To Liam it sounded as if the keys jingled a great deal, and he knew her hands were shaking, though her back was to them. ''With it, we can force him back into his tomb.''

''Then we need the Jewel,'' Liam said, not wanting to go into the crypt again, his conviction growing that Grantaire was being careless.

''I have it,'' she responded, and swept through the open door into the antechamber. Liam hurried up behind her and put a hand on her shoulder. The gate before her was closed.

''Grantaire,'' he whispered, aware in a frightened way of the black crypt beyond the gate, ''this is not safe.''

''Don't be simple, Rhenford,'' she said, but he noticed that she was whispering. She noticed it herself and raised her voice. ''Mistress Priscian, if you will?''

''Wait,'' Liam said. ''Let's think a little bit more about this. If it is Eirenaeus, how do we know what he can do?''

Grantaire held up the sack. ''We know what he can't do, Rhenford, and he can't stand against this. All we have to do is wait until he returns. Now, Mistress Pris-

cian?'' She swung the sack in the direction of the lock.
The older woman hung back for a moment, her gaze
darting from Liam to Grantaire, and then she stepped
forward, the gate key already in her hand, and put it in
the lock.

The gate swung away on its own, after a few long
seconds clanking against the inside wall. Grantaire held
up her lantern, throwing light as far as the middle of the
crypt; then, satisfied, she threw Liam a triumphant look
and went in.

Despite her apparent nonchalance, Liam was happy to
see that she walked along the left-hand bays, approaching Eirenaeus's sarcophagus circuitously, the sack with
the Jewel in it raised as high as the lantern. He followed
her, whispering.

''Are you sure that will stop him?'' Without understanding why, he was suddenly convinced that Eirenaeus
had come back, that he had killed the beggars, that he
was waiting by his sarcophagus for them now.

Grantaire refused to whisper. ''Quite sure. The only
reason he could come out at all was because the Jewel
was removed—and even then, it was only Oakham killing the beggar that allowed him the spirit to actually
rise.'' She sounded sure, but Liam crept close, warily
peering into the bays they passed. *One loud noise,* he
thought, *and I will explode.*

She slowed as they approached the sarcophagus of the
first Priscian; a slow draught of air swept around them,
and Liam smelled the sea. Grantaire held up the lantern
and waved it towards Eirenaeus's bay.

The sarcophagus stood undisturbed.

For some reason this relaxed Liam; the tension
flooded away. His shoulders slumped a little, and he
shook his head. To compensate for his nervousness, he
walked forward to stand by the sarcophagus, resting one
hand on the stone foot of Eirenaeus's effigy.

''So we just put the Jewel back, and then he can't
come out?''

Grantaire joined him. ''He may not be there,'' she
said, handing him the lantern.

"And if he isn't?" It occurred to him that there was no reason for Eirenaeus to return at all. Why did they assume he would come back? *If I had been kept in a tomb for hundreds of years, I would never come near it.*

"He will return—this is his home, his place of refuge. And when he returns, we can use the Jewel to keep him here. Now please be quiet." She handed him the sack as well, and gestured for him to back away from the sarcophagus. When he had, she laid both hands on the stone and bowed her head, mumbling under her breath.

Liam could not make out any of the words, and as he stood listening, his nervousness began to return. Mistress Priscian had followed them, and stood now at the foot of the first Priscian's sarcophagus, her back to the balcony corridor.

His nervousness grew, but it was fueled now by logical thought. If Eirenaeus had indeed come back, they should be looking for him out in the city, not in the crypt. Why should he come there? Who was to say that he was not killing someone else right that very minute, stealing their spirit? Liam supposed that he might return, because the crypt was a safe place from which to go forth to kill, but would he return with the Jewel there? Grantaire had said that the closer it was to Eirenaeus, the weaker he was—surely he would avoid it.

His eyes fell to the bag in his hand. The Jewel was inside, the thing he had spent two days looking for, for which two men had died and for which he himself had almost been killed. Curiosity overcame him; he put the lantern down by his foot, opened the drawstring—and stopped, his fingers just inside the soft leather mouth.

Something from beyond the far gate, the one that led to the Oakhams', had made a noise. His mouth went dry, an instant dessication, and then he heard it again, a quick, chittering squeak.

A rat. Liam let out a pent-up breath, then walked over to the Oakhams' gate, the sack still in his hand. He pulled at the bars and the gate moved towards him, unlocked. If Eirenaeus returned, he assumed, that was how he would come, and Liam was not sure he could stand it—stand waiting in the crypt. At the very least he should tell Coeccias what was going on.

Fingers still touching the gate, he closed his eyes and projected. *Fanuilh, are you far from here?*

As always, the dragon responded immediately. *No, master.*

I want you to watch the Oakhams' front door. If anyone comes, I want to know immediately.

Yes, master.

"He is not there," Grantaire said from behind him, satisfaction audible in her voice. Liam turned.

"How can you be sure?" *How can you be so calm?*

"A spell." She shrugged and then held out her hand. "The sarcophagus is empty. Give me the Jewel."

Liam brought it to her, still in the bag, all of his questions bubbling out. "Are you sure this will work? Are you sure he will come back? What if he doesn't? Won't the presence of the Jewel warn him? Won't he be able to sense it?"

She snatched the Jewel from him, but once she had it she answered his questions thoughtfully, almost as if she were convincing herself. "He will come back. This is his home, after all, and for the moment the safest place. It will take a great number of lives for him to regain his former strength, and in any case he will not want to be too far from the Jewel. Not too close, but not too far. He will come back," she said, nodding firmly.

Liam was not convinced. "He kept the Jewel in a warehouse, Grantaire. What does he care where it is?"

"He let the Jewel get away from him once," she countered, "and Dorstenius used it against him. He will want to know where it is now. Besides, we don't need to wait here—we can wait upstairs. Fanuilh can hide down here, and let us know when he arrives."

"Oh, no he can't," Liam started to say—he was certainly not going to expose the dragon to that sort of danger—but Mistress Priscian's faint cry stopped him.

Both he and Grantaire turned to the older woman, and
the thing that stood behind her.

For Liam, there was a terrible familiarity to the scene,
as if time had doubled on itself. For the second time that
evening, he faced someone across the first Priscian's sarcophagus, and for the second time, he wished he had a
weapon.

It was impossible to see any resemblance between the
creature behind Mistress Priscian and the stone effigy
behind Liam, but he had no doubt it was Eirenaeus, and
that it had been hiding on the balcony, listening to
them—had returned from its spirit-hunting before they
came down to the cellar, in fact, and then been trapped
there by the proximity of the Jewel. The thing was tall,
towering over the old woman, around whose neck it had
thrown one of its arms, so that her chin rested on its
bony elbow. Its height accentuated the terrible thinness
of its limbs; the arm it raised above Mistress Priscian's
head was thinner than the handle of the mace it held,
and its body was completely hidden by the woman's thin
form.

Grantaire reacted faster, yanking the Jewel from the
sack, but Eirenaeus gestured threateningly with the
mace, letting it dip just a little. The movement reminded
Liam oddly of a drummer hesitating before a stroke.

"Let her go," Grantaire commanded, cold and self-
assured. Out of the corner of his eye he saw her hold
up the Jewel, a spot of pure white in the shadowy crypt,
dangling from her hand by a gold chain, but the sight
of Eirenaeus held him facing forward.

He can't be alive, Liam marveled, watching Eirenaeus try to speak. Its neck was a rotten branch, a bundle
of bone-dry twigs that seemed more likely to snap than
move, but move they did, and a dry cough whispered
out. Its eyes had sunk so deep the sockets looked
empty, except for the bright sparks far within; sparse
black hair hung in wisps down either side of the skull-
like head.

It coughed again, and a puff of dust dribbled out and

onto Mistress Priscian's head. She stared pleadingly at Liam.

"*... get away...*" Eirenaeus managed, barely audible.

"No," Grantaire said firmly, advancing a step with the Jewel held high. Liam tensed, readying himself to jump forward. *Why isn't he weaker?* "Let her go," Grantaire said again.

Atrophied over centuries, Eirenaeus's voice sent a literal shiver down Liam's spine; he gritted his teeth, helpless and horrified.

"*It is mine.... Leave it ... and go.*" With slow majesty, it leveled the mace, pointing at Grantaire, and then drew it back up, back behind its head, and Liam was sure it was going to come down on Mistress Priscian's head.

Grantaire must have thought so, too; she shouted, "No!" and started forward, and then Eirenaeus threw the mace.

Even before it hit Grantaire, the long-dead wizard had pushed Mistress Priscian aside; Liam, though, hardly noticed this. He only saw Grantaire spin away, the Jewel flashing past him, and then she fell.

He jerked away, as if he had been hit himself, and heard the Jewel fall somewhere behind him, by the Oakhams' gate, and Eirenaeus was clambering over the first Priscian's sarcophagus like an obscene spider, crouching amid its own long limbs. For a nightmarish moment it stared at Liam, head sunk to the level of its knees, long stick-fingers curled around the edge of the stone.

And then Liam was turning and running, two steps only, and he saw the Jewel gleaming, a white star in the gloom just beyond the bars, and he leapt, hitting the ground hard, grinding his hip into the stone. The bars were not far; his hand went between them, grasping the Jewel. He had expected it to burn, it glowed so, but it did not hurt; it fit his hand perfectly.

Eirenaeus landed on him, and it was like being trampled by horses, most of the weight on his right thigh, and the snap that echoed in Liam's mind, a bone, his

bone, another foot coming down in the small of his back,
driving the air from his lungs, his chin into the stone,
the Jewel from his hand.

He could not breathe; he bucked, more a reaction to
the abuse than a thought-out offensive, and Eirenaeus
tottered. The weight on his back lifted for a moment,
descending on his thigh, on the broken bone there. The
pain was a jolt through his entire body, from his toes
through his head and up to his grasping hand. It seemed
to terminate in the Jewel, just beyond his reach, the
bright white physical manifestation of his incredible
pain, and he dragged it back into the crypt by the necklace of gold to which it was attached.

The Jewel seemed to bring breath back with it; air
came into his lungs and he twisted on the floor, unaware
of his own howling. The Jewel followed his twisting,
arcing up from the floor, and he followed it in the long
second as it flew—of its own volition, it seemed to
him—flew up at Eirenaeus, the terrible stick-thing
crouching over him.

In the even longer second as the Jewel struck, he saw
the face, the permanent grin, flesh dried and stretched
taut around the jawbone, the evil flicker of the deep-
sunk eyes.

And then the Jewel struck, and Liam shut his eyes a
second too late, the silent white flash lancing through
into his brain.

The last thing he knew was that someone was screaming, but he was not sure who.

CHAPTER 18

LIAM DREAMED, CONVOLUTED visions that drifted imperceptibly from the nightmarish to the merely confusing. He drifted with the dreams, helpless and to a certain extent apathetic, as if the things he saw were of no concern to him personally, even though many of them happened to him. He felt a curious detachment, so that kissing Countess Perenelle meant as little to him as opening Eirenaeus Priscian's sarcophagus and placing his father inside. He just watched, floating.

Eirenaeus, a pyre of burning twigs, sat beside him in a temple, tearing pages from a book and tossing them, flames licking at their edges, at Grantaire; he climbed a long, black curtain just below Oakham, the other man's boots continually grinding on his head, and when the curtain fell, he swept out over the sea, flying with frightening speed in long, arcing loops. His legs were on fire, burning while he patted at them in amazement. Once again he walked through the ruined villa north of the King's Range, Mistress Priscian at his side, and the old woman identified each statue; the statues crumbled at her touch, and he wearily tried to support them, handfuls of gritty dust that trickled through his fingers, always too much until he gave up.

There were more peaceful dreams, long interludes of sunshine and warmth, and occasionally Fanuilh sat by his side. It was during one of these interludes that he kissed the countess, ten or a dozen languid, almost passionless kisses.

After that there was Eirenaeus again, crouching on the first Priscian's sarcophagus, talking and talking and talk-

ing in a vicious little whisper. Liam could not hear him,
but he did not want to go closer, though the other man
continually curled his long fingers in a come-here gesture.

And then there was Grantaire, bending over him, her
hand cool and firm against his cheek, better than a pil-
low. He leaned into it, closing his eyes, and slept.

Then there were no more dreams for a while.

When Liam was awake and knew it, he lay still, unwilling to open his eyes. He was in a strange bed, softer
than the divan in the library, but it was comfortable, and
he could feel sunshine on his hands where they rested
on the blankets. His right leg ached, but not too much.

He lay there for a long time, the bed too perfect a
nest to leave. Even the scratching of claws somewhere
out in the room did not make him open his eyes; but
when he felt a weight suddenly land on the bed, stretching the blankets tighter over his stomach, he grunted and
forced his lids up.

Fanuilh stood on the bed beside him, staring at him.
It was shaking a little bit, a gentle quivering in its legs.
You are awake.

"Not for long," he mumbled, and raised a weak hand
to pat clumsily at the dragon's head. It flopped down
next to him, snug against his side.

It was not a room he knew; there was a window, but
all he could see was blue sky. He assumed it was Mistress Priscian's house, and he was vaguely happy that it
had not burned down; his last impression had been of
intense heat.

He closed his eyes, letting his hand lie on the soft,
clothlike scales of his familiar's back. The steady rhythm
of its breathing lulled him back to sleep.

When Liam woke the second time, his head was much
clearer. A great flood of moonlight lay across the foot
of his bed. He stirred, trying to raise himself up, but a
twinge in his leg warned him and he fell back.

His movement woke Fanuilh, though; the dragon

raised its head. The moon silvered its black scales, but its face was dark.

You are awake.

"Again," Liam whispered. "We're in Mistress Priscian's house?"

Yes.

"How long have I been here?"

Five days.

He blew out a long breath, lacing his hands together behind his head.

Mage Grantaire is gone.

That brought his head back up with a jerk.

"Gone? When?"

This morning. When she was sure you were well.

"Where did she go?"

She did not say. She left a letter with Mistress Priscian. She stayed with you while you were ill. The Aedile has been to visit you many times as well.

His neck ached from the awkward position; he laid his head back, staring up at the ceiling.

"What was wrong with me?"

Your leg is broken.

"I know that," he said. He could feel the splint, holding the leg rigid. The foot below it was numb. "Why was I asleep for five days?"

The dragon's thought was hesitant. *Eirenaeus . . . exploded . . . over you. Mage Grantaire said there was a backlash of magic. In a sense, you were blasted.*

"So am I lich, then? Something hideous, less than human? A monster all right-thinking people will run away from?"

No, you are not a lich. As usual, Fanuilh had missed his attempt at humor; Liam smiled to himself and closed his eyes. After a while he felt the dragon lower its head.

They slept again.

Liam was awake the next morning when Haellus came in with a pitcher and a cloth.

"Master Rhenford, y' are with us again!"

"Yes," Liam said, smiling. He had managed to pull

himself up to a sitting position with only a little pain from his leg. "And glad to be so."

The servant held up his pitcher. "I am come to wash you, on which score Mage Grantaire was plain."

"I think I can wash myself." He had looked himself over on waking, surprised to find just how clean he was. The shirt he was wearing had been fresh the day before, as were his linen smallclothes. Knowing that Haellus had been responsible relieved him.

"Ah," the servant said, "Mage Grantaire warned that you'd essay that, and expressly forbade it. Y' are not to stir from the bed for a week entire—for that your leg may heal."

"I don't need to get up to wash," Liam said patiently, and in any case, the leg looked very well to him. He had seen enough broken limbs to know that his could never have healed as much as it had in five days. It would not do to walk on it for a while, even with a crutch—but he was sure Grantaire had done something magical for it.

Haellus was stubborn, but after several minutes of haggling it was agreed that Liam could wash himself, provided he did not move too much.

"Your back'll wait," the servant said, putting the pitcher and the cloth on a stand by the bed. "I'll see to it later, if you wish; you mustn't do it for yourself. Absolutely mustn't: Mage Grantaire was most clear. And I'll get you a bite, and Mistress Priscian'll wish to see you, when y' are ready."

Liam agreed to all this, particularly the food—he was starving. When Haellus finally left the room, he threw back the covers and hastily scrubbed those places he could reach, careful not to jar his leg or strain himself. Even so, he was tired when he was done, and he was slumped wearily on his pillows when the servant returned with a tray.

There was broth and bread, and he ate too much, refusing Haellus's many offers of help. Liam would never have suspected that the servant had such a nannying streak in him.

"Look—not a drop spilled," he said at last, but the other man still eyed him critically, finally giving a grudging nod and collecting the tray.

"If y' are well enough, Mistress Priscian earnestly desires a moment. But only if y' are well enough," he said.

"I am well enough," Liam said. "Please tell her I would be happy to see her."

Mistress Priscian inquired immediately about his health, and appeared greatly relieved when he told her he felt very well. Greatly relieved, but not entirely relieved; Liam noticed the way she clasped her hands before her, holding them tight as if she had no idea what they might do.

He frowned unhappily at her hands, and then she burst out: "Master Rhenford, I offer you my apologies. I can only plead that I could never have guessed the danger involved."

Liam goggled for a moment. The apology had come out almost defiantly, but he did not doubt the woman's sincerity; he was simply amazed that she was apologizing to him. He had meant to apologize to her.

"What—what for?"

It was her turn to goggle; for a moment, she was speechless, as if this was not at all what she had planned. Her hands flew apart, one to her ear, the other out to wave in his direction.

"Why, for all of this. Your leg, your . . . illness. That wizard." He was not sure which wizard she meant, but she went on in a low, mournful tone. "Mage Grantaire and the Aedile have told me everything, and as I said, I can only plead my woeful ignorance."

Liam could think of nothing to say. He really had meant to apologize to her—he had arrested her niece's husband, after all—but he could not ignore the relief he himself felt.

"You must not . . ." he stammered at last. "Really, I should apologize. I mean, Lord Oakham—"

"Nonsense," Mistress Priscian said firmly. "You

quite rightly warned me that I should expect unpleas-
antness. And I must say that his low character is not
entirely surprising to me. The Aedile informs me he will
be taken before the Duke and tried for murder, and I for
one think it quite right.''

She had regained control of her hands, Liam was
happy to see; she folded them complacently at her waist
and gave a little nod. Liam could not help but wonder
about Lady Oakham, but he did not want to say anything
that might spoil her composure.

''Well, there is nothing you need to apologize for,''
he assured her.

''Hmmph. When y' are up and walking, we'll see
about that. For the moment, there is this for you.'' She
produced a thick sheaf of paper, triple-folded, from her
pocket and placed it on the bed near his hand. ''Mage
Grantaire left it, with her apologies as well. Pressing
business took her from Southwark, or she'd have attended your recovery. As it was, she sat with you from
morning till night.''

''Yes, so I heard,'' Liam murmured, holding up the
letter. His name was on the outermost sheet, visible
where it was folded. She had misspelled it: LIAM
WRENFORD. *At least she got the first name right,* he
thought.

''I'll leave you to it,'' Mistress Priscian said quietly.
''If there's aught you need, call Haellus.'' She slipped
out the door before he could respond, and he turned his
attention to the letter, eager and curious.

It was five pages long, all but the last written on both
sides; Grantaire's letters were so compressed the words
looked like series of slashes, but he found that he could
puzzle it out after a few lines.

> *Wrenford,* it began, *please forgive my leaving be-
> fore you were well, but it is not safe for me to stay
> here, and you will be well soon in any case. I have
> seen to that. The leg will heal cleanly, and there
> will be no permanent damage from the Jewel.*

The first three pages were an extraordinarily detailed explanation of Eirenaeus's return and his eventual destruction. A great deal of it went over Liam's head—she sprinkled the description liberally with quotes from Eirenaeus's notebook and Dorstenius Priscian's diary, as well as a number of references to the work of other magicians—but he managed to grasp the general outline, with Fanuilh's help.

The Jewel had, in effect, blasted Eirenaeus; he was nearly immortal, but he had to provide himself with vast amounts of spirit, since the Jewel continually drained him. And the closer it was to him, the more it drained; in explaining this, Grantaire had included a long series of what Liam assumed were mathematical formulae, but he could make neither heads nor tails of them, so he skipped them.

There was a point of equilibrium, where the Jewel stopped draining him but left him completely incapacitated. When, at the head of an angry band of townsmen, Dorstenius Priscian had entombed his brother, Eirenaeus and the Jewel had been at that point. Grantaire was quite sure that the brother had not known he was condemning his brother to life eternal in a stone box—his diary made it quite clear that he fervently hoped his brother would die shortly. She was less sure what the intervening centuries had been like for Eirenaeus, though she entertained a few gruesome conjectures.

Liam skipped those as well. "She certainly flinches from nothing," he commented to Fanuilh, a hint of admiration in his voice.

There is no way to be sure, the dragon replied, peering over the edge of the paper.

Liam rolled his eyes.

The removal of the Jewel for Duessa Oakham to wear had only set the stage for Eirenaeus's resurrection; it was the murder of Malskat that had allowed it to happen. Oakham had apparently confessed to cutting the beggar's throat directly over the sarcophagus, but Grantaire stated that she did not think such proximity was strictly necessary. Anywhere in the crypt would have done, she

wrote. The sarcophagus, it seemed, had been designed
by Eirenaeus himself, sometime after he enchanted the
Jewel. At the back there was a hidden exit; Grantaire
seemed impressed by this, calling it "extremely clever,
and well hidden." Apparently Eirenaeus believed in preparing for all eventualities.

The rest, she thought, was obvious: the gradual series
of murders—the second beggar, the two maskers, then
the three beggars together—as a way of building up his
strength. A single life would have provided him enough
spirit for a day or two, but she speculated that he would
have required more to work any magic.

She dedicated a full page to explaining what she
called "his final and irrevocable demise," but the simple
fact seemed to be that bringing the Jewel directly into
contact with him had allowed it to completely drain him
of spirit. The reason for the explosion—which had apparently done no damage at all to the crypt, only to
Eirenaeus and Liam—was beyond her, but Liam had his
own ideas about it.

"If a single life gives off a flame," he said to Fanuilh,
"wouldn't the three or four he had stolen give off a
much larger flame?" He was thinking of Mother Japh's
blue plane.

The dragon cocked its head at him. *I do not think so.
The flame is more of a symbol.*

Liam waved his familiar's skepticism away; the idea
appealed to him. It seemed appropriate that Eirenaeus
and his Jewel and his stolen spirit should mix explo-
sively. "I like it," he said, grinning at the dragon, "and
you will not disagree with me. I am sick."

You are not very sick.

"Sick enough," Liam said. "Don't contradict me."

Fanuilh gave up on the letter, and Liam read on alone.

The fourth page was a brief, maddeningly cryptic description of the events of the past five days. She referred
to the two maskers twice, but did not explain how they
had been connected to Eirenaeus, and she spoke of Oakham's confession without mentioning any of the details.

Lady Oakham had "taken it badly," but Grantaire
would not say how. She mentioned Quetivel's departure
and a visit by Earl Uldericus, but nothing about the duel.
There was a great deal of praise for Mistress Priscian,
her calmness and good nature.

All in all it frustrated him, raising more questions than
it answered—he wished she was there to answer. And
somehow, he had expected more, something . . . personal, he realized. The moment when he had thought he
might kiss her recurred to him. The letter gave no hint
that she remembered that. *She might as well be writing
to her brother,* he thought. Had he imagined the whole
thing? He was turning to the fifth page with a sour expression when Haellus poked his head in the door and
announced the Aedile.

"Come," Coeccias chided, standing at the end of the
bed with a broad grin, "y' are too lazy here, Rhenford.
Waited on hand and foot, and for what? A scratch!"

"How else can I relax? If I had known that breaking
a leg would keep you away for five days, I would have
done it long ago."

The Aedile chuckled, but his expression quickly grew
serious. "Truth, Rhenford, it likes me to see you well.
Aye, it likes me well. It was nearly a bad end to the
whole affair."

Liam was not sure if he thought that was a vast un-
derstatement, but decided to give Coeccias the benefit of
the doubt. He rattled the letter. "Grantaire says Oakham
confessed."

The Aedile's face lit up. "Truth, confessed isn't the
word for it! He fair drew us a map of his evils, from
the Jewel through the beggar and the thief to that Desiderius. He's gone up to Deepenmoor these two days,
for trial before the Duke. For that he's a peer, he must
go before the Duke, but I don't doubt the outcome. He'll
be hanged, not least for attempting your life."

Strangely, the thought gave Liam little satisfaction; he
certainly did not object, but he was surprised to find that
he was mostly indifferent to Oakham's fate.

"The Jewel, in course," the Aedile continued, "was destroyed—but then, I'm not sure that isn't for the best."

"Destroyed? Grantaire didn't mention that."

"In your bonfire, Rhenford. There was as little left as there is at the bottom of a tipster's bottle—a fine powder was all. Not that Mistress Priscian took it poorly. She is a fine woman, not given to airs. Unlike some," he said, leaning over and dropping his voice confidentially. "That Lady Oakham, for an example. It is well that she took herself off to Deepenmoor, or I'd have had to post a man at your door. I imagine after the hanging it'll be a temple of seclusion for her."

Liam could think of worse things than temple life, and he could manage no sympathy for the spoiled girl.

"And what about those maskers? Grantaire says it was Eirenaeus."

The Aedile grimaced. "Aye, it was. We only found them two nights past, in an old cistern. A beggar found them, to be fair—I'd naught to do with it." He hung his head sorrowfully. "The same wounds, and no spirit. They were but children—no more than twelve. They should never've been let out."

There was a long silence while Liam digested this, imagining Coeccias telling the parents. He knew the Aedile would have done it himself. *And to think I thought my responsibilities were too much. . . .*

After a while the silence grew lighter, and Liam ventured another question: "What about Uldericus and Quetivel? Was there a duel?"

Heavily at first, and later with growing relish, Coeccias described the earl's arrival a few days before at Mistress Priscian's door, bearing a fistful of papers that he claimed were Oakham's debts to him. "He tried to come all over the gallant, and offered them to her, saying that he would not trouble her in her sorrowful time, and that she might destroy the markers at her convenience, but that he must see Quetivel, who was dancing attendance on the distraught Lady Oakham at the time."

Mistress Priscian had told him off in no uncertain

terms; according to Coeccias she had threatened him with a poker, the thought of which set the Aedile laughing. "She packed Quetivel off that very afternoon, and brought the markers to me. I had a quiet word with the earl—he was much annoyed, but finally saw sense. Most especially after I told him that Oakham had confessed to cheating for him, so that he could take Quetivel for greater sums."

"Ha!" Liam shouted. "I knew it!" *There was no way I could be that bad at Alliances.*

"Aye, they had a scheme—Uldericus forgave a fraction of his debt, and Oakham did something for him. I doubt not that y' understand it better than I; I don't game much. And then there's this: Uldericus never asked to buy the Jewel. It seems Oakham offered it to him, in return for his markers. The earl refused, quite rightly. I can only think that he must have guessed that Oakham was responsible—but there's no proof, and it's not a crime, though it should be. In fine, though, Oakham was still as far in debt to the earl as we could have hoped." He named a sum, and Liam blinked, appropriately impressed.

"You could raise a fleet on that," he said.

Coeccias agreed. "Aye, but it was only the half of what he said Desiderius was going to give him for the Jewel. Can imagine? And here's more—the ship he booked passage on, the *Sourberry*? He had only booked one. I've told Mistress Priscian, but she asked me to keep it dark."

"I imagine she wants to tell her niece herself."

"Aye, there's that. She was most surprised, for that it seems he has no family in Torquay."

They considered this in silence, Liam gazing out the window. Then a different thought occurred to him: he had been in bed for five days.

"I have missed the whole Banquet," he said.

"Y' have, y' have," Coeccias said sadly, and then snapped his fingers. "I near forgot—there was a message for you. That maid, the one you sent me after. I never found her that night, but she came around the next day. She asked that you remember her gift. Does that signify? She was a rude little thing.''

Liam laughed, amazed at Mopsa's audacity. *Does she call that keeping a low profile?* "I will have to think about that," he said, refusing to answer the question implicit in the Aedile's raised eyebrow.

When it was clear that no explanations would be forthcoming, Coeccias coughed into his fist. "Well and well; I should leave you to regain your strength. It would like me, though . . . truth, I needs must—well, there is this, Rhenford: I am sorry for that with the beggars, and that I doubted you.''

The Aedile's blush appalled Liam; was everyone going to apologize to him today? He had forgotten his anger with his friend, had explained it away to himself in that walk up the Point.

"Forget it," he said, and then repeated himself more forcefully. When Coeccias still appeared uncomfortable, he held out his hand. "Shake, and we will both forget it. Doubting me is never a bad thing.''

The Aedile took his hand and pumped it twice. "It ran through my mind when I saw you in the crypt, that my last words to you were angry. I would not have us part that way." He seemed more comfortable now, but the sentiments embarrassed Liam a little.

"Forget it," he said again.

"I will," Coeccias promised with a smile, "and I will leave you now. This lazing about can't last.''

"It will last as long as I can make it last," Liam called after him, and to prove it he sank himself down into the pillows, even as the door closed behind the Aedile.

Liam sat up a little later and finished the rest of Grantaire's letter. There was only one more page, but it was very different from what had gone before. From the very first sentence it seemed much less assured, a complete departure from the dry, almost scholarly tone of the first four pages. Even the letters were different: they were easier to read, better formed, as if she had spent more time tracing each letter, using the time to think about what she was writing.

I should thank you for letting me stay in the house, she wrote. *It has been over a year since I stayed in a house. I have stayed at Mistress Priscian's for the last three days; it is very comfortable and she is a fine woman. But I think I like your house better—you are a better cook than Haellus.*

He laughed at this, and then wondered if she meant it as a joke. As far as he could remember, he had never seen her smile.

Tanaquil was right about you. When he came to me, I was in Carad Llan. (The Guild chapter house there is very small.) He told me to go to Southwark and take his things, but he also said I should meet you. He said you could be trusted, that you might be a useful friend. I must admit that on my journey here I did not think much about it; you are not a mage, after all, and it has been a long time since I have dealt with anything but. But he was right.

There are things I have to do now, people I must visit. Other mages, mostly. Harcourt represents a serious danger, and they must be warned. It may be that from time to time mages may come to Southwark—that I may send them here. The Guild has no presence in the Southern Tier, and the closest chapter house is Torquay, which is so disorganized as to present no danger. I may give them your name, and I hope you will be as kind to them as you were to me.

Liam frowned, torn by the last sentence. He did not think he had been overly kind to her, but it was exactly the kind of personal sentiment for which he had been looking. On the other hand, he was not sure he wanted to be drawn into a conflict between wizards. He shook his head; Grantaire had only said she might give out his name—he would worry about it if another wizard arrived on his doorstep.

> *I would like to come back sometime, if I get a chance. In the summer, I think. Tanaquil said you used to swim in the ocean from his beach, that was how he first mentioned you: "A man who used to swim from my beach." I have never been in the ocean—I think it would be very cold.*
>
> *However, I do not think it will be for some time. I have a great many things to do, and I must leave today.*

There was a line across the page, as if to mark off separate thoughts.

> *It is very early in the morning. I have been watching you sleep—you will recover today or tomorrow, I am sure. You look very lonely when you are asleep. I think you are like me, Wrenford.*
>
> *Rif says he thinks you were going to kiss me, that night when we talked in the kitchen. I don't think so, but he is quite sure. Were you?*
>
> *I wonder what would have happened if you did?*

She signed her name below that, a large, sprawling signature. There were two names, and he thought the second one was Fauve, or Fauvel. He puzzled over it for a minute, trying to work it out, then gave up and reread the last three paragraphs again.

"Fanuilh, what was Grantaire's cat's name?"

The dragon raised its head from the blanket. *Rif, master.*

Liam nodded ruefully. "Smart cat." *I should have kissed her,* he thought, but then his conviction wavered a little. If she wondered what would have happened, that probably meant that she was uninterested in being kissed.

And what did she mean about his being like her? *She*

doesn't mean she looks lonely when she sleeps, he thought. *Does she think I'm lonely?*

"Fanuilh, am I lonely?"

Master?

"I'm not lonely, am I?"

You are not alone, the dragon thought, after a long moment of consideration. *I am always here. And Aedile Coeccias is your friend.*

"Right," Liam said, but he wondered—not about Coeccias or Fanuilh, but about whether she might mean a different kind of loneliness. Exactly what kind, he was not sure, but he thought that was what she meant.

The letter lying facedown on his stomach, he turned to the window to think about it. He remembered then the feel of her hand on his cheek, and how it had helped him sleep.

Much later, he turned from the window and called Haellus's name as loudly as he could without shouting. The servant must have been waiting, because he arrived only a few seconds later.

"Is there something you need, Master Rhenford?"

"Yes," Liam said. "I need to buy a Banquet gift."

"But the Banquet is over," Haellus said, puzzled.

"I know that, but I need one anyway." When the servant looked at him as if he had lost his mind, Liam pointed to his leg and added: "I meant to get it earlier, but I didn't have a chance."

"Ah," Haellus said, comprehension dawning. "In course, Master Rhenford. What will you need?"

Liam frowned. His thoughts had turned to the two children killed by Eirenaeus, how they were no older than Mopsa, and he had decided that he would have to do something to help her, something permanent. It would have to wait until he was back on his feet; in the meantime, all he could do was remember his promise.

"Something big," he said, and then he waited for Haellus's suggestions.

DANIEL HOOD

FANUILH   0-441-00055-X/$4.99

The wizard Tarquin valued the miniature dragon Fanuilh as his
familiar—and the human Liam as his friend. And when Tarquin
was murdered in bed one rainy night, both were left to grieve—
and to seek justice.

WIZARD'S HEIR   0-441-00231-5/$4.99

Despite what people think, inheriting a wizard's familiar did not
make Liam a wizard. But he is shaping up to be quite a detective.
When his late friend Tarquin's magic artifacts are stolen, and then
used to commit further crimes, Liam must solve a mystery that's
already caused one death and threatens to start a holy war.

BEGGAR'S BANQUET   0-441-00434-2/$5.50

Liam agrees to help solve the theft of a priceless—and magical—
family heirloom stolen from his business partner. And he recruits
his dragon familiar, Fanuilh, to help. Because what's a little magic
among friends?

VISIT THE PUTNAM BERKLEY BOOKSTORE CAFÉ ON THE INTERNET:
http://www.berkley.com/berkley

Payable in U.S. funds. No cash accepted. Postage & handling: $1.75 for one book, 75¢ for each
additional. Maximum postage $5.50. Prices, postage and handling charges may change without
notice. Visa, Amex, MasterCard call 1-800-788-6262, ext. 1, or fax 1-201-933-2316; refer to ad #717

Or, check above books	Bill my: ☐ Visa ☐ MasterCard ☐ Amex _____ (expires)
and send this order form to:	
The Berkley Publishing Group	Card#
P.O. Box 12289, Dept. B	Daytime Phone # ($10 minimum)
Newark, NJ 07101-5289	Signature

Please allow 4-6 weeks for delivery.   **Or enclosed is my:** ☐ check ☐ money order
Foreign and Canadian delivery 8-12 weeks.

Ship to:

Name	Book Total	$_____
Address	Applicable Sales Tax (NY, NJ, PA, CA, GST Can.)	$_____
City	Postage & Handling	$_____
State/ZIP	Total Amount Due	$_____

Bill to: Name

Address _____ City _____
State/ZIP

DAVID DRAKE

__**IGNITING THE REACHES**__   0-441-00179-3/$5.99

A remarkable world where renegade pirates race to the farthest reaches of space to seek their fortune trading with the star colonies. It's a journey of incalculable odds and unpredictable danger as rival ships, strange aliens, and human hybrids all seek the same reward—the countless wealth to be earned in the Reaches.

__**THROUGH THE BREACH**__   0-441-00326-5/$5.99

Their mission is called the Venus Asteroid Expedition, but it has little to do with legitimate trade. Their destination is the Mirror, the impenetrable membrane of another universe—a universe that holds all the riches of the Federation. And their only point of entry is Landolph's Breach.

But the last person to pass through was Landolph himself. And most of his men never returned...

__**FIRESHIPS**__   0-441-00417-2/$5.99

Enter the heart of the Venus rebellion and join forces with the legendary Piet Ricimer and Stephen Gregg. Captain Blythe knew it meant risking everything she had—her ship, her crew, her life. But hey, why not?

VISIT THE PUTNAM BERKLEY BOOKSTORE CAFÉ ON THE INTERNET:
http://www.berkley.com/berkley

Payable in U.S. funds. No cash accepted. Postage & handling: $1.75 for one book, 75¢ for each additional. Maximum postage $5.50. Prices, postage and handling charges may change without notice. Visa, Amex, MasterCard call 1-800-788-6262, ext. 1, or fax 1-201-933-2316; refer to ad #700

Or, check above books   Bill my: ☐ Visa ☐ MasterCard ☐ Amex _____ (expires)
and send this order form to:
The Berkley Publishing Group   Card#_____

P.O. Box 12289, Dept. B   Daytime Phone #_____   ($10 minimum)
Newark, NJ 07101-5289   Signature_____

Please allow 4-6 weeks for delivery.   **Or enclosed is my:** ☐ check ☐ money order
Foreign and Canadian delivery 8-12 weeks.

Ship to:

Name_____   Book Total $_____

Address_____   Applicable Sales Tax $_____
                                 (NY, NJ, PA, CA, GST Can.)

City_____   Postage & Handling $_____

State/ZIP_____   Total Amount Due $_____

Bill to: Name_____

Address_____   City_____

State/ZIP_____

NICK O'DONOHOE

T·H·E
HEALING OF
CROSSROADS

Veterinarian BJ Vaughn spends her days traveling throughout different
realms, both real and imagined. She finds that outside of Crossroads, the
creatures of myth and magic are falling ill—and the land she loves is now in
danger from the evil that has followed her home...

__0-441-00391-5/$5.99

UNDER
T·H·E
HEALING
SIGN

As the creatures of Crossroads battle among themselves, a sinister
outsider breeds mistrust and mayhem, BJ wonders if wisdom will be enough to
defeat the powers of ill will—and brute force...

__0-441-00180-7/$4.99

T·H·E
MAGIC AND THE
HEALING

BJ has been chosen as part of a special group that will
venture not only to the frontiers of science, but beyond it...To Crossroads, a
world where the creatures of the imagination live
and breathe—and hurt. BJ will discover the joy of healing—
and the wonder of magic...

0-441-00053-3/$4.99

Payable in U.S. funds. No cash accepted. Postage & handling: $1.75 for one book, 75¢ for each
additional. Maximum postage $5.50. Prices, postage and handling charges may change without
notice. Visa, Amex, MasterCard call 1-800-788-6262, ext. 1, or fax 1-201-933-2316; refer to ad #678

Or, check above books and send this order form to:	Bill my: ☐ Visa ☐ MasterCard ☐ Amex _____ (expires)
The Berkley Publishing Group	Card#
P.O. Box 12289, Dept. B	Daytime Phone # _____ ($10 minimum)
Newark, NJ 07101-5289	Signature

Please allow 4-6 weeks for delivery. **Or enclosed is my:** ☐ check ☐ money order
Foreign and Canadian delivery 8-12 weeks.

Ship to:

Name	Book Total	$
Address	Applicable Sales Tax (NY, NJ, PA, CA, GST Can.)	$
City	Postage & Handling	$
State/ZIP	Total Amount Due	$

Bill to: Name

Address	City
State/ZIP	

PUTNAM *pb* BERKLEY

online

Your Internet gateway to a virtual
environment with hundreds of
entertaining and enlightening books
from the Putnam Berkley Group.

While you're there visit the PB Café and
order-up the latest buzz on the best
authors and books around—Tom Clancy,
Patricia Cornwell, W.E.B. Griffin,
Nora Roberts, William Gibson,
Robin Cook, Brian Jacques, Jan Brett,
Catherine Coulter and many more!

Putnam Berkley Online is located at
http://www.putnam.com/berkley

• •

Once a month we serve up the dish on the
latest science fiction, fantasy, and horror
titles currently on sale. Plus you'll get
interviews of your favorite authors, trivia,
a top ten list, and so much more
fun it's shameless.

Check out PB Plug at http://www.pbplug.com

• •